MARTIN SHEPHERD spent over thirty years in various businesses before pursuing a passion for writing. After selling a company in 2008, Martin gained an MA in Creative Writing from Chichester

TOO FAST A LIFE

Martin Shepherd

SilverWood

Published in 2015 by the author
Revised in 2015

SilverWood Books Ltd
30 Queen Charlotte Street, Bristol, BS1 4HJ
www.silverwoodbooks.co.uk

ISBN 978-1-78132-319-9 (paperback)
ISBN 978-1-78132-320-5 (ebook)

Contents

Author's Note

I have been asked many times why I attempted to write a lightly fictionalised biography of someone about whom so much has already been written, not least by the man himself. That's easy. I wanted to convey all aspects of Mike Hawthorn's dramatic life in an intimate way, unfettered by excessive motor racing jargon and detail, whilst never forgetting that his abiding interest and profession *was* motor racing.

Although this is not usual biography, I have tried to ensure that all relevant facts and dates are accurate and to avoid unwarranted embellishment, for I believe his story is extraordinary enough. Only incidental situations and conversations are imagined, and only then for the purposes of aiding the known narrative. Any errors of fact will therefore be mine and mine alone.

With the notable exception of the narrator, Tom McBride, all the principal characters in the story are real and their names have not been changed. Tom is a fictitious amalgam of various close friends of Mike's and only exists to get us 'up close and personal'.

My goal was to see how Mike's experiences, in the context of the values of that time, might have influenced his personality, and to try to give reason to the often contradictory accounts of this sometimes over-lauded – and over-criticised – charismatic and driven young man.

Prologue

By Frank R W England (aka 'Lofty'), 1974

Motor racing pits must be one of the few places on Earth where one could remain oblivious to twenty people or more being decapitated less than forty yards away. Beheaded in a single moment. No warning. No head.

Even though I was that close, I can still hardly believe it. The accident happened two and a half hours into the Le Mans 24 Heures race in northern France, at twenty-six minutes past six in the evening, on Saturday, 11 June 1955. It remains to this day the worst crash in the history of motor racing. An estimated eighty-four people died and a further 120 were seriously injured. The overwhelming majority were simply spectators, mostly French.

The eleventh *and the twelfth* of June…dates I'll never forget, as the horror lasted for two days.

It was a contest I had been keenly anticipating. This was Jaguar versus Mercedes. Britain versus Germany. Our lads against the bloody Krauts. As far as I was concerned, it wasn't so much a race as a battle, and we had the ammunition to pull it off.

The race was scheduled to start at four in the afternoon. The weather was perfect, not a cloud in the sky. Ironically, it began with an amusing incident. The reigning world champion, Juan Fangio – *El Maestro* – was one of three drivers starting for Mercedes in their all-new 300 SLRs. There was never a less likely-looking racing driver than Fangio: short, barrel-chested and bandy-legged, with a high, tinny voice. Yet the Argentinian was utterly brilliant behind the wheel.

As the tricolour flag dropped, Fangio dashed across to his car and tried to vault into it, copying the 'run and jump' style of his younger teammate Stirling Moss. It didn't go well: the gear lever got stuck up his trouser leg. The crowd burst into laughter as he sat there struggling.

Prior to the accident, the race was extremely exciting. It was fought like a short Grand Prix event rather than an endurance one. The Italian Eugenio Castellotti, driving a scarlet Ferrari 121, made a terrific start and led the race for the first hour.

Fangio quickly caught up with the front runners and, eventually, he and Mike Hawthorn began to challenge Castellotti for the lead. By lap 16, Castellotti had to settle for third place. Mike and Fangio were going quicker and quicker. For lap after lap, first Mike's dark green Jaguar would come flying past, with Fangio's sleek silver Mercedes hard on its tail, only for the order to be reversed the very next lap. Lap records were established and then beaten every few minutes, with Mike taking the final honours, posting a 4 minutes 6.6 seconds lap – an average of 123.4 miles per hour. Not bad considering this was on public roads, not a racetrack. After two hours of flat-out racing, only one second separated Mike and Fangio.

Mike was going like the clappers, fully justifying his ranking as our top driver. When he was driving like this, I thought he was unbeatable. He could power-slide round a corner better than almost anyone, except perhaps Archie Scott Brown, and he was fearless. What's more, he was the only driver I ever saw who smiled when going flat-out. Of course, I did worry whether such nervelessness would ultimately be his undoing.

I was looking out onto the track when the accident happened. I'd decided to rest Mike and give Ivor, his co-driver, a stint at the wheel. The car also needed refuelling. I was holding up the last of three countdown boards that we used to advise drivers to come into the pits.

On lap 35, I watched 'Golden Boy', as the press had begun calling Mike, come haring down the outside of the track, lapping several cars. Fangio was right behind him. These faster cars were decelerating from nudging 190 miles per hour as they approached the gentle bend leading into Dunlop Curve – the bend that would later be the scene of so many horrific deaths.

As Mike approached the kink, he drifted towards the inside line, crossing the path of a slower Austin-Healey, braking all the while to come into the pits. This wasn't such a strange thing to do, but a second or so later Lance Macklin, the driver of the Austin-Healey, swerved violently outwards, which certainly was.

Realising that, as Mike had overtaken him, others would soon be swarming behind, Macklin may have glanced up to his rear-view mirror rather than steered around Mike who was now braking hard in order to pull in to the pits. This momentary lapse prevented Macklin from taking a smoother line to repass Mike. Aside from ramming Mike, this left him only two choices: either to brake hard and risk being run into, or to swerve left. He chose to swerve and, in doing so, locked a wheel.

At the same time, Frenchman Pierre Levegh, driving the third Mercedes, was hurtling down towards the melee on the outside. It was clear that either he hadn't sufficiently anticipated what was happening up ahead or was slow to brake. The Mercedes' drum brakes were nowhere near as efficient as the disc brakes on either our cars or the Austin-Healey. The only way those Mercedes could compete on braking was to deploy their revolutionary auxiliary air brake, resembling a large boot lid which opened forwards to create massive air resistance. It was operated by a lever on the dashboard, so it was not as intuitive as pressing a pedal, and it required a little more time to be effective. Maybe precious time Levegh didn't have.

The next thing I registered was Levegh's car taking off, having ridden up the back of Macklin's Healey, exactly as if it had shot up a waterskier's ramp. It must have flown twenty feet up into the air, heading straight for the grandstand. I was still intently watching the track in front of me, so I missed what happened next in the grandstand. I realise it sounds callous, but all I cared about was that my lads were okay.

I'm grateful too as I didn't have to witness that large sheet of steel, flying horizontally into a packed grandstand taking the heads off all those poor men and women. From film footage, one can just make out that it was the bonnet that turned into a mass guillotine, once it became detached from the rest of the car. It was all over in seconds. The poor buggers didn't stand a chance. Beheaded in the blink of an eye. The rest of the car ploughed on into spectators, the engine separating on impact. It then bounced up onto the so-called safety wall where it caught fire.

Having been shunted from behind, Macklin's car went into

a spin and ran into three spectators: a gendarme, a photographer and a race official. All three were killed. The car continued spinning and ended up not so far from where Mike had pulled up. Macklin appeared unscathed as he leapt from his wrecked Healey.

Mike pulled over a little way past us, and I watched him scramble out. Relieved to see both Mike and his car in one piece, I glanced back towards the grandstand and saw what looked like the after-effects of a fire bomb. An intense white ball of fire was sending flames high into the evening sky, shrapnel spitting out noisily in all directions. People were scurrying everywhere, their screams and desperate shouts intermittently audible over the noise of the speeding cars. It was like something from the war.

Conscious of the carnage behind him, Mike had failed to stop in time and overshot our pit. Reversing was strictly prohibited so Mike ran back to us, via the Cunningham pit, undoing the straps of his helmet as he ran.

Conversations in the pits were always difficult. High-performance engines with minimal silencing revving to full throttle were never far away, so we'd have to shout.

'What have I done?' he kept repeating. 'There are dead people out there on the track.' He was shaking and his hair was soaked with sweat. 'Is the Bishop all right?' The Bishop was the drivers' nickname for Pierre Levegh.

Macklin came striding over towards us. 'That was all your *fucking* fault!' he shouted at Mike.

Mike recoiled as if he'd just been shot.

'Mike,' I snapped, 'you just get back in the car and bring it round.' All I could think was that I didn't want to relinquish the lead, not all the time that the driver was okay and the car drivable.

Mike looked at me defiantly but, big chap though he was, at six-foot five, I was bigger still, older and his boss.

'Don't just stand there. Get your arse into gear,' I shouted.

He turned away, put his helmet back on, and ran back to the car.

In the minutes following the crash, I was preoccupied with the progress of our other two cars and making sure Ivor was ready to take over.

In the middle of all this kerfuffle, a race official came running over. '*Excusez-moi, monsieur,* do Jagwuar wis' to stop?' he asked.

'*Non!*' I replied, rather curtly.

I turned away and carried on with what I was doing, hoping the little fellow would get the message that I didn't want a debate. Why would we want to stop? We were in the lead. It simply didn't occur to me to stop racing. We were all so caught up by the adrenalin of competition that we weren't thinking rationally. Huge preparation and lots of money went into those races, and so much could go wrong, one tended to press on regardless. Anyway, press on we did.

Nowadays, officials would have stopped the race immediately. Then, the clerk of the course thought that hordes of departing spectators would prevent the emergency services getting onto the circuit. It was a brave and unpopular decision, but he was absolutely right.

Five minutes later, Mike brought the car round. He'd slowed right down. He was in a frightful state, quite hysterical. 'That's it! I'm finished. I don't want to drive again – ever.' He was trembling and staggering about.

'Michael, snap out of it!' I shouted. 'You can win this thing! Now, go and get some rest.' I had no time for girly hysterics. Moreover, he wasn't my only concern. Jaguar had two other entries, so I was relieved when Rob and Lois Walker volunteered to take Mike off to their caravan for a spot of TLC.

The next thing I realised was that Ivor hadn't jumped into the D(-Type) straight after Mike had got out.

Ivor was just standing there, looking at me. 'Bloody hell, this is suicide! I can't drive in this…' he said.

I thought for a second I was going to have a mutiny on my hands. Fortunately, Norman Dewis, another of my drivers, grabbed hold of Ivor and practically pushed him into the car, shouting, 'Come on, Ivor, the race is still on.'

Thankfully, although he was still shaking his head, the moment Ivor was seated he found first gear and was away.

Rob Walker was a reliable sort. I knew Mike would be fine with him. Like me, he'd been a pilot in the war. Although not nearly as quick as Mike behind a wheel, he was more experienced, and I knew Mike was fond of him. I learnt afterwards he gave Mike a couple of stiff brandies and a bit of a talking to.

Once I'd seen all three cars refuelled and generally sorted out, I went to find Mike. Sitting in the Walkers' caravan, he still looked shaken up, but I knew I couldn't give him any quarter. 'I want you back at the pits in exactly an hour from now. Got that? And in top form. Understood?'

'Lofty, please, I c-can't,' he stammered. 'I'm finished. I can't drive any more.'

'Pull yourself together,' I said. 'You're going out there to finish what you started.'

Mike's eyes went down to the tumbler he was holding. He said nothing.

'Just how bad is it, Lofty?' asked Rob.

'Haven't a clue,' I replied. 'There's still smoke rising opposite, and I believe there've been a few fatalities, but the race hasn't been stopped, so we just crack on.' I looked back at Mike. 'Listen, Mike, nothing you or I do now will alter the consequences of the accident. We've come here to win this race, and that's what we're bloody well going to do.'

'Whoa...you're all heart,' said Rob with half a smile. And then, addressing Mike, 'But you know, Mike, Lofty's right. You don't really want to be beaten by the Krauts now, do you?'

Bless Rob for that. As far as his friend was concerned, he knew exactly which buttons to press. It was a challenge that a few years later would prove extraordinarily profound.

Meanwhile, Ivor was doing okay. The poor chap inexperienced, as he'd seldom driven such a high-performance car, and his only practice laps at Le Mans had been in the dark. But he was holding onto second place behind Stirling Moss, who had taken over from Fangio. Ivor wasn't in the same league as Stirling so he was doing well to lose only a few seconds each lap.

I admit I was slightly surprised to see Mike when he walked into the pits bang on time. I imagined I might have to go and get him. He looked drained, expressionless. I didn't care. I wasn't going to take the pressure off.

'Right, Ivor's now lost ten minutes to Moss, so you'll have your work cut out.'

No one spoke for a while but, when Ivor pitted around ten o'clock, Mike duly clambered in and off he went. By this time,

roughly three and a half hours after the accident – the *first* accident
I should add, for there had been subsequent lesser ones elsewhere –
there was a lazy plume of black smoke rising from the grandstand
opposite. A new crowd had formed to watch the race from the very
scene of the disaster. It was like a scab had quickly formed, almost as
if the accident hadn't happened.

Amazingly, Mike was not only back driving but he was reeling
in the Mercedes' lead.

Information was scant but as the night wore on so the whispered
death toll rose. The official tally was eighty-four, although some later
accounts claim it was over a hundred. As dramatic as the impact itself
was, they say the majority of deaths resulted from shrapnel or burns
from the flaming Mercedes. Its novel, lightweight magnesium body
burnt white hot. Some poor buggers died from their burns long after
the accident.

Around half past one in the morning, some seven hours after the
accident, I was informed by Alfred Neubauer, Mercedes' manager,
that his team were pulling out. Mercedes' board of directors had
been convened at midnight to debate whether or not they should
continue. Greatly concerned about Franco/German relations, they
took the reluctant decision to stop.

I suppose I should have consulted with the Jaguar management
back in England, but I so much loathed that great fat self-righteous
German, I took pleasure in telling him that we had no intention of
quitting. My public line was that the race had not been stopped, we'd
come here to race, and race we would – with or without Mercedes.

In the absence of any serious competition – no Mercedes, and
the Ferraris already out due to mechanical failure – there was nothing
to stop us winning. Even the torrential rain later didn't stop Mike and
Ivor from comfortably reaching the chequered flag first. But Mike's
mistake was to behave as if nothing had happened – waving around
champagne bottles and grinning at the cameras. The extraordinary
transformation of his mood from twenty-odd hours earlier was as
night is to day. In time, I wondered whether Mike had accepted
the trophy in memory of his late father, whose funeral had clashed
with the previous year's Le Mans, and so had prevented Mike from
entering.

I've subsequently come to realise there were many reasons for this unprecedented accident, but I believe Mike's manoeuvre was a catalyst, not the cause. Of the chain reaction that followed, Macklin was arguably more at fault than either Mike or Levegh, because he reacted late and suddenly. That said, Levegh was going too fast and, as a consequence, rode straight up the back of the ramp-like Austin-Healey and took off.

Old Levegh died when his car landed. I say 'old' not in a pejorative way but because, at fifty years of age, he was considered far too old to be racing at this hugely demanding level. Whilst it doesn't seem gallant to pin blame on a dead driver, I do to this day query whether a younger driver might have slowed down in time.

The biggest culprits were those in charge of the race. This major event, held on ordinary public roads, had first started in 1923 – when the winning car lapped at just fifty-seven miles per hour. Thirty years later, our cars could lap at over twice that speed, and yet the track had scarcely changed. Another problem, all too common at that time, was that cars of markedly different performance were allowed to run in the same race.

It was probably because the recriminations rumbled on that I kept questioning our part in the tragedy. Initially, I'd convinced myself that there had been nothing wrong with Mike's driving. Later, as I ran the accident over and over in my mind, and replayed the image of Mike distressed and blaming himself, I was struck by a terrible thought. What if Mike had briefly blacked out?

Mike's blackouts, although thankfully rare, were known to just a handful of trusted people. He'd only confided in me a few months previously.

But what if that *had* been the reason? Would I too have been culpable...for allowing him to drive? Should I have said something or kept quiet?

Chapter One

1955 – Killing Time

The Manchester Guardian   12 June 1955

Two young boys were decapitated, one next to his dying father. His mother, blood coming from a gashed arm, screamed as she clutched the mutilated body to her. The packed enclosure along the grandstand straight was a terrible scene. Hundreds of spectators went to help rescue teams, police and firemen. A priest moved slowly among the dying, administering the Last Sacraments, while volunteers covered the bodies with newspapers and torn clothing.

Levegh, killed instantly, was dragged from the blazing wreckage of his car and other bodies were carried away on stretchers and ladders. Most of the dead were French, but a police list of dead included the name of Jack Diamond, aged 24, of London, and Robert John Loxley, aged 24, of Worchester.

Two British are among the injured – Mr W.T. Saunders of Rugby, and Mr John Chapman, whose address was not given.

One of the injured, M. Jacques Lelong, said after leaving hospital today with his head in bandages, 'There was a terrific explosion and two car wheels whistled over my head. I saw a little girl in a light-coloured dress who had been trampled on by panic stricken spectators, lying in a pool of blood. A piece of metal hit me square on the forehead and I saw a headless man beside me collapse like a rag doll.'

On the other side of the track, it was several hours before many people knew of the crash as they danced in the open air and rode on the fun-fair roundabouts—

I couldn't read another word. I put down the paper, reached for my pint and drained the last inch. This was three days after the crash. After Le Mans. I'd been thinking about it, Mike and little else. I wanted to see him, of course I did, although I didn't know what on earth I should say, not even to my best friend.

I began to reflect on when we were last together. It had only been eleven days ago. We'd said our au revoirs in Paris, the day after the Belgian Grand Prix at Spa, where Mike had had a very disappointing race driving a little-known racing car called a Vanwall. I hadn't been able to get to Monaco, but the Spa circuit was much more accessible for a weekend, and Mike had indicated he'd welcome the company.

After the race, Mike invited me to join him for dinner. I knew from his mood that 'drink would be taken' that evening. We were joined by a little clique of other drivers and mutual friends in the Pierre Le Grand restaurant. Everyone was boisterous, and Mike was in fine, opinionated form. Well into the meal, Vanwall's team manager David Yorke came over to the group and tried to make polite conversation. 'What did you think of the race then, boys?'

'It would have been nice to have been in it,' quipped Mike.

David looked a little hurt. 'Don't you worry. We'll get it sorted.'

'How's that then? Found a five-lap Grand Prix...something a Vanwall can actually finish?' There was a stunned silence.

I intervened. 'Come on, Mike. That's a bit rich.'

'A bit rich? It's me who risks his neck in a bodged car that can't finish a single bloody race. The Guv's got pots of money but no know-how. His mechanics in their smart white overalls are all bloody useless. It's a bloody Fred Karno's – and they know it.' He paused to look around the assembled faces. 'David, why don't you go and tell the Guv he should sign up a half-baked driver to go with his half-baked car. I've had it with Vanwall.'

David looked as if he was about to say something. Instead, he turned on his heel and walked off.

'Fucking Vanwall!' Mike said, to no one in particular, and then laughed too loudly. It had only been the briefest of conversations but that was basically the end of Mike's contract with Vandervell. One which, as I was to learn later, would cost him dearly.

The whole Vanwall thing wasn't going well during 1955. Mike had decided to leave Ferrari to drive for Tony Vandervell, once a racing driver and now wealthy innovator. Vandervell was a man he knew and liked. It meant Mike being based in England and, moreover, driving for a British team. However, the car, beset with problems, wasn't ready for the start of the season.

Its first outing was on 7 May that year at Silverstone. Mike's teammate had crashed his Vanwall irredeemably and Mike, who had briefly held the lead, had to pull out due to an oil leak. It had pained Mike to watch another young British gun, Peter Collins, win in a Maserati. In Mike's mind, if he had been driving that Maserati then he would have surely won.

The next race was the Monaco Grand Prix. Mike had a reasonable practice session and thus qualified in the middle of the grid. That was okay, the car was fast, and these were early days. However, during the race, the fuel injection system, which was still a new concept then, failed and Mike's race came to a stuttering end after just twenty-three laps. Both Mike and Vandervell were deeply disappointed, and their relationship began to sour.

It was at this third outing, the Belgian Grand Prix, where it started to really unravel. Vandervell, widely referred to as the Guv, indulgently forsook his own Bentley in order to drive the Vanwall the short distance from the out-of-town garage to the circuit, and in doing so largely wore out the clutch. Shortly after practice commenced, the clutch had to be replaced giving Mike very little familiarisation time. Starting once more from the middle of the grid, Mike gave it everything he could in the race but the gearbox packed up on lap 8 of the thirty-six-lap race.

The morning after that awkward exchange with David Yorke, and a couple of strong black coffees, we were both on surprisingly good form, considering the evening we'd had. I asked him what would happen if Vandervell got to hear what he'd said to David Yorke. Mike said he couldn't care less. If he'd have known how dramatically Vanwall's fortunes would change, I venture he might have cared a great deal.

From Spa, Mike was due to drive directly on to Le Mans in France and had kindly offered to drop me in Paris, so I could fly back to England. This meant travelling with him in his new pride and joy, a dark green Lancia Aurelia B20 GT – something I wasn't going to turn down.

As we left the town, Mike spotted Fangio, the reigning world champion, who was driving a swanky Mercedes 300 convertible, and overtook him. Sitting three abreast with Fangio was his wife and an Argentinian radio commentator. We all smiled and waved at one another. Fangio looked totally nonplussed: one hand on the wheel, the other dangling over the door. It only strikes me now how similarly attired he'd been for the Grand Prix. For both occasions, he was driving in short-sleeved shirts. Almost the only difference was the absence of helmet and goggles.

Once we were out of sight, Mike floored the accelerator and drove like stink for two hours. Apart from through the odd village, I seldom saw the speedo needle fall below 100 miles an hour. It was one of the best rides I can remember. Although I felt in constant danger, I didn't want it to stop – it was too thrilling. Eventually, a closed railway crossing forced us to stop. Both Mike and the Lancia were completely out of breath. We'd only been sitting there for a minute or so when Fangio's Mercedes glided up alongside us. The recent Grand Prix victor was looking as relaxed as you please, still driving one-handed and greeting us with his infectious grin. The Old Man, as we affectionately knew him, was pure class behind any steering wheel.

What a lot has happened since then. On that drive, Mike had seemed so joyous and carefree – the outburst at poor David Yorke the previous night and his problems with Vanwall all seemingly forgotten.

But what must he be feeling now? I asked myself. You couldn't compare the frustration of not finishing races with being blamed for the world's *worst* ever motor racing crash. In recent years, Mike had become inured to the odd fatality at a race, as I suppose to a lesser extent we all had. It was all so common, and expected. Providing we didn't know the deceased personally and they too were racers, we seemed to accept each new fatal accident as the inherent risk of the sport. But for Mike to be held personally responsible for killing nearly one hundred spectators, well, that was an altogether different matter.

I'd read acres of newsprint about 'Le Crash'. Our own newspapers were referring to Mike as 'Mr X' – the man perceived to be responsible but who could not be named – and yet everyone knew his identity. There were no such niceties from the French media. They all but called him a murderer. I'd read so much, knew the characters so well, felt I'd been there, had actually witnessed that awful, surreal spectacle. What's more, I should have been there, was due to be there, but for my bloody employers cancelling my leave at short notice. Although I was part qualified as an accountant, I was still very junior in the practice, and far too lowly to put up any resistance. If I'd have been at Le Mans, I could have supported Mike. Equally, it wasn't lost on me that I could have been haunted for life had I seen with my own eyes that calamitous moment of impact.

I was there to support Mike at Le Mans two years earlier, when he didn't even finish. The year in between, despite having entered, he'd been forced to pull out following the tragic death of his father, Leslie. Leslie had been returning home from a day of motor racing at Goodwood – a day spent spectating, chatting and drinking steadily. He'd stopped off at a pub in Midhurst where, apparently, he reconvened with some of his cronies, for 'a couple of drinks, no more'. Later, he stopped again, this time at a friend's house near Haslemere, for 'a nightcap'. It was around eleven o'clock when he finally struck out for home, and it was raining hard. On the Churt road from Hindhead he struck another car, and was thrown out of his own, a Lancia Aurelia, whilst it was rolling over. The door must have burst open. He died of his injuries the following day, aged fifty-one. The inquest returned a verdict of accidental death, although his friends all said the non-standard Perspex windscreen was to blame. Notably, there wasn't a single reference to alcohol having been taken. Today, he'd have been well and truly over the limit. Back then, there were no limits.

Leslie's funeral was held on the same day as the 1954 Le Mans 24 Heures. Poor Mike was barely able to walk behind his father's coffin due to the horrendous burns he'd sustained two months earlier at the Sicilian Grand Prix. Clearly, the Le Mans weekend was not a good one in Mike's calendar – not even when he won.

Despite everything I'd read, I still didn't know what to think. Obviously, Mike was no murderer, but could one of my oldest and closest friends really be guilty of mass manslaughter? Driving so fast and so recklessly that he endangered the lives of others? Yes, quite possibly. How thin was the line between driving dangerously and driving on the very edge of one's own ability, and that of the car, in order to compete at the highest level?

It struck me then how fickle the press were. Only a couple of years before, on 5 July 1953, at Reims in France, Mike had claimed his first, and finest, Grand Prix victory, in a stupendous battle that became known as 'The Race of the Century'. The press had loved it: *Plucky Young Brit Beats World Champion*. And it *had* been truly remarkable. For lap after lap, there was nothing between the front runners. Sometimes, all three of them would be side by side, charging down closed public roads at speeds of 160 miles per hour. After a gruelling 312 miles (today's Formula One races are less than 200 miles), Fangio finished only one second behind Mike, with three other renowned racers, Gonzalez, Ascari and Farina, still pressing hard. Less than eight seconds separated the first five cars. Our Mike, the Farnham Flyer, had beaten the very best in the world – fair and square. In my opinion, it was his best ever performance, his golden moment – and his day didn't even finish there. But more of that anon.

So, John Michael Hawthorn was now the principal character in two of the most written-about motor races: Reims Grand Prix of '53 *and* the '55 Le Mans 24 Heures. In the first, feted as a national hero, and in the second, denigrated as an international villain.

I'd come to the pub alone, in the reasonable expectation of bumping into him. Mike was a creature of habit, and last orders at The Bell was a pretty safe bet. He never stayed away for long. On some occasions, he'd get back to Farnham for a last beer even when he was competing in Europe. Having his own aeroplane helped, of course.

I looked at my watch. It was just gone ten twenty. All our nearer regular haunts in Surrey would have closed at ten, but here in Dockenfield, a few yards into Hampshire, closing time was a heady ten thirty.

I emptied my pipe, and gathered up my tobacco, matches and newspaper. I was on the point of leaving when Mr X stooped under the front door of The Blue Bell, seconds after Muriel shouted last orders.

Leading across the threshold was his unmistakable, unruly mop of white-blond hair. It was a slow entrance by Mike's standards. He straightened, stood still for a couple of seconds, and looked around. The pub was practically empty. We caught each other's eyes. He raised his eyebrows in acknowledgement and headed towards me. I was used to seeing him look pretty ropey – nearly always the result of the night before – but today he simply looked older and wearier. His English gentleman's uniform, immaculately tailored Saville Row sports jacket, Van Heusen shirt, cavalry twill trousers and polished chukka boots, handmade by Lobbs of London, seemed incongruous with the careworn young man within.

I stood up, my hand outstretched. 'Cutting it a bit fine,' I said, immediately regretting my choice of verb – remembering too late he stood accused of cutting in front of Lance Macklin. I needn't have worried.

'Ah, at last…a friendly face,' he said, forcing a smile. 'Get me a beer, old chap. I really don't want to speak to anyone.'

'Present company excepted?' I punched him gently on the shoulder and headed off to the bar.

'Make that two, would you, Tom?' he shouted after me, his voice uncharacteristically flat.

While I was waiting for our four pints of light and mild, I pondered how perverse it was that I, on my pathetic salary, should be buying a successful racing driver not one but two drinks. He'd let slip that his retainer alone from Vandervell was £3,000 that season. In addition, he'd receive half of all starting and prize monies and bonuses. His accent may have been classic Home Counties, but he was frequently, and rightly, criticised for his legendary Yorkshire thrift. However, as I turned to look back at him, all such thoughts rapidly melted away. He was slumped forward, staring down into his lap.

As a friend of nearly twenty years, I'd witnessed most of his highs and lows. And although the press had referred to him as Golden Boy almost from the start of his career, Mike had already had more than his share of life's problems. His parents, fiery, volatile characters both, had finally split up when Mike was nineteen. Rather than stay with Leslie, his dad, and whichever floozy happened to be in favour, Mike came to live at our house for six months when his mother Winifred moved into a flat. Despite having to share my bedroom, we got on exceptionally well. It was like having a brother, and we talked about anything and everything, except his parents. It was the one subject on which he never said a word. I never knew whether this was through familial loyalty or if he was ashamed of their behaviour.

I set down our glasses and pulled round a chair so I could face him. 'To Mister X!' I was still standing, my glass raised in salute. When he looked up, I could see he was on the verge of tears.

'That's not funny!' His voice was cracking. 'I can't carry on like this…not knowing if I'm going to kill myself, or someone else. It's a bloody nightmare.'

It was clearly as bad as I feared. 'Hey, come on, Mike, what's changed?' I leaned forward and rested a hand on his shoulder. 'You always said motor racing is a lethal game, but you're still alive, right?'

'Do you know how many people they're now saying died at Le Mans? It wasn't the odd driver. They reckon it could be as many as 100 spectators. What's more, they're saying it was all my fault.'

'Well, they're bloody wrong then, aren't they?' I determined I would show my solidarity.

'How the hell do I know? I've thought about nothing else since. Lofty says it was mostly Macklin's fault. Macklin himself is going round telling everyone I'm solely to blame.' Mike took out his pipe and tobacco pouch from his jacket pocket.

'Aw, come on, Mike, you know Lofty. He's old school. If he thought you were responsible, he'd bloody well say so.'

'I hope you're right. But don't forget, as far as he's concerned, I'm Jaguar's main driver. He's got a vested interest.'

'No, Mike, he's more than that, he's a friend. He'll look after you.'

Mike banged the bowl of his pipe repeatedly against the sole of his shoe. The ash fell onto the stone floor. 'That's the point – he can't. Drivers are just cannon fodder: the cars aren't safe, the tracks aren't safe. Look what happened to Chubby the other day – best fucking driver I ever saw, quicker than Fangio.' He stuffed the pipe with fresh tobacco, lit it with a silver Dunhill lighter, and drew upon it heavily.

I'd read about the 'Chubby' accident. Barely a month before, Alberto 'Chubby' Ascari, two times World Champion and latterly Mike's teammate, had died during testing for Ferrari. Mike had been devastated. Whether this was because it could so easily have been him, or whether Ascari and he had become close whilst both driving for Ferrari, I wasn't sure. The British newspapers had given Ascari's death substantial coverage. However, in Italy, the story was huge. They said one million mourners, all dressed in black had gathered to watch his horse-drawn hearse pass through the streets of Milan. Even if one allows for Italian exaggeration, it must have been a momentous occasion.

It wasn't just the loss of a charming, popular national figure. It was the most extraordinary coincidences around his death which gave the papers so much material. Alberto was the son of a famous pre-war motor racing champion and was notoriously superstitious.

It was at the Monaco Grand Prix that year when Ascari Junior had his most spectacular crash. His car left the track, plunged straight into the harbour, and sank out of sight. Fortunately, Chubby quickly bobbed up and was rescued by frogmen. He'd got away with only a broken nose and various cuts and bruises. Four days later, he unexpectedly pitched up at Monza, Ferrari's home circuit, where his teammate Eugenio Castellotti was testing a 750S Ferrari sports car. Alberto surprised everyone by announcing that he ought to get into a car again quickly, in case he lost his nerve. He didn't have his lucky blue helmet with him and so had to borrow one from Castellotti. The first two laps he took steadily. As he started the third, he really went for it. And it was on the third that he lost control. The car overturned and he was killed.

As for some of the coincidences: both Alberto *and* his father died aged thirty-six, and on the twenty-sixth day of the month. Each left behind a wife and two children. They had won thirteen Grands Prix apiece. Both were killed exiting easy left-hand corners whilst racing four days after surviving serious accidents. The papers thought it was some weird supernatural occurrence. Mike thought otherwise.

He slammed down his glass. 'And why did he die?' His voice was unnecessarily loud. 'Simply because a fucking tyre came off a rim! One stupid accident, and, hey presto another widow. Two kids without a father. He wasn't even racing, for Christ's sake!'

I took a long draught of my beer and attempted to change the subject. 'So, do you have much planned before you have to go off again?'

'I was hoping to have a few days catching up with Mum at the garage, but I have to go up to London tomorrow. Lofty wants me to appear on the television with Rudi Uhlenhaut of Mercedes, describing the crash and our reflections on it. There's really no bloody end to it.'

I made a mental note to look out for that broadcast. Rudi, despite his German name, spoke perfect English, and I could imagine he'd be eloquent on behalf of Mercedes. I doubted that I'd learn much, but I was curious to see how Mike would cope in front of the TV cameras.

We chatted on until, eventually, Muriel accused us of not having homes to go to. The Blue Bell was a lovely old pub in a tiny rural settlement a few miles to the south of Farnham and less than ten minutes from our respective homes. We'd been using it for years. The police never came by, which was the main reason we'd started frequenting it long before we were legally entitled.

As we headed for the door, Mike spotted a pair of youths. I recognised one of them as an apprentice at the Tourist Trophy Garage, the Hawthorn family business. The lads, probably barely seventeen, looked at us warily.

Mike marched up to the apprentice. 'What are you staring at, you little shit?'

'Er, nothing, Mr Hawthorn, sir. Only, me and me mate – we only wanted to say "well done".'

'Bollocks, you did. Listen up, if you're so much as one second late in the morning, Sunshine, you'll be looking for another job. Oh, and one other thing, I don't ever want to see you in here again. Have you got that?'

'Er...yes, sir...right, sir. Goodnight, Mr Hawthorn.'

We walked out in silence. This was a side of Mike I wasn't used to seeing, and it made me uncomfortable. He'd been inclined to moodiness for some time and could often be tetchy, yet seldom really aggressive. I knew that his irritability was usually linked to bouts of back pain, but he would never excuse himself or explain. I think that is why people said he had two characters – a bit of a Jekyll and Hyde.

Mike was routinely described in the newspapers as 'genial', 'unassuming' and 'polite'. I wanted to believe that it was the events of the past few days that had brought out this aggression, but unfortunately it chimed with recent stories about him bullying his staff since he'd taken over the garage from his father. It was a trait that I would witness increasingly as Mike became more famous.

Our cars were almost the last in the car park: my dad's flat grey Austin Somerset right next to Mike's glossy dark green, sleek Lancia.

I was reminded of another Lancia, and another time. It was only four years earlier, yet we seemed to be different people then. Mike had recently joined the Steering Wheel Club in Mayfair, and one of the members had invited him up to London for a New Year's Eve party. Mike had duly 'borrowed' a Lancia Aprilia from his dad's garage for the expedition. We'd set off, thinking we'd stop at a couple of pubs en route for a little 'social lubrication'. Predictably, we stopped rather more than we intended and, having only got as far as Ripley, decided that London seemed far too far away. Instead, we decided we'd go to a different party, one we'd heard of in nearby Haslemere.

By this time, we were sharing the driving. Mike had full steering responsibilities and I had gear-changing and observation duties. We were coming off the Hog's Back section of the A3, going like the clappers – with Mike singing for all he was worth – when the Lancia's back end suddenly went sideways. I had no idea what a portentous event this would prove to be. The car flipped onto its side and skidded down the road. It was the weirdest sensation. When the car stopped, almost nothing had changed. Mike was still clutching the wheel, singing away. I was in the passenger seat, and the rear wheels were still whizzing round. The main difference was that we were at ninety degrees to the road – me with my face only inches off the tarmac, and Mike wedged in his seat above me looking as if he was going to fall on top of me at any moment. We managed to scramble out of the driver's door, as if clambering out of a submarine, and a passing lorry driver kindly helped us push the car back over. We then drove onto the Haslemere party – a little more gingerly, but still giggling all the way.

Mike's current, distinctly exotic Lancia, registration JMH 21, was an altogether superior beast. It was a two-door coupé, styled by Pininfarina, that had cost Mike somewhere around £3,500 – not much less than an Aston Martin. Looking back, the Lancia Aurelia might seem an unusual choice for a British racing driver but it's worth pointing out that, in 1951, this car had finished first in its class at Le Mans, and second overall in the Mille Miglia endurance race. Moreover, the greatly admired Fangio had owned one. Ominously, it was the only car Fangio was known to have crashed off the track. He'd swerved, spun twice, and had been thrown clear, grazing his elbows as he fell.

As we approached our cars, it struck me that Mike shouldn't be driving. Neither of us was exactly what you'd call sober. I'd had four pints, and I was certain that Mike had had all that or more even by the time he'd arrived at The Blue Bell. He could handle it. Probably better than me. No, always better than me.

I held the door for him as he clambered in and sank down into the beige leather bucket seat. He gripped the large wooden steering wheel for a moment before firing up the V6 engine. A rich, rasping growl shattered the still quiet of the country night. An electric aerial rose as if by magic from the right front wing.

He then turned to look up at me and, with a big smile, the first proper Hawthorn smile I'd seen all evening, he said quietly, 'Thanks for that, mate. Thanks for believing in me.'

Instantly, I felt ashamed that I hadn't actually said that I did, at least not outright. I slammed the door, and he took off, just like the Mike of old, spraying gravel noisily against the fence.

The four chromium exhaust pipes picked up what little light there was and sparkled. I watched the receding tail lights until they disappeared. The spectator, not the player. All my life, I'd had conflicting feelings about my friend: consuming jealousy and deep affection. Ever since we were seven years old, he'd effortlessly won whatever competition lay before us. Mike first, Tom second. It didn't matter whether it was running, jumping, cricket or shooting. I was better than average. Mike was outstanding. My mum kept an old photograph of Mike, two other lads and me racing in our pedal cars shortly after we met. No prizes for guessing who was in the lead. And later, when we were pursuing girls, it was always me fighting for them and Mike fighting them off. Before Mike began racing cars, we both tried our hand at scrambling (it's what they call motocross today). There was no way I could keep up with him.

I had tried blaming my parents, and my schooling, but the truth was, come what may, Mike would always be faster, more handsome, more popular, more flamboyant…more everything. Yet, I counted him amongst my very best friends – and, to his great credit, he had stayed in touch, not only with me, but with all 'the Members' – our gang of friends who'd grown up together with a common fondness for motorbikes, beer and girls. I couldn't have said it then, and perhaps I shouldn't say it now, but I think I was slightly in love with Mike.

Back home, I went straight to bed. Sleep wouldn't come. I had so many thoughts racing round my mind that my skull felt like a race track. Mike seemed to keep so much anger and frustration, even self-pity, below the surface. Maybe these emotions could only be vented in a racing car? Could he carry on competing at the highest level or were his best days behind him? Could he ever get over Le Mans? Was he really going to be convicted of manslaughter?

I began to think about Mike's mother and how upset she must be. Michael was her only child. It dawned on me then that Mike's new car, the Lancia, was exactly the same model as the one in which his father had killed himself a year ago. I wondered what lay behind such a grotesque choice. I knew Mike genuinely liked Italian cars – we all did – but there were plenty of other cars he could have chosen. What must his poor mother have felt when she saw him driving it?

Chapter Two

Cherry

The following Saturday, Tim Miers, another of the Members, and I went to see a film at the Regal, a substantial red-brick Art Deco picture house in East Street. The film was *Sabrina*, starring Humphrey Bogart and Audrey Hepburn. I don't think either of us knew much about what we were going to watch. The sole reason for going was Miss Hepburn. She was our ideal girl – a real glamour puss – and we were rewarded with a few shots of her long, shapely legs. As it turned out, it was also quite a good flick.

We were still shuffling out of the auditorium when Tim turned to me and whispered, 'Hey, isn't that Cherry Huggins in front?'

It clearly was – she was unmistakable. 'Who's she's with?' I asked.

'No idea. Shall we see if they want to come for a drink?'

'Phwoar...you'll be lucky.'

Cherry Huggins was Farnham's answer to Audrey Hepburn. She was easily the most attractive girl of our acquaintance. And the most posh. Her parents, Lord and Lady Huggins, had recently retired to the UK from the West Indies, where her father had been the Governor of Jamaica and Trinidad, and had settled very near the Hawthorns. Word got out that Lady Molly had the hots for Mike and would frequently go to his garage to buy tiny quantities of petrol in the hope of seeing him. Needless to say, we ribbed him about this something rotten.

Lady M would pull in towards the pumps and 'accidentally' park miles away so that the fuel hose wouldn't reach. Then she'd flounce out of the car saying to whoever was serving, 'Don't worry, dear boy, I'll get Michael to move it.' Which, invariably, he did.

We caught up with Cherry and her companion as they stepped out onto the street.

Tim wasted no time. 'Well, Cherry, fancy seeing you. I don't suppose you lovely ladies could be persuaded to join Tom and me for a drink, or perhaps a coffee?'

I so wished I could have done that: gone straight up to them and asked them out.

Cherry's friend was a right plain Jane. I wondered why it was that smashing girls typically hung around with girls who were, shall I say, less fortunate in looks. Was it that the less fortunate perceived it raising their own currency, or the more fortunate girls' way of ensuring little competition?

'Oh yes, that would be great, thanks. I don't think you've met my cousin, Ella.' Cherry's smile was bewitching.

I began to picture how the rest of the evening would unfold: Tim smooth-talking Cherry into a date, leaving me with Ella, both of us pretending to be interested in each other when it was patently not the case.

We agreed on the Nelson Arms, which Cherry said would have to be strictly for one drink. Apparently, having recently signed up with a modelling agency, Cherry needed to go to London the next day and Ella would be travelling with her. The Nelson was only a short walk away and was almost certainly nominated by Tim because it was dark, beamy and intimate.

Cherry was looking wonderful, her brunette hair cut short like Hepburn's, emphasising her large eyes and fine features. The conversation was a little stilted at first. Tim asked whether they were intending to see *The Ladykillers,* a new comedy starring Alec Guinness, which was coming to Farnham in the next week. Just as I thought he might be on the point of suggesting that he take Cherry, she interrupted with, 'Oh yes, it does sound awfully good, doesn't it…Mike's promised to take me.'

There was a moment's silence. Tim shot me a glance. We must have had the same thought. Mike? Not *bloody* Hawthorn? How could that be? He was always abroad somewhere.

Fortunately, Ella picked up the conversation, but the atmosphere had subtly changed. Tim was no longer leaning forward and had started to include Ella in his remarks. How come we hadn't heard that Mike was now walking out with Farnham's best girl? And what about his present girl – the sexy Moia? Had he even told her? I sat there quietly, amused that Tim had been so royally thwarted, but also a little upset to think that there were things Mike hadn't told me.

I caught up with Mike a few days later. He'd just got back from the Dutch Grand Prix and telephoned that afternoon to propose we meet at 'the Pond' for an early beer. The Frensham Pond was an old haunt of ours, and invariably an early start here would lead to a pub crawl – or, more accurately, a pub car sprint, as most of the nearby pubs had unofficial timed stages between them.

Mike was already there when I arrived bang on time. He looked in great shape, sharply dressed, and his blue eyes were sparkling. 'Come on, bo, you're missing valuable drinking time. What'll you have?' Calling each other 'bo' was strictly a Members' thing. How it started, no one could remember.

'I'll have an IPA, thanks. By the way, how was the Dutch?' Even though I knew the answer, I couldn't resist asking the question.

'Don't ask. It was a fucking disaster. Bloody Krauts...First and second, the bastards. Couldn't get close to them. Ours simply aren't good enough. The gears stick, they understeer...even the Masers were quicker than us. You probably heard I was seventh.'

I knew this wasn't the whole story. It had been reported that Mike himself had underperformed, but I wasn't about to rub it in. Mercedes' superiority had virtually guaranteed Fangio and Moss first and second places. And yet the Ferraris should have been highly competitive with the Maseratis who took third, fourth and sixth. One Ferrari split up the Maseratis, coming fifth, although not with Mike at the wheel but his teammate Castellotti. An on-form Mike would never have come second to 'Casti'. I'd hoped that, following Vanwall's mid-season retirement, Mike's fortunes would improve now he was back with Ferrari.

'Maybe it's just not your sort of circuit?' I ventured lamely.

'I dunno how Stirling can live with himself – driving for the Krauts. Bloody traitor.' Mike clearly didn't want to dwell on his own performance.

'Hey, steady on. The war finished ten years ago – Germany's part of NATO now – and, anyway, you're driving for one of their allies.' I was surprised to find myself defending Stirling.

Mike took the glasses off the bar, placed them on a small table, and sat down heavily. 'Would *you* buy a German car?'

None of our circle approved of the Germans much. The emotional scars on our parents' generation were still quite raw, but still Mike's hatred was excessive. I wasn't in the mood for an argument. 'Look, I can't afford any decent car – German or otherwise. Enough about all this. Give me some low-down on the Dutch crumpet.' I was on a fishing expedition, hoping he'd spill the beans about Cherry.

That smile again. 'What can I say, Tom? At least, what can I say that won't get back to Moi?'

'Moia?' He was clearly holding out on me.

'Yeah, Moia. Who else? Anyway, what happened after Reims a couple of years ago has rather put me off all that sort of thing.'

After Reims. Now there's a story. Mike's first taste of Grand Prix success, the French of '53, wasn't only newsworthy for his driving. Having surmounted the winners' podium for the first time and sprayed the champagne, he'd decided it was time to really celebrate.

It is said Mike blagged his way into a Reims Tennis Club 'soirée' the night before the race and had met two local sisters there. The girls, having watched the Grand Prix from the grandstands, managed to fight their way through the throng of well-wishers to add their appreciation. Mike introduced them to Lance Macklin, who was a good friend back then, and they in turn had introduced Mike to their father. Papa suggested they all go back with him to celebrate with more champagne, which they did.

Being particularly attracted to the older sister, Jacqueline, Mike asked if he could take her out for dinner. Papa consented, with the proviso that Lance took sister Monique along to act as chaperones. Which, given Lance's matinee-idol looks and his lascivious reputation, was a shockingly irrational call on the father's part. After the four had dined together at Auberge de la Garenne, a chic restaurant situated directly on the race circuit, Mike and Lance took the sisters back to the hotel at which they were both staying. It wasn't an innocent move. Suffice to say, Monique, the nineteen-year-old younger sister, managed to say '*non*' to thirty-three-year-old Lance whereas her slightly older but less wise sister said '*oui*' to twenty-four-year-old Mike. Poor Lance was forced to sit with Monique making small talk when neither could really speak the other's language. The following day, Mike and Lance packed up and left for England. Three months later, Jacqueline discovered she was carrying Mike's baby.

It was from Lance that I'd first learnt about Mike's night of French passion, but I was fairly sure Lance knew nothing of the unplanned outcome. That was so hush-hush that even Mike's mother didn't know. If Lance had known, I reasoned, he'd have blurted out something to the press by now. He was that angry with Mike over the Le Mans crash.

By now, more people were drifting into the Pond – many we knew. There was a buzz about the place and the air was thick with tobacco smoke. Mike singled out one new arrival. 'Hello, look who's crawled out of the woodwork!'

I turned to see Don Beauman, an old school friend of Mike's. 'Hello, boys, whose round is it?' he demanded, boisterously.

'Ah, if it isn't the brigadier's little boy! How come you're down? Who's looking after the hotel?' asked Mike.

'I can give myself the odd day off, you know. I heard you were back in town, so I thought I'd come and cadge a drink off you.'

'What'll you be having?'

'Hmm, what are *you* drinking…? A snowball?' Snowball was a nickname Mike had acquired immediately he started at Ardingly College, aged thirteen, on account of his shock of white blond hair. This is where, as dormitory captain, he had first met Don, and they had remained firm friends since. I made a point of never calling him Snowball.

'You'll get a bloody snowball if you're not careful! And it should be *you* buying *me* a drink, seeing as how I got you into Jaguar.'

'I suppose my exceptional driving talent had nothing to do with it?' Don shot back.

'Nope. I only wanted you in because it would make me look quicker.' Mike seemed to have shifted up a gear. He loved this sort of banter, especially in front of an audience.

I felt my status change. Up until then, I'd been sitting with Mike in my capacity as his oldest, and I thought, most trusted friend. But Don was becoming a proper racing driver, and it was Don who'd met Mike from the airport when he'd come back for his father's funeral. It didn't really matter that he wasn't in the same class as Mike. All that mattered was they were *drivers*, and I wasn't. And they

34

were both public school. It wasn't that either man was deliberately rude or exclusive; it was just that they would automatically fall into technical discussions to which I could contribute little. Mike was busy sounding off about rain tyres. I sat down alone, wondering if he'd told Don about Cherry.

'Hey, Mike,' boomed Brian, an old school friend of ours, who'd just spotted him, 'how's it going? Are you still seeing the lovely Ann?' Redheaded Ann had been a friend of Brian's sister, and someone whom many of us fancied.

'Ann? Now, let me think...' said Mike, looking puzzled. 'Ah, yes, I remember her. Now, she was before Marjorie, I think...' He paused before continuing slowly. 'And definitely Rosemary... and Valerie...and Kathy...and Dorrie...' He paused again before speeding up. 'But *after* Norene, Sarah and Diana – or were they at the same time?'

As he tailed off, he looked around his audience and beamed. There was spontaneous applause. Impressive though the list was, I knew that it was far from exhaustive. And it wasn't lost on me that Moi and Cherry had escaped inclusion, not to mention Jacqueline.

Feeling unnecessary, I took myself off to the gents. What was it about Hawthorn that made him so irresistible to girls, and men come to that? I caught sight of myself as I approached the urinal. Taller even than Mike, and he was considered tall, slicked brown hair, brown eyes, and regular features. What was it my mother used to say? 'Just smile a bit more, dear'? Was that it? I didn't smile enough?

Fortunately, we quickly moved on from the Pond, and by the time we got to the Cherry Tree at Rowledge we'd been joined by Ray and the two Johns, Waghorn and Nicholson, none of whom were proper racers. Someone then suggested we go on down to The Greatham Inn which, despite its name, wasn't exactly great, or nearby. When the idea was greeted with groans, the proposer tried to convince us that the barmaid there had the best pair of 'bazooms' in the county. I didn't really mind either way, for the undulating route had lots of gentle bends and took in a fast, wide section of the A325 where we would commonly see if anyone could get over the ton. I persuaded Ray to let me drive his MG and we set off just ahead of Don, Mike and the two Johns. I drove as fast as the little car would go, wanting

Don to see that I too was capable of driving quickly.

Ray and I arrived comfortably ahead of the others. We piled into the lounge bar and immediately ordered six pints of light and mild, and two light and bitters. We then sat down, affecting to have been there for ages as the others trooped in.

After a while, Mike proposed that we play Spoof, a game similar to Liar Dice but using coins rather than dice. The forfeit was that the loser would have to steal the bugle off the wall beside the bar and play it for at least a minute. Mike was calling some outrageous numbers, as if he wanted to lose. In the all-important head-to-head, Mike lost. Mike asked Ray to pop round to the public bar and order a drink. The moment the barmaid's attention was diverted, Mike reached up, grabbed the bugle and put it to his lips. To my astonishment, Mike managed to play something short and almost tuneful. With a full minute to fill, and with a limited repertoire, he proceeded to repeat the piece a couple of times. As he went to put it back, there was applause from both sides of the bar.

'That was pretty impressive,' commented the landlord who'd appeared from nowhere.

'I'm a bit rusty.' Mike was flushed and panting a little.

'I know you,' said the landlord. 'You're that Mike Hawthorn, aren't you?'

'The very same,' said Mike as he smiled and extended his hand.

Mike was such a regular sight around Farnham most locals left him alone. It was a bit of shock to realise he'd become a household name, and face, further afield.

'Well, I never. Would you care for a drink? On the house, of course,' added the landlord.

Mike was always being offered free drinks, though God knows he needed them less than the rest of us. And what was with the bugle playing? Another bloody talent, and one I knew nothing about. Or maybe one I'd forgotten. No wonder his calling had been so poor – he'd intended to lose.

'So, when did you learn to play the bugle – or can you just do everything?' I asked, intending to sound jovial but coming across rather bitter.

'Have you forgotten I was in the JTC band at school – not that I was any good.' JTC was the Junior Training Corps, and the 'school' he was referring to was Ardingly College, not the little pre-prep school we'd both attended. 'There's really nothing to it. I bet you could learn in a week.'

I silently bet myself I couldn't.

I'd cycled to the Pond, with little intention of cycling back. Mike kindly offered me a lift home which I accepted. If he was tipsy, he didn't show it. I wasn't sorry to leave the others. They were all good blokes, in their way, but Mike was forever playing to the gallery – and they couldn't help but fawn. I don't know if they even realised they were doing it. Mike drove us slowly. He only had two speeds: flat out or sedate. He seemed suddenly pensive. He turned on the car wireless. *Dreamboat* by Alma Cogan was playing.

'What do reckon to her?' Mike demanded.

'She's okay,' I said, hedging my bets.

'But not a looker?'

I didn't exactly disagree, although I felt Mike was being harsh. The next record was *Ain't That a Shame* by Pat Boone, which I liked a lot. 'Now this *is* good,' I said.

'S'okay, but Fats Domino's version is far better.'

I wondered whether Mike genuinely thought that or was being deliberately provocative, showing off his cosmopolitan status. We didn't speak again until we arrived at my parents' place.

'Do you want to come in? Say hello to the old man if he's still up?' I asked.

'Sure that's okay?'

'Of course, he'll be pleased to see you.'

No one was still up. I shouldn't have been surprised: it was midweek and both my parents would be going to work the next day. We tiptoed through to the kitchen and closed the door. Mike sat down and rested his elbows on the kitchen table, one hand cradling his head. I made some coffee. I was embarrassed we only had Camp. Mike didn't say anything. I guessed he was starting only to drink the real stuff by then.

'Tom, can I trust you?'

'Depends.'

'Don't mess about. This is important. I'm in a spot of bother. I need to talk to someone.'

'Do you think now's the time? We've both had quite a bit...'

I thought he was going to witter on about Jacqueline's paternity claim. 'Is it about the butterfly who kissed a frog?' I quipped. Mike had been christened 'Le Papillon' by the French press, prior to Le Crash, on account of his trademark bow ties.

'What on earth are you on about?' he replied sharply.

I thought he knew perfectly well, but I let it go. 'Is it about Moia, then?' I asked. I'd become quite fond of Moia. Mike had first chatted her up at the '53 Earls Court Motor Show, where she'd been hired as a glamour girl for the Michelin Tyres stand. We all pulled Mike's leg about him going out with a pneumatic woman, although the truth was she was yet another very slim and beautiful Hawthorn conquest. I wondered what my chances might be with Moia if Mike was moving on. Of course, I wouldn't be able to buy her expensive presents, or drop the odd hundred quid into her account, like he did.

'Moia? No, don't be daft.'

'Is it true you're now walking out with Cherry?'

'Bloody hell, you've got your ear close to the ground! What've you heard?' After a slight pause, he continued in a quieter voice. 'Do you think Moi knows?'

So it was bloody true. 'I don't know. I've not told her – but you've got to. She can't hear about this from other people.'

I told him about Tim and me seeing Cherry after the pictures, and how I thought Tim was going to pluck up courage to ask her out only to discover 'bloody Hawthorn' had beaten him to it.

Mike smiled, fleetingly. 'I'm still very fond of Moi, you know, but this isn't about her.'

'So, if this isn't about crumpet, what's the big secret?'

'You got any Scotch?'

'Only my father's and he's asleep.' This had all the hallmarks of another evening I would live to regret.'

'Your old man likes me. He won't mind. I like all your family. You're really, really lucky, you know.'

Mike, envious of me? That sobered me up a bit. Well, I suppose I did have what he didn't: parents who actually liked each other. I went to fetch the Scotch from Dad's little mirror-lined drinks cabinet in the lounge. 'Oh, all right, just a wee one,' I said as returned. I poured out some Bells, about two fingers for Mike and about half as much for me. 'Now, come on. What's the big secret?'

'I'm going to die.'

He'd spoken softly. His tone hadn't changed. I nearly missed it. I sat down opposite him. I wanted to look into his eyes, but he was staring down at his hands. I wanted him to suddenly laugh.

'Yeah, yeah, we're all going to die,' I managed.

He glanced up again. 'Ah, the difference is you're going to make seventy, maybe eighty. Me – I'll be damned lucky to get to thirty.'

He lifted his whisky and drained what little remained.

'Only if you drive like an idiot. Look at Fangio – he's *really* old. He's well into his forties! The best will always survive. And you and Fange, well, you *are* the very best. That's what the papers called you after Reims.' I sensed I was sounding scared, and I instinctively knew I mustn't.

'It's not racing that's going to kill me.' Still the uncharacteristic, expressionless delivery – so unlike him.

It wasn't like Mike to be melodramatic. He'd already experienced more drama in his twenty-six years than I would in a lifetime. In the past eighteen months alone, he'd been hounded by the press for draft dodging, nearly burnt to death in Sicily, pursued for paternity, had lost his father – and many friends – and was now accused of killing almost 100 people. Maybe the irrepressible Golden Boy had finally met his Waterloo. Either way, the gulf between his and my staid, boring life was humbling.

'If you really want to jack it all in, well…let's face it, you've had a good innings. And you've always got the garage to fall back on.'

'You just don't get it, do you?' Mike was now staring intently at me, his blue eyes wide open.

'Well, obviously not.' I was tired and beginning to get irritated.

'You know that I've complained about having backaches for years?'

I nodded.

'And that sometimes it hurts to pee?'

'Yup.'

'They're related symptoms. It's my kidneys, they're packing up. The quacks think I've only got five to seven years left.'

I was struck dumb. I wanted to believe this was a classic Hawthorn wind-up, but it didn't feel right. I scoured his face, desperate for clues. He looked deadpan, deadly serious. And yet so very far from death. He looked positively healthy. 'I don't know what to say.'

'There's not much to say.'

'They could be wrong?' Conversationally, this was uncharted territory for us.

'Fat chance. It was last year, in Rome. You remember when I was being treated for burns...the doctors thought I had kidney troubles then. They told me to see my doctor when I got home.'

'Which you did?'

'Sort of. I saw Pat and he told me to see a urologist.' Pat Kendall was a close doctor friend of Mike's. Mike had lodged briefly with Pat and his wife Jill when he first went up to London

'A what?' I'd never hear of a urologist.

'A consultant chappie. Straight after Pop's funeral, I went up to London to see him. He wanted to know all about my back pains and my trouble peeing. He reckoned it was a congenital kidney defect.'

'Meaning?'

'It means he thought my kidneys were on the blink and they'd soon give up altogether. He also thought I had a bloody great kidney stone...'

'What's that when it's at home?'

'I don't know...it's not good. He wanted to operate there and then but I persuaded him to wait until after the end of the season.'

'Didn't you want to get it sorted?'

'What, and have to explain to Enzo Ferrari why I was AWOL for the Belgian, the French *and* the British Grand Prix? I'd have been sacked. As it turned out, the season only got better for me as it went on.'

It was a fair point. He'd come second in both the British and the Italian, and won the final GP in Spain, to finish third overall in the Championship, only half a point behind Gonzalez. I remember Mike seemed happier about finishing ten places above Stirling than he did about coming third. I couldn't believe he'd not told me before now. 'And then?'

'I had to go up to Guy's Hospital – obviously on the QT. They were meant to just deal with the kidney stone, but the bastards were obviously enjoying themselves so much they took out the whole bloody kidney.'

'What? You mean you've only got one left?'

'Uh-huh. I was kept in for a couple of weeks. It was pretty dire. I doubt you'll remember but I told people I was on holiday with Moi.'

'Oh, mate, I wish I'd known. You know I'd've come to see you.'

'Until now, Moi's the only person who knows – apart from Mum. Moi was great – came to see me nearly every day. That's when she was living in Earls Court.'

'You mean even Lofty doesn't know?'

'Um…I had to tell him – he'd have found out eventually.'

Of course, Lofty would've known. Ever since Mike's father died, Mike had leant on him like a surrogate father.

'But not old man Ferrari?'

'Christ, no! He'd never trust me with his precious cars again.'

'Why ever not?'

'Because I might black out again, that's why. Plus he's a heartless bastard.'

'Black out? Again? What, whilst you're driving? Christ—'

'It's possible. Although it hasn't happened yet.'

'But you've told Lofty?'

'He was there once.' Mike looked me straight in the eyes. 'Look, Tom, you mustn't breathe a word of this. If the press get wind, they'll have a field day. Just think of the fuss. I'd lose my racing licence. It'd be far worse than all that draft-dodging malarkey…' Allegations of Mike avoiding his national service had by then largely died down, mostly because Mike had turned twenty-six and was therefore no longer eligible.

'Why are you telling me, then?'

'Because you're my best mate.'

I was really touched by that. He was easily my best mate, but I thought Don or Duncan Hamilton or Rob Walker or any other of his many racing chums would now be a new best mate. 'I won't tell a soul, I promise, but surely the press are bound to find out about your op sometime?'

'Not if everyone keeps schtum,' he said, pointedly.

'Is it possible to live normally with just one kidney?' I knew nothing whatsoever about kidneys. I wasn't even sure where in the body they were.

'Seems to be working so far – although it's likely to be about as reliable as a Vanwall.'

'What happens if it plays up?

'That's the point. It's not *if*, it's *when*! And when it does, I've been assured it'll be sheer bloody agony. I don't want to think about it.' Finally, his expression said it all. He was scared stiff.

It had taken a while but the enormity of what he was telling me had finally registered. 'It's not if, it's when' was the phrase that had managed to penetrate my thick skull. I'd gone from wanting to believe he was overreacting to some potentially dangerous condition to now understanding that he'd been handed an immutable death sentence. A chill ran down my spine.

I wanted to stay positive for him. 'Please don't say that. There *has* to be some kind of cure, surely?'

'Not yet. My consultant thinks that one day they might be able to transplant a kidney from one person to another.'

'God, that would be incredible.' I noticed Mike's empty glass. 'Did they say anything about drinking?'

'They suggested I regularly flush my system through – by drinking a lot.' He had brightened again.

I couldn't keep up. 'Presumably they meant water?'

'I must have missed that bit. But, if you're offering, I'll have another little one for the road – perhaps this time with water?' he said, handing me his glass.

The combination of unburdening his secret and more alcohol seemed to have lifted his mood. With another small Scotch in his hand, Mike spent the next few minutes reminiscing about his time in hospital, talking about tubes coming out of every orifice, and the nurses he tried in vain to chat up.

'You know, I thought all this was going to be about your little French problem,' I ventured.

For months after she learnt she was expecting, Jacqueline had tried every means at her disposal to contact Mike, even managing a 'chance' encounter at the Paris Motor Show that October.

He'd said afterwards, 'This bloody French girl came up to me and told me she was carrying my child. She didn't look a bit pregnant to me. I thought she was having me on – saying I had to marry her and so forth. Well, we've all heard about blokes being had like that so I told her to clear off. I told her I didn't love her, and if she was pregnant it was her own stupid fault. She created the most God-awful scene...screaming and crying. She's a nice enough girl, and of course I felt bad about it, but how could I even know if the child was mine?'

And that would have been the end of it had Jacqueline decided not to keep the unborn child. Her old man, a strict Catholic, was apparently outraged and had banished his daughter to the servants' quarters for the duration of her pregnancy. Once Mike's son, Arnaud was born, the charming man threw them both out.

'Ah,' said Mike, 'the "little problem" has now become a big problem.'

'In what way?'

'She's started writing to me.'

'Blimey, how does she know how to reach you?'

'She writes to me at the garage. Fortunately, lovely Annie hides all the envelopes before Ma gets to see them.' Ann was tall, dark, slim and jolly attractive. She was also barely sixteen – ten years younger than us. It amused me to see Mike's mother, Winifred, practically growl at Mike if she thought he was unnecessarily hanging around her young assistant. 'Jacqueline's saying I must marry her for the sake of the boy. I've been telling her it's impossible.'

'Impossible?'

'I'm meant to be going out with Moi – I'm even having trouble staying faithful to her. I don't know whether it's the racing or what, but, honestly, I'm constantly surrounded by the most fantastic crumpet. Anyway, I can't marry her – imagine what Mother would say.'

'What are you going to do?' I tried imagining Mike married to this French girl. I had a picture of them walking along, each of them holding the hand of a little boy between them. No, Mike would be a nightmare father, and husband – he knew it and I knew it. And what would be the point? It would only be for a matter of a few years, and then she'd be a widow. That is, if she didn't divorce him sooner.

'She says that, if I won't marry her, I must give her money for the boy.'

'That's not totally unreasonable, is it?' Emotionally, I was all over the shop by now due to a heady combination of the beer, the Scotch, and the news. But I reckoned it was highly likely Mike was the father, and I suspected him of being typically tight-fisted.

'The problem is, I'm absolutely boracic.'

Did Mike really think I was going to buy that? 'Oh, pull the other one.'

'No, I'm serious. I owe Ferrari literally hundreds because of Sicily. The insurance paid out something towards patching me up but Enzo picked up the rest – on the understanding it would be deducted from my earnings.'

'So he takes it out of your salary?'

'I don't get a salary from Ferrari. Not even a bloody retainer. I only get a share of any prize money.'

I was momentarily speechless.

He went on, 'And now, because of all this fucking Le Mans nonsense, half the Grands Prix have been cancelled. To make matters worse, I've had to hand back much of what I got from Vanwall. It was nothing I did. It was totally their choice to pull out.'

I was genuinely shocked at the thought of Mike having to hand back a large chunk of £3,000. I knew he also had his Jaguar earnings and his other commercial interests, but that retainer alone would have been sufficient to buy a nice house outright. 'Okay, but you've still got the potential to earn loads, haven't you?'

'Depends on how long I live, doesn't it?'

Another nail of realisation punctured my cranium. 'Yeah, I suppose so,' I muttered. I got up saying I needed a slash. While I was relieving myself, I began to imagine how I would react if I was told I only had a few years to live. What would I do? How would I cope? Would I want others to know? If there was nothing that I or anyone else could do about it, maybe I would want to travel the world – make the most of my remaining time. Then again, surely I'd want to spend the precious time with my family and friends. It wasn't resolvable: wanting to go everywhere and stay put at the same time. I couldn't work it out.

As I re-entered the kitchen, I said, 'You know, if there's anything, anything at all, you've only got to ask.' I knew the futility of the offer the moment I'd made it, but I desperately wanted him to know that I cared.

'That's very kind, old chap.' He suddenly flashed me a smile, a Hawthorn special. 'So, once they work out how to transfer kidneys, I'll know where to come.'

Shortly after that, I felt desperately tired. Mike also looked all-in. I told him I had to be at work in just a few hours and suggested he drink up and drive home, carefully. That at least provoked a chuckle. We got up simultaneously from either side of the kitchen table, and I stuck out my hand. He took it, and we squeezed each other's hand for all we were worth.

As he headed out the door, he turned and said, 'You know what I'm going to do? I'm going to drink too much, bed every pretty girl I can, and never lose a race to a fucking German.'

'In other words, you're going to carry on exactly as before, only faster!'

'Exactly!' And, with that, he strode off into the night.

I went up to my room and closed the door gently for fear of waking my parents, and fell face first onto my bed. It was then that the tears began. I couldn't remember the last time I cried. I was a grown man, for Christ's sake. It was all I could do to keep quiet. I wanted to yell at the blasted unfairness of it all.

Mike was still a young man. We were both twenty-six, but he'd be lucky to live much beyond thirty. He was always talking about the possibility of killing himself in a car, but this was different. This was a non-negotiable death sentence, with an absolute certainty, irrespective of whether he ever raced again. This was worse, much worse.

I'd been preparing myself for the 'big' accident, the final one, for years. I always comforted myself with the knowledge that, if it happened, at least he'd be doing what he loved best. And it kept nearly happening.

The first time was Monza in '53, when he'd fallen out of a Cooper as it was going over. He lost a lot of skin from his back and shoulder and had liquid on his lungs. He was hospitalised for weeks afterwards.

There was also the time in Sicily when he swerved to avoid a collision and hit a low wall so hard the car's fuel filler cap flew open. Petrol sloshed out onto the exhaust pipe, setting the whole car, and Mike, alight. He was sliding backwards, trapped in a bath of fire. When the car finally stopped moving, Mike managed to get out and roll around to put out the flames. In hospital the resultant second-degree burns to his left hand, wrist, elbow, both legs and back were

45

completely smothered in sheep's fat and swaddled in bandages. With typical Hawthorn luck, his cherubic face was unmarked.

And then there was the gassing incident at Spa. He was still in bandages from his Sicily burns and greatly shaken up by the loss of his old man, so I flew out there with him. Mike had asked me to film the race, using Mike's new 8mm movie camera, and after a few laps, he started driving like he was blind drunk. Granted, we'd had a few the night before, but that didn't explain why he was weaving all over the road, bumping off one kerb, then the other. I thought he was going to create the most almighty pile-up.

When he managed to get back to the pits, his crew had to lift him out of the car. A cover plate had come off the exhaust, right by his elbow, allowing carbon-monoxide fumes to pour into the cockpit, some getting trapped under the visor of his helmet. He was made to drink milk – which must have been a novelty. The medics said that one more lap and he'd have gone for a Burton.

But compared to this – this latest, terrifying revelation...death through total kidney failure? That was simply too much. To learn that when his remaining kidney no longer functioned, he would rapidly go downhill and die in pain, doped up on painkillers. How could he come to terms with that? Tears flowed as I silently punched my mattress.

I'd always thought his backaches were the result of driving, not ill health. In his first full season of racing, Mike had driven a pre-war Riley Sprite with terrifically hard cart springs. He'd said the ride was 'like a stone bounding down a tin roof'. The previous generation of drivers had all worn wide stiffened belts to keep their insides in place. Knowing that Mike had occasionally complained about having a sore back, even when he lodged with us, it struck me then as crazy that he didn't wear such a belt.

'No way am I wearing a woman's corset!' he'd protest.

Once, years ago, after an Ulster Trophy race which was held on poorly maintained public roads, he'd told me his body had taken a real pounding, so much so that he'd passed out without warning the following evening and was despatched to bed with whisky and hot milk.

Thinking back to that event, I began to question whether he'd passed out from the pounding to his body or whether it was an early indication of kidney malfunction. I didn't know then that they were almost certainly connected.

Even though I had work in the morning, I was too agitated to sleep, so I paced gently back and forth across the bedroom in my bare feet, the floorboards creaking. I had so many questions: Would the symptoms worsen? Did he take medication? Would he know when to stop competing?

Mike's revelation cast the Le Mans episode in a whole new light. Had his kidney condition affected his driving that day? Had he actually blacked out? Would he have even known? Could it have been just for a couple of seconds?

If he thought the authorities would take away his racing licence, shouldn't he, in all conscience, retire now? It wasn't as if he'd be without work. He could go straight into the family business. He'd be great at selling luxury cars. His mother Winifred had acquired a Jaguar franchise, and business was booming. I began to convince myself that his best racing days were behind him. Okay, he was still competitive, but his truly heroic drives were increasingly a thing of the past. Would history, I wondered, deem his first Grand Prix win, Reims in '53, the pinnacle of his career?

His unbridled, carefree happiness of that time was in stark contrast to his obvious desperation now. I decided I would try to talk him round into temporarily giving up racing, if not for his own safety then for other people's, in the hope that a cure might be found in time. I was also being selfish: I didn't want to lose Mike any sooner than I had to.

To think, only a couple of hours previously, I'd been mightily pissed off with Mike for two-timing Moia and Cherry – and God knows who else. And I was cross with him for showing more interest in Don than me. And even cross with him because he could play a stupid bugle. Those things all seemed so trivial now.

Eventually, I sat down at my bureau. My eyes were drawn to the faint lettering etched with a hard pencil years ago onto the painted surface: *M H – World Champion!* He'd written that one night when we'd staggered back from the pub, under-age and pissed. I kept it covered over for ages but, inevitably, Mum discovered it. Although she tried to sound cross, she could never really be cross with Mike.

Being a champion was his true goal – or at least his father's. Even if he did carry on racing, would he live long enough to achieve it? I undressed and tried to sleep, but the opening refrain of *Ain't That a Shame* had slid into my mind where it stuck, repeating over and over, my tears falling like rain, until I finally fell into a fitful sleep.

Chapter Three

Not Guilty

I saw Mike only a couple of times between that unforgettable late night *tête-à-tête* and his next race, the British Grand Prix. The unusually long break between the Dutch and the British was due to the French cancelling their Grand Prix – a direct consequence of the Le Mans crash.

The first time I saw him was when he telephoned and suggested we got some of the lads out for a 'swift one'. I jumped at the opportunity.

It was just gone six o'clock when I arrived at the Duke of Cambridge – the small hotel which was used by the Hawthorns and some of the staff of the Tourist Trophy Garage like a works' canteen and private bar. Mike was already surrounded by others. He was laughing and joking and, as always, the centre of attention. He only had a few platitudes for me; the subject of our chat a few days previously seemingly erased from his consciousness. As early as seven, he made his apologies and left abruptly. One chap reported Mike as having said that he was off to see someone 'considerably more attractive than present company'. That had to be Cherry.

The second time our paths crossed was on the evening of 9 July. I had taken some work home, although whether I would have done any is a moot point. We'd just finished supper when there was a loud knock at the door. Dad went to answer it.

'Evening, Mr McBride.' Mike's smooth Home Counties delivery was easily audible from the kitchen. 'These are for you. I'm afraid I rather helped myself to your Scotch the other night.'

'Michael, dear boy! As if I'd begrudge you a wee dram. Come on through.'

Dad appeared at the kitchen door with a bottle of single malt in one hand, a bottle of champagne in the other, and the broadest grin

I'd seen for a long time. Mike strode in behind him.

'Won't you stay and have something to eat?' asked Mum, notwithstanding that we'd consumed every morsel of our supper. She would willingly have cooked something from scratch for Mike. He really was Golden Boy as far as my parents were concerned. Thankfully, my sister was out visiting a friend. Otherwise, there would have been even more hero worship, not to mention flirting.

'That's most kind, Mrs McBride, but really I only popped round to take Tom out.'

The bloody cheek! Take Tom out? What, like a child, or a dog? Presuming I'd be free! Before I could say anything, Mum answered for me, 'Oh, that's most kind, Mike. Tom doesn't go out so much when you're not around.'

Oh, thanks, Mum. Why not make me seem even more pathetic? 'Actually, I was intending to do some work this evening,' I said limply.

'Hang the work, old chap. You know what they say: all work and no play...' A smiling Mike leant forward, resting his hands on the back of a kitchen chair. He really couldn't have appeared more different from when he was last in this kitchen.

There was a moment of silence when glances were exchanged. We all knew I would go. Dad slyly winked at me in encouragement.

'Give me a minute to wash my face,' I said.

Outside, the Lancia was gleaming from top to tyre and even the dark green, gloss-painted dashboard sparkled. Mike had obviously had one of the lads clean it for him that afternoon. He wasn't lazy, or at least he didn't used to be, it was simply that valeting cars was a job for the TT juniors – quite possibly the poor sod I'd seen when Mike came back from Le Mans.

'Bell all right with you, bo?' he asked, as he selected first gear and the car shot away from the kerb.

'Fine. You seem in good spirits,' I shouted over the noise of the engine.

'Got a letter today. I'll show you over a pint,' he bellowed back.

It was a fine evening, the sun still warming despite the hour. We flew down the narrow lanes that threaded around and between the woods and farms of the beautiful leafy Surrey hills. Fortunately, there were few other cars on the roads, but the drivers we met often had to swerve violently or brake hard simply to avoid an accident. For a number of years, we must have been the curse of every decent motorist to the south of Farnham and, come to that, every pedestrian, cyclist and horse rider, for there were precious few pavements.

Mike was clearly in the mood for driving. I could tell from the way he was keeping the Lancia's power on, refusing to let the revs drop, that he was totally focussed. His steering inputs were constant and fluent, his attention unwavering.

When he was like this, I felt perfectly safe, although I suspect many others didn't. I remember Mike once telling me that he'd given Stirling a lift and frightened him half to death. Stirling had said he never wanted to be driven again by Mike. Far from feeling affronted, Mike thought it was hilarious.

As we dropped down from Frensham towards the River Wey, we passed the driveway to Frensham Manor, a seriously historic mansion originating from the tenth century. A few years earlier, shortly after Mike had started driving competitively, he told me he'd buy Frensham Manor once he became World Champion. He would also be married to a beautiful woman, keep Boxer dogs, drive Jaguars and collect exotic Italian cars. Why that particular house? I'd asked. He told me that when he was much younger he'd been invited to tea there. In his typically uncomplicated way, he justified his choice: it was in the nicest part of England; it was suitably grand for a world champion; it would be near the garage and his mother, but, most of all, because it had a long equestrian cross-country circuit which he would turn into a race track.

Neither of us mentioned the Manor this time as we sped past the drive that night on towards The Blue Bell at Batts Corner.

With pints in our hands, we went out to the garden and sat at a wooden table. It was the most perfect summer's evening. Mike pulled a telegram from his inside pocket and handed it over. It was addressed to Jaguar Cars and written in French.

I was hopeless at French so handed it back. 'What's it say?'

'I'll read it to you. It says, Mussyour Awthorn eez not responseeble for zee crash.' He looked up and smiled. 'That, my friend, is the finding of the official inquiry. I'm exonerated. In plain English, I'm in the ruddy clear!'

'Beezer!' I exclaimed, and raised my tankard to him. 'Let's drink to that.'

As the sun fell, the temperature dropped rapidly and we were forced inside. It was quiet in The Bell that evening, and homely. Mike sat down and continued to study the telegram as if not quite believing what he was reading. Meanwhile, I went to the bar to order beers. I recognised one or two of the locals although not the couple of spotty herberts perched on bar stools at the far end of the bar with a few empty glasses, a full ashtray and one raided manila pay packet in front of them.

One old local saluted Mike's presence with a gruff, 'Evenin', Mike' as he was going outside to the gents.

On hearing Mike's name, one of the youths whispered too loudly to the other, 'Ain't that the upper-class prat who bought his way out of national service?'

'Yeah, s'all right for some,' said his mate. 'I mean, how difficult can it be to drive fast when Daddy buys all the petrol?'

I wasn't having that. I also thought if I involved Mike it could get nasty, very quickly. They were obviously emboldened by alcohol. I slowly edged over towards them until I was towering over them, well inside their comfort zone. My build was handy sometimes. 'So, boys, you think driving a Formula One car is easy?'

The darker-haired lad looked up and said nonchalantly, 'Can't fink why not. I've been driving a year. It's hardly difficult.' His face was greasy. His many whiteheads were picked out in the low shafts of sunlight coming through the pub window. His top lip glistened. I sensed he was more anxious than he sounded.

'Well, sunbeam, why don't I tell you what it's really like? That way you won't carry on talking bollocks.'

'Oright,' said the youth, with a little flick of his head.

'You think you've driven fast, yeah?' I said. 'Eighty miles an hour, perhaps?' The boy nodded. 'That's eighty on the clock, right?' Another nod. 'Okay, so you were probably doing just over seventy. All speedos over-read.'

'What's your point, mate?'

'Now, imagine you're going nearly three times that speed. You're cramped – sitting down very low. There's no windscreen. You're wearing a helmet and goggles. You can't see properly for all the oil and insects plastered over your goggles...'

'So... it's a bit uncomfortable. That don't make it difficult.' His words bolder than his appearance.

'In some countries the temperatures will be well over 100 degrees in the shade.' I continued. 'You'll suffer dehydration and begin to feel faint. Together with the noise of the exhaust, this'll give you a splitting headache...'

'And...?

'What if, just ahead of you, there's a sharp corner? You'd start braking, wouldn't you? I would. But long after you've begun to brake, real drivers like Mike there, and Stirling Moss, would have shot past you as if you're going backwards. And you'd be thinking they must be insane. They do brake, of course, but only at the last possible moment. And they daren't brake hard and start turning, 'cos if they do, they'll end up flipping the thing over and possibly dying.' I paused, aware I now had their full attention.

'As they go round the corner, they'll experience sickening G-forces. The car will slide outwards, jittering... threatening to go over at any time. Those guys will be hauling the wheel in the opposite direction as fast as they can. And then, at exactly the right part of the corner, they'll accelerate flat out. If the front wheels aren't pointing the right way, or if they change their mind about which direction to turn the wheel, it's literally game over – they roll over, or spin. Either way, it won't be merely 'uncomfortable'. Mark my words, laddies, you need big balls to be a racing driver.'

'Over 200 miles an hour...? Come off it,' piped up the mousey one.

Clearly he was brighter than he looked. 'Okay, not quite,' I conceded, 'but not far off. Norman Dewis was recently clocked doing over 192 in a Jaguar down the Mulsanne Straight.'

That provoked an almost silent whistle.

'How come you know so much about this?' asked Acne Face.

'Because I've tried it – and I know how difficult it is, and exhausting. It's one thing to drive flat out for thirty minutes; an altogether different thing to keep it up for three hours. Not only that, you can't be afraid of dying. Would either of you enter a race when you know that, on average, one driver will die?' I didn't know for sure whether that was true but, if it wasn't, it couldn't be too far from the truth.

'So, you must be upper class too then, if you've done racing' said the smaller lad.

'I'm certainly not – and neither is Mike. Alright, his dad runs a garage, and, okay, he did get him started but, without the raw talent, Mike would never have been taken on by Ferrari. Think how many Italian boys dream of driving for Ferrari.'

It wasn't desperately late when he dropped me back. We'd each had five or six pints which I'd declared was quite enough for a weekday evening. Although our conversation had largely been about Le Mans, we'd also ranged over many of the usual subjects: his garage, cars, girls and upcoming races. It was easy conversation, helped no doubt by the beer, but the huge elephant sitting slap bang on the table between us, about which nothing was said, was the subject of his health.

For the next few days, I kept wondering whether I should have asked if there had been any developments. I'd had the ideal opportunity to try to talk him into giving up racing. I came round to the idea that Mike had decided to try to put it out of his mind. After all, there was nothing he could do about it. He could plan for next month, perhaps for next year, but not really 'the future'. He had no long-term future. This was a slow ticking bomb, over which he had no say. And it seemed well and truly strapped to him.

Chapter Four

Mike's 'Reign' Over Stirling

Two days later, I learnt Don Beauman was dead. He'd had a fatal accident on 9 July at Wicklow, the very day Mike and I were celebrating Mike's exoneration from blame. He'd been racing Sir Jeremy Boles' 2-litre Connaught and had crashed, straight after setting the fastest lap of the day. A chap I knew had witnessed the accident. He said that Don had rounded the sharp right-hander by the Beehive Inn when the car mounted a bank, crashed and caught alight. Don had been thrown clear and appeared to be okay. He sat down on the bank and put his hands to his head before keeling over, never to regain consciousness.

Even though I hardly knew him, I was terribly upset. It didn't seem like five minutes since we'd been out drinking with him. His smile, his voice, his laughter were all fresh in my mind. A man couldn't have been more alive. I could scarcely imagine what Mike must have been feeling.

Although they were the same age, Don had effectively become Mike's protégé and was comfortable deferring to him. Mike had encouraged Don into the sport by selling him his old pre-war Riley. More recently, Mike had persuaded Lofty to sign him up to drive for Jaguar and, controversially, had lobbied for Don to be one of the six drivers for Le Mans, over the equally experienced Ivor 'the driver' Bueb.

Don's funeral was held the following Friday, the day before the British Grand Prix. I didn't go, it didn't seem appropriate, but I'm sure that Mike did. The GP that year was held at Aintree, within the confines of the famous equestrian racecourse and using the same grandstands. Mike finished a disappointing sixth, sharing the honours with Eugenio Castellotti. The official line was that Mike had been suffering from the heat, and had therefore handed over the Ferrari to his teammate. The story from the pits was that Mike had certainly been suffering, although more from a massive hangover than the effects of the sun. It's my guess he'd started drowning his spirits after the funeral.

Other first-hand accounts told of a blazing row he'd had with Moia that previous evening and how, as a result, he had drunk himself senseless. My sister heard it on good authority that this row had continued straight after the race. According to witnesses, in an admirable act of defiance, Moia stormed off and instead went out to dinner with Castellotti – or Il Bello, the Beautiful One, as he was called in his native Italy. I had imagined that would be the end of Moia and Mike's relationship yet, surprisingly, he continued to see her, off and on, for the next few months. It didn't even seem to dent the comradeship between Mike and Eugenio.

Lance Macklin, who was still trying to convince anyone who would listen about Mike's culpability for the accident, finished a respectable eighth in the Grand Prix, much to Mike's irritation.

The winner, by half a car's length, was Stirling. The papers said he'd been gifted the win by Fangio, who was by then a triple world champion, because the Argentinian knew what it would mean to Stirling to win his first Grand Prix on home soil. Mike, of course, was typically disparaging about both of them – driving their 'bloody Mercs'.

On 30 July, there was a prestigious non-Championship International Trophy meeting at Crystal Palace. Although Stirling had entered a Maserati 250F, he couldn't attend as he'd had to go to Stuttgart for the Mercedes presentation of his famous Mille Miglia victory – a remarkable feat of endurance and fast driving by any yardstick, then or now. He'd driven almost 1,000 miles along Italy's public roads, over mountain passes, brushing past countless crazy spectators, at an average speed of ninety-eight miles per hour, setting a record that would never be beaten. I was not allowed to mention this subject in front of Mike, who dismissed it as 'not real racing'. The truth was that Mike probably couldn't have lasted a race of this length, and didn't wish to be reminded of the fact. Mind you, many years later, Stirling admitted that he'd taken amphetamines, or 'pep pills' as he called them, in order to keep himself alert for such a long, arduous race. Not that they were banned in those days, and he wasn't the only driver to take them. Knowing he couldn't be in two places at once, Stirling had offered his car to Mike. As it happened, Stirling made it back to the UK in time for the start of the race and sportingly invited Mike to drive in his stead. Driving the Maserati for the very first time, Mike won both the heat and the final, much to Stirling's apparent delight.

The enduring Maserati 250F, designed by Colombo, had the familiar classic fat cigar-like roundness of its peers, but was curved in a pleasingly sensual way. Its svelte looks were accentuated by a long, rising two-into-one exhaust pipe, shallow wrap-around windshield, wire wheels, and anti-splash fins for wet weather. It had a generous quantity of rivets over the rear fuel and oil tanks. The 250F cockpit was Spartan yet spacious − for one − with a blue corduroy-covered seat and no belts or harness, and a collection of gauges behind a large three-spoked wooden wheel. The Jaeger tachometer (rev counter) dominated the dash, with three smaller dials giving oil and fuel pressure and water temperature. The gear lever was on the driver's right. No one made as beautiful a shift gate as the Italians − chromium finished steel plates with precision slots cut out in an H pattern. They were genuine works of art, appearing to be lovingly handcrafted. Only Vanwall fashioned a gear shift gate to compare with the Italians. Oh, and 250Fs were almost always painted bright red. The car was a testament to the Italian sense of shape and proportion.

The relationship between Mike and Stirling Moss was curious. They were simultaneously friends, but never that close, *and* arch rivals − for over seven years.

They'd both started their professional driving careers on the very same day. When Mike was on form, they were well matched on the track, but polar opposites off it. Moss was short, intense, serious and highly consistent. He considered himself a professional driver. He would prepare himself properly for every race. This would include foregoing alcohol the night before, not that he drank much anyway, and making sure he was fully rested. He couldn't have been more different from Mike. And yet, despite some of the quips which Mike would make about Stirling, including some slightly uncalled for ones, I believe they had a healthy respect for each other's talent.

The irony was that when Mike had started driving for Ferrari back in 1953, Stirling had remained proudly patriotic, driving various British marques, including BRM, HWM and ERA (we Brits clearly felt most comfortable with three initials), all of which had great potential but were hopelessly unreliable. And then, in 1955, exactly as Mike changed from driving Italian to British, Stirling changed his allegiance from British, via a brief Italian dalliance, to German. Having been constantly thwarted by mechanical failure, it is understandable that Stirling would be attracted to the prospect of reliability that a better funded team would offer. However, in Mike's rather myopic view, patriotism meant British if at all possible, Italian by necessity, but driving for Germany, the sworn enemy, never.

Back then, the nationality of a racing team was nearly always conveyed by the colour of cars: Italian marques, such as Ferrari, Alfa Romeo and Maserati, were invariably red; German marques, such as Mercedes, Porsche and Auto Union (which would become Audi) were usually silver; French marques, such as Bugatti and Peugeot were blue; and British marques were mostly green. It made spectating a great deal easier than it is today.

It was therefore something of a surprise, indeed a huge compliment, that when Mike first went out to South America to drive for Ferrari in 1953, Enzo Ferrari had Mike's cars painted British Racing Green. It wasn't to last, however. Once back in Europe, all Ferrari's cars were red again. Mike knew it was pointless to try persuading Enzo to continue giving him a 'British Ferrari' and so decided to give up his impractical all-white overalls in favour of a new dark green windcheater. This was well before the introduction of fire-retardant racing overalls or sponsored clothing.

He said to me at the time, 'If I can't drive a green car, at least I can wear a green jacket.' To do so was, of course, a very public, patriotic statement.

Stirling didn't live round our way, but once or twice he came down to spend an evening with Mike. I remember well the time Mike invited some of the Members to join him and Stirling for an evening of drinking. It had been brilliant fun, and everyone was on great form. We'd even managed to get Stirling to have a couple of pints. Come chucking out time, we realised that Mike had gone missing. We knew he couldn't be far away because his car was still in the car park. Thinking Mike must have gone outside to the toilet,

Stirling dutifully waited by his car to say goodnight. The next thing he knew was that it had suddenly started 'raining' – all over his car and Stirling himself. We all looked up into the trees above the cars and could just make out Mike precariously braced in the branches, liberally sprinkling all below him.

Diving for cover, Stirling shouted, 'You bastard, Hawthorn!'

To which came the laughing reply, 'That's for driving for the fucking Krauts.'

Chapter Five

Lofty Encounter

Less than a month after Don's funeral, there was more sad news for all of us. One of the members, Julian Crossley, was reported to be in a coma, following an accident sustained in a motorcycle race at Dundrod, Northern Ireland. Mike and I had known Julian for the past ten years, ever since we'd begun frequenting pubs. We three had founded the Members. Mike flew out to Belfast the day after we heard the news. Julian's mother was either too poorly or upset to make the journey herself. Despite Julian remaining in a coma, Mike stayed with him until Mrs Crossley was fit enough to travel and be reunited with her son.

No sooner was he back than Mike was needed for a long-distance race. Although this was going to be racing at the highest level, at least it was relatively close to Farnham, and there were no championship points at stake. Nevertheless, I did wonder whether I should've cautioned Mike against taking part, given the events of the past month *and* all the preceding months. Mind you, he'd probably have said, 'No choice, old chap'.

The Nine-Hour endurance race staged at Goodwood in August, then only in its third year, had already become a mandatory fixture for the Members – a summer holiday treat. It was designed to start in broad daylight, carry on through difficult twilight, and end in pitch-darkness, or moonlight, depending on the phase of the moon.

With the race not starting until three o'clock that Saturday afternoon, we Hawthorn supporters could have a leisurely start. This usually involved having a 'proper breakfast', meeting up for a 'sharpener' at The Bush around midday, and then hacking down to Goodwood in convoy for about two o'clock where we'd immediately have another pint or two. If the weather was fine, we'd stay right through to the midnight finish which, naturally, involved downing a few more pints. We'd then drive back to Farnham, really quite squiffy. This sounds completely irresponsible today, but I can honestly say that back then there was hardly any stigma associated with that sort of behaviour.

This was Mike's first time competing in the Nine-Hour. I was concerned for him primarily because long races didn't suit him, despite the fact that he would be sharing the driving with a co-driver. With no official Jaguar entry, he was free to represent Ferrari. He was to drive a sleek red Monza 750S and would have as his partner de Portago, a Spanish marquis – and every inch the jet-setting playboy. Alfonso Antonio Vicente Eduardo Angel Blas Francisco de Borja Cabeza de Vaca y Leighton, Marquis of Portago, was the product of wealth and privilege, but he was no idiot. 'Fon', as he was known to us, was now twenty-six years old, he'd been married twice and was now separated, had fathered two children, and was expecting a third. He spoke four languages, flew his own plane, had twice ridden horses in the Grand National, and represented Spain at bobsleigh. Needless to say, he was also fabulously wealthy, although surprisingly this was courtesy of his Irish mother, Olga. Alfonso was gregarious, charmingly snobbish, and invariably accompanied by glamorous girls. It was no hardship for us to hang around with Fon when it was Mike's turn to drive.

I'd travelled down to Goodwood in Tubby White's car, an old Vauxhall. With no Julian in our party, we were noticeably more subdued than usual.

It was gone two thirty by the time Tubby and I had managed to talk our way into the pit area. As we approached the Ferrari pit, we saw Mike. He was dressed ready to go: distinctive bottle-green cotton windcheater jacket, white shirt with trademark spotted bow tie, white linen trousers cuffed around the ankles, battered brown shoes, string-back driving gloves, and carrying his blue crash helmet with visor. He was standing stock-still, vacantly staring into the middle distance. He didn't see us approaching.

I called out, 'Hullo, Mike, how you doin'?'

He registered us and smiled instantly. It was a Pavlovian reaction for as soon as the smile appeared it was gone. 'Bloody hell, what do you two buggers want?'

'Well, that's charming,' said Tubby.

'We've come to cheer you on,' I said. And then, nodding at the car, added, 'She's a beauty.' I meant it too – the Ferrari Monza was all sweeping curves and sat low to the ground. It was sexier even than a Maserati 250F. The car could be worth around £2 million today.

'She's that all right, and she goes like the clappers. Or rather, has done so far. All I want is something that'll bring me back in one piece.'

'Who's got pole?' I enquired tentatively, in case practice hadn't gone well.

Mike smirked. 'Number 6, of course.' The Ferrari in front of us was wearing that number on both sides and its bonnet.

'Hey, isn't that Stirling over there?' asked Tubby, gesturing towards a silver Porsche.

'Yeah, why don't you go and ask him where his Nazi uniform is?' quipped Mike.

'Is the Porsche any good?' I asked.

'It's quick enough, but it's the Astons we're worried about. They've won this thing twice already.' He looked around him before continuing, 'Look here, chaps, good of you to come and all that, but you'd better scarper now. I'm only minutes from being called.'

Right on cue, one of the mechanics started the car. The noise from the big 3-litre, 4-cylinder engine was deafening.

'Best of British!' I shouted.

'Thanks.' With that, Mike pulled on his helmet and climbed into the car.

'How's he seem to you?' I asked Tubby as we walked away.

'Not his usual self.'

As we left the pits and headed for a corner known simply as Woodcote, I reflected on how times had changed. It was only six or seven years earlier, when the wartime Westhampnett Airfield first became Goodwood motor racing circuit, that we all used to pile down here together, Mike included. We were all in our late teens then, and none of us had much cash. Even the price of the entrance ticket was a big consideration. But it was always Mike who'd volunteer to climb over the fencing, scrounge a couple of tickets and pass them back and forth until we all got in for free. And now here he was: one of the event's main attractions.

There were a lot of spectators but we managed to muscle our way into half a space against the trackside fencing, immediately after the corner. From here, we could see the cars during their warm-up laps, deliberately snaking down Lavant Straight at half throttle, braking, and then lining up exactly the right approach for the chicane.

It was a Le Mans-style start, and Mike must have made a terrific job of it for he was leading the pack as the cars came thundering past us for the first time. The thrill of seeing a phalanx of cars, all roaring and popping as they came charging into a corner, desperately searching for that tiny clear route through the pack, never waned.

I watched Mike come belting down Lavant at full chat before hammering through Woodcote. (Coincidentally, there is a Woodcote Corner at both Silverstone and Goodwood.) I could see the bright red bodywork of the Ferrari quiver slightly as it drifted sideways, its tyres screeching, its engine popping on overrun, whilst Mike was holding the steering on modest opposite lock. On his heels was Stirling in the silver Porsche. Then, some five seconds after the main pack had passed, there came that heady, rich smell of racing exhaust fumes – a smell without parallel. The atmosphere around the circuit was buzzing.

Mike continued to lead for the first half-hour before having to pit early with what I later learnt was a gearbox problem. The Ferrari stopped for far too long and by the time Fon took over they stood little chance of a decent finish.

While Mike was resting back in the pits, I decided to walk around a bit. My back was stiff after standing still. I was passing the entrance to the main Start-Finish grandstand when I saw Lofty England striding towards the entrance. At six foot five inches tall, and with a rugby player's physique, he was easy to spot.

I'd encountered Lofty a few times before, but never to speak to. The last time had, in fact, been acutely embarrassing. I'd arranged to go out flying with Mike in his Fairchild Argus aeroplane one day the previous summer, with no particular destination in mind. When we met up, Mike told me that he, along with Norman Dewis, had been summoned to Silverstone to help test-drive Jaguar's new D-Type. I argued that he should go alone but he insisted it wouldn't take long.

Once we landed at Silverstone, we wandered over to see Lofty and some of the other Jaguar lads. Mike went straight up to

Lofty and said, 'Excuse me, Lofty, what am I here for? Why've you got me down here?'

'Well, the D for starters. You haven't driven it yet. I thought it might be a good opportunity,' replied Lofty.

Mike just stared at him, pushed his cap to the back of his head, and said, 'I don't want to drive the car. I wish you hadn't got me down here. I was busy. Anyway, Norman's doing that, and when he says it's all right then I'll drive it. That's good enough for me.' And with that, he turned on his heel and strode back towards his aeroplane. He was so rude. I was mortified. Neither of us spoke until we were airborne again. Mike was resolute. In his opinion, it didn't take two of them to test it, and Norman was contracted as a test driver.

Lofty first met Mike in only his second year of serious competition, driving a Formula Two car. Lofty had gone down to Boreham specifically to scout for promising young drivers. Even though it was August, the weather was foul, really pissing down, and Mike was driving right on the limit. It is rumoured that when Mike overtook a 4.5-litre Ferrari on the outside, in his 2-litre Cooper-Bristol, Lofty turned to his assistant and pronounced, 'That's my boy!'

As it happened, Lofty would have to wait two years. Prior to then, Mike was contracted to drive for Ferrari in both Grand Prix and sports car events. When he left Ferrari to join Vanwall, he was free to drive sports cars for Jaguar.

Mike later recounted that some 'big chap' had come up to him and asked him his name. He'd also asked Mike why he wore a ridiculous bow tie. Totally unfazed, Mike told him that a regular tie flapped in his face. It's odd to think that, from that inauspicious meeting, a friendship would flourish that would last for the rest of Mike's life. Lofty soon adopted the role of an indulgent uncle to Mike. A week after the Boreham encounter, Lofty got him up to Silverstone, put him in a C-Type, and within five laps he'd beaten the course lap record.

Having now spotted Lofty again, and emboldened by beer, I took a couple of steps forward, semi-blocking Lofty's path. It was most out of character. I hardly recognised my actions. At six foot six myself, I seldom had to look up to anyone. I did now. The uneven grass bank on which we stood gave Lofty a slight height advantage. I began to regret stopping him. His bulk and military bearing, plus his reputation as a disciplinarian, made him seem doubly unapproachable, but Mike insisted that, at heart, 'Lofty was a softy'.

'Ah, Mr England!' I said. The great man looked alarmed momentarily, as if I was going to demand something of him. 'Tom McBride, friend of Hawthorn's. Hope you don't mind me saying hello?'

His expression softened. 'No, not at all, young man, not at all. So, a friend of Mike's, are you?'

'Yes.' There was a pause. I hadn't planned what I should say next, which was something of an error. Fearing an awkward silence, I continued, 'He seems to be doing awfully well this season...'

'Well, he's a hell of a driver – when he wants to be. Having the right car helps.'

'He'd be going even better if he was on one of your D-Types.' Why ever was I gushing? I felt childish.

Incidentally, in the fifties, it was standard practice to describe drivers being 'on' their cars, rather than 'in' them. Racing cars then were latter-day steeds. It was, of course, a more apposite term for Mike than most of his smaller rivals.

'Maybe.' After a pause, Lofty added, 'Though he's a bit bloody hard on cars. Drives more like a wrestler. Whereas Moss – he drives like a sculptor.'

Lofty's candour took me slightly by surprise, but even to my untrained eye, I knew he was right. In small pre-war cars, Mike had actually looked ridiculous. His torso stuck out high above the car, his beefy shoulders overhung the flanks, and his elbows flailed as he fought the wheel. Even in a modern car like the Ferrari, Mike still looked oversized. By comparison, Moss sat lower in the cockpit, his arms out straight. Lofty had a point – Mike may have been effective, but he wasn't the prettiest driver to watch. Mind you, Mike was a good six inches taller than Stirling, and had often relayed to me the battles he'd had with constructors, trying to persuade them to make the cockpits big enough.

Lofty turned back to face me, 'So, how do you know Mike?' We had to lean in and shout over the noise of the track.

'I've known him since I was six. We were at school together,' I bellowed back. I was hoping he wouldn't ask whether that was Ardingly.

At this point, a stocky, much shorter man with a dynamic

manner and a rather cuboid head joined us. He was someone else I recognised, but I was certain he wouldn't know me. It was John Cooper, the former racer and now builder of racing cars.

'Afternoon, Lofty,' he shouted breezily. 'Sorry to interrupt. Just wondered whether you'd be at the dinner tonight, and if you were, whether you'd fancy sharing a table?'

'Sorry, John, leaving early. Promised the memsahib I'll be back by eight. I've no excuse today as I'm only meant to be spectating. Actually, it's a treat nowadays to spend the odd evening at home.' He waved a big hand in my direction. 'Have you met this young chap? He's an old friend of Hawthorn's.'

Cooper stuck out his hand and said, 'Don't think I have. John Cooper, and you are...?' He had the dry, vice-like handshake of a mechanical engineer.

'I'm Tom,' I managed, feeling a little star-struck in the presence of two motor racing gods. However, I clearly wasn't worthy of much further investigation as both men promptly turned their attention back to the track.

Aside from his father Leslie, Frank England, universally known as Lofty, and John Cooper were two of the most influential characters in Mike's career. It was John who had designed and built a car in which Mike found instant success, and Lofty had lined up Mike for a career with Jaguar before he was snapped up by Ferrari.

The story of how John Cooper, together with a character called Bob Chase, was pivotal to Mike's meteoric rise is worth retelling. Early in January of '52, a detailed description of John's proposed Cooper-Bristol Formula 2 car was published in *The Motor*. Bob Chase, an eccentric friend of Leslie Hawthorn and alleged alcoholic, read the article whilst ill in bed. He telephoned Leslie and proposed that, if Leslie looked after it and Mike drove it, he'd buy one off the drawing board. It was nearly £2,000. Today, that sum would be worth well over £40,000. It's no wonder the Hawthorns jumped at the chance.

The first three examples of the new Cooper-Bristol were scheduled to make their debut at the Goodwood Easter meeting of '52. Two were for the Ecurie Richmond Team and one for John himself.

Cooper's tiny factory in Surbiton had been struggling to get the three cars ready for Easter, let alone a fourth for Mike. Consequently, Mike and one of his TT mechanics went to the factory to lend a hand. Everything was eleventh hour. Mike even roped me in, a couple of days before the race, to go with him to collect the Bristol engine and gearbox. However, in testing on the Lashham Aerodrome, the car just got worse and worse. When the guys took the engine apart, all the valve seats were distorted. I remember being horrified that an engine and gearbox assembly which had cost 660 quid had failed straightaway. That was on the Good Friday, and as practice started on Easter Saturday, those amazing TT mechanics had no option but to work right through the night to rebuild the engine.

Prior to that Easter meeting, neither Mike nor his car had had any exposure in Formula 2 racing. That didn't seem to faze him at all. It was his first major race, and yet he treated it all as a big joke. As usual, he was in the pub the night before drinking beer and holding court.

Mike was easily the fastest of the four Cooper-Bristols in practice. One had to feel sorry for John. Driving his own prototype car, he was completely outgunned and outcornered. Mike absolutely murdered him. In the end, John handed over his car to Juan Fangio, but incredibly even the Old Man couldn't better Mike's times! Come the Monday, Mike won the Formula 2 race easily – and also the Formule Libre (a race in which unequal cars compete). But his crowning glory was to finish second to Gonzalez's 'Thin Wall Special' in the Formula 1. Second, to a pukka Grand Prix Ferrari! Now that was something special. As were the Hawthorn celebrations that followed.

Shortly after that Easter Monday, Mike and John were back in their cars practising again. John was going through a corner, right on the limit, as fast as he reckoned the car could possibly go. Suddenly, Mike, on an apparently identical car, came belting round the outside of him, steering with one hand and giving John a two-finger salute with the other. That was the moment, so legend has it, that John decided to give up driving racing cars and stick to building them.

I don't know whether John ever knew the secret behind Mike's success, but it was largely due to the tuning of the car's carburettors by Les, *and* his special home-brew 100-octane, nitro-methane fuel. Such things were legal then. And it probably explains why not even Fangio could catch Mike on a seemingly identical car. Of course,

Mike was amazingly fortunate to have been given a Cooper-Bristol in the first place, but I've often wondered whether Mike's career would have ever taken off had it not been for his dad's 'rocket fuel'.

Back at Goodwood and the Nine-Hour race, I began to study the frenetic activity of the pits obliquely opposite where we were standing. Cars were screeching to a halt beside their designated pits, sometimes just for fuel, sometimes for new tyres, and sometimes for more radical repairs. Their wheels, mostly wire-spoked, were flamboyantly removed in seconds by mechanics hammering off the spinners with hide-faced mallets. Refuelling was undertaken by one of the crew throwing an absorbent sheet around the filler aperture and inserting a large open funnel. Another pair of mechanics would rush out carrying a ten-gallon churn and tip it in, as fast as they could. Of course, fuel spilled everywhere. It is incredible there weren't more serious accidents in the pits.

'Hey! Look here,' Lofty suddenly shouted. Immediately below us, a lone Cooper-Bristol had come round Woodcote and hit some spilt oil. Having lost much of its forward momentum, it began an elegant, slow-motion pirouette along the track. We could just make out a silver streak haring down the Lavant Straight coming towards us – and the errant Cooper-Bristol. I knew that the silver car would be decelerating from around 140 miles an hour, and the driver wouldn't have a clue what awaited him around the corner. I saw a yellow flag being frantically waved by a marshal as the approaching car, number 34, revealed itself to be Moss's Porsche. The light was fading, and the warning flag was too little, too late. Stirling was clearly braking as hard as he could. It wasn't enough. He slammed right into the side of the Cooper with a resounding metallic crunch and a squeal of protesting rubber.

'Ouch,' said Lofty, almost casually. 'One of yours, I think, John?' No one else spoke. 'Do you reckon the oil was a little present from Mike to Stirling?' And then, turning to Cooper, he said, 'Anyway, where were we?'

Although I'd heard about Lofty's reputation, I was still shocked. I guess he knew straight away that we weren't looking at a fatality so, to him, it was merely another shunt – an everyday hazard of racing. The red flags came out, the race was duly suspended, and the tow trucks trundled onto the track.

John looked up from the scene and appeared to carry on as if nothing much had happened. 'Indeed, yes. Let's hope they're both okay.'

They were, thank goodness. Stirling, on that occasion, was certainly luckier than James Dean[1], the Hollywood film star, who died a few weeks later, driving an identical silver Porsche to a race meeting in the USA.

The sun was now low in the sky. It was around nine o'clock. Two thirds of the race had been run. Predictably, I found Tubby leaning against a beer tent. He told me I owed him a pint because he'd just spotted the best-looking girl of the day. It was the barmaid who'd pulled his last pint. This facile, but fun, competition had become a custom amongst the Members over the years – it was always a pint to the bloke who first identified the most attractive girl at the circuit. Obviously, these nominations were often highly contentious. He urged me inside the tent where I ordered a couple of beers and we both studied form. I reminded Tubby about the attractive Coca Cola salesgirl with blonde hair, bright red lipstick and figure-hugging dress that I'd pointed out shortly after we'd arrived. She'd been selling chilled bottles from a tray around her neck. She looked very modern, very American. He thought for a while and then, only after I'd paid for the drinks, admitted that I was right. 'She certainly had a great chassis,' he conceded.

We decided to venture back to have a word with Mike, who'd been out for some time with mechanical failure, yet again. It would be scant consolation but we were going to congratulate him on breaking the course lap record.

As we approached the pits, we saw him from a distance. He'd already changed out of his racing togs, and he wasn't alone. He was with Cherry Huggins! There they were, side by side, smoking cigarettes, leaning up against his brand new regency-red convertible Jaguar XK140. I didn't know which I coveted more: his girl or his car! Cherry looked fantastically dishevelled, doubtless in a contrived way: her dark wavy hair piled up; blouse sleeves rolled up to the elbow like a mechanic's; and her tight pencil skirt gathered ferociously at the

---

1 *Coincidentally, Dean also managed to avoid US National Service due to having a 'mental disorder'. His 'disorder' was homosexuality.*

69

waist by a wide leather belt. Tubby wasted no time in relegating our Coca Cola vendor from her pole position. However, both Mike and Cherry were looking sombre, their eyes fixed on the ground in front of them. Had they had a row, or was Cherry simply trying to console him? Either way, their body language didn't look welcoming.

'Aw, come on, let's shoot off. We're not needed right now,' I said to Tubby. We turned around and went back to the trackside.

During the race, we heard about another Cooper-Bristol that had somersaulted spectacularly and caught fire, but it wasn't until the following day we learnt that Mike Keen, the driver and a close colleague of Mike's, had died. It's highly possible that learning of another fatality at Goodwood would have brought back memories of his dad. All things considered, it was hardly surprising Mike had been looking sombre.

To add insult to injury, at midnight that night, one of the two privately entered D-Types came in just behind the winning Aston Martin. Who knows – if Mike had been behind the wheel of that Jaguar, it might have finished first.

Chapter Six

Dropping Like Flies

Two days later, I received a phone call at work. It was unusual for Mike to call my office, so I was immediately on high alert.

'You okay, Tom?'

'Uh-huh.'

'Listen, there's no easy way to say this. Julian's not made it.'

I couldn't think what to say. I pictured Julian sitting up at the bar in the Pond, smiling.

'Are you still there?' Mike asked.

'Er, yes. Okay, thanks. Thanks for letting me know.'

'I don't know when the funeral is. If I hear first, I'll let you know?'

'Thanks. Do the others know?'

'Doubt it. I've only just heard from Mrs C. I'm ringing round. I started with you.'

'Thanks.' My repetition was involuntary.

'Do you realise they both died in Ireland?' He meant Don and Julian.

'No.' And then for want of anything else to say, I asked, 'Are you out for a drink tonight?'

'Bloody right. Let's meet in The Bush at eight. I'll see who else I can get.'

I don't know about *a* drink, we must have had ten. When we met, everyone was close to tears. By the time we left, we were laughing and joking and telling ourselves that Julian would be laughing with us.

It was all so very different at the funeral, however. The church was packed, as I knew it would be. I'd already attended three Members' funerals before this one. It was beginning to feel like *Ten Green*

Bottles. The first was Simon Hayter's. He was just seventeen years old when he'd crashed his motorbike because he'd turned to check out some crumpet walking down the pavement. Another was Mike Currie's, a promising racing driver, whom we all called 'Black Mike', to distinguish him from 'White Mike' Hawthorn. Black Mike had entered a Frazer Nash Le Mans Replica with cycle-style mudguards, in the 1953 Nurburgring 1,000km. The scrutineers would not pass the car unless the gaps between the mudguards and the body were infilled. It seemed an impossible request at such short notice.

Meanwhile, 'White Mike' had been deprived of a drive, due to his Ferrari being requisitioned for the reigning world champion, Ascari, and so he set about saving the day for his friends. He insisted that Black Mike and his co-driver Don Beauman go to bed while he and his ace mechanic Brit Pearce stayed up all night and worked on the Frazer Nash until it was fully race compliant. Their entry not only competed but won its class. It was a wonderful little-known act of selflessness and camaraderie on Mike's part.

After the race, Mike and his two friends went their separate ways. Don and Black Mike, driving in convoy through the night, happened upon an American car that had crashed into a tree. Two of the occupants were dead. A third was badly injured. Don agreed to stay with the casualty while Black Mike drove the Frazer Nash back to the German-Belgian frontier, in the hope of finding a doctor. Apparently, in his haste, Mike didn't notice an unlit pole barrier across the road, at around head height, and was himself killed instantly.

The life expectancy for a Member seemed unduly poor – even if one wasn't a Grand Prix driver with a life-threatening health problem. I remember making many resolutions during that funeral service – chief amongst them was to make the most of every day.

Notwithstanding the loss of other Members, Julian's untimely departure shook me up the most. Perhaps it was because Julian, Mike and I had been like brothers almost. Perhaps it was because I was getting older and more sentimental.

Julian and Mike had done a lot of motorcycling together, before Mike graduated on to cars. And, because Julian was able to work more flexibly than me, he'd been able to accompany Mike to the inquest of Mike's father, Leslie. They'd both recently learnt to fly, and Julian's career as a motoring journalist was just beginning to take off, no doubt with a little help from Mike.

I managed a few minutes alone with Mike at the wake.

'Can it be worth it?' I asked.

'Worth what?' he asked, knowing full well what I meant.

'Risking your neck every week. Causing this sort of grief. I mean, it's not like you need the money.'

'I'm good enough to survive. Anyway, I enjoy it.' He took a draught of his beer.

'Does your mother? Does Cherry?' I was on a roll.

'Ah, they don't really mind.'

'Have you asked them? Listen, they say life's short – well, yours is going to be shorter than most, so why don't you try to have as much as you can?'

'I'm still here, aren't I?'

'That's got nothing to do with your chances. It's pure Russian roulette, and you know it.'

'Tom, sometimes you're as bad as the women.'

'I just don't see the point of risking your life when you have a choice.'

But, Tom, that's *exactly* the point. My life's already going to be cut short because of my bloody kidneys. I don't have that retiring-to-the-country thing to look forward to. If anything, it's the opposite. I'm *absolutely* the right material for a racing driver. Know which I'd choose – dying quickly in a car next year, or slowly and painfully in a hospital in three years' time?'

'You told me it was seven years.'

'No,' he said forcibly, 'I said they *thought* it could be five to seven years. What if they're wrong? What if the margin's the other way? What if it's only three years?'

'There's a big difference,' I protested.

'Anyway, I never feel as alive as when I'm driving right on the limit. There's no feeling like it. And to win…well, it's what Pop always wanted. The crowd all waving…crumpet coming up to you afterwards. I can't think of a better way to risk my life.'

'Yes but it's not always like that, is it? Have you forgotten the low times…the lonely hotel rooms, mechanical failures…the crashes, for God's sake? And the burns? What about Syracuse? And Le Mans?'

'There's always another day. Another victory, another girl!'

I knew then that I'd never talk him out of racing. No one would.

Incredibly, between our own private wake-cum-piss-up and the funeral proper, Mike had raced at Oulton Park and picked up a second place, driving the same beautiful red Ferrari we'd seen him drive at Goodwood. I marvelled at his inner strength – or insensitivity.

Shortly after the funeral, Mike had to travel to Monza, in preparation for the Italian Grand Prix. He sent me a postcard afterwards. All he wrote, in his neat hand, was:

> Bo, Didn't finish. Gearbox bolts snapped off – doing 160mph! What a bloody Fred Karno's! Wouldn't happen on a Jaguar. Best, Mike

He hadn't had time to come home to Farnham before going off to Belfast for his next race. It was there, at the 'Dreaded Dundrod' circuit for a major endurance sports car race that we next caught up. The seemingly invincible Streamline Mercedes took first, second and third, courtesy of Moss, Fangio and von Trips. Mike, driving a D-Type Jaguar, was partnered with Desmond Titterington, a local Belfast lad and well regarded driver. I suspect it was because of Lofty's loyalty to his top driver that he instructed Mike to take the first two-hour slot, Desmond the next two hours, and then for Mike to finish with a final stint of about two and a half hours.

Mike started well enough, running second behind Stirling's Mercedes but, in the third lap, they encountered a bad crash. I was unaware of it. From where I was standing, I could only see a column of smoke rising from beyond Deer's Leap. Mike told me later that he came upon a couple of crashed cars and, having no time to stop, had to drive through dense smoke which obscured the track. All he could do was hope he didn't hit anything, or anyone. Fortunately, he didn't. It was only later he learnt that there had been an almighty pile-up involving seven cars.

Although the Mercedes cars were known to be quicker than the opposition, their manager, Neubauer, had inexplicably broken up the ideal partnership of Fangio and Moss, giving each of them a slower co-driver. It was a huge mistake because, having covered over 600 miles, Mike and Desmond looked assured of a glorious second place, until Mike spun off on a pool of oil on the penultimate lap.

As the race ended, I was standing almost opposite the pits. I saw Alfred Neubauer stride towards and then square up to Lofty England in a most confrontational way. Neubauer was a large man with a huge girth. His team drivers called him Der Fette Mann, a moniker which requires no translation. His podgy features were sandwiched beneath his wide-brimmed felt hat and a white shirt. He had no neck and wore thick-rimmed round glasses. His vast woollen jacket gaped open, exposing the hard-working braces which suspended his trousers at the maximum diameter of their wearer. His tie, resting upon his shirt like a ski jump, ended well short of the belt line.

It was obvious to all that the two 'had words'. It was quite comical really because, whilst they were both very large men, Neubauer was the shorter by over half a foot. That didn't stop him poking Lofty in the chest or waving his Stetson-like hat in his face. After putting up with this for a few seconds, Lofty disdainfully turned on his heel and walked away. I'd love to have known what was said.

I decided to go and find Desmond to ask him what had happened to Mike.

'He over-revved the engine – and that was that.' Des was clearly not overjoyed.

'Blimey, I was told he'd hit some oil.'

'He did – his own! He found first gear instead of third when he was accelerating out of a corner. A rod came straight out of the side of the engine, and with it most of the oil.'

'That's not like Mike,' I protested.

'Maybe. But let me tell you, he was too tired to race. My wife says he was lying down the whole time I was driving. She reckons he was completely whacked.'

Had today, I wondered, been a bad kidney day?

'The strange thing is,' Des continued, 'I was furious that the bastards hadn't allowed Archie to race, all because of his so-called disability. But, having seen all that bloody carnage, I'm only pleased he wasn't. Any one of us may have been killed.'

Archie Scott Brown, who I knew to be a long-standing friend of Des's, was a remarkable driver who enjoyed considerable success at the highest level, despite his physical handicaps, which included being born with no right hand.

That one Dundrod race was responsible for no less than three fatalities. And Mike had known all the casualties personally: Jim Mayers, twenty-four years old, who'd started his career at the same time as Mike; Richard Mainwaring, twenty-six, who had been to school with Mike; and Bill Smith, just twenty, who Mike considered 'very promising' and with whom he'd been enjoying a beer the night before the race. All gone. Five friends. Three months. All died while racing in Ireland.

Pals dropping like flies. This was more akin to what our fathers had endured, yet the war had ended ten years earlier.

Chapter Seven

Warm Crumpet

By the autumn of '55, I was still working hard and periodically enjoying myself, despite still living with my parents. I wasn't, however, properly happy. It was as if something was missing. There was too little excitement in my life – I felt as if I was suspended, watching real life rather than participating. I thought it must be because there was no girl in it. I'd been thinking a lot about Moia, wondering whether she and Mike were no longer officially together. Mike had once asked me to return his call when he'd stayed over at her place and I'd deliberately held onto her telephone number.

After one particularly dull day at work, and a couple of 'sharpeners' for Dutch courage, I decided I would call her on the off chance. I jogged down to the telephone box at the end of our road. Fortunately, it was empty, and, better still, no one was lingering outside waiting for a call. I stepped inside and immediately lit a cigarette. I realised I hadn't planned this at all and only had a few coppers on me. The few I had I fed into the slot. Then I fished in my wallet for Moia's number and dialled it.

She answered it flatly, giving just the four digits of her number.

I pressed Button 'A', 'Is that you, Moia?' I ventured, knowing full well that it was.

'Who is this?'

I felt a tingle of excitement at hearing her dulcet voice. 'It's me, Tom. I was just, erm, wondering how you were.'

'Well, I've been better. Your *friend* has seriously embarrassed me.'

'Why? What happened?'

'He only swore at Sir Jeremy Boles! It was dreadful...truly awful. You do *know* who Sir Jeremy is, I take it?'

I did. He was a wealthy chap who had first sponsored Don

77

Beauman to go racing. 'Yes, I know who you mean, but surely Mike wouldn't have meant any—'

'Oh yes, he did, and it was deliberate. We were upstairs at the Motor Show when some chap told Mike that Sir Jeremy was about to buy a Gullwing Mercedes. Mike's reaction was, "Oh no, he's not! He's not buying a fucking German car. Come on – let's get down there." He grabbed my arm and whisked me downstairs, and there was Sir Jeremy writing out a cheque. Mike jumped up onto the stand and said, "What the hell are you buying a bloody Kraut car for? Why don't you buy a Jaguar from me, you silly bastard?" There were lots of people within earshot. I just wanted to disappear.'

'He actually called him a silly bastard?'

'He did.'

'Then what happened?'

'Sir Jeremy slowly stood up, looked at Mike and told him he happened to like that particular Mercedes better than any Jaguar and then carried on writing the cheque. Mike then called him "an unpatriotic old sod" and stormed back upstairs.'

'What about you?'

'I came straight here.'

'With Mike?'

'No. He came round quite a bit later. He'd been drinking. He was all coy and asked if he could stay over. I told him to clear off and only come back when he was sober. That was at least two hours ago.'

'Oh, you poor thing.' I actually thought the whole thing was a bit of a hoot, but I wasn't going to let Moia know that.

'I'm okay. It's just…well, you know what he's like…One minute he's all arrogant and stand-offish, the next he's a little kid. You should have seen him after that TV thing with Rudi What's-his-face. He came round here in a terrible state, bawling his eyes out, he was.'

I wasn't desperately surprised to hear that. It would have been the first time he'd have had to publicly confront the enormity of the Le Mans disaster. I wasn't going to defend him. Not now.

'I know he's my mate…but he's not really worthy of you, you know.' I couldn't believe what I'd just said. I felt such a creep.

'Look, I'm sorry. I shouldn't be moaning to you. Presumably, you called to speak to him?'

'No, that's all right. It wasn't anything urgent...' In that one sentence, I missed my chance.

We said our goodbyes. Moia's sounded indifferent. I pressed the bar to disconnect the line while I held onto the handset, staring at it, wondering if Moia had any idea how I felt about her. Eventually, I replaced it and trudged back home, feeling sorry for Moia – two-timed and now seriously embarrassed. And then I reminded myself that I should feel sorry for Mike too. By the time I walked indoors, I had also begun to feel sorry for myself.

Chapter Eight

To BRM, or Not To Be…?

Apart from at Christmas, I saw little of Mike as he was spending more time in London and abroad. My concern that Mike's best days of racing were behind him was growing, knowing what I did about his health, and wondering whether he might be losing his nerve. Had he peaked between '51 and '53? It certainly seemed that unless Mike could get to drive the very fastest cars he was now destined to be an also-ran. How would he take it if he was never to climb those podium steps again? He was a gracious loser, mostly, but I knew how much he hated to lose.

Seeing less of Mike didn't stop me avidly following motor racing. I was deeply shocked when I read that Stirling Moss was out of a job. Without any warning, Mercedes, for whom he had driven so successfully, decided to pull out of both Grand Prix and sports car racing. This left him and another young British talent, Peter Collins, in search of new teams for the following year, 1956. On one of the foulest November days, both men were offered test drives at Silverstone in three British cars – a BRM, a Vanwall and a Connaught.

Publicly, Stirling said that he would like to drive a British car again, and no doubt he would have done, had they been competitive. However, for Stirling, winning races and earning a decent living trumped patriotism and, in the absence of a decent British Grand Prix outfit, he opted to drive a Maserati. This would not be directly for the company but in a privately entered Moss family-funded car. In fairness, he also opted to drive for Britain's Aston Martin team, in all sports car events.

It was much the same for Pete Collins. He'd had a disappointing season driving for BRM, and was equally disillusioned with British offerings, and hence promptly signed for Ferrari.

Mike too was facing exactly the same dilemma. I remember many pints being consumed while he agonised over his options. His heart wanted to stay with a British team while his head knew that, to stand a chance of winning races, he would have to 'go foreign' once more. Enzo Ferrari invited him to Italy to discuss the forthcoming season. Lofty, meanwhile, was lobbying hard for Mike to stay driving for Jaguar. Mike went to off to Maranello in the hope that, if he drove for Ferrari in all the Grand Prix events and any other races not entered by Jaguar, Enzo would accept Mike driving half a dozen times for Jaguar.

Enzo would have none of it. Neither party would back down. Which is how Mike ended up swapping teams with Pete Collins and driving a contraption called a BRM Type 25. Almost all the components of that car were made in Britain, with the notable exception being the Italian Weber carburettors. Finished in British Racing Green, the BRM was a glorious-looking car. However, its reputation led to one Member deciding the initials stood for Bum Reamer Machine. Stirling Moss commented that it was 'the worst car I've ever sat in' and Mike called it 'an absolute time bomb'!

All in all, 1955 was, I'm sure, Mike's personal 'annus horribilis'. However, the following year wasn't exactly beer and skittles either.

Chapter Nine

1956 – The 'Lucky' Year

Abstinence

By 1956, Mike had become a very high-profile celebrity and was consequently in great demand for public appearances around the world. As I saw less of Mike in person, I had to rely upon news broadcasts on the BBC, race reports I read in magazines, or anecdotes gleaned from mutual friends and acquaintances – of which there was no shortage.

In January that year, his signing for BRM was conducted live and with much fanfare on the BBC's Sportsview television show. Ironically, the more well known he became, the less success he enjoyed. The BRMs would prove just as hopeless as the Vanwalls had the previous season. His public profile seemed to be growing all the while, not through his prowess on the track but by his performances on television and his photogenic face in newspapers.

Uncharacteristically, he'd asked my opinion about joining BRM. The offer made by BRM's financier Alfred Owen looked, on paper, another extremely generous one. Not only would Mike receive a healthy retainer, effectively a modest salary, but also fifty per cent of all the prize money, starting money and 'component bonuses'. Being a natural pessimist, I pointed out that, if the BRM didn't perform, those generous incentives weren't going to materialise. Mike told me I was being a typical bean counter and that he was bound to get a few good podium finishes. As the season unfolded, my pessimism proved prescient. Mike was only able to enter a BRM in six races. In four races, the car failed to finish at all. In one, the car wasn't considered capable of even starting. And in the other, BRM wasn't even able to enter a car in working order By any reckoning, it was a lousy season – for podium and pocket. When

I reminded Mike of my misgivings, he denied that I'd said anything.

As BRM only built racing cars, Mike was free to continue driving for his beloved Jaguar sports car team. However, Mike had little more success here, achieving only one second place and one sixth place all season – both in shared drives.

It could have been worse: he could easily have been upstaged by Stirling. At the beginning of the year, Stirling was without a sports car drive despite being at the top of his game, popular and British. It came as a surprise to no one when Jaguar offered him a contract. But Stirling didn't want to be perceived as inferior to Mike and thus made his acceptance conditional upon being named the team's number one driver.

That must have thrown Lofty somewhat as Mike had already assumed that mantle. Mike said there was no way he was going to be number two to Stirling, although he did at least suggest that they could share the top billing. Perhaps only Lofty knows what actually transpired, but the upshot was that Stirling rejected Mike's counter-offer and duly secured his position with the Aston Martin team, with whom he went on to enjoy considerable success.

There are many factors which influence the success or otherwise of racing drivers. Not least is the reliability of the cars they drive. And it's true: there is luck – both good luck and bad luck. I began to think that Mike was starting to lean on his bad luck rather too much. The car he was driving, the Jaguar D-Type, was doing really well, for the works' team as a whole as well as the quirkily named Scottish Ecurie Ecosse team, and in the hands of private entrants.

Mike was to score a measly four Grand Prix Championship points in the whole of 1956 that year. Granted, that was four more points than the previous year although none was courtesy of BRM. Four points hardly began to compare with his twenty-four points and nineteen points of 1954 and 1953 respectively. I began to wonder what it would be like if his star were only to wane from here on. I pictured him travelling around the globe, occasionally lonely and always preoccupied about his failing health, his career flagging, and his earnings diminishing. Although I'm not sure I needed to have worried about him being lonely as the thing with Cherry was really taking off.

His racing campaign in this year started, as ever, in South

America, commencing with the Argentinian Grand Prix at Buenos Aires. I used to shudder at the thought of the Argentine GP. It was all so chaotic and disorganised. I remember Mike telling the Members all about his first campaign out there in 1953. There were six Argentinian drivers, including Juan Fangio and Gonzalez, out of the sixteen entrants, and such was the excitement amongst the local populace that the authorities proposed making no admittance charge. It was estimated that over 400,000 spectators occupied the Buenos Aires Autodrome, spilling all over the track. Even today, it's hard to imagine that number of spectators attending any race, anywhere. The crush caused many of the safety barriers to break. Despite the best efforts of the marshals, some spectators refused to move off the track surface, taking off their jackets and shirts and playing matador to the charging cars! Predictably, there were many accidents, the worst of which involved Mike's teammate Nino Farina. Someone actually ran across the track in front of Farina. At racing speed, Farina swerved to avoid hitting them, skidded and ploughed into the crowd, killing fifteen spectators. An ambulance, racing to the scene, lost control and killed two more.

This year, the BRM wasn't ready in time for the South American leg, and so Mike again drove a Maserati 250F, perversely but generously supplied by BRM's Alfred Owen, and in which Pete Collins had campaigned the preceding year. I remember Mike telling me afterwards that the exercise of flying the Maserati out and back had cost Owen around £3,000. I was incredulous. That was the equivalent of ten years of my annual salary – for 'bean counting', as Mike used to call it.

Juan Fangio notched up yet another controversial victory in front of his home crowd while Mike finished a lucky third, due to a catalogue of accidents and incidents which befell faster cars. It was to be Mike's best solo performance in the World Championship all year – and not in the car he was being paid to drive.

The next GP, a fortnight later, was held at Mendoza, a small city in the foothills of the Andes, 600 miles west of Buenos Aires. Here the Maserati's steering column broke, which effectively put him out of contention for any points. However, remarkably, the mechanics managed to patch it up, and he finished in ninth place. Fangio on a Ferrari and Moss on his Maserati picked up first and second respectively. All this, of course, I'd had to glean from the radio and newspapers.

Notwithstanding that Mike's next big race was on the same side of the Atlantic, in Florida, it was over six weeks away, and hence Mike came home. This was ostensibly to spend time with BRM testing brakes, although from what I could see he'd come back to spend as much time with Cherry as possible.

I would have dearly loved to have gone out to Florida with Mike, but I was having difficulty even affording travel to some of the European circuits. As it was, I'd have probably got in the way. Mike and five other Jaguar drivers flew out to New York and then on to Palm Beach, via Washington and Miami. They then drove themselves all the way out to Sebring before competing in a 1,000-mile endurance race. The weather there was beautiful: hot and windy. The circuit was flat, open and, in parts, very wide, quite unlike European circuits.

Mike and his Jaguar partner Des Titterington were given the débutante, fuel-injected D-Type. The other pairings had carburettor-fitted Ds. Sadly, for Mike and Des, their car, which had been in the lead after four hours – the first two hours of which had been wheel-to-wheel dicing with Moss on an Aston and Fangio on a Ferrari – lost all its brake fluid, forcing retirement. Victory was once again secured by Fangio, this time partnered with Castellotti.

Just a week later and Mike was back in Farnham – and out on the town, in some style. Flying visits like this were getting rarer, but whenever Mike had a whole evening free, he'd be the catalyst for a major drinking session – with all available Members. A lot of us were there, and the mood was particularly jolly. A couple of conversations stayed in my memory: one about the new car and one about Stirling Moss.

This was two days before the new BRM Type 25 was to make its Formula One debut in the hands of Mike and his new teammate Tony Brooks at Goodwood, and we all wanted to know what it was like. Mike put it in simple terms: 'It's effing fast, doesn't go round corners, and doesn't stop too well.' When pushed to elaborate, he said that the car was really twitchy, and the slightest provocation could 'send the tail out'. As for its poor stopping ability, this was all down to one designer's insistence on persevering with a single inboard rear disc brake, despite all the evidence pointing to its inherent weakness.

In reply to one chap who asked whether Mike was worried about driving it, he replied, 'Worried? Why should I worry about this, and not all the other contraptions I've been expected to drive? If your number's up, your number's up. Don't worry about me. I'm bloody immortal.'

If only. The other subject we all wanted to talk about, which Mike obviously didn't, was Stirling. Stirling had finished second behind Fangio in the last World Championships whilst Mike had finished without a single point – a reversal of fortune from the year before when Mike had finished fourth to Stirling's thirteenth. It was widely held that Moss was Britain's first world champion in waiting – waiting upon Fangio to retire. As a consequence, Stirling's PR was in the ascendancy, and he was already enjoying a strong start to the season. The lads demanded to know if the only difference between Stirling's success and Mike's lack of it was in the cars, many of them wanting to believe that their 'Farnham Flyer' was peerless on the track. I felt sure that none of the others knew what I knew, so I deliberately kept quiet.

Fortunately, just as Mike was beginning to articulate a technical answer, Simon interjected with, 'Nah, I know what the difference is. Moses (our politically insensitive name for Stirling, coined due to his part Jewish roots) won't *do it* for at least four nights before a big race...whereas Mike only stops doing it once he gets into a single-seater!'

'Do what exactly?' asked someone just as the collective penny dropped. Well, that was it. The bar exploded with guffaws and questions and comments. It was already well known that Stirling would go to bed at nine o'clock the night before a race and seldom drank. In comparison with Mike, he was practically teetotal, yet none of us had heard of this latest abstinence. Like most racing drivers, Stirling was renowned for attracting his fair share of decent-looking crumpet, and this revelation was quite something.

Mike was in his element. 'I'll tell Moses he should send them round to me before a race. I'll keep 'em nice and warm for him,' was one of the more repeatable things he said.

Over and Out

Mike divided the next day, a Sunday and April Fool's Day, between his BRM team and Cherry Huggins. I'd bet a pound to a penny against Mike's abstinence of any kind. His immediate race preparations, to which I can personally attest, usually comprised little more than a cup of tea, a cold flannel, and sometimes a hair of the dog.

Once again, a big Farnham contingent trooped down to Goodwood on Easter Monday, me included, to witness Mike's first race in the BRM. It certainly looked the part: its svelte, tapered barrel-shaped body in British Racing Green hanging between its novel steel wheels. It was even perfectly proportioned, up until Mike clambered into the cockpit. The top of the low Perspex wind deflector in front of the driver, there to deflect the worst of the air resistance, was about level with Mike's shoulders. Once again, there was that slightly comical look, as if he was piloting a child's pedal car.

In the pits, I was fleetingly introduced to young Tony Brooks, 'Hey, Tom, come and say hello to Tony, the racing dentist'. I'd heard that Tony had originally trained to be a dentist, but this neat little chap with a reedy voice had the all the charisma of a nervy office junior. Was he really any sort of racing driver? He was a mouse, not a lion. Looking back, this unfavourable initial impression seems grossly unfair, given how he developed into one of the best racing drivers of the late 1950s and an asset to British racing teams. This was only his first season in Grand Prix, and I now realise he was probably in awe of some of the company he was keeping – not least Messrs Hawthorn and Moss. He was, though, young and skilled, and I was jealous. I should also mention that, in contrast with so many drivers mentioned in these pages, he, like Stirling, was one of the very few survivors of this era.

The thirty-two-lap Glover Trophy was *the* race of the day. Mike got the BRM away brilliantly and led for the first lap. We were watching the race close to the start/finish line so we couldn't assess how Mike was getting on through the corners. What we could see was that the straight-line speed was impressive. Once through the chicane, he came screaming past us, hotly pursued by Stirling Moss and Archie Scott Brown.

Minutes before, I'd bumped into Winifred Hawthorn, Mike's mother, when I was returning from a visit to the gents. I said 'hello' in passing, and noticed that she was standing near to Cherry Huggins and a few other people I didn't recognise. Winifred was a rare spectator by then. However, this was a high-profile race and one that was practically on our doorstep. It's likely that someone, perhaps Cherry, had given her a lift. She wouldn't have driven alone.

By the time Mike came past for a second time, he was lying third, behind Scott Brown and Moss in that order. Everyone who knew how difficult it was to drive a Formula One car right on the edge was a massive fan of One-Arm Archie. It amazes me still that Archie was a driver who was the equal of Mike or Stirling and yet was severely disabled. Mike must have been hugely frustrated to have been outcornered by Stirling and Archie, and was clearly looking to optimise his straight-line speed.

We heard of Mike's crash long before we knew what happened. The words 'Oh no...this looks very bad...yes, it's Hawthorn's BRM that's gone over...' were the first his mother and friends heard of it. It happened at Fordwater, which is more of a gentle bend than a corner, and thus tempts drivers to take it flat out.

Mike told us afterwards – and yes, by some miracle he did survive – that having slowed right down for Madgwick Corner, he'd accelerated up to over 100 miles per hour when the BRM became difficult to hold. The car then spun, hit an earth bank and flew up into the air. Once Mike sensed the car was going over, he knew he'd have to get out. He let go of the wheel and began to drop out. Momentarily, his ankle snagged against the seat, and then the next moment he was launched into mid-air. For a split second, he was floating away from the car, seemingly defying gravity. Then, as he described it, came a 'bone-jarring shock' as he hit the ground. Incredibly, apart from being dazed and having a painful ankle, he was remarkably unscathed. It simply wasn't necessary to articulate what would have been the outcome had he not managed to get out of the car before it landed upside down. If he'd have been wearing one of today's racing harnesses, that would have been his last race.

The moment I heard of the accident, I ran straight towards Fordwater. I don't know what I could have done if Mike had been seriously hurt. I just felt I had to be with him. Whilst I was trying to jog through the crowd, I began to fear the worst. Should I instead have gone to be with Winifred and Cherry? Looking back, that is of course what I should have done. However, back then I was still very gauche.

By the time I reached Fordwater, Mike was up on his feet, walking unsteadily towards his upturned green car. It only had three wheels. One had obviously sheared off on landing. I shouted across to Mike not to get near the car, fearful that the petrol could ignite. I'm not sure he heard me, but I was relieved when he groggily veered away and headed for the trackside. I knew Mike would go straight back to the pits via the infield so I headed back to personally deliver the good tidings to his mother and girlfriend. Of course, I needn't have bothered because the tannoy had already briskly advised the spectators, 'Good news. Hawthorn is now up on his feet and is looking fine'.

Of course, I was hugely relieved to see that he was okay, but the extent of his good fortune didn't fully register until I learnt later that day that two other drivers, novice Tony Dennis and Bert Rogers, had also gone over in their cars during that race and died of their injuries.

I remember afterwards spending an hour or so sitting alone on the grass, nursing a pint and ruminating about this wretched sport. Motor racing was at that time a relatively young sport, if sport is what it is. Formula One had only begun in 1950 and had immediately attracted big crowds and a huge media following. Were all these people fascinated by the latest automotive technological advancements or by ear-piercing exhausts? No, of course not. What many, perhaps most, spectators came to see was raw danger. Had the cars gone round the track, one at a time, hardly anyone would have been interested. The public bayed for wheel-to-wheel racing, where drivers were right on the edge of their ability, ideally for their own nation's pride. They wanted accidents. That was the drama. That was the excitement. Of course, they were appalled by loss of life, but provided there was no personal connection, it was accepted as part and parcel of an exciting contest...not so different from the gladiatorial battles of ancient Rome.

The sport today is far more sophisticated, the drivers no less talented, the competition as close as ever, and yet it is incomparably safer. As I write, there has been no fatality in a Grand Prix race for twenty years. As someone who might have enjoyed many more enduring friendships during the past sixty years, I think this is a wonderful thing, but I do wonder what keeps the interest of the vast numbers who follow Formula One today.

Some hours later, a few of us caught up with Mike and Cherry in The Richmond Arms. Imagine…thrown out of a somersaulting car in the afternoon and having a few beers in the evening! We drank to lucky escapes, and went on to have a rare old time. Naturally, a toast was made to those who didn't make it.

Brakedown

Mike was immediately to encounter more luck – he deemed it good luck. Most rational people would think it was the polar opposite. His BRM had not been totally written off when it crashed at Goodwood. The front suspension and body was badly damaged, but the chassis was carefully checked and found to be free of distortion. Consequently, BRM rebuilt the car and arranged for Mike to test it at Silverstone. He'd only completed a few laps and was just coming into the straight before the pits when the bonnet came clean off and hit him straight in the face. Fortunately, he was wearing a helmet with a visor. The visor, which was smashed, took most of the impact. Mike was taken directly to see a doctor who advocated stitching the wound on his face. Mike flatly refused stitches and so returned to the track with a sticking plaster instead. It transpired that the bonnet had not been the one belonging to his car and had been fitted in error. Mike said afterwards that he felt lucky because had it flown off at a different angle he could have been beheaded. As he evoked the memory of decapitation at Le Mans, there was a discernible pause in our conversation.

Days later, he took the very same BRM to Aintree for a 200-mile race. I couldn't be there, but I did hear all about it. Archie Scott Brown had pole position, and Mike was alongside on the front row. Mike got the better start. They were clearly the quickest two cars on the day, and Archie nipped past Mike on one corner. The lead then kept alternating between them. With Mike in front, approaching Cottage Corner at speed, and with Archie hot on his heels, Mike went to press the brake. To his utter disbelief, the pedal had vanished. Thinking he must somehow have missed the pedal, he stamped down again. All he managed to do was to snag the accelerator and ended up careering off the track and onto open grassland. Amazingly, he didn't crash. He motored back to the pits, at little more than walking pace. He was almost purple with rage. It was soon established that a clevis pin (which secures the pedal assembly to the braking gear) had dropped out because no one had fitted a securing split-pin to hold it in place. It was yet another example of how something so seemingly insignificant could so easily have cost the life of a driver.

By now, Mike had developed an abiding aversion to endurance races run on public roads rather than race tracks, and so I was not surprised when he turned down an invitation to drive in the gruelling Italian race, the Mille Miglia, at the end of April. It was probably a combination of factors, not least his own physical limitations, but Mike's public stance was that they were too dangerous for both spectators and drivers. Mike clearly wasn't alone in this stance because the only two works' teams to enter were Ferrari and Maserati – both Italian.

Unfortunately, Mike's anathema was Stirling Moss's forte – and Stirling had been much feted for his bravura drive of the previous year. Mike was, however, totally vindicated in his views as there was the usual carnage. Six people were killed during the race: three drivers and three spectators. The spectators seemed oblivious that the drivers' vision of the roads, along which they lined, in torrential rain through plastic visors and windshields, was severely degraded, and there were no pedestrian barriers anywhere.

When Mike heard that at one point during the Mille Miglia Stirling's brakes had failed and his car had been hanging perilously over a precipice, he laughed and made some wisecrack about God looking after Moses.

At Silverstone that May, Mike continued to be plagued by unreliability and misfortune. He entered three races – one with the hapless BRM whose engine gave up on the thirteenth lap after he'd taken the lead, and two for Jaguar. He failed to reach the chequered flag in any of them. Mike spoke about how 'bloody uncomfortable' he was in the BRM because, despite adjustments, the seat still didn't fit him. He would be astonished, not to say very jealous, to see today's constructors pouring molten latex into flexible moulds around their seated F1 drivers to ensure a totally bespoke fit.

Chapter Ten

Ins and Outs in Paris

These weren't, however, entirely dull times. One week later, Mike invited me to accompany him to Monaco for the Grand Prix. I didn't need to be asked twice. We were to fly in his four-seater Fairchild Argus, one of three ex-RAF planes his father had bought after the war. This American-built aeroplane was originally known as a Forwarder – an appropriate name given the character of the pilot. Mike had never flown to France before and decided to take it in easy stages, stopping at various small airfields en route.

The flight afforded a chance for us to talk; the noise of the little aircraft seeming to help rather than hinder, in the same way a crowded bar can be surprisingly conducive to an intimate chat.

'Your dad'd be very proud of you,' I ventured.

'Why do you think that?' Mike replied.

'Well, for a start, you're now really famous.'

'I was more successful when he was alive.'

'You're still successful. Do you miss him?'

'All the time. When I'm struggling and I really need to try hard, I try to win for him. He'd have loved me to win the Championship one day...but I can't see that happening now, can you?'

I paused, wondering whether he meant that his form wasn't good enough, or that his cars weren't good enough, or whether his health would now preclude him from being physically able. I'd hesitated too long.

'You don't think I can either, do you?' He glanced across at me.

'If you get the right car, of course you can.' I said, without enough conviction. I was thinking how much like his dad Mike was becoming. Father and son were equally passionate about cars and planes. They were unabashed womanisers. They could both be charming – Mike more so – but, at the same time, they could be feisty and confrontational. And both were serious drinkers. By now, I was certain that drink had indirectly killed his father. Mike had idolised his father, and I wondered whether he'd eventually go the same way.

The transformation of Leslie Hawthorn from fiery, irascible disciplinarian parent of our youth to Les, colleague, confidante and champion of his son, in the couple of years before his death was absolute. He and Mike were great pals at the end.

Mike had put me in charge of navigation. That is to say, he handed me a road atlas of France! Much to my amazement, shortly after we'd run out of sea beneath us, we identified Le Touquet, our first scheduled stop, where both plane and pilot were rapidly refuelled. Our next stop was to be Abbeville, only we couldn't find it.

'Oh, bugger it,' said Mike. 'Let's push on. See if you can find Beauvais.'

'How do you spell that?' I asked.

He spelt it out and reached across, dabbing a finger where he imagined it might be on the map. 'It's around here, somewhere.'

'Got it,' I said. 'It's some way away, roughly south of us. Well, south-south-east, I suppose.'

Mike adjusted the plane's course slightly and then settled back into cruising mode. 'What are the chances of BRM sorting out their cars within my lifetime?'

I was about to answer this seriously until it dawned on me that he was making a point about his short life expectancy.

'Pretty slim, if your flying's anything to go by.'

Mike responded by violently pushing back the joystick so the plane's nose pointed directly at the ground.

'You can't scare me, Hawthorn,' I lied.

He laughed loudly and pulled out of the dive. 'I bet I can.'

Mike flew on for what seemed like an eternity until we eventually spotted a huge conurbation with a tall skeletal tower right in the middle. We'd completely missed Beauvais and stumbled upon Paris.

Mike landed at Toussus le Noble Airport and immediately paid for an expensive taxi to take us into the city.

I thought, considering his catalogue of failures so far that season, he seemed in remarkably good spirits. Which probably accounts for what happened next.

We headed straight for Fred Payne's bar in Rue Pigalle. The upside of having been hired by BRM was that Mike was feeling in the money again, and that day he was in a truly expansive mood. He ordered half a bottle of champagne, which cost ten bob. That was soon emptied. Another followed, and another. We were drinking the stuff like lemonade. There was a brothel right next door, and there were always girls looking for customers at Fred's. The more we drank, the better-looking the girls became…to the extent that two of them became absolutely irresistible and we found ourselves going next door – a long way removed from sober.

A short while later, Mike appeared in my room stark naked and announced, 'I've had enough of mine. Shall we see if we can find some prettier ones?'

I'm ashamed to say that that's exactly what we did, neither of us wearing a stitch. We went barging into some of the other rooms, shoving two unsuspecting chaps out of the way so that we could check out their girls. We thought it was a hoot but our humour wasn't appreciated by all the clientele, some of whom were Algerian manual workers. A commotion ensued, and we had just enough wit about to us to grab our clothes and leg it before we lost anything more precious than a few francs.

To this day, I can't tell you how we found our way to the Hotel Miami where we had a reservation, but we did. The next thing I recall was waking up about twelve hours later wondering where on earth I was and why my head hurt so much.

We'd missed dinner and were only just in time for breakfast, which comprised lots of black coffee with bread and jam. I felt a bit better seeing that Mike was obviously suffering too and could barely manage more than one or two words. That is, until I realised we had no time to lick our wounds: we had to be in Nice by nightfall, and Mike had to fly us there.

By some miracle, we made it…well, to Lyon anyway, which was about as far as Mike could fly in his delicate condition. At least the flight had given us a chance to sober up a bit, and so we set about hiring a car to take us on to Monaco. Mike asked for a *voiture economique* which, if interpreted as cheap, was exactly what we got. It was a little Renault Dauphine, a gutless little four-seater. I informed Mike that it had just thirty-one brake horsepower.

'How do you know that stuff?' he demanded.

'I read a lot,' I said. 'Did you know Renault were going to call it a Corvette?'

'Best hold onto your hat, then,' he said with a laugh.

As we set off towards Monte Carlo, all I could think about was the lecture I'd been given by Raymond Mays, the boss of BRM who, a few days earlier, had said that on no account was Mike to be let loose in Paris. Clearly, neither of us was going to be too popular.

On the drive, Mike was in pensive mood. He asked whether I thought 'the old kidney problem' could be contributing to his feeling particularly awful. I didn't think anything I said would make much difference and I was actually feeling pretty lousy myself.

'You understand, don't you? I've got to live for the day. Who knows how long I've got.'

'Yeah, but, you know, you could be making it worse,' I ventured.

'I guess so, but surely there's no harm in the odd drink or two?'

'Mike! Last night was a bit more than *one or two*. It was more like twenty-two!'

Mike laughed. The truth was it had been a heavy session, even by our standards.

It was late by the time we reached Monaco. Mike confidently threaded his way down towards the waterfront until we were just above the harbour.

Oh please, Mike, I thought, not the Casino. We weren't dressed for it, and I doubted I could afford a single drink. And then there it was, straight in front of us: that magnificent floodlit edifice. This was no sleazy gaming joint; this was a late nineteenth-century fairy-tale palace. Beautiful cars lined up outside, chauffeurs waiting patiently for their affluent owners. My heart sank.

Mike slowed right down as if to stop, but then carried on driving around the manicured island in front. It was dark outside. Few people were on the street, and the architecture of the Square was intimidating. He finally came to a halt directly outside the equally imposing Hotel de Paris, Monte Carlo's finest old hotel.

'What's up?' I asked.

'Thought you'd fancy a nightcap,' he said as he got out of the car. An immaculate, expressionless doorman approached us. Far from embarrassed about our *economique* set of wheels, Mike flashed a smile and handed over the keys and a sizeable franc note. 'Bon soir,' he said smoothly. He then looked back at me.

I was still sitting in the car.

'Come on, chap, I'm thirsty,' he said.

I followed him into the hotel's huge lobby – all marble floors, glass and ornately-detailed white stucco columns and domed ceilings. I felt so scruffy. We were dishevelled, unshaven and dirty. If Mike felt the same, he didn't show it. He merely spied a sign to a bar and continued marching. I trotted along behind, worrying about what might be happening to our rented car, our luggage, and when I would be getting some sleep.

Although Mike never once treated me other than an equal when we went somewhere truly expensive or exclusive – and this was both those things – I seldom felt worthy. Indeed, I was often uncomfortable. I was only too conscious that I was the hanger-on. It was Mike who deserved to be in this place, with these people. Actually, it was more than that: he seemed at ease with it all, as if he'd never experienced anything else. It had only been a handful of years since somewhere like the Regal, Farnham's picture house, and one of its nicer usherettes were our idea an impressive building and a pretty girl. Now, it was the Hotel de Paris and a girlfriend who worked for Vogue magazine.

And yet, as I reflect upon those times, I feel so lucky to have been to so many amazing places and seen such incredible sights – simply because I was a friend.

As Mike strode into the bar hoping for a quiet, reviving hair of the dog, he got a heck of a shock. Who should be sitting there alone, seemingly waiting for us? None other than Mr Mays. He took one look at Mike's face and said, 'My God, Hawthorn – what *are* we going to do with you?'

Some minutes later, one small drink and properly chastened, we slunk off back to Reception. After a brief exchange with the receptionist, at whom I'm convinced Mike winked, our car was duly brought to the door for us. Mike thanked the doorman, and we set off into the clear night to find the more modest lodgings into which we were booked. When my head finally hit the pillow, I was so desperately tired I couldn't even worry whether everything would be all right in the morning.

The first practice session was not until 4pm the following afternoon, which was just as well seeing how Mike and I managed to snooze our way through 'til midday. Brunch consisted of coffee, bread and beer. The later practice sessions commenced at the extraordinary time of 5.45am on the Friday and Saturday mornings. This, I assume, was to keep the disruption of the Principality to a minimum. It also served to separate the disciplined, sober drivers from non-disciplined party animals.

Sometime around six o'clock on the Friday evening, I was able to join Mike to drive around the circuit. It is very much an urban race over the twisting, undulating roads of Monte Carlo. One lap is just less than two miles and is devoid of any decent straight sections. The start is close to the quayside, immediately after which is a hairpin bend which doubles back on itself at the gasworks. In little more than quarter of a mile, the track turns sharp right at Sainte Devote and then winds up the hill to Casino Square before plunging down towards another hairpin past the railway station. Another two sharp right-handers take one down to the harbour front once more and the long tunnel. Emerging from the tunnel, the track would be straightish if it wasn't for the chicane which acts to slow the cars considerably. The chicane leads to an abrupt left turn and back to the start.

Whenever the road was deserted, Mike tried to drive the wheels off our little rear-engined Renault. However, try as he might, he couldn't get the rear to swing out. In fact, it never really lost its composure.

'What's the matter with this thing?' he complained.

'Nothing,' I volunteered, 'apart from having about a seventh of the power of your BRM'.Even though we were going round at a stately pace, I was amazed at the tightness of the two hairpins. It felt as though you could only get around them at walking speed.

As luck, of some description, would have it, both Mike's and his teammate Tony Brooks's BRMs were plagued with valve trouble during practice – the inlet valve heads fell off – and their cars were consequently withdrawn from the race. This was probably terrible news for Mike's opponents who were still racing, as Mike urged them to attend every party and explore every bar with him.

For me, undoubtedly the best thing about being Mike's 'escort' at these parties was the bevy of fantastic crumpet who seemed to shadow the motor racers. Not that their interest was ever directed at me. It was as if I wore a big badge proclaiming, 'I'm not a Driver – I'm Ignorable!' How did they know?

Amongst the lovelies present, I distinctly remember a stunning American girl with the most fabulous smile being at the Cahiers' party. Bernard Cahier was a renowned racing photographer and journalist, and he and his wife Joan had the reputation of hosting the best parties in Monte Carlo. This one was at his villa on the Moyen Corniche. The girl, a former model turned actress, was introduced to all of us as Louise King. I remember thinking that she was one of the most beautiful girls I'd ever seen, whereas both Mike and Pete seemed a bit blasé about her. I most certainly wasn't…but who was I? A bag carrier, that's what.

We all briefly encountered Louise again later that week, on a beach where her 'tidy chassis' could be fully appreciated, but it would be another year before she became significant in all our lives.

It is telling that Pete, with whom we spent many happy, mostly squiffy, hours qualified the slowest of the four Ferraris. By comparison, Fangio, on another Ferrari, qualified in pole position. No matter how young, fit and fast, no one could party all night and drive at their best the following morning.

Watching the race with Mike was a treat. He was able to provide a running commentary. The start was a fantastic spectacle. The noise of the cars' exhausts was deafening as they thundered away; their deep, straining growls reverberating off all the tall apartment blocks where spectators hung off every balcony and out of every window. The smell of the exhaust fumes lingered well after the cars had gone out of sight. It was a heady, exciting and glamorous atmosphere, and yet I sensed amongst us a ghoulish minority who were there solely in the hope of witnessing some awful crash or pile-up.

The upside of some unexpected time away from the trackside, prior to the race, was that it gave me a few hours to appreciate the astonishing beauty of a freshly-scrubbed, floral Monaco. Everything had a crisp contrast: the neat lines of white yachts which swayed gently on the blue water of the harbour; the tall terraces of hotels and apartments with their white walls and terracotta roofs rising up against the green of the mountain backdrop, interspersed with palm trees enlivened by shocking pink and purple bougainvillea. Only a month before, the eyes of the world had been focussed on this wealthy and immaculately buffed Principality when its Prince Rainier III married the beautiful American actress Grace Kelly. Those watching eyes had included most of my family's as we'd gathered round a neighbour's black and white television set.

My mother had turned to the lady of the house and asked casually, 'Vera, did I mention that our Tom will be in Monaco next month?' In Mum's eyes, there was nowhere more exotic in the world, and her son was actually going there!

It was probably the most glamorous wedding the world had ever seen. It was said that some thirty million people globally watched the ceremony live on television. It's possible that that number was exaggerated, for not many ordinary people could afford a television in 1956, but absolutely everyone I knew had watched it.

When we were there, Mike took me to a fancy restaurant and helped me decipher the menu. Amongst the starters was *escargots de bourgogne*. I vividly remember shuddering when Mike told me these were snails, 'Yes, Tom, snails like in your garden'. He ordered them for himself and declared them delicious. It took twenty years before I risked eating one myself.

The flight back to England was pretty tiring but much less eventful. We took off from Nice at eight in the morning and, after stopping for fuel at Lyon and Le Touquet, we finally touched down in Surrey at seven in the evening. Naturally, we avoided Paris like the plague. Mike was tired and subdued. Though he was clearly upset with BRM, he was equally upset that Stirling had beaten Fangio in the Grand Prix.

We were back down to Goodwood a week later for some sports car fun. Mike seemed to have forgotten all about his 'lucky escape' less than two months previously and was in ebullient mood. Here, at last, Mike enjoyed a rare taste of success, picking up a second place behind Colin 'Chunky' Chapman in the Whit Monday Trophy. Both men were driving Lotus Elevens. It had begun as a scintillating dice between the two, the lead swapping time and again, balletically, at Madgwick Corner on the thirteenth lap. They both rejoined the circuit but only Chapman was able to drive unimpeded to the finish. Mike had to limp round to the pits to pull some bodywork away from a tyre before charging on once more. He achieved a creditable second place although, to be truthful, none of the other top-flight British drivers of the day, such as Moss, Collins, Scott Brown, Brooks or Salvadori had entered. Still, the weekend as a whole turned into a jolly fine piss-up.

Mike's 'luck' was to stalk him all season. Next up was the 1,000km at Germany's Nurburgring, at which he again shared a D-Type with Des Titterington. Mike led the race initially but was quickly overtaken by Stirling in a Maserati. He was holding third place when he was twice black-flagged for overtaking on the right instead of the left.

During a pit stop, Mike was warned about this by Lofty, who told him the German officials were getting pretty agitated. Back out on the track, Mike came upon a slower car which cut straight across his line and caused him to ram it, albeit not very hard. The D was still driveable, and it was only later, when Mike brought the car in and the mechanics looked at the damage to the nose, that they realised that the auxiliary fuel tank, positioned where there would normally be a passenger seat, had started to leak. Mike had looked really groggy from the petrol fumes as he clambered out of the car. Fortunately for Des, the mechanics were able to patch up the fuel tank before he took over. Not that it really mattered as the car failed to finish.

Mike's problems didn't stop with their premature retirement. The German press, who were already anti-Mike for his pyrrhic victory at Le Mans in '55, accused him of overtaking misdemeanours. It didn't seem to matter that the then boss of the Porsche team, whose cars Mike had overtaken and rammed, pointed out that his drivers were all in the wrong, for they were slower cars and so should have pulled over to allow Mike to overtake on the correct side.

Despite having a busy if relatively fruitless season in '56, Mike was still finding time to pursue girls, and one girl in particular: Cherry. There'd been many other girls breeze in and out of Mike's life up until then but I can honestly say that he seemed more infatuated by Cherry than any previous girlfriend. And, let's face it, she was *gorgeous*. I didn't mind being sidelined for Cherry whereas I did resent Mike being monopolised by other guys. However, as much as I wanted it to, I didn't expect the relationship to last. They never did with Mike.

Chapter Eleven

Mini Mike

Notwithstanding the three-week interval between Monaco and the Belgian Grand Prix on 3 June, BRM were still unable to resolve their production difficulties. Consequently, Mike was again offered a Maserati for the Spa race. He was, however, still out of favour with the Germans, and they campaigned to bar him from the race because of his dangerous driving style.

I suspect that Enzo Ferrari was also no ally to Mike at this time, as the negotiations to secure his services had come to nothing. What transpired was that Mike was advised to honourably withdraw his entry and let the heat die down. In his absence, his compatriot, but not yet teammate, Pete Collins easily won the Grand Prix with a handsome margin of nearly two minutes.

In mid-June, Brit Pearce, Mike's chief mechanic, took the Lotus Eleven out to Italy in readiness for the Supercortemaggiore 1,000km race. Mike, who'd travelled down with 'Drunken' Duncan Hamilton, took it for a run along an autostrada. An oil pipe burst, and the car caught fire. Mike was unharmed, and Brit quickly effected repairs which enabled Mike to drive it on to Monza. Just as he arrived, the gearbox completely locked up. It's a shame back then we didn't know that Lotus would become an acronym for 'Loads Of Trouble, Usually Serious'. Mike would have thought that hilarious.

Without a working car, Duncan and Mike offered their services to the Ferrari team. Mike was teamed up with Pete Collins in a Ferrari 500 TR, in which they led the race from start to finish. However, towards the finish, Mike was called into the pits in order that Pete, the 'official' Ferrari driver, could take the chequered flag.

Tasting success again after a catalogue of disappointments, and finding a kindred spirit in Pete, Mike was as happy as a sand boy.

Although I was not there to witness the celebrations, I'm certain this occasion marked the beginning of the great friendship between Mike and Pete – the 'Mon Ami Mates'.

A few days later and the whole motor racing caravan had moved up to Reims for the annual French Grand Prix. Mike's employers, BRM, were having a torrid time and were so busy trying to resolve their engine problems they couldn't enter that race either. Again, this left Mike free to drive for a competitor. Tony Vandervell must have been unbelievably forgiving, or very ambitious, because he jumped at the chance to have Mike drive his Vanwall car once again. Mike, however, also agreed to drive a Jaguar D-Type in a twelve-hour sports car race which was programmed to end only four hours before the Grand Prix was due to start.

One unique feature of that French GP was the offer of 100 bottles of fine champagne for the first driver to lap at 200 kilometres per hour in practice. Needless to say, there was a big scramble amongst the quicker cars, and, typically, Mike was the first to achieve the goal, something which did his popularity no harm back in Farnham afterwards.

On the second practice day, Mike was just slowing down for a corner when another Vanwall ploughed into the back of him, driven by none other than Colin Chapman – the man who had played a large part in the car's design. Mike's Vanwall was shunted down an escape road. Colin maintained that his brakes had locked on. Initially, I was a bit sceptical at what I thought was a convenient excuse, but Mike concurred that the Vanwall's brakes did require a lot of pushing and were inclined to stick. Fortunately, Mike was unhurt, and Colin only slightly. Colin's car looked to be a write-off – it was badly crumpled and the chassis bent. Mike was reassured by the apparent strength of the car that had allowed Colin to escape without more serious injuries.

In order to extend the short rest period between the sports car event and the Grand Prix, Lofty suggested that Mike hand over the Jaguar to his teammate Paul Frère a couple of hours before the end.

Having established a decent lead, Mike handed over the car and set off into town, in the hope of getting some sleep. Despite this being in the early hours of a Sunday morning when there should be little traffic, road closures forced Mike to drive a long way round into Reims, about twenty-five miles, before reaching his hotel. Once there, he couldn't sleep and soon returned to the circuit, tired and in a foul mood – a mood that wasn't much improved when he found out that his old mucker, Duncan Hamilton, driving another Jaguar works' D-Type, had overtaken Frère – contrary to instructions from the pits – to claim victory, thereby downgrading Mike into second place.

A good pal told me that Mike looked 'shot to pieces' as he clambered into his Vanwall for the GP. On the grid, he was placed behind the Franco-American Harry Schell who was at the wheel of another Vanwall.

Mike made a reasonable start but he knew he was spent, and the pace was relentless. Uncharacteristically, he'd suggested to Vandervell before the race that, if anything was to go wrong with Schell's car, he would be happy for Harry to take over his car. By the grace of the gods, that's exactly what happened, and it was a mightily relieved Mike who relinquished his car after just five laps.

Harry went really well after that, mixing it with the formidable Ferrari-engined Lancias of Fangio, Castellotti and Pete Collins. His chances of a respectable podium finish were sadly dashed by fuel pump problems. He ended up a valiant tenth, with Pete Collins winning his second ever GP, straight after his victory in Belgium four weeks earlier. Admittedly, Fangio had had problems with a leaking fuel line, but Pete was clearly hitting his stride.

That brief excursion in the Vanwall marks Mike's last ever drive in a British racing car. Thereafter, he only ever drove Italian Grand Prix cars. He would, however, continue to race for Jaguar in sports car races for a little while longer.

From Mike's perspective, that French Grand Prix might have been rather forgettable had it not been for the drama which took place off the track.

Mike's plan was that Cherry, who had recently acquired her pilot's licence (it didn't take nearly as much time or money as it does today), would fly his Fairchild aeroplane to Reims, and they would fly back together. This turned out to be terrific news for me. A few days ahead of the race, Mike telephoned to ask a 'huge favour'. He asked if I would accompany Cherry on the flight, as she wasn't yet comfortable flying solo, escort her around the circuit, and drive his Jaguar back to England. I don't know about 'favour' – I'd have jumped at any one of those three offers. It was like a Christmas and birthday present rolled into one.

Cherry proved to be a charming companion and very competent pilot. She flew so much more 'by the book' than Mike. She may have been lacking experience, and therefore confidence, but I never felt unsafe at any time. She mostly wanted to chat about Mike. She wanted to know what he was like when he was young, about his previous girlfriends, about his father, and so forth. She was so bewitching, I could easily have said too much. Thankfully, I don't think I gave away any great secrets.

On entering the circuit, Cherry and I were approaching the grandstand before the race had started when we saw something which stopped us dead in our tracks. There was this little blond-haired boy – an infant wearing white trousers, a short bottle-green windcheater, a white shirt, and blue spotted bow tie. It was 'White Mike'...in miniature! Cherry walked a couple of steps towards him, and then her knees appeared to buckle so that her eyes were almost at the same level as the child's.

'Hello, little chap. What's your name?'

The child looked stunned.

'Eee iz Mikel,' said the young woman holding the boy's hand. The boy beamed at the mention of his name.

Cherry popped up like a champagne cork. I thought she'd been stung. She turned to me and whispered, 'Tom, he looks *exactly* like Mike. He's even got the same smile.'

'Bloody hell, you're not wrong!' I replied.

'Maybe you know eez father?' asked the woman, I assumed to be the boy's mother. Cherry shot me a glance. I couldn't interpret it. There was anxiety, some curiosity too.

Meanwhile, my mind had raced to the finish line. This *had* to be Jacqueline, with Mike's son – the son Mike had never seen, the son he'd never owned up to. Although the penny had well and truly dropped, I didn't know what on earth to say.

'Er, no. I don't think so, mademoiselle. Should we?' I blustered.

'You 'ave not 'eard of Mr Mike Hawthorn?' she demanded. 'Ee iz famous, *non*?'

I touched Cherry's elbow gently. 'Come on, Cherry. There's been a mistake. The race is about to start.' I began to walk on.

Fortunately, Cherry came too. We walked in silence until we took our seats in the grandstand. Then, she turned to me and fixed me with her huge brown eyes.

'Come on, Tom, for God's sake, spill the beans.' She didn't blink; her penetrating eyes daring me to lie.

'About what?' I didn't sound convincing.

'About back there.'

'Oh, the child?'

'Yes, Tom, the child.' And then, slowly, she added, 'Is he Mike's?'

'How would I know?'

'Tom, it's a bloody good job you don't play poker.' She was right, of course. I've always been a lousy liar.

'I've never seen either of them before – promise.' At least, that was true. Though I knew with every exchange I was fighting a losing battle.

'I saw your face when she mentioned Mike's name. You already knew—'

'I didn't know anything – well, not for certain. I mean, I still don't...'

With that, Cherry turned away, as if she was contemplating her next move.

Meanwhile, I was desperately trying to weigh up how little I could disclose. I was also thinking what I could possibly say to Mike if he thought I'd blabbed. This whole thing seemed like a car crash in slow motion.

Cherry recommenced her interrogation. 'How often does he see her?'

'Never. Well, hardly ever...I don't know.'

'Tell the truth.' Her eyes never left my face.

'Honestly, I don't think he's seen her for years.' I was starting to feel hot.

'It can't be that many years...the child's hardly a teenager,' Cherry said, with a hint of a smile.

'I'm not sure if Mike's ever seen him,' I offered lamely.

'Not seen his own child?' she demanded. This was getting more uncomfortable by the minute.

'He didn't believe it was his.'

106

'Not his?' Her voice rose an octave. 'Well, if it's not his, I'd like to see who the father is. Mike's double?'

I feigned a wave of acknowledgement to someone in the far distance, hoping to force a change of subject. We stood in silence for another minute or two. It occurred to me that, rather than allow this interrogation to run its course, I could appear to volunteer all I knew and then close the subject.

'Listen, all I know is this. Mike had a brief fling with a French girl, and it was all over by the time she found out she was pregnant. The silly girl decided to have the baby so she contacted Mike in the hope that he would return to look after them both. Mike thought it was a con. He'd heard of scams like that and didn't want to be played for a fool.'

'And that's it?'

'Yup.'

'So, how come I've never heard about this?'

'No one has.'

'Except you?'

'He wouldn't have wanted to upset you.'

'Upset me? Embarrass himself, you mean. How irresponsible can you get?' Cherry's expression, thinned lips and flashing eyes, hinted at the fire within.

I said nothing. There was nothing more to say. I just hoped that I could get to Mike first. After a few minutes of awkward silence, I offered to get us both an ice cream.

Due to Mike's unexpectedly early retirement from the race, we didn't have that long to wait. When we learnt of Mike's stoppage, we made our way down towards the pits to find a tired and grumpy Mike, which was lucky for him. If he'd have been elated in any way, he'd have been cannon fodder. When he had that deflated look, you could only feel sorry for him.

The three of us chatted about the race, the 'useless' car, and his disappointment of the day before. We also spoke of our flight over and where we would be staying. We spoke of many things, but not of seeing Jacqueline, or of 'Mini Mike'. I thought Cherry would bring up the subject at any moment, but she didn't. I soon began to feel like a gooseberry and, without a chance to tip him off, I made my excuses and wandered off.

Mike told me afterwards that, once they were alone, Cherry had 'given him hell' about the whole thing – being 'so bloody mean' and 'so bloody stupid'. In my naivety, I thought it would all work out for the best. She was bound to find out eventually and, well, at least they were still together.

Initially, Cherry appeared satisfied that the *affaire* was well and truly over. She even encouraged Mike to get to know his son. And although Mike seemed genuinely taken with the notion of having a son, he offered nothing more than to help out financially. The nature of that financial support was typical Mike. Rather than commit to a regular contribution, he would occasionally gift her sizeable sums. For example, at the Reims Grand Prix in '57, and again in '58, he asked Ferrari if he might receive all his starting money in France, in order that he could hand over much of it to Jacqueline. When Ferrari's newly appointed team manager, Romolo Tavoni, asked why he wanted all the money in Reims, Mike replied that it was 'for humanitarian reasons'.

The eventual outcomes were, on reflection, rather tragic. Jacqueline spectacularly failed in her mission to win back Mike as a partner and a father, even having played her trump card at the circuit. Mike had now to face the facts, and live with being an absent, disconnected father. And Cherry would never view, or trust, Mike in the same way again.

Amazingly, the story of Mike's paternity never reached his mother's ears, or at least I don't think it did. I bumped into Winifred shortly after Reims and was dreading what she might say. Her main preoccupation appeared to be marrying off her son to Cherry. Winifred was usually perceived as intimidating where Mike's girlfriends were concerned. However, she clearly doted on Cherry. It was a closeness that had doubtless intensified as they'd stood together watching Mike being thrown out of that tumbling BRM at Goodwood. Two women contemplating a shared loss – one of a son, the other a lover. And how much worse for Winifred, recently widowed, as the result of her husband having been thrown out of a car.

It was a shock to everyone when Cherry suddenly announced that she was going to live and work in New York. It was her parents' idea, apparently. She had been offered a job by Vogue magazine. She maintained that it was a career move and would only be temporary. She also said that it didn't matter quite so much as Mike was coming home less and less.

It was much later that I learnt that, as keen as Winifred was on their pairing, Lord John Huggins, Cherry's father, was dead against it, believing that Mike would make a wholly unsuitable husband for his middle daughter.

In the light of what was to transpire just a couple of years later, that was truly ironic. In the summer of 1958, I read a newspaper story about Lord John. He was then aged sixty-eight and had run off to Italy with a married lady who ran a women's dress shop in Farnham. The lady in question was reported to be in her forties whereas poor 'old' Lady Molly was exactly fifty and still a good-looking woman. Incredibly, he'd booked into the same hotel he'd taken his wife for their honeymoon twenty-nine years previously. There was a wonderful quote from Molly: 'He is being very silly. I don't think I shall follow him to Italy. I don't suppose he will be there long. He's a little old for that sort of thing.'

What Cherry's departure for America did do was give Mike a serious wake-up call. Mike maintained he really missed her, and I'm sure he did. But I can't help feeling it was the thought of 'his girl' – young, free, and incredibly attractive – alone in a city like New York which provided the catalyst for his next romantic move.

Chapter Twelve

Transatlantic Engagement

The racing season was in full swing. No sooner had Mike said a tearful goodbye to Cherry, as she boarded her New York flight, than he had to prepare for the British Grand Prix at Silverstone. The top four constructors of that time, Ferrari, Maserati, BRM and Vanwall, unsurprisingly attracted the top drivers. There was no doubting that the BRMs were the fastest – in a straight line. They were also easily the most unreliable.

I attended the race and was lucky enough to spectate from above the BRM pits with a mutual friend, Bill Cotton. We'd noticed that Mike was slowing down and were not surprised when he pulled into the pits beneath us. He jumped out of the car, tore off his crash hat and threw it across the pit, saying, 'If I want to commit suicide, I'll do it without your help, thank you very much!' He then marched out and straight into the beer tent in the paddock.

I turned to Bill. 'Do you think we should join him?'

'Well, we came to see him, didn't we?'

We caught up with him at the bar. He was fuming. 'That *fucking* car is an absolute time bomb!' He told us he was sure that the oil seal to the drive shaft had failed, and if he had carried on, he would have had a repeat of his recent Goodwood accident. He was later proved right, and BRM withdrew from racing for the rest of that season.

We were soon joined by Jabby Crombac, whom I suspect had been earwigging our conversation. Jabby was a French journalist who worked for Autosport, and with whom Mike had become quite pally. Although Mike could speak only a few words of French and Italian, he'd amassed any number of European friends – none German, of course. Jabby soon took Mike away, ostensibly in search of his photographer and arch-party thrower, Bernard Cahier. This was probably in the knowledge that, if he left it any later, Mike would not be capable of coherent dialogue.

I don't think it was an accident that, when Mike disappeared, Tony Rudd, BRM's development engineer, appeared. I'd got to know Tony a little and had time for him. However, I knew that he and Mike had had their differences so I found myself torn.

'Hello, chaps. Can I get you a beer?' Tony asked brightly.

'Well, well, fancy seeing you here,' I replied.

'Listen, Tom, I'll get straight to the point. Do you know what's eating Mike? He's as miserable as sin right now.' It was a fair question, only I couldn't tell him half the answer.

'And you're surprised?' I shot back. 'He thinks you're trying to kill him every fortnight.'

'He knows what the problem is, and he knows we're trying to fix it. Well, I am.'

'What's stopping you?'

'Peter, mainly. It's not helped that Mike won't try fitting in with the rest of the team. He's got no rapport with the guv'nors or the mechanics. He just about turns up in time for practice, says bugger all, and then pushes off. Can't you have a word?'

'It's a bit late for that. He's lost faith in the car.' I felt a bit sorry for Tony, partly because I knew he himself was at loggerheads with Peter Berthon, one of the owners of BRM, and partly because Mike had only ever been really happy driving for Jaguar or, to be more accurate, Lofty *and* Jaguar.

Driving for BRM was Russian roulette compared to the relatively reliable Ferrari-Lancias driven by Fangio, de Portago and Collins — all of whom mounted the podium that afternoon. Of Mike's two teammates, Ron Flockhart lasted only two laps, and Tony Brooks was going round Abbey Curve on lap 39 when his throttle jammed open. The car somersaulted, landed upside down, and caught alight. Luckily, Tony was thrown clear, sustaining breaks of his ankle and jaw.

It wasn't much better for the other principal British marque. None of the three Vanwalls made it to the chequered flag either: they all broke down before the finish.

*

During the week Mike was free between the British GP and his return to Le Mans, he suggested we meet up.

We met in Farnham town centre one evening, with a couple of other Members. Mike positively fizzed with boyish enthusiasm and bonhomie. It only encouraged him when the barmaid practically offered herself to him. It was like the good old times – way too much beer, much laughter, a bit of singing, and lots of tobacco smoke.

Two days later, and I was expecting more of the same. His car was already outside the Pond when I arrived. I walked in, braced for a greeting from Mike such as I usually received from our family's spaniel. He didn't even look up from his pint.

'What's up, bo?' I asked.

'It's all one bloody great mess…' His eyes looked moist.

'Why? What's happened?'

'Oh, it's everything. I should never have signed with BRM. I think their cars are dangerous, and they don't like me.'

'Is that all?' I said. 'I thought it was something serious. Look, I need a drink. Can I get you one?'

He shook his head. I wandered off to the bar, thinking about his predicament. When I sat down, it was clear he just wanted to unburden himself.

'And what about that French kid who could be mine?' he asked. 'I don't think Cherry's going to forget about that too quickly, do you?'

'Listen, Cherry's lovely, really she is, but there's loads more fish in the sea, especially for you bastard racing drivers.'

'I'm missing her, Tom. You probably don't believe me, but I am.' There was real conviction in his voice.

'She'll be back soon enough. Is that what's *really* eating you? Or is it that you're not feeling well?'

'I'm okay, I suppose. I'd rather not be going out to Le Mans tomorrow.'

I saw then that it was the prospect of returning to the scene of what was still referred to as the World's Deadliest Crash that was the final straw.

'Hey, chin up,' I said. 'You've been officially exonerated. You're in the clear.'

'Yeah, but you know what the Frogs think.'

112

He had a point, but I wasn't going to encourage his wallowing. 'Bollocks to them. If I was you, I'd speak to the press before the event and say lots of nice things about the French and the race. Get them on side early.'

Still resting his head heavily in one hand, elbow on the table, he managed, 'You could be right.'

'Okay, if you really can't face it, why don't you pretend to be ill?'

'I can't do that.'

'Why not?'

'Because I'd be letting down Lofty. Anyway, I've got to – it's in my contract.'

'Face facts, Mike. You're probably not well enough for long-distance stuff right now.'

'So what? So I black out...lose control and die. Does that matter?'

'It matters to me. And it'll matter a great deal more to Cherry.'

He had no answer and so promptly changed the subject. He didn't want to go and he couldn't not go. But go he did, this time with me in tow.

The Le Mans circuit which greeted us was transformed. The Automobile Club de l'Ouest had spent 340 million francs on the facility – equivalent to about £6 million today – much of it safety-related. In my view, that was a clear admission that a major contributor to the previous year's disaster had been the location of, and the approach to, the pits. The road there had been widened, the much improved pits moved back, and a service road inserted between the track and the public enclosure. Unsurprisingly, there was also more protection for the spectators.

The organisers had also changed the rules for the cars, in order that they were more akin to cars the public could purchase. This involved the requirement for a full-width windscreen, a passenger seat, and the introduction of a maximum fuel consumption figure (10.8 mpg) which obliged some manufacturers to weaken their mixtures. This last requirement was disastrous for Jaguar's legendary reliability.

On the day before practice, Mike had agreed to give a live

commentary about the improved Le Mans circuit whilst driving around it. This was cutting edge technology. A cine camera was mounted off the boot, to one side of Mike's head, and a large microphone was supported by a metal yoke around his neck. Tape recorders were stowed in the passenger footwell.

This five-minute footage (which can be viewed via the Internet today) is remarkable for two reasons. Firstly, Mike comes across as a man completely at ease with himself, with not a care in the world. His calm, articulate commentary is delivered in a faintly upper-class accent, and his evenly modulated tones give his words real authority, as if he'd done a hundred such broadcasts. The second is the blatant lack of consideration Mike gives to all other users of the roads, particularly cyclists, as he blasts past them in his Jaguar at speeds not too far short of those he'd be using in the race. At one point, he comments: '...somebody in the way!...Never mind... Cyclists everywhere!...Ha! Ha!...typical French!' This is said as he swoops past a car and cyclist coming in the opposite direction! And then immediately carries on with: 'We're on the Mulsanne Straight now...going down here...in the race, we get up to about 185 miles an hour...One advantage for us having a long straight like this is you can relax a little and get back some of your energy.'

It's that word 'relax' in the context of driving at that speed – in competition, and sometimes in the dark – which tells you succinctly why Mike was a racing driver and I never was.

On Mike's first practice run, the engine of his D-Type faltered and smoke billowed out. The mechanics took off the bonnet and got the engine going again. There was an almighty bang! Hot oil spewed all over the place. The weak mixture had burnt a hole in a piston and so, when the engine was restarted, the fuel exploded in the crankcase rather than the combustion chamber. The engine was a write-off. Later in practice, in a different car, Mike was again haring down the Mulsanne Straight, doing about 140mph, when he felt the car begin to shake. He correctly guessed that this was due to a tyre disintegrating and so quickly slowed the car down and got it safely off the track.

That night, it was a subdued Mike with whom I shared a few drinks and offered reassurances. He kept saying he had a bad feeling about the race.

The rain started about ten minutes before the drivers ran across the track to their cars. In these slippery conditions, it was obvious Mike was doing all he could to keep his car from going off whilst trying to fend off a persistent Aston Martin being driven hard by Stirling.

Mike came round Mulsanne Corner for only the third time to find his team's other two D-Types lying wrecked by the roadside. Only two laps gone of a twenty-four-hour race and Mike's was Jaguar's only remaining car. By the fourth lap, he began to experience various fuel and ignition problems. He was in and out of the pits like a yo-yo. The problem was eventually diagnosed as one of the injector pipes. It took seven hours to fix. By the time Mike and his co-driver Ivor Bueb were off again, they were in twentieth place and stood no chance of catching the leaders. But there *was* the prospect of a consolation prize.

Knowing that a D with a working engine was more than a match for any of the other cars, Mike went hell for leather to post the fastest lap. Once he received a signal from the pits that he'd succeeded in this endeavour, he brought the car in to swap with Ivor. In the handover, Mike said, 'Well, at least we've made a little money. We'll get 500 for the fastest lap.' And so they would have... the preceding year. However, in 1956, the organizers had withdrawn the prize for the fastest lap.

Mike's earnings for that race, for risking life and limb, were £15. Even to me, at the time, it seemed paltry. It was barely enough to pay for the celebrations that followed. Quite early on in that session, Mike disappeared for an hour or so. He returned to the bar a changed man. He was grinning from ear to ear. He was buying drinks as if he'd won the 24 Heures. My repeated enquiries were fruitless, at least until we were the last ones standing.

'Listen, Tom,' he slurred. 'Will you be my best man?' And then he winked.

'You know I will. Only one problem. You don't have a fiancée.'

'Ah, there you're wrong. Cherry's practically agreed to marry me!' His face lit up.

'Practically...?'

'She said it sounded like a nice idea.'

'That's not actually saying yes...'

'She said "probably". Said she'd like to see me.'

'When did you ask her?'

'About three hours ago.'

'How? When? On the blower?'

'No, stupid. I flew over to New York, bent down on one knee—'

'You asked her on the phone?' I was genuinely struggling with this.

'You're really quick tonight. She said lots of nice things, but she also said it wasn't right to say yes over the phone. So I have to go and visit her.'

'Blimey. Do her parents know?'

'Of course. I went round to see the old man before I left and asked him outright.'

'I thought he didn't approve.'

'Nonsense, that was ages ago. He said it was Cherry's decision, and if it would make her happy, then they'd both be happy.'

And he sounded so happy. I was truly delighted for him. It was the following day that I started asking myself questions. The first was whether he'd told Cherry about his life expectancy? And, if he hadn't, when would he? Is that why she wanted to see him? Also, did Cherry know about Moia? More importantly, had he properly finished with Moia? He must have done...surely? And if he had, could this possibly open a door for me? What if Moia had met someone else in the meantime?

To my lasting regret, I did nothing about contacting Moia immediately, stupidly believing it would be easier to say something if I happened upon her by chance. Of course, when I did bump into her, about two months later, she was with another feller.

That was so typical of me back then. I'd agonise for weeks over what to do, or what to buy – even what to say – and then end up missing the boat altogether. I remember trying to be philosophical about it, and telling myself that, if she'd have been at all interested in me, she could have phoned. Not, of course, that it worked like that in those days. A girl who did such a thing would be considered 'very forward'.

Mike did indeed hop on a plane to New York, especially to see Cherry and to ask her in person, and she did say 'yes' to him. He could only afford to be there for two nights as the next big event on the calendar, the German Grand Prix, was scheduled for the following week at the Nurburgring circuit.

It was no surprise, after Mike's outburst at the British Grand Prix, that BRM chose to release Mike from his contract. That was the second consecutive year that Mike had parted company with a British racing team mid-season. It did, however, leave him free to drive for a competitor, and Ferrari was quick to make him an offer.

In the days leading up to the Nurburgring race, the German authorities dropped a bombshell: Mike was not permitted to enter because the insurers refused to cover him, citing his 'lack of self-discipline' (referring to the allegations of overtaking on the wrong side) during the 1,000km race earlier in the season. This was seen as blatantly anti-British. Our press explained the ban thus: 'The Germans have no racing cars this season – and no drivers even if they had cars' and 'They're still trying to blame Hawthorn for last year's Le Mans tragedy when a *German* Mercedes, driven by a Frenchman, hurtled into the crowd'.

It turned out that Mike himself might have been guilty of sensationalising this story for he complained to the press even while negotiations were in progress. The RAC, who were trying to broker a resolution, asked Scuderia[2] Ferrari whether they could provide suitable insurance for Hawthorn. This they duly did, and it was accepted by the German authorities.

As far as Mike was concerned, the accusations of 'lacking self-discipline' merely deepened his hatred of Germans, and he would do everything in his power to discredit them. In the end, Mike chose to be a martyr about it and refused to drive.

If Mike was to miss any race this year, this wasn't a bad choice. Of the twenty-two cars that started, only six finished, one of which was disqualified. Fangio won, driving a Ferrari. Stirling, who took second place, and the other four finishers all drove Maserati 250Fs. Pete Collins's short spell of success ended abruptly when a fuel line on his Ferrari split. The high-octane petrol vapour within the cockpit made him so groggy he nearly lost consciousness.

---

2 *Scuderia literally meaning a stable reserved for racing horses, but became widely used for motor racing teams. The equine analogy in these early days of Formula One was carried through to the expression of racing 'on' rather than 'in' one's car.*

Chapter Thirteen

Over and Out – Again!

Rather than sit at home feeling sorry for himself about the German GP, Mike suggested we all go down to Brands Hatch where Ivor Bueb had generously offered him a drive of his little Lotus Eleven. Ivor intended to drive his other small car, a Cooper.

It wasn't a lot of fun for me, or most of the spectators, as it was raining all day. However, there were compensations. One was the hilarious sight of Mike in such a tiny car. He looked too big for most racing cars, but this image took me right back to when we both had pedal cars. I took a picture of him seated or, more accurately, squashed into the Lotus. I had it framed and placed it alongside the one my mother took of us in toy cars when we were kids. The other compensation was that, in all the frenetic cut and thrust of the racing, Mike, who admittedly had been shunted himself, shunted another driver clean off the track. Mike swore at the time he didn't realise it was Ivor. Fortunately, it was nothing that couldn't be patched up over a pint or two afterwards.

Brands Hatch proved to be good for Mike's mood. Although he only picked up a sixth place, this wasn't about winning. It was about having fun. And Mike was certainly in high spirits as he left to go to Sweden for the last of the World Sports Car Championship races.

Jaguar had chosen not to enter, so Mike was offered a drive by Ferrari. This was another occasion where one's chances of survival were helped by driving a Ferrari. All the Maseratis retired – Behra's after it had caught fire during refuelling. And all the non-works' Jaguar D-Types were eliminated through accidents. That said, Mike told me that the car he shared with Duncan Hamilton and Fon had feeble brakes initially and then no brakes at all. At one point, Mike didn't brake hard enough for a corner and ended up barrelling down a bank and into a cornfield. Apparently, the crop was so tall he had to drive half standing up in order to navigate his way out.

Stories of the utter mayhem and unruly behaviour which went on in the hotel after the race trickled out for weeks afterwards. It was alleged that, after staying up until the wee small hours drinking whisky, when Mike and Duncan Hamilton finally turned in for the night, Mike grabbed a fire bucket full of water and threw it over Duncan's head before running to the sanctuary of his bedroom.

Duncan promptly found a fire hose, unfurled it, connected it to a water supply and went in pursuit of Mike. He forced open the bedroom door and found Mike undressed, changing into his pyjamas. The force of the water knocked Mike clean off his feet and drenched most of the room. The retreating Duncan panicked when he found he couldn't turn off the water and thought he should find an open window. And so, now pursued by Mike, he opened the door of a neighbouring room. Unfortunately, that room was occupied by a lone woman who, on seeing two men approaching, one naked, the other carrying a gushing water hose, screamed for all she was worth. The boys fled and tried another room. This proved much more fun, for not only was it occupied by a colleague of theirs but he was not alone – and nor was he sleeping. Needless to say, Duncan and Mike had no qualms about dousing the couple's passion. The water damage to that floor of the hotel was extensive.

The following morning, Mike and Duncan were hugely relieved to see the secretary of the Swedish Automobile Club turn up at the hotel (having been summoned by the very grumpy hotel management) to negotiate a settlement. Neither Mike nor Duncan would let on how much it cost them. Mike simply said it was 'oodles of kroner'. I told him he was lucky the police weren't called. My guess is that they only got away with it because the hotel management might have been in trouble themselves as the boys had clearly breached Sweden's tough anti-drinking laws.

It's funny that hotel trashing stories became the preserve of flamboyant rock and pop stars – characters like Keith Moon, John Bonham and Keith Richards – when, nearly a generation earlier, some racing drivers were behaving just as badly. The difference, not only in this particular but in so many other aspects of their private lives, was simply these events were seldom reported.

Mike found himself drenched again the following week. This time, it was back in England for the Daily Herald International Trophy at Oulton Park where it poured with rain all day long. I'd been looking forward to this race, despite it not counting towards championship points and despite the weather forecast. It was a chance to see how Mike would fare in the little Lotus against Stirling and Roy Salvadori in their rear-engined Coopers competing for the Sporting Life Trophy.

Oulton Park, although one of the few purpose-built motor racing circuits, had similar characteristics to the former wartime airfields such as Goodwood. Two drawbacks of flat circuits are that excessive surface water is slow to drain away, and they don't make especially good spectator circuits – unlike, say, Brands Hatch which is largely within a natural bowl. If you're spectating from the wrong place, you can easily miss the action.

The conditions that day were truly appalling. Fire pumps and men with brooms were trying in vain to clear the track. Unfortunately, the heavily laden black clouds overhead were easily equal to the men's labours. The racing was always going to be dicey.

I saw Mike initially vying for the lead with Stirling and Roy. Stirling was just ahead of the other two drivers. The next time they came past, Stirling was alone. It was far too early for a pit stop. These mouth-drying moments are vivid even as I write now. What's happened? How bad is it? Nothing on the tannoy.

And yet, because innocuous stoppages were so commonplace for all manner of mechanical breakdown, lack of fuel, or even spinning off, the chances were that it wouldn't be serious. This time, for some reason, I felt differently: genuinely alarmed. It was probably the weather. Plus I sensed Mike was really going for it.

I waited for what seemed like an eternity before the commentator dryly announced, 'I'm told Hawthorn and Salvadori have both gone off at Knicker Brook.' Silence for a few seconds, and then, 'Ah, it looks as if Salvadori is okay and is making his way back onto the track...'

I ran towards that part of the circuit. The first thing I noticed was Mike's Lotus lying upside down, one of its wheels still spinning. As I got closer, I could see a small huddle of spectators were crowded around a motionless prone figure some distance from the overturned car. It had to be Mike.

I asked the first chap I saw what had happened.

'He fell out the car, just as it was going over...'e fell right out, he did...didn't half hit the ground.'

For a second, I was frozen. Was that it? The end? No, it couldn't be. Although, of course, I knew that Mike himself would have preferred this ending to the one he feared. Also, for the first time, I realised I was concerned for someone else: his brand new fiancée, Cherry. Until now, my anxieties for him barely went beyond me and his mum, and maybe his grandmother. Now, there was someone else who could be bereaved in a moment. I forced myself to continue walking forwards towards the huddle.

I edged closer still and thought I could hear someone talking to Mike, 'It's all right, Mike, you're all right'. I eased through the bodies until I could see Mike lying on his back. He was alive – very still, but obviously alive.

I was about to say something when a man roughly pushed past me and another chap. His action irked me and I felt my hackles go up.

'Oi, watch it!' I said sharply.

'I'm a doctor,' came his equally brusque response.

Damn – I should have guessed. The doctor immediately took control of the situation by ordering people to stand back and give him some space. He then started firing questions at Mike, looking into his eyes, listening to his breathing and so forth. I withdrew slightly, transfixed, and watched as the doctor instructed a couple of marshals to carry Mike gently to a safer position. Here, the doctor began a more thorough examination, seemingly oblivious to the rain which continued to pour down upon us all.

Mike was duly shipped off to a local hospital for further tests, and although he was not kept in, it was nearly a week before I caught up with him again. He was staying with his mother who was trying her best to manage his convalescence. He was clearly feeling better, for they were bickering well. Mike was wearing bandages on a wrist and an ankle and was hobbling about a bit. He told me I mustn't make him laugh; it hurt too much.

All he'd been trying to do, he said, was wrest second place back from Roy by taking him on the outside of Knicker Brook. The Lotus had appeared to hold the line beautifully and then, in an instant, the tyres gave up their adhesion and the car slewed violently sideways. 'The car bounced off the bank and flipped over in mid-air. I was heading straight for a tree. I realised I had to get out and so I struggled for all I was worth. I can't honestly remember anything after that.'

'Did you pass out?' I asked.

'Don't think so. I think I was knocked out. What I do remember was someone moaning and groaning and wondering who on earth it was making all the fuss. It was me! There was this bloke standing over me, telling me that I was quite all right, and I was thinking how the devil does he know?'

'What have you done to yourself?'

'Apart from spraining my wrist and my ankle and bruising my hip, my ribs and my back…very little, as it happens.' He smiled.

'And the car?'

'You heard about Roy, I take it? After I fell out, my Lotus somersaulted straight over his Cooper, smacking him on the helmet as he passed underneath it. Talk about a lucky escape…a few inches lower and it would have taken his head off…' Mike's amused expression suddenly collapsed.

Why did this image keep recurring? Would it haunt him forever?

'Was he hurt?' I asked. We both liked Roy Salvadori. He was a popular, talented and self-financed British driver, albeit the son of immigrant Italian parents.

'Thankfully, not badly. He also went off the road, but somehow managed to get back on and made it back to the pits. He was all over the shop, by all accounts.'

'Did he continue?'

'No, he was too groggy for that. Apparently, Lofty rushed up to him and asked what had happened to me. He told Lofty I was dead.'

'Dead! Oh, that's dreadful. Poor old Lofty.'

'Poor old me. This has put paid to my season. The quacks don't reckon I'll be fit to race for a couple of months yet. I am jolly sore round here,' he said, waving his good hand all over his torso, 'so they're probably right.'

And right they were. Mike was forced to sit out the rest of the season. Mind you, it hadn't exactly been his best – only three Grands Prix entered, four measly championship points, nothing won for Jaguar, and he'd had two serious crashes, either of which could easily have been fatal. Lucky old Mike.

Chapter Fourteen

Ferrari to the Rescue

I got to spend more time with Mike that autumn than I had for a while. His injuries were healing quickly, and he was soon out and about but seemingly listless. Although we'd socialise at weekends, work was keeping me fully occupied during the week, whereas Mike seemed to be drifting. He was often hanging around at the garage, when he wasn't in the Duke of Cambridge. He became quite demoralised during this period, telling his friends that he'd had enough of racing and he'd return to the life of a garage proprietor.

Of course, his timing for that move wasn't exactly ideal, courtesy of the Suez Crisis. Following the Egyptian seizure of the Suez Canal some four months earlier, supplies of petrol had been running low. By the end of November, the Government released details of petrol rationing which was to come into force on 17 December 1956. Private car owners had an allowance of just 200 miles per month. Needless to say, prior to the introduction of the scheme, there was panic buying, and prices soared to six shillings a gallon. Within weeks, garages were closing and traffic levels plummeted. Many of us had resorted to using bicycles we hadn't used in years.

To those who were close, Mike's life seemed to be unravelling at a pace. If the catalogue of woes I've recounted wasn't bad enough, it was about to get a whole lot worse.

My mother called me saying Mike was on the phone.

'I need to see you, Tom. Are you free now?' was his opening gambit.

Oh Christ, what now? I thought. 'Yeah, I guess I could meet you in The Bush in about an hour's time.'

'Make it The Ball and Socket – one hour latest. See you there,' he said.

I thought that The Ball and Wicket (its real name) on Upper Hale Road was a telling choice, for it was unlikely we'd know many people in there, if any, on a mid-week evening.

By the time I arrived, Mike was well in his cups. I guess he'd started drinking even before he phoned me. He had a couple of empties in front of him. He must have driven straight there after he hung up. There were no preliminaries.

'It's over, Tom. She doesn't want to marry me.' His eyes were wet. He looked like he'd already had a good cry. The pub was quiet, as I expected.

'Hold on a sec,' I said. 'What makes you think that?'

'She rang – this afternoon – from New York. She said she doesn't think she's the right girl for me.' He was slumped forward, seemingly utterly defeated.

'Had she been drinking?' I didn't think for a second Cherry would be; I was buying thinking time.

'No, it was in the middle of the morning, her time.'

'Oh.'

'But *why*, Tom? What the hell does she mean – not the right girl?' There was anger in his tone.

'I've no idea,' I replied. Which, of course, was a lie.

'Do you think she's met someone else? Is that it? Or is it her old man? All I want to know is *why*, damn it.'

It was undeniable that Lord Huggins wasn't Mike's biggest fan, but I didn't think that was the most likely explanation. At least three other plausible explanations occurred to me, none of which would make comfortable conversation. One was Cherry's recent discovery of Arnaud, Mike's bastard son. It would have been completely under-standable if Cherry had begun to envisage starting a family together and how that special, novel moment had been sullied by Mike's history – and which might continue to haunt them. Then there was simply the mortal danger of his occupation – she was well aware of the statistics. It also occurred to me that tales of Mike's recent dalliance with other girls may have made their way across the pond. After all, Mike's photograph had appeared in the press in July standing next to Renny Lister, a pretty actress eight years his junior. All things considered, it was a miracle Cherry had ever considered marrying him.

'Well, say something,' he demanded.

'Erm, d'you think hearing about the wee French laddie might have—'

'Of course not! That was all over, three years ago.'

'Yeah, but it's not like Arnaud doesn't exist.'

'No, it can't be that,' he said huffily. 'She must have some new feller.'

The rest of the evening carried on in a similar vein: Mike repeatedly asking why, and me either being evasive or trying to change the subject. How would I know whether she'd found someone else? It wasn't exactly unlikely, given her looks and her nature. I also thought it was a bit rich, Mike castigating her for possibly looking elsewhere when he was at it all the time. Even if I had pointed out his own infidelities, I know he'd have thought they were perfectly acceptable, whereas the very thought of Cherry seeing other men would have been unacceptable.

As it transpired, I don't believe she had found someone else in New York – or at least if she had, they may have only been casual dates – for she married a British pilot, Peter Twiss, a short time later.

I can't ever remember Mike being openly jealous of others' successes – he desperately wanted to be a champion and yet was modest enough to accept that he might never be as good as 'the true greats' – Fangio and Ascari, and maybe Farina and Nuvolari before them. Those were his heroes. But he wasn't so keen on adulation being heaped on his peers when he wasn't receiving attention. And not only was Stirling still making front- *and* back-page news but Peter Collins, two years younger than Mike, was coming up fast on the rails, courtesy of his recent Grand Prix victories.

Coinciding with one of the lowest points of Mike's career, Peter was elected 'Driver of the Year' by the Guild of Motoring Writers. I was with Mike when he read the eulogy, '…like Moss, the real measure of his skill has been brought to light in the hard school of World Championship events, under the guidance of a man whose name will probably live longer than any other in the memory of motor racing enthusiasts – Juan Fangio. In his first season with a foreign team, Collins has won two Championship events, shared second place three times, and set an example of sportsmanship throughout the season…one can understand why Collins is considered by many as the best all-rounder in the game.'

'Huh!' was Mike's response, when he finished reading. 'You know that could have been me, had I chosen to drive for Ferrari instead of trying to kill myself in a fucking BRM.'

I was a pal – a good pal – so I wasn't about to point out that Mike hadn't had much success driving for Jaguar, either. Nor was I about to point out that Pete had been widely lauded for relinquishing a potentially winning drive, thereby allowing Fangio to win his fourth Championship title. I'm not sure Mike would have done that.

Privately, I thought that if Mike's career was going downhill fast, it was due to his own dwindling performances. His chances of joining a properly competitive team in Formula One racing for 1957 looked remote. There were seemingly enough decent drivers for the top two or three constructors without them risking someone now considered erratic. And, if that wasn't bad enough, in October, Jaguar announced they would be quitting sports car racing altogether. Mike's luck, his bad luck, seemed limitless.

He'd burnt his bridges with BRM in some style, and any thoughts he may have had about rejoining Vanwall were dashed when, also in October, it was announced that Stirling was to be Vandervell's lead driver with young Tony Brooks as his number two.

Although Stirling and one or two of the other top drivers had a manager, it was not unusual then for drivers to manage their own affairs. Apart from Les, Mike's father, in the early days, Mike never did have a manager. It felt, from the sidelines, as if he was being squeezed out of the top tier.

He wouldn't speak about his plans or aspirations. He was either playing his cards close to his chest or not playing them at all, which was much more likely considering how low he was.

One of the few things that did seem to interest Mike during this 'downtime' was the opportunity to do a little test driving with Norman Dewis for Jaguar, which was ironic, considering the scene he made at Silverstone a couple of years before. This time, it was for a new sports road car, designed for the public, with many elements carried over from the D-Type. It would be known as the E-type – an iconic car which has subsequently been described as the most beautiful car of all time.

That autumn, Mike didn't mention whether he'd held discussions with Enzo Ferrari. All I do know is that, in mid-November,

Ferrari named his five drivers for the forthcoming season as Fangio, Castellotti, de Portago, Musso and Collins. If Mike was to remain a proper Grand Prix contender, this left him with Hobson's choice: Maserati. Not that that would have been such a bad thing. Stirling had campaigned well throughout 1956 in a Maserati and had finished second in the Championship, narrowly behind Fangio. Some, myself included, thought Moss was daft to leave Maserati when they had a car as good as their 250F. Maybe the unpatriotic thing was getting to him?

However, the merry-go-round hadn't quite stopped. Within a couple of weeks, it was announced that Fangio, the Ferrari-driving reigning champion, had decided to quit Ferrari and would return to Maserati for the coming season. I reckon there were two principal reasons behind this abrupt change of allegiance: personalities and remuneration.

Firstly, he was Argentinian, not Italian, and, despite being Ferrari's best driver, he never felt especially valued by Enzo. Plus, he had got on well with, and respected, Ferrari's former manager Nello Ugolini, who had defected to Maserati the year before, after enjoying great success with Ferrari between 1952 and 1955.

The second reason may have been money. Fangio was one of the few drivers who did employ an agent. Maybe it had been especially important in his negotiations with Enzo Ferrari, as there was little warmth between the men. To cut what were doubtless lengthy negotiations short, Maserati offered twice the remuneration offered by Ferrari. It was a foolhardy move. Maserati couldn't actually afford Fangio's wages, let alone compete in Formula One, for it was on the edge of bankruptcy.

Enzo Ferrari, having previously maintained his stance of refusing to nominate a number one driver, now surprised everyone by bestowing this honour on Pete, something he could and should have done for Fangio. It was a blatant case of favouritism.

Mike was painfully aware that Fangio's dramatic exit left a single vacancy within Scuderia Ferrari, but Enzo didn't contact him, and initially he didn't contact Enzo – until prompted by a true friend.

By a stroke of good fortune, both Pete and Mike attended the premiere of the film *Checkpoint* at Leicester Square Theatre, in London's West End. It was shot in 'Glorious Technicolor' – quite a rarity at the time. As the film featured Aston Martins, loaned by the marque's racing team, speeding through Europe, Pete's presence as one of their professional drivers was expected.

Mike, like every other top racing driver in the country, had been invited to the screening to maximise publicity for the film. I remember Mike telling me that he heard rumours about it being a lame plot. He gave me the impression he wouldn't bother to attend – despite my dropping repeated hints that he might like to take me. I only learnt afterwards that he decided to go because he wanted to take a new girlfriend – whose name I probably knew, but have since forgotten (there were so many) – somewhere which was free to enter.

Pete was already in the foyer chatting to David Brown, the boss of Aston Martin, when Mike strolled in. Pete rushed up to Mike and said, 'Mike, you need to go to Modena right now. The Old Man's looking for another driver, and you could be the captain of the team.'

This was beyond considerate, as Pete had had this very status conferred upon himself only a fortnight earlier. It could be that Pete genuinely thought Mike was the better driver, which wasn't rational, or he was feeling uncomfortable being the lone favoured Englishman in a nearly all Italian team – or he didn't relish the responsibility.

If driving that rocket-powered Cooper-Bristol at Goodwood back in '52 had been the launch pad of Mike's career then this amazing lifeline, at a time when Mike was firmly in the doldrums, was to make the difference between fading notoriety and enduring fame.

Thankfully, Mike took Pete's advice and acted upon it. The next day, Mike sent a typically Yorkshire telegram to Enzo Ferrari. It read: 'I am interested, if you are.' Ferrari replied that he was interested, and so on Monday 17 December, Mike boarded a flight to Milan to 'talk turkey' with Enzo Ferrari.

'Do you know how long that bastard kept me waiting?' asked Mike that Christmas Eve when he was back in Farnham. 'I was pacing about outside his office for nearly an hour.'

'I suppose he knew you were there?' I asked.

'Oh, he knew all right. He does it to everyone. His secretary, Romolo, had told him I was waiting.'

'So, did you chat her up while you were waiting?'

Mike laughed. 'Ah, the dark, mysterious Romolo Tavoni...so

tall...and so thin...' Mike drawled, in an exaggerated Italian accent, '...and who wears such thick glasses. In fact, I'd have to say *he* looks half scarecrow and half schoolmaster!'

I felt such a charlie, I quickly pressed on. 'Well...how did it go?' I was confident I knew the answer: his body language said it all. Mike was looking and sounding brighter than he had for months.

'The offer he made was terrific – way better than '54. The only sticky point was Sebring.' Mike had been asked by Briggs Cunningham's company to drive a D-Type at Sebring in March, and Mike passionately wanted to represent the team. It would mean linking up with Lofty and Ivor Bueb once more as Jaguar Cars would be supporting the entry.

'Did he refuse?'

'Naturally. But I told him it was only one race in the whole year, and anyway Jaguar had played fair with him, releasing me when I was needed by Ferrari.'

'And...?'

'He didn't really have a leg to stand on. And he's always allowed Pete to drive for Aston. Plus I got the impression he really wanted me on board.'

The comparison with Mike driving for Jaguar and the Pete Collins/Aston Martin tie-up wasn't as simple as Mike liked to postulate, so I suspect Ferrari's capitulation was more down to the second reason: they needed each other.

'And is Pete still going to be number one?' I asked with some trepidation.

'No. Ferrari's gone back to his usual nonsense – each man for himself for the first three races; then it's whoever's leading gets the nod.'

On the face of it, such an arrangement might seem equitable. It was, in fact, unnecessarily dangerous. The reality is that, when one team has all the fastest cars in any race and its fastest drivers are all vying for the top slot, it's a recipe for, at best, pushing the cars to breaking point and, at worst, encouraging accidents between team members. But, this was the Enzo way – and he'd been running his Scuderia for more than twenty-five years.

That Christmas was a generally happy time for Mike. He gave the impression of having mostly got over Cherry, if his increasing dalliances with other girls was any yardstick, and was buoyed by the prospect of returning to Ferrari – specifically, to more reliable and, in his mind, safer cars.

I look back on that Christmas fondly. It was probably the last time Mike and I spent a lot of time together, driving around from pub to pub, laughing a lot and generally having a rare old time.

Chapter Fifteen

New Best Friend – 'Mon Ami Mate'

Mike and I met less frequently the following year. It wasn't that our friendship had diminished. It was, I guess, that our careers were keeping us apart. I'd moved up to London and had got a reasonable position as a junior accountant with British Petroleum, and Mike was spending more time abroad in the company of his new friend, Pete Collins.

Although Mike had known Peter Collins for some time, it was only when Mike rejoined Ferrari for 1957 and became Pete's teammate for the first time that the two men really bonded. It's not difficult to see why. Pete had been the lone Englishman in Ferrari's Scuderia throughout the preceding season, and then along comes not only another native English speaker but another completely irresponsible, fun-loving one. Their mutual predilection for women and alcohol, the latter often resulting in outrageous behaviour, meant they became bosom buddies overnight.

Initially, this was a difficult time for me for as Pete's star waxed so I felt mine wane. Sometimes, months would go by without me hearing from Mike. Increasingly, I was having to learn about his racing from the newspapers and word of mouth. Mike was never anything less than very friendly towards me – it was simply that he had a new soulmate, one to whom he would become practically joined at the hip.

It's worth a brief detour at this point to look at Pete Collins's career to this point, which was remarkably similar to Mike's. Pete had started racing competitively a couple of years before Mike, despite being marginally the younger man.

When Mike was experiencing his first proper race in his Riley, at Gamston near Nottingham on Easter Monday 1951, Pete was doing battle with Stirling Moss in little Cooper 500s down at Goodwood. Mike and Pete were both sons of garage owners and had, at different times, driven for Ferrari and Vanwall, yet had never been teammates until 1957. That's not to say their friendship hadn't begun. It had, and they'd got up to mischief from the off.

After the Swedish GP, the scene of the dramatic fire hose fight, Mike and Duncan hitched a lift to Copenhagen Airport in Pete's distinctly unracy Ford Zephyr. While on board the ferry, the lads came across a Swedish chap who was bragging about the performance of his new Cadillac 'automobile'. During the crossing, Pete surreptitiously found a heavy rope and tied one end to a railway goods wagon and the other end to the Caddy's rear 'fender'.

On their arrival at Copenhagen, as the Swede was preparing to drive off, Pete made some quip about British cars being quicker than any 'Yank Tank' and revved his engine. It had the desired effect. The Cadillac shot forward leaving its rear bumper on the deck of the ferry. Exactly who was the architect of this jape, I wouldn't like to say. It could have been any one of them.

If, by the end of '56, Stirling and Mike still occupied the front two places on the grid of British public profile, fuelled by their overhyped rivalry, then Pete had quietly drawn up alongside them, having been voted Driver of the Year and nearly winning the Drivers' Championship. That he actually finished third overall is a little story in itself.

The final Grand Prix of the season was the Italian, held at Monza in September. This fast, purpose-built circuit comprised substandard roads with steeply banked corners, and had a frightening reputation for eating up tyres and destroying suspensions. Going into the race, three drivers each had a theoretical chance of winning the Championship: Fangio and Collins driving for Ferrari, and the Frenchman Jean Behra for Maserati – although Fangio had a substantial eight-point lead over the other two.

Fangio, as Ferrari's most successful driver, could expect to take over another teammate's car if his was in any way failing. Except, in the middle of the season, Enzo had given Pete an assurance *he* would not be obliged to give up his car in favour of Fangio. This was clearly special treatment.

Before long, and not unexpectedly on this circuit, Fangio's car did break down, terminally – a steering arm had broken. Some laps later, his teammates Musso and Castellotti were brought in on the same lap for a tyre inspection. While a front wheel was being changed on Luigi Musso's car, Fangio stepped forward to take over. Musso sat resolutely looking the other way, deliberately making out he hadn't seen Fangio. Then, when the wheel was secure, he roared off. Luigi wasn't giving up his car to an Argentinian in an Italian Grand Prix!

Pete, who was then lying in third place, with sixteen laps still to go, was also brought in for a tyre check. Seeing Fangio hanging around without a drive, Pete immediately vacated his cockpit. Fangio slapped his teammate on the back, climbed in and rejoined the race, still in third place. The leading car, Stirling's Maserati, then ran out of fuel, which allowed Musso to take the lead. With only three laps to go before a certain victory in front of his home crowd, Musso's front wheels parted company on the banking. It was the fourth Ferrari retirement due to broken steering arms. Meanwhile, Stirling had managed to get round to the pits, had some more fuel sloshed in, and went on to take the chequered flag. Fangio, closing fast, finished less than six seconds behind him and was duly awarded half of the six points for second place. The other three went to Pete.

Had Pete carried on, without either accident or incident, *and* had managed to beat Stirling to the flag, he would have earned the maximum eight points, bringing him level with Fangio. And, because he would have had three outright victories to Fangio's two, he would have been awarded the Championship. All of which can be picked over with the benefit of hindsight. At the time, Pete thought he had no chance of catching Stirling and therefore little to race for, whereas Fangio – his teammate – needed only one more point to secure the Championship. He felt it really wasn't such a big deal.

And hence Fangio won the Championship for the third year in succession. Almost more galling was that because Stirling garnered nine points – eight points for the win and one for the fastest lap – he finished the season two points ahead of Pete.

When asked about why he'd thrown away the chance of winning the title, Pete was reported to have said, 'It's too early for me to become World Champion – I'm too young. I want to go on enjoying life and racing, but if I become World Champion now, I would have all the obligations that come with it. And Fangio deserves it anyway.' This race alone did a huge amount for Pete's reputation as a 'gentleman driver'.

In between Christmas and New Year, I'd had to go back to proper work, whereas Mike affected the role of part-time garage proprietor, something which must have mightily upset Bill Morgan, the then general manager, not to mention Mike's mother Winifred who had single-handedly administered the business since the death of her husband.

Chapter Sixteen

South America and Louise

The motor racing calendar started very early in '57. This was probably just as well for Mike, and everyone around him. He was getting bored and had been upping his drinking.

The first Grand Prix, the Argentine, was scheduled for Sunday 13 January. Mike was required first to go to Italy to meet up with the rest of the Ferrari team, before flying out to South America to acclimatise and practise a full week before the race. He was pleased to get racing again. He was not so pleased to leave behind a brand new dark green Jaguar 3.4-litre saloon, registration VDU 881 – a car provided for him by Jaguar.

I remember Mike telling me about the long flight out to South America, from Milan to Buenos Aires via Lisbon. On board were most of the Ferrari team and the Maserati team. This was a lot of competitive young men to have holed up in a smallish space. Someone suggested playing poker. Naturally, Mike was in like a shot, although it wasn't long before he was fifty pounds the poorer. To the lads he was playing with, 'Fon', Musso and Perdisa, fifty quid was an insignificant sum, but it was too much for Mike, so he gave up his place to Jo Bonnier, a tall, goateed Swede who drove for Maserati.

Although these peer racing drivers were all well remunerated, there was a tremendous discrepancy in their wealth. The likes of Joakim Bonnier, Luigi Musso, Alfonso de Portago, Eugenio Castellotti, and Castellotti's great friend Cesare Perdisa were all born into very wealthy families. Whereas others, including most of the Britons, could at best be described as having come from families who were comfortable rather than wealthy.

Mike watched in fascination as the stakes, like the aeroplane, climbed ever higher. Cesare Perdisa was on a roll, largely at the expense of Bonnier and Luigi Musso. Despite Musso being Mike and Pete's Ferrari teammate, neither Briton particularly liked the Italian. Mike once described him as 'precious and religious'. By the time Musso bowed out, he owed Perdisa 8 million lire – around £4,500. Mike thought this was hysterical.

Luigi Musso and Eugenio Castellotti were, I surmise, regarded in Italy approximately as Stirling and Mike were in Britain. At that time, they were the top two Italian drivers, and there was always rivalry between them, something which Enzo Ferrari positively encouraged.

Pete had not been on the flight as he had elected to travel across the Atlantic from Genoa with the cars. This had entailed setting off in mid-December on a mid-sized passenger steamer with his new German teammate 'Taffy' aka Wolfgang von Trips. It was on this voyage that Taffy would get a taste of what life with Pete (and Mike) was going to be like.

The two men immediately got on well, sitting on deck for hours recounting their individual adventures. Bound eventually for Buenos Aires, after two weeks at sea, the boat docked at Montevideo for two days. No sooner had it moored than Pete vanished into the city with a young Brazilian girl he'd met on board and then failed to show up when the ship was leaving. Taffy was beside himself worrying about what Pete was going to do without luggage, clothes or money.

In vain, he begged the captain to delay departure. And then, as the steamer slipped its moorings and edged away, Pete came running into view, weaving between the piles of quayside freight, dragging the poor girl behind him. After only a minute's hesitation, Pete jumped into an old skiff moored against the quay and, with a combination of smiles and some cash from his pockets, successfully persuaded its startled crew to 'follow that boat'. The deckhands of the bigger vessel threw down a rope ladder in anticipation but the smaller boat couldn't keep up. Taffy again implored the captain to stop. He wouldn't stop, but fortunately gave the order for 'Slow Speed Ahead'. It proved just enough for the skiff to catch up and come alongside. Pete and his recently acquired crumpet only just managed to catch hold of the ladder and clamber aboard.

*

Out in South America, it was ferociously hot. Mike described that first GP of the year, the Argentine, as being as 'hot as Hades'. The temperatures soared to over 100 degrees Fahrenheit in the shade.

Meanwhile, I was worrying over whether Mike would hear about the death of Ken Wharton, yet another motor racing friend of his, before he competed in the Grand Prix. Ken, four times British Hill Climb Champion, had been racing a Ferrari in Auckland, New Zealand when he had his fatal accident. He was some thirteen years older than us, and Mike talked about him being 'good ol' boy'. They were to have been teammates at Vanwall but for Ken's car bursting into flames, and they'd both driven D-Types for Jaguar.

I calculated that it was probable that news of that magnitude, happening on 12 January, would have been picked up the next day in South America, especially with Auckland being some sixteen hours ahead. However, if the results are anything to go by, it didn't seem to faze him.

One amusing story of the South American series which travelled back was about the starting flag. It had been entrusted to a politically prominent dignitary ('an effing idiot' according to Mike), who was first required to drop a yellow flag and then raise the Argentinian national flag. Apparently, he wouldn't stand still while the cars were on the grid, engines revving, and when eventually he did lower the yellow flag, he was unable to raise the national flag because he was standing on it. By the time Mike relayed the story to me even he thought it was farcical, but at the time the drivers were furious because it was disastrous for their engine temperatures and clutches. Three of the four Ferraris were forced to retire during the race with clutch failure. The fourth Ferrari, Castellotti's, lost a wheel at speed. Fortunately, it shot over the heads of the crowd without causing injury to driver or spectators.

Mike was pleased that, although he didn't finish the race, he still felt he had been competitive with Fangio who, for Mike's whole career, was his standard bearer.

One poignant thing I remember hearing, prior to the 1,000km race due to take place the following week, was that all the English drivers, including Stirling, Pete and Mike, received threatening notes, anonymously, about Britain's 'illegal occupation' of the Falkland Islands.

Mike handed his over to me in a pub back in Farnham. It read: '*You are robbers, robbers, robbers! By the Grace of God, may your cars blow up and crash.*'

When I expressed shock and disbelief, Mike simply laughed it off and said, 'So what, our cars are always blowing up and crashing anyway.' Thankfully, nothing ever came of those threats, but I remember thinking racing was dangerous enough without being caught up in political strife, too.

I was reminded of that apparently innocuous incident some twenty-five years later when Argentina invaded the Falklands, and wondered whether Mike and the others would have taken the threats any more seriously if they'd appreciated just how widespread and passionate the anti-British feelings were amongst the host nation. It's strange to think how, even now, this dispute over those faraway little islands grumbles on, another thirty years later.

The weather for the 1,000km race was, if anything, even hotter. Mike said that when he stepped out of his air-conditioned hotel the heat practically knocked him over. It was 100 degrees in the city, and 131 at the track. The heat haze shimmering off the tarmac actually clouded the drivers' view. For that year only, the race was run on the six and a half mile Costanera road circuit in Buenos Aires. It largely comprised the long, straight, tree-lined boulevard running parallel to the seafront, along which the drivers would, unbelievably, pass in opposite directions. This was, of course, madness: unreliable racing cars driving past each other at a combined speed of up to 340mph, with only the odd bale of hay to separate them! The organisers had also thoughtfully stretched thin wires between the trees to keep the crowd back, little appreciating that, if a car went out of control, the wires were at the perfect height to swiftly decapitate the driver.

'As if the cars aren't bloody lethal enough,' Mike said afterwards.

The attrition rate of the cars was dramatic, necessitating the 'better' drivers to swap cars, sometimes more than once, but, amazingly, no one died.

Mike had two weeks to fill before his next big race, the Buenos Aires City Grand Prix, back on the Autodrome where the Argentine GP had been held. He couldn't justify returning to England, and so this fortnight turned into one luxurious, indulgent holiday. He and his colleagues were forced to endure those spare, sun-filled days sailing, swimming, water-skiing, attending barbecues and drinks parties, etc, with just the odd official reception thrown in.

He told me that, during this time, Taffy had expressed an interest in taking some aerial cine footage of the river and the yachts. Somehow, Mike managed to get his hands on a tiny Piper Cub aeroplane and volunteered to take him up.

Mike was flying low in order that Taffy would get some decent footage when suddenly the engine stopped. Coincidentally, he'd just been assessing the slim chances of their survival should they have to make a forced landing because, in every direction, all Mike could see was either water or trees.

Fortunately, rather than panic, Mike glanced down and noticed that the throttle was in the closed position. It turned out that as Taffy, who was sitting behind Mike − tandem style − had wriggled to lean out of the cockpit, in so doing he had unwittingly shut down the dual-control throttle with his elbow.

By the time the boys returned to the Autodrome for the Grand Prix, the weather had become hotter still. It was now 104 degrees in the shade. Not only were the engines overheating again on the grid but so were some of the drivers.

After a dreadful start to the first heat, in which Mike fluffed his gear changes and then tried to keep the engine revs below 7,000pm, he eventually managed a creditable fourth place, behind Fangio, Pete and Stirling. Mike confessed that he was so affected by the heat that he needed to be helped out of the car.

He didn't think he was going to be able to go out again for the second heat, but he found someone to drill lots of holes in his crash helmet and stood under a cool shower for twenty minutes. He was also given some salt tablets.

Mike did go out and messed up the start. Masten Gregory, a short, square-jawed young American, with bottle-top glasses, and a newcomer to Ferrari, shot into the lead, impressing all his teammates in the process. Probably spurred on by this young upstart, Mike pulled out all the stops and briefly managed to take the lead. By this stage, he was really suffering from the effects of heat exhaustion and was forced to slow down. He conceded the lead and was beaten to the finish by Fangio, of course, and Jean Behra and Pete Collins.

Mike drew into the Ferrari pit and sat there, unable to move. Mechanics lifted him bodily from the car, and Mike practically collapsed. He told me that at that very moment he would have happily signed an undertaking never to step into a racing car again. The mechanics dealt with heat-exhausted drivers by lying them down and wrapping them up in wet towels containing ice. It wasn't elegant, but it was effective. He said he felt worse when he saw Pete prancing about 'lively as a cricket'.

'That was a pretty good effort, Pete,' he said with conviction.

'Thanks. Weren't those pills wonderful?'

Mike thought he meant the salt pills. However, whilst Mike had been monopolising the shower, a medic had done the rounds distributing 'heart pills' which had made the other drivers more or less immune to the heat.

By this time, Enzo Ferrari had ceased attending Grands Prix in person, although there was no question as to who pulled the Scuderia Ferrari strings. It was the team manager's responsibility to telephone Mr Ferrari immediately after each race to apprise him of exactly what had happened. A new manager, Eraldo Sculati, had been in the role for only a matter of weeks, following Nello Ugolini's 'defection' to Maserati.

Apparently, so the story goes, Ferrari was pacing around his office in Italy with his personal assistant Romolo Tavoni until late, waiting for Sculati's report. Sculati never did call from Argentina.

Upon Sculati's return from South America, Ferrari took him to lunch at a fine restaurant where he was able to hear first-hand what had happened in South America. Having received the information, Enzo promptly sacked him – paying him off with cash out of his pocket!

It was a massive shock to the whole team when it was announced that Sculati's successor would be Tavoni, Enzo's personal assistant for the past seven years. Tavoni was not an engineer and had no direct racing experience. What he did have was Enzo's trust. Poor Tavoni was really thrown in at the deep end as his first race was to be back over the Atlantic for the demanding Twelve Hours race at Sebring, Florida.

Another significant event, which would greatly touch Mike's life, was what Pete Collins got up to after the Argentina series.

Whereas Mike flew up to Nassau in the Bahamas to spend a few days with…none other than Cherry Huggins, Pete flew to Miami for what he thought was a blind date.

Pete was travelling with Masten Gregory with the intention of staying with him at his home in Kansas until it was time for them to go to Cuba for the next race meeting. The detour to Miami came about simply because of Stirling Moss's suggestion to look up an American actress he'd met a couple of months prior – '…Louise, a very beautiful girl and great fun'.

On Monday 4 February, Pete duly called Louise King on the telephone and asked whether she would meet him for a drink after her evening performance in *The Seven Year Itch* at the Coconut Grove Playhouse. She accepted. Pete thought Louise was indeed beautiful – an American Ingrid Bergman with freckles. Their first date was dinner for three, which included a mutual friend, Bob Said. Two days later, Louise spent the afternoon lazing around the pool of the motel where Pete and Masten were staying. While the three of them quietly sunbathed, Louise stretched out between the two guys, Pete managed to propose marriage, sotto voce, and Louise managed likewise to accept.

Masten hadn't the faintest idea what had occurred. Incredibly, neither Pete nor Louise remembered meeting the other at the Cahiers' party in Monte Carlo some ten months earlier – despite this encounter appearing like 'love at first sight'.

Pete told Masten that he'd like to stay on a while in Miami, omitting to say why, and so Masten flew on home alone. Exactly one week after their first date, Pete and Louise were married – to the enormous consternation of both their parents, particularly Pete's. The first Masten knew of their marriage was when he heard it on the radio the following day.

Mike was also flabbergasted when he heard the news. He, and many others, thought Pete was about to marry someone else. He'd been with Pete down in Buenos Aires only a few weeks earlier when he'd witnessed Pete's whirlwind romance with Eleanor Herrera, a twenty-one-year-old heiress to one of Argentina's grandest families. She was tall, shapely, with perfect olive skin, big eyes and high cheekbones. They'd met at a swimming party one week before the Argentine GP. They became inseparable over the next three weeks, dining together in the best restaurants, going to night clubs, and receiving invitations to the palatial homes of cattle barons.

As was clearly his modus operandi, Pete proposed to Eleanor one week after meeting her. He bought her a £200 platinum band with a pearl set in diamonds, and their engagement was announced at a family banquet. Mike and the other Ferrari drivers enjoyed many jokes along the lines that Pete was as quick with women as he was in a car.

By the time the lads all left South America to fly north, some wondered whether Pete was having second thoughts although, by then, all concerned thought that Pete couldn't very well back out. But, a few thousand miles and one week later, and, hey presto, another fiancée! It's fair to say that Eleanor didn't take it at all well.

Cuba was host to the next race – the inaugural Cuban Grand Prix – a race that would be run for only three years. At the time it seemed unfair that Pete, who'd only been married a week, was included in the Ferrari team whereas Mike was not. However, given Mike's propensity for attracting trouble, it was probably just as well. Fidel Castro's rebel forces were raging against the government so, on their first night in Havana, all the principal drivers were allocated bodyguards. Stirling and Pete managed to slip away to watch a boxing match. They had just taken their seats when Castro's men fired shots into the ceiling. The ensuing panic resulted in several people being crushed to death.

There were twenty-seven further casualties when a temporary wooden footbridge collapsed during practice. Sabotage was strongly suspected as flyers had been distributed around Havana which read:

Don't go to automobile races – avoid accidents. Revolutionary Movement of 26 July.

Chapter Seventeen

Castellotti's Chips and Enzo

Mike had a break of nearly two months before his next outing: the Sebring Twelve Hours sports car race. He shared his time between Farnham, London and New York. He was already in much better spirits than he had been at the end of '56.

I think it was because he was back in contention, and not on a slippery slope out of the sport. that I even found myself forgetting that not all the problems that had plagued Mike in recent years had gone away. Whilst the accusations of draft dodging and his culpability for the Le Mans tragedy had dimmed considerably, and even young Arnaud's paternity claims appeared to be semi-resolved, Mike's health – both physical and mental – was another matter, although he continued to remain intensely private about such things.

Many people who first met Mike around this time formed the opinion that, in spite of his many terrifying accidents, here was a young man in his prime – perfectly fit and well.

I well remember a time when there was a big crowd one evening at The Bush in Farnham and there was a right old sing-song going on – Mike at the centre of things, as usual. He had a great repertoire of rude rugger songs. At one point, he slipped away to the gents. I followed a couple of minutes later, and as I walked in I saw Mike alone, still addressing the trough. Completely unaware he was not alone, he emitted a quiet, strangled cry of pain, 'Agh!'

'Are you okay, bo?'

He turned and said, 'Yeah, just sometimes it hurts like hell when I pee. It's like pissing tacks.'

What could I say? He'd told me the prognosis. And he knew that I knew. Half-heartedly, I said, 'Get yourself another pint and I'll pay for it in a sec.'

Mike did up his flies and cursorily flicked a hand under the cold tap, ran it roughly through his hair, and paused by the mirror as he went to rejoin the party. I saw him smile broadly at his reflection, push his shoulders back, and walk out. I heard someone shout out in a shrill falsetto, 'Oh look, he's fallen in de water!' It was one of Spike Milligan's catchphrases from the Goon Show. Quick as flash, Mike shot back with another Goon classic, one of Peter Sellers', delivered in dramatic style, 'It was hell in there!' And with that, there was boisterous laughter, and a spontaneous chorus of the Ying Tong song began.

After Nassau, Mike flew back to Rome in order to call into Maranello and report back to the engineers on the problems they'd experienced in Argentina. Whilst he was there, the subject of the Sicilian Grand Prix in April cropped up. Mike admitted that this was his bogey event, having raced there twice, and twice crashed and been burned. Enzo was surprisingly sympathetic and excused Mike until the Naples Grand Prix.

Just as Mike and most of the other drivers were preparing to depart for Sebring, they were in for yet another shock: 'Casti', Eugenio Castellotti, their dear friend and teammate, lost his life at Modena Autodrome. He was testing a Lancia-Ferrari.

It was widely promulgated afterwards that Castellotti had been much troubled at the time of his death. He'd been dating a hugely successful singer named Delia Scala. It is said that, whilst they were both keen to marry, he wanted her to give up her singing career and she wanted him to give up motor racing. It didn't help matters that Eugenio's mother was far from approving. The story goes that one day Castellotti took Delia home to meet his mother. Straightaway, she took Delia's arm and said, 'You look like a waitress – the kitchen is this way'. Notwithstanding that little hurdle, the couple were due to marry twenty-five days after his fatal accident.

I heard the news at the same time as Mike. It was on the BBC. Within a few minutes of hearing the announcement, the telephone rang. It was Mike.

'Have you just been watching the news?'

'Yup.'

'Can you bloody believe it?'

'Yes, sadly.'

'I need a drink. The Duke in half an hour?'

'Done.'

He was already there when I arrived. We spent a couple of hours together, chatting about the unfairness of accidents, the probability of actually retiring from the sport without getting killed, and other related cheery topics.

Although Mike would not have described Casti as a really close friend, they'd spent a great deal of time together and had a healthy respect for each other. What I saw in Mike wasn't raw pain, such as I'd seen following the deaths of his old muckers like Black Mike, Julian and Don, but a stark resignation to the inevitable. It was almost like seeing someone on Death Row...in his mind, it wasn't so much a case of 'if' but 'when'. Naturally, we went on to get extremely pissed and drove home.

Castellotti's death was all the worse for it not happening in a race. In fact, as the circumstances of the accident leaked out, many people began to view Enzo's autocratic, bullying style of management as mortally dangerous.

The story I heard was that Enzo was having a cup of coffee at the Biella Club in Modena when he learnt that Jean Behra was busy setting new records at the Autodrome circuit in a Maserati 250F. Incensed at the thought of losing face on his home turf, and still smarting from Maserati taking first, second, third *and* fourth in the first Grand Prix of the season, Enzo set about tracking down Castellotti who was in Florence with his fiancée.

Enzo demanded that Casti come to the circuit the very next day to 'defend the honour of Ferrari'. This required the twenty-six-year-old to leave Florence at five in the morning and drive flat out to Modena, in order to pit the Ferrari Tipo 801, a new grand prix car, against the impressive times being set by Jean Behra in the latest Maserati.

Certainly tired, possibly emotionally strained, and under huge pressure from Enzo to perform, Castellotti clearly pushed the car, and/or himself, beyond the limit. A Ferrari employee, who was present when Enzo learnt that Castellotti had been killed, said the Old Man simply responded thus: '*Castellotti? Morto? Poverino! E la macchina...?*' Roughly translated, that is: 'Castellotti? Dead? Poor devil! And the car...?'

Ferrari's official line wasn't much more sympathetic: 'He (Castellotti) was going through a confused and conflicting time emotionally, and probably his reflexes failed him for a moment.'

Castellotti had become what Ferrari termed 'a true *garibaldino*', his shorthand for a driver who was prepared to put courage and verve before cool calculation. Stirling wouldn't have got on well in the Scuderia Ferrari.

During that beer session in the Duke of Cambridge, I asked Mike, 'What if you'd been in Florence rather than here? Would you have been called up?'

'Very possibly. Ferrari would have had us all out there, if necessary. If it wouldn't have weakened his bloody team, I doubt he'd have cared too much if we'd all crashed, just so long as he kept his precious lap record.'

'What? Even blue-eyed Pete?'

'Okay, maybe Pete would be the exception – the bastard.' He smiled.

It was widely acknowledged that Enzo had developed a particular fondness for Pete. Scuderia Ferrari was not dissimilar to a big Italian family, and certain drivers were favoured over others. Musso and Castellotti were favoured simply because they were Italian, even though they were like chalk and cheese. Castellotti had been intense and desperately self-conscious about being short in stature whereas Musso was considerably taller, more confident, and appeared to treat life like a game.

It should, therefore, be something of a surprise that Pete Collins, an Englishman, was also favoured. Enzo appears to have adopted him in place of his own son, Dino, who died of muscular dystrophy in the summer of 1956 aged just twenty-four. Pete's innate charm and easy-going nature made him universally popular. That coupled with being almost the same age as the Ferraris' only son meant that Pete was, at least for a while, cherished by Enzo and his wife as a surrogate son.

This was no mere perception. Enzo had insisted that Pete took up residence in his late son's apartment, over the Ristorante Cavallino, free gratis. Enzo and his wife Laura were hugely appreciative of Peter's warmth and friendship of their dying only son, and in the months afterwards showed it in many ways, this being one of them.

Peter, before he was married, would brag about how Signora Ferrari would make his breakfast and do his laundry. That caused a few raised eyebrows back in Farnham, I can tell you.

Mike made too many references to Pete's 'dago father' and Pete 'brown-nosing' Ferrari, leading me to think Mike was a wee bit jealous. My concern was simple: if Ferrari was going to endanger one 'pilot', one driver, more than the others, Mike was higher up the list than Messrs Musso or Collins.

It was many years later that I learnt something of Ferrari's self-awareness. To the many people that imagined Ferraris were designed by him personally, he would say, 'No, no, I'm not the designer. Other people do that. I am an agitator of men.' An agitator of men, indeed.

Chapter Eighteen

Fon Memories

Within a few days, it was time for Mike to fly back out to the USA for the Sebring Twelve Hours race. We said a fond farewell over a few beers. Increasingly, these au revoirs felt like adieus. I was the father sending off his son to war.

Enzo must have regretted his decision to allow Mike to drive a Jaguar at Sebring, for he was now without three elite drivers in his squad. Following the death of his friend Castellotti, Cesare Perdisa had decided to retire. Consequently, new drivers had been enlisted, including the American Phil Hill.

Sebring was won comfortably by Fangio and Behra, with Stirling and Harry Schell taking second place, both pairings driving Maseratis. It was becoming incontrovertible: Maserati had competitive cars which were more reliable than Ferraris, *and* they had the world's best drivers.

Mike's D-Type, although not an official Jaguar entry, which he shared with Ivor-the-Driver, had also gone well over this gruelling circuit. Their car was running in second place after eleven hours before loss of brake fluid and an engine misfire slowed Mike considerably, allowing Stirling to beat him to the chequered flag. The best placed Ferrari was fourth.

Back home, Mike's recounting of his latest American trip was far more about Pete and Louise than it was about the racing. Although he'd heard about Pete's new wife, this was the first time the two had met (if we discount Monte Carlo), and clearly he was smitten. To say that he was envious of his friend would be an oversimplification. He was genuinely pleased for Pete and undoubtedly charmed by Louise, and, perhaps for the first time, seriously attracted by the prospect of settling down.

Mike was clearly a lot more impressed with Louise than he was with his travel arrangements. He'd flown out to Sebring with Lofty and Ivor in a Douglas DC-7s, a sleek modern aeroplane with four propellers. He said it wasn't much fun being cooped up for the whole flight. Despite it taking nearly two hours longer to cross the Atlantic, he much preferred the 'fat old Stratocruiser' (a Boeing 377), a luxurious aircraft in which one could wander around and even pop down to the lower deck by way of a spiral staircase where there was a lounge and, of all things, a bar to prop up.

Having flown into New York, Mike and Ivor decided they wanted to go up inside the Statue of Liberty. Mike was surprised to discover the lift only went as far as the top of the plinth. The final hundred or so feet they had to ascend on foot, discovering in the process neither was as fit as they thought they were. There's another gulf between Formula One drivers then and now.

Pete and Castellotti hadn't been the only ones with marriage on their minds. Even Stirling had announced his engagement to Katie Molson, a twenty-two-year-old Canadian heiress to a brewing fortune. I repeatedly asked Mike how he'd missed that one – attractive and with an inside track to a successful brewery!

Upon his engagement, Stirling, not renowned for his witty remarks, did come out with this belter: 'Of course, I realise this is a foolish time to get engaged because Peter Collins has just got married and released a flood of crumpet onto the market, and now I can't do anything about it!'

With hindsight, that wasn't the most tactful thing to say in front of one's young fiancée. The Mosses' honeymoon in Holland lasted just four days as Stirling wanted to get back to London to judge the Miss World competition! Mike was so jealous. I really wasn't surprised to hear that Stirling and Katie split up two years later.

Mike had to sit it out for a month before his next Grand Prix, unlike Pete who, with Luigi Musso, went to Sicily for the Syracuse GP – a race Pete won. So much for Ferrari's assertion that wives were bad news for his drivers. Mind you, Pete's win was rather fortunate. Stirling Moss had now left Maserati to join Tony Brooks at Vanwall, and during the race, Moss's Vanwall had created something of a sensation, lapping significantly quicker than both the Ferraris and Maseratis, and setting a new lap record.

Unfortunately for Stirling, an enforced stoppage of ten minutes in the pits meant that he was never able to catch Pete or Musso, but still he got third place. Vanwall's ascendancy had started.

Pete and Mike were reunited for the Naples Grand Prix, a race that was to prove exciting despite the absence of works' Maseratis. Mike and Pete flew out to Milan, drove to Modena to pick up Louise, and then all of them piled into Pete's massive American Mercury station wagon for the drive down to Naples.

The most amazing thing about Mike and Pete's friendship was it didn't change one iota when Pete got married. I assumed that Pete would withdraw into matrimonial bliss and Mike would resume coming back to Farnham at every opportunity. Only that never happened. It almost seemed as if both Pete *and* Mike had got married: they still went everywhere and did everything together.

Practice was, initially, a disaster for Mike. He wasn't remotely able to match the lap times of his teammates Pete and Luigi. He said that he began to think he'd either lost his nerve or, worse, his ability. Fortunately, all was explained when the mechanics discovered that the offside drive shaft had seized on its splines. Once fixed, Mike matched Pete's best time, putting the Englishmen on the front row of the grid. Mike's long held admiration for his late hero, Alberto Ascari, only grew when he learnt that even their best practice times hadn't beaten Ascari's lap record – a record he'd set four years previously in a less powerful car.

Pete suggested that if, by the end of the race, their two cars had established a comfortable lead over the rest of the field, he'd be happy to take second place, given that he'd won at Syracuse. I thought Mike would never have made that offer to Pete. Naturally, such thoughts went unspoken. For all his off-track, apparently easy-going nature, once he was racing, Mike wanted one thing and one thing only: to win.

As it turned out, they did finish first and second – although it was Pete then Mike – and not quite in the way Mike would have wished. For the first dozen or so laps, their Ferraris were dominant, and as a result of pushing each other hard they were swapping the lead regularly. Mike then felt a welcome cooling spray on his face. Initially, he thought it was water. Then, some got into his eyes and he realised it was petrol. It 'stung like stink', he said. The leak continued to get worse until fuel was streaming out of the louvres of the bonnet.

Mike had no choice but to stop. The mechanics discovered the pipe to the fuel pressure gauge had split. They effected a technical repair: they cut off the pipe and sealed it by bending it over. Driving without a fuel pressure gauge was of little consequence.

This running repair cost Mike more than a full lap, and so he was down in seventh place. That seemed to bring out the best in him. He went charging after those in front, picking them off one at a time. He overtook the lot, including Pete who was in the lead. But, being a lap behind, he had to overtake three of them again! The third placed car, driven by Lewis-Evans, retired with mechanical failure. The car in second place was Musso's, his teammate. Driving absolutely on the limit, and at one point mounting a footpath, Mike managed to scream past Musso right on the start/finish line. Publicly he maintained he'd have caught Pete too if there'd been a few more laps to go. Privately he was gracious enough to concede he probably wouldn't have won because he didn't think Pete was driving flat out.

One of the things which contributed to Mike's performance that day was as basic as the car fitting him – as opposed to the usual situation where he was cramped in a Ferrari cockpit built for much shorter drivers. No driver then was ever what might reasonably be thought of as 'comfortable', but it's worth a moment's pause to imagine what it must have been like to drive flat out for 200 miles with one's kneecaps jammed hard against the bottom of the dashboard. As no more leg room could be found within their 'standard' car to accommodate this long-legged driver, Ferrari had taken the unusual step of lengthening the chassis and mounting the engine further forward.

As a measure of his bravura driving during those last few laps, Mike managed to post the best lap time of the race and, in the process, beat Ascari's long-standing lap record.

I was delighted for my friend when I read the reports of this race. I could picture him standing on the podium next to Pete and Luigi, all of them Ferrari drivers, with a beaming smile and spraying champagne over each other. They would, of course, not be identically dressed in scarlet overalls, as today, but in their own clothes. It was, according to the press, 'a vintage Hawthorn performance'. I would have loved to have seen that race. It was about then I started to believe in his potential once again.

After Naples came the Mille Miglia, the long-distance road race around Italy. Enzo asked Mike whether he'd like to compete in it. I was so relieved when I heard that Mike had sensibly declined. It was widely, and accurately, considered to be one of the most dangerous races, and the endurance aspect of it would have made Mike particularly vulnerable to having an accident.

Pete didn't share Mike's qualms about the race, having finished second the year before. It was a contest he positively relished. In the days leading up to the race, Pete and some of the other drivers took some exhilarating white-knuckle drives up into the mountains to the south-west of Maranello by way of practice.

On the eve of the race, a number of competitors, wives, girlfriends and journalists – thirteen in all – found themselves dining at the same restaurant. The drivers included Pete, Fon, Olivier Gendebien and Taffy von Trips. I gather it was some party. Now, that part of the event, Mike *would* have greatly enjoyed.

Fon was not one of the original Ferrari entrants for this race and was only included because Musso had contracted hepatitis in Sicily. At one point during the evening, Fon pronounced, 'Life has to be lived to the full. It is better to be wholly alive for thirty years than half dead for sixty'.He may have looked Spanish, like his father, but his scruffy appearance and devil-may-care attitude might well have come from his spirited Irish mother.

Ferrari entered five cars for this Mille Miglia: four similar sports cars of around 4 litres, and one V12 3-litre car – a 250 GT Tour de France. Fon had been instructed to drive the 250 GT, a car in which he'd already had considerable success, including winning the Tour of France 1956. In this regard, he wasn't alone: Olivier Gendebien, a Belgian former paratrooper and one of the other drivers, had also known success in this car, having won the Tour of Sicily a few weeks earlier. A few days before the race, Enzo decided to swap these two drivers, telling them, 'You (Gendebien) will take the 250 GT, and you (de Portago) will now take the sports car' – a Ferrari 335S. Addressing de Portago, he added, 'I will be surprised if you go as fast as Gendebien does in the GT.'

That was so typical of the Old Man, the agitator, throwing down challenges to his drivers. And, as Mike commented afterwards, there is no doubt that such a gibe would have spurred on Fon to give it his all.

There were no definitive accounts of Fon's accident, but it was thought a shock absorber failed, causing a front tyre to rub on the bodywork. At a checkpoint only forty miles from the finish line, Fon, who was lying in third place, was advised by a mechanic to change the wheel. He was also advised that his time was practically identical to Gendebien's. He apparently responded by saying, 'If I change the tyre, Olivier will beat me.' And, with that, he waved away the mechanic.

He and his navigator, Ed Nelson, reached a dead straight road and built up their speed to an estimated 160 to 170mph when the tyre shredded. Fon lost control and the red Ferrari swerved and rolled spectacularly, first to one side of the highway, killing five spectators, then to the other side, killing another four. Fon and Ed were killed instantly, and their Ferrari was so damaged as to be unrecognisable. Eleven dead, five of them children – four more fatalities than had died the previous year in the whole race. Thankfully, it was also to prove the death of this crazy race.

Enzo was widely criticised. He was portrayed, not unfairly, as an old man who sat at home and sent out young men to mow down women and children. It wasn't an entirely balanced view, but because I felt he was endangering the lives of my friends, it was one I vehemently shared. It was only much later that I began to ask myself why it was that a father who'd lost a dearly held son of a similar age to his drivers could behave in such a callous, cavalier fashion. Or, indeed, was that the reason?

It was also later that I began to see that it was the race organisers, the all-important but faceless 'authorities', that were again more to blame than anyone else. Who in their right mind would allow child spectators to line the streets along which half worn-out cars would be driven flat out?

It wasn't just criticism that Enzo faced: it was a manslaughter charge. He was accused of specifying the highly respected Belgian Englebert tyres which were considered not fit for purpose. The judiciary also cited Englebert Tyres (which eventually became Continental) with the same charge. It would be four years before both accused parties were exonerated.

It was yet another death I learnt about directly from Mike. He was driving back from London and heard it on the car wireless.

He rang me when he got home. 'Tom, have you heard? Fon's had it!'

'Had what?' I asked. As the penny dropped, I immediately felt stupid.

'He crashed...he and Nelson...both killed.' He sounded upset now.

'In the Mille Miglia?'

'Yup. I don't know any more yet, except a load of spectators got it too. Apparently, Pete had led almost to the finish when his back axle broke up, allowing Taruffi to win.'

Mike said he'd phone Maranello to try to get more detail and suggested we meet later for a beer. I didn't say as much, but convening upon learning tragic news was becoming a ritual.

Mike was deeply affected by Fon's death. It was another close colleague, a good friend, and a fearless teammate. I hadn't fully appreciated how much time they had spent together on and off the circuits.

Obviously, drivers at the time did discuss their own mortality, and Mike quoted Fon as having recently said something like, 'I won't die in an accident. I'll die of old age – that or I'll be executed by some gross miscarriage of justice.'

It was that evening when I became totally certain, as I sat there with my tearful friend, that he too would die in a car accident. It was only a matter of time. I felt so maudlin. I had known Fon, too, not well, but well enough, and now I began to mourn Mike's death in anticipation.

That I openly wept surprised Mike. He had no idea what I was feeling. I hated Ferrari, but I loved Ferraris. I hated motor racing, and yet I loved the speed and excitement. I hated their Russian roulette lives, but I envied their lifestyles. I wanted Mike to stop. I couldn't ask him to quit for my sake, and with Cherry probably out of the picture, there was no one special girl whose name I could use to spare her from bereavement.

Word from the Ferrari camp was that Romolo Tavoni was so upset by the death of Fon, he asked Enzo for his old secretarial job back. He had never wanted to be the team manager anyway. Enzo refused and insisted that he stay on.

Weeks later, when I was talking to Louise Collins about the

Mille Miglia, I was astounded to discover how differently the racers out there in Brescia had responded to the news. Understandably, Pete was bitterly disappointed not to have won, having led for practically the whole race. He was, however, typically gracious about the victor, Taruffi – the fifty-year-old campaigner driving in his last ever race.

As for Fon, although he had been a very popular guy, it was as if no one was greatly surprised by his death and no one was terribly upset about it. In fact, the Collinses and their friends went out for dinner in Brescia that evening and, in Louise's words, 'danced the night away'. I didn't mention about Mike and me weeping into our beer in a small pub in Farnham.

What strikes me most forcibly now is how the drivers then simply blamed themselves if they succumbed to an accident. It was Pete's view that both Castellotti and de Portago died because they went beyond their limits. It was never the car's fault. Perhaps that was the only way he could see it?

Chapter Nineteen

Monza Madness

The Monaco GP immediately followed the Mille Miglia, and two teams were shorn of some of their top talent. Ferrari, who had now lost Castellotti and Portago, were also without Musso, who was still poorly. Similarly, Maserati's number two, Jean Behra, was also out, having crashed and broken his arm during practice for the Mille Miglia. Stirling Moss, however, was in fine form, behind the wheel of the rejuvenated Vanwall. In fact, the British contingent was starting to look quite potent. BRM had Scotsman Ron Flockhart and Roy Salvadori; Connaught had Ivor and Stuart Lewis-Evans; and Vanwall had Tony Brooks as number two to Stirling. Was the pendulum starting to swing?

To compound matters for Ferrari, they missed the first day of practice because their cars were still being examined by the authorities after the Mille Miglia crash. Stirling set a blistering time in practice and won £100 for the fastest lap of the day, despite having had a hefty prang at the chicane and writing off one of the three cars available to him and Brooks. Pete, in his Ferrari, was fairly fortunate when he narrowly avoiding plunging into the harbour, in the style of Ascari the year before. He was 'luckily' stopped by a concrete bollard right on the harbour wall. Amazingly, Pete was okay; the car less so. As it was Mike's especially lengthened car, Mike wasn't best pleased with Pete.

Later practice sessions established an older order once more, with Fangio on pole, Pete second, Stirling third, Tony Brooks fourth, and Mike fifth. Stirling got off to a good start and led the race. On the fourth lap, however, he once more failed to negotiate the chicane and ploughed straight into a barrier – a barrier incredibly placed there to mark an escape road – sending poles and sandbags everywhere. Pete then crashed into the scattered debris while Fangio picked his way delicately through the resultant mayhem.

Tony Brooks, trying to avoid the poles, braked so hard that Mike clipped him, lost a front wheel in the process, and then went careering into Pete's now stationary car which was again parked alongside the harbour wall. The broken front suspension of Mike's car ended up just inches from Pete's head. Pete jumped out and started to run to safety. Mike followed, as did Stirling, dodging the other cars which were still travelling at racing speeds. Stirling had a particularly lucky escape as he was sprayed by nitromethane fuel which burnt his back.

When Mike was telling me all about this, I was horrified. Apparently, when he saw that all three British drivers were safe, he'd burst out laughing, probably out of relief.

From the trackside, Pete and Mike made their way together back to the pits. Pete found he had sustained bad grazes to his legs whereas Mike, for once, seemed fine.

On arrival at the pits, Tavoni, the new and inexperienced manager, decided that Mike – having just been in a high-speed, head-on collision – might fare better than Taffy, who was still going, and so instructed Mike to take over Taffy's car. Mike tried arguing that he couldn't physically fit in Taffy's car, but Tavoni insisted. So, without the mechanics allowed to make any alterations to the cockpit, at the next pit stop, Taffy hopped out and Mike got in. He managed a couple of laps, but it was hopeless. His hands kept hitting his knees. He handed the car back to von Trips. Suitably motivated, Taffy went really well, getting himself up to third place when the engine blew up. The car spun, then crashed, and came to rest precipitously among shattered stonework on the edge of a thirty-foot drop.

While all this was going on, Pete and Louise jumped into their new speedboat and tore around the harbour, having a great time.

Behind the apparent glamour, daring and spectacle, all was not well with Formula One motor racing. There were problems everywhere. The race organisers felt they needed to economise, and one of the simplest ways to achieve this would be to pay the drivers and manufacturers less for entering. They proposed that only the reigning world champion could be a 'Grade 1' driver and that he would receive nearly twice as much money (£180) as drivers in Grade 2, of which there would, quite arbitrarily, be three.

The larger, more established manufacturers would also receive less. However, this wasn't as catastrophic for them as it was for the small teams such as Connaught who would receive nothing. These proposals provoked a big hoo-ha from all the competing teams, large and small.

The organisers decided to cancel the next Grand Prix after Monaco, the Dutch, due to spiralling costs. The drivers felt very anxious about this, and the day after the Monaco race they held a meeting in secret. The catalyst for their coming together was undoubtedly the question of fair starting money and the summary cancellation of an established race. However, once they realised they might have some influence as a collective body, they soon turned their attention to matters of safety. And so the first motor racers' union, the l'Union des Pilotes Professionels Internationaux (UPPI), was formed. Eligibility required the driver to have finished three Grands Prix or to have won one. The first elected president was elder statesman Louis Chiron, the grandfather of the sport (who at nearly fifty-six years of age holds the record of having been the oldest ever participant of a Grand Prix race). Fangio and Taruffi, two other elder statesmen of the sport, were vice-presidents. Britain's interests were to be represented by its top three drivers: Stirling, Pete and Mike. 'Militant Mike', I called him.

When he first told me about the UPPI, I thought he was joking. However, when I learned that one of their first campaigns was to have telegraph pole barriers, such as those which nearly decapitated Stirling, replaced with straw bales, I could see enormous sense in it. 'After all,' said Mike, 'if we all collectively refuse to drive, there will be no Formula One – at least, not straightaway.'

The races scheduled to follow the Dutch included the Belgian and German Grands Prix, where the new starting money was to be first implemented. Ferrari and Maserati promptly withdrew, causing these races to be cancelled too. This was a disaster for the top drivers for the rules of the World Championships stated that there needed to be six qualifying races, and without the Dutch, Belgian and German there could only be five.

There was yet another storm cloud on the sport's horizon: the

Monza 500, which was also to be known as the 'Two Worlds Trophy' race. In simple terms, this was an attempt to pitch the American fast racing cars, designed for banked circuits, against the predominantly European cars, designed for flat, twisting road racing. It was ambitious, to say the least. The American cars *were* certainly fast but didn't handle. They didn't need to; they just had to go round and round, flat out. Astonishingly, these big Yank Tanks were actually designed to race only turning left, anti-clockwise. They were also built to run on smooth surfaces. The deal was the best ten American drivers were to take on the best ten European drivers.

It was controversial for another reason: sponsors' adverts were to be plastered on the cars. Hitherto, cars had only been painted in their national colours – with very few exceptions, such as Mike's British Racing Green Ferrari of 1953.

The drivers, using their new mouthpiece the UPPI, refused to enter, saying that it would be too dangerous, and that the banked circuit of Monza was too hard on both cars and drivers for a race of this sort. There was big prize money at stake – the equivalent of about £600,000 today – but neither side would back down, and so the race went ahead with nine American cars and drivers competing against three D-Types of the Scottish Ecurie Ecosse team.

Despite the track doing its damnedest to destroy the cars, the race passed without major incident. Indeed, it was considered a thrilling spectacle. The press, who had been all for it, crowed, and the drivers who'd refused to race were made to look a bit precious. Predictably perhaps, an American won comfortably. The Scottish-prepared Jaguars all did well to even finish the three heats, but ultimately were out-muscled by the bigger American cars. More of the Yank Tanks would have fared better but they needed constant attention because the racing surface was so poor.

Mike didn't go straight home after Monte Carlo. Instead, he 'spent a pleasant day with Pete and Louise aboard Sir James Scott Douglas's yacht'. These were Mike's official words, and from them one could be forgiven for picturing a formal and genteel cocktail party. Not so. 'Jamie' Douglas was a contemporary of his invitees and a party animal. In the early fifties, he had dabbled a little in racing sports cars, notably with Ecurie Ecosse, when he could still fit into them. The expression 'larger than life' has seldom been more apt for, although Jamie was already too large to fit into a racing car, he would continue to expand in later life when, financially obligated to work for a newspaper, he had to travel by goods hoist to his second-floor office because his enormous mass proved too much for the passenger lift.

Jamie was born into a Scottish Borders dynasty and was extremely well-connected if not actually extremely wealthy. He lived for the moment and was not exactly thrifty by nature. His 'yacht' had been a Royal Naval destroyer before it was kitted out as a luxury pad. The purchase and running of it practically bankrupted him. Mike told me that the party had been 'an absolute belter' and, having briefly met Sir James, I could well believe it.

Chapter Twenty

Bloody Everything

Mike went to Modena to see Enzo en route to the 1,000km race at the Nurburgring circuit in Germany. There was some doubt as to whether he'd be racing. The Italian authorities threatened not to release the Ferrari sports cars which were still impounded following Fon's death at the Mille Miglia. Fortunately, they did, and these were duly lined up against the best of the Maseratis piloted by the likes of Fangio, Moss and Schell.

Mike and Pete were paired with Maurice Trintignant and Olivier Gendebien respectively while Taffy was to partner Masten Gregory in a 250GT.

Poor Taffy was used to driving Ferrari sports cars which had the accelerator in the middle and the brake on the right, whereas this new 250GT had the throttle pedal on the right, as is common today. Consequently, during race practice, Taffy stamped on the right-hand pedal, thinking it was the brake and promptly went straight through a hedge, breaking a vertebra in his back, and ending up in hospital.

The race didn't start well for either Mike or Stirling. They both ran to their cars and leapt in. Mike said that he fired up the engine, depressed the clutch, put it in gear, and let the clutch out, but nothing happened. It was only after the roar of the departing cars diminished that he realised he had mistaken his engine firing for Pete's car next to him. He sat there on the grid with the engine churning and not firing until the mechanics arrived. Bizarrely, the same thing happened to Stirling, and he left only shortly before Mike, some way down the field.

According to Mike, it was 'a funny old race'. It was won by a new car, Aston Martin's DBR1, driven superbly by Tony Brooks. Pete and Mike managed to come second and third respectively, a Porsche slipped in at fourth, and a big Maserati came fifth.

What annoyed Mike most after the race was how Maserati had played 'musical chairs' with its drivers. 'Once Stirling had a wheel come off, he and Fange should have been out of it. Simple as that.'

'So, what happened?' I asked, albeit I knew where this was going.

'They took over Hans and Harry's car, until that conked out, too.'

'That's happened before, surely?'

'Ah, but then Stirling, Harry and Horace all had a go in Jo and Georgio's Maser, and ended up coming fifteenth. Plus, Stirling, Fange, Georgio *and* Horace all had a crack in Paco's car, and ended up coming fifth! So, you tell me: which driver should get the points? It's bloody farcical!'

He passionately believed that the original entrants, a pair in an endurance race like this, should stay with their car throughout the event. It was, I have to agree, a real mess, although like most of Mike's beefs, he wasn't nearly so critical of Ferrari who used to do much the same as Maserati.

Due to the cancellation of the Belgian and Dutch GPs, Mike had a break of nearly a month between the 1,000km and Le Mans. He spent much of this time in Farnham, a little in London, and some with Pete and Louise. The Collinses had gone to visit Taffy in hospital, then bobbed around Monte Carlo harbour for a week or so before returning to Pete's family home in Kidderminster. I found myself resenting the time Mike spent with Pete and Louise. Partly because this meant he spent less at home, and thus with the Members, and partly because the Collinses were so obviously his most exciting friends.

I remember saying to him once: 'Look, Mike, don't you think that they might want some time to themselves? They've only recently got married.'

He would have none of it. 'No, no, they love having me around, and, anyway, they're such fun.'

Thankfully, I didn't express my automatic reaction which was: Oh, what, I'm not much fun, you mean? I think there was another dimension to this, which I didn't pick up on at the time, and that was celebrity. Mike, when pictured with Peter, seemed to have more currency than if pictured alone – they were the golden boys of British motor sport, the handsome, smiley, ladykiller ones. Plus, it was true: Pete and Mike did get up to a lot of mischief together, *and* had the wherewithal to buy their way out of trouble, unlike most of his old friends.

To be fair, when I did see Mike during that summer, he was practically back to his best, in terms of japes, drinking and womanising. When I saw him out, especially with people neither of us knew well, I found myself wondering whether I worried more about his well-being than he ever did. He was, in many ways, a consummate actor.

I knew he again wasn't looking forward to Le Mans. One evening, shortly before he was due to fly out there, he became maudlin, talking about the futility of racing and the inherent risks. I think Mike needed these periods of melancholy in order to get things off his chest, even if it was short-lived. But, being more sensitive than he was, this emotional roller coaster became exaggerated in me. It was rather like he'd flick one end of a rope, and I'd be left feeling the effects for longer, and sometimes more deeply, long after he'd dropped it.

I was so concerned about his mood for Le Mans that I offered to accompany him on the flight. He thanked me but told me that he'd agreed to take Pat Massey-Dawson, another friend and ex-Fleet Air Arm pilot. Pat was another guy I was slightly jealous of. He appeared to have inherited so much money that he didn't need to work and accordingly hung around the TT Garage most days. The problem was that he was actually a really genuine, likeable and generous gentleman. It was no surprise when, a little later, Pat bought the first E-type Jaguar sold by the TT Garage and also married the firm's attractive Ann, Winifred's much guarded office assistant. As they say, some guys have all the luck.

When I discovered that Mike had also given Ivor Bueb a lift, I immediately felt slighted. I assumed this was simply because Ivor was a racing driver and I was not. It was later that I heard Ivor's car had broken down while driving towards the coast and he was fairly stranded. It had meant Mike delaying his flight and jettisoning some twenty gallons of fuel – and even then he was probably overloaded, for Ivor was no rake. Not only was Ivor's need more pressing than mine but, as he went on to win the damned race, I was left feeling quite churlish.

As for Le Mans itself, I was pleased not to go. As a chum of Mike's, I'd become an avid Ferrari supporter, and the team was having a torrid time. Ferrari was trying out new pistons, and three of their four entered cars all retired through piston failure. Of a race in which the winners would complete over 300 laps, Pete's car didn't even manage two laps, Mike and Musso's managed fifty-six, and Gendebien and Trintignant's just over 100. The only Ferrari to finish, indeed post a respectable fifth place, was driven by newcomer Stuart Lewis-Evans and test driver Martino Severi.

The Maseratis were not having a lot of luck either. They were still competitively quick, especially in the right hands, but they, too, were unreliable. Both Stirling's car and Behra's car went out due to broken axles. The furthest any works' cars managed was Bonnier and Scarlatti's seventy-six laps. It was a shame really, because Ferrari and Maserati arguably had the world's top drivers between them and, when the cars were running well, the crowds could be assured of some spectacularly close racing.

I read one story about the race that did intrigue me. It was that, in practice, Fangio set the fastest time in his Maserati and then declined to enter the race. It was said that he no longer enjoyed endurance events and was never again going to drive the Mille Miglia or Le Mans.

Not that he needed to have worried about the Mille Miglia for, after Fon's fatal accident, the race was never again staged. A lot of barroom pundits including, it must be said, most of my friends at the time couldn't understand why such a talented driver would pull out when he was clearly one of best, if not the best, drivers of the time.

Looking back, it now seems far easier to understand. He would have celebrated his forty-sixth birthday during the second day of the race, if he'd made it. And that's probably the point. He'd enjoyed a fantastic career. He'd already won the World Championship four times, and so why should he expose himself to the extra risks which would come with fatigue? He was old enough to be a father to the majority of the drivers, and his thoughts must have been on self-preservation. And, if that was the case, he was ultimately very successful, for he went on to live to the ripe old age of eighty-four.

From a British perspective, the '57 Le Mans was a triumph. The D-Type Jaguar was unassailable – taking five of the top six positions. Perhaps all the more remarkable as there were no official Jaguar entries. The Scottish Ecurie Ecosse team finished first and second, courtesy of the pairings of Ivor-the-driver and Ron Flockhart, and Jock Lawrence and Ninian Sanderson. Mike's pal Duncan Hamilton, aided by Masten Gregory, finished sixth in his privately entered D.

Although they didn't finish, Pete, Mike and Stirling all led the race at some point, while their cars were working. Pete recorded a new standing-start lap time with his Ferrari, and Mike, too, managed a little personal glory by posting the fastest lap time of the race: 3 minutes 58.7 seconds – an average speed of 203kph, a fraction *slower* than that of Fangio's during practice!

When Ron Flockhart took the chequered flag, he was joined by Ivor and several of the pit crew who jumped on top of the car as he brought it round towards the enclosure. At that moment, a low-flying plane passed overhead and dropped countless rose petals, all as part of the event's twenty-fifth anniversary. It was a magnificent spectacle.

On his return, I'd fully expected Mike to be cursing about Ferrari's experimentation with new pistons, but he wasn't. Or, at least, he was philosophical about the need to try new things, some of which only ever got tested in the most extreme environments such as a twenty-four-hour non-stop race.

What really bothered Mike was brakes. Having driven for Jaguar, who had adopted disc brakes some time ago, Mike was convinced of their superiority over drum brakes. However, the difference was much more significant for an endurance race such as Le Mans. Mike said that once brake shoes need to be changed mid-race, so much time is lost that Ferrari could never again hope to win a race such as Le Mans.

'I can't seem to get through to the Old Man,' Mike said. 'Sometimes, he takes on board innovation. At other times, he refuses to listen to reason.'

During his previous spell at home, Mike had spoken about wanting to get a new aeroplane, something a bit faster. Mike was still fairly passionate about some cars, but I sensed that planes had become his abiding hobby, whereas cars had become work.

During the break between Le Mans and the French GP, a fortnight later, Mike bought a second-hand Percival Vega Gull. It was a classic, dear little aircraft, constructed of wood and fabric. Although it was no larger than his old Argus, the Gull could fly fifty miles an hour faster (at 174mph, this about the same speed as the cars Mike was used to driving) and had a fifty per cent longer range, making it far more suitable for touring. It was also highly manoeuvrable. One of its unusual features was its folding wings, allowing it to be stowed in unused corners of hangars.

I was one of his first passengers in the Gull, and I have to say it was pretty exciting. The view from the cockpit was much greater than the Argus because the fuselage sat above the wings rather than being suspended from them. This was especially demonstrated when Mike flew upside down with his eyes closed.

Mike was in good spirits for the flight out to Rouen. I think, Arnaud apart, he had fond memories of the French GP and always expected to do well. He told me later that each day after practice, he would fly Louise and Pete off to Deauville for some 'fun in the sun'.

The French Grand Prix was held on a country road circuit called *Rouen Les Essarts*, an exciting course comprising steep uphills, fast sweeping bends, and tight hairpins. Vanwall was without its top drivers. Stirling was out with sinus trouble, and Brooks was in hospital with leg injuries sustained from a crash at Le Mans. Salvadori and Lewis-Evans replaced them. However, neither Vanwall managed to finish. The two BRMs suffered the same fate. Ron Flockhart was lucky to survive after his car hit some oil, crashed and overturned, while first-time Formula One driver Herbert Mackay-Fraser was forced out through transmission failure.

In the end, it turned into an all-Italian victory. Fangio, by all accounts, drove faultlessly on an unfamiliar circuit and claimed his third GP victory out of three for Maserati. The three Ferraris of Musso, Collins and Hawthorn all chased hard, but finished behind Fangio, in that order. Fangio's teammates Schell and Behra took fifth and sixth respectively. The novice Mackay-Fraser apparently had a tremendous tussle with Mike until his BRM packed up. There's a name to watch, I thought.

Straight after the race, Mike again flew to Deauville where

there was an air rally going on. Pete and Louise joined him the next day by car. Pete told a lovely story about Mike who was determined to go to the end-of-rally black-tie dinner but had no dinner jacket.

'As only Mike would,' Pete started, 'he asked around as to where he might hire a DJ – on a Sunday evening!' His hotel directed him to a dry-cleaner's where the proprietor proceeded to go through his customers' clothes until a large enough jacket and a long enough pair of non-matching trousers were found. All he had for his feet were his oil-stained, brown racing shoes. These he blackened up as best he could. With a borrowed tie, he managed, just, to look the part. The smile did the rest, and he was in.

On the Wednesday, the three of them went down to Reims, in anticipation of the Grand Prix de Reims – a non-Championship race. Again, there was a prize of 500 bottles of champagne for the fastest driver in practice. Stuart Lewis-Evans set a blistering time in his Vanwall and twice broke the lap record. This was beaten only by Fangio, lowering it three times further, but only by the smallest of margins. Stuart was awarded 200 bottles and Fangio 300. So typical of the man, Fangio gave 100 of these to his Maserati mechanics and then, more surprisingly, fifty bottles to the Ferrari mechanics with whom he'd worked so closely in the past.

Louise Collins told me a while later that she and the 'two boys' had spent the days leading up to this GP lounging around, reading novels, and drinking beer and wine. She said it had been a most relaxing and peaceful time.

However, immediately prior to the GP, there was a Formula Two race in which two popular drivers, both known to Mike, were killed. They were: Bill Whitehouse, a friend of Bernie Ecclestone and considered to be 'past it' at the grand age of forty-eighty, driving a Cooper, and the promising thirty-year-old American Herbert Mackay-Fraser or 'Mac', in a Lotus. Mac had also been entered for the Grand Prix. He'd only ever driven in one GP.

Mike started way back, on the fourth row of the grid, something he wasn't at all used to and was, I felt, indicative of his sadness in light of the latest tragedy.

Lewis-Evans and Musso got away quickly, with Fangio and then Mike running a little way behind. As Mike fought to stay on terms with Fangio, the duel between them was shaping up to be very similar to the same race of '53 – the encounter which Mike eventually and narrowly won. For the first few laps, Mike trailed in Fangio's slipstream and, by braking later, was able to pull up alongside, but he just couldn't get past – the Maserati's acceleration was too great.

According to Mike, Fangio would wait until they were just level, turn to Mike with a grin, and then floor the accelerator. And then, on lap 8, Fangio uncharacteristically spun, allowing Mike to shoot past, flicking a V-sign at his old rival as he did so. Mike's supremacy was short-lived for Fangio soon caught up and overtook Mike, only for Mike's Ferrari to develop terminal piston trouble. Blue smoke poured from the bonnet, and his race was over after only twenty-six laps.

The race was eventually won by Musso, on the sole surviving Ferrari, ahead of Behra on his Maserati. Vanwall drivers Lewis-Evans and his teammate Salvadori came in third and fifth. However, the race was again dominated by Maserati's 250F which took eight of the top eleven places. This was fast becoming a vintage year for Maserati, at exactly the same time the company's finances were falling apart.

Feeling disappointed, Mike attempted to fly home from Reims as soon as he could. However, a massive thunderstorm prevented him from getting any further than Amiens where he was obliged to spend the night.

Mike only had a day or two at home before he was due up in Liverpool for the British Grand Prix. He was in a bloody mood. It was all: 'Bloody Ferrari'…'No bloody safety'…'Bloody Tavoni'…'Bloody Musso', and so forth. This last one was relatively recent. Ferrari's strategy of playing all his drivers off the others was seriously effective, especially where Musso was concerned. Musso wasn't at all happy about his *Italian* team having two English drivers, and Pete and Mike thought that Musso sometimes was given favourable treatment by the management, or at least by the mechanics. Mike believed it was no coincidence that Musso's car finished the Reims GP when none of the other Ferraris did, and had bettered them in the French GP. It was a schism that was only to worsen as time went on.

Naturally, I attended the British GP. I drove up to Aintree with a couple of the Members. I am pleased to say that whilst there was plenty of racing drama, it was all of the right kind, with no serious crashes. The Vanwalls were still in good form and were more than a match for the Italians. We joked amongst ourselves that there wasn't likely to be a bad outcome for us.

Fangio was suffering from some sort of tummy bug so victory was most likely to go to either a British car or a British driver, or both. For some reason, we'd not factored in Jean Behra who had recovered from a road accident and really was too good to overlook.

From the off, Stirling's Vanwall led Behra's Maserati, with Mike and Pete in hot pursuit. Stirling's car eventually developed a misfire, and so he took over Tony Brooks's car. We'd heard that Tony wasn't fully recovered from his Le Mans crash. It had only been a month since the accident, and so this was always on the cards. Behra duly inherited the lead and began to look invincible. Stirling was down in ninth position.

One of the Members, it may have been Tubby, said, 'Don't worry, chaps, it's only a matter of time before the Frenchman breaks his car.'

We all drank to that, of course, and, what's more, that's exactly what did happen. Behra's clutch disintegrated. Mike inherited the lead, which caused me to rashly propose another round of beers. No sooner had I bought the round than Mike came in with a puncture. Apparently, he'd run over bits of broken clutch.

Moss, meanwhile, had not been gathering any: he'd been positively flying round, carving through the field and setting new lap records. Whilst Mike was in the pits, Stirling overtook Lewis-Evans resulting in a terrific roar from the crowd.

Briefly, it seemed as if Vanwall might finish first and second, and then Lewis-Evans's Vanwall conked out, leaving Musso to take second place, and Mike, with a replaced wheel, to pick up third. From a British perspective, it was a fantastic day for not only had Stirling won his home GP but a British-built car had finally won a World Championship race – the first to do so since a Sunbeam in 1924. The green cars had finally made it.

A few of us jostled to get to see the prize-giving. The atmosphere was carnivalesque despite the crowd being smaller than anticipated. This was due to it being the first day of a week-long busmen's strike in which 100,000 drivers went out on strike demanding a rise of a pound a week.

I still have the dog-eared black and white photograph I took of

Stirling and Tony Brooks being presented with the winner's trophy – a large silver cup. Looking at it now, the first thing I notice is their faces. They are comically blackened by a combination of road dirt, oil and exhaust fumes. Tony Brooks, the taller of the two by some margin, is wearing a dark shirt whereas Stirling is wearing a lighter-coloured one. Both men are smiling and, with their white teeth and large white patches around their eyes (protected by goggles), they resemble incompetently made-up Black and White Minstrels. At the time, I wouldn't have given it a second thought. It was the look of every post-race driver. Full-face helmets were still more than a decade away.

I'd like to say that Mike was pleased for Stirling but that wouldn't be entirely true. Stirling's consistency and fluency as a driver were winning him a lot of professional and public approbation. As far as Mike was concerned, Stirling had just 'got lucky' going to Vanwall when they'd finally made a fast, mostly reliable car. He may have been jealous of Stirling's success but, fortunately, Mike was generally pleased with his own efforts. He'd been clocking up far too many 'DNF's – Did Not Finishes – for his liking which, in his opinion, could all be attributed to Ferrari, whereas when the car lasted he would usually finish in the top four. And, in fairness, that was a reasonable summation. Mike was still a very quick driver, by anyone's measure.

Chapter Twenty-One

Flying Fangio

The teams had a fortnight to anticipate the German GP, which was to be held at the Nurburgring in August. The Collinses first went down to Dartmouth to spend a few days aboard their boat Genie Maris before driving over to Germany. There they were to stay with Wolfgang Alexander Albert Eduard Maximilian Reichsgraf (Count) Berghe von Trips, or 'Taffy' as we all knew him, at his parents' small ancestral castle complete with two moats, parks and gardens.

Even though Taffy was out of hospital, he was still not in any shape to drive but was much buoyed by their visit. Mike was never as close to Taffy as Pete had become, although there was no animosity between them. It was simply that Taffy was a German, albeit not a stereotypical one for he had a droll, mischievous sense of humour.

Mike remained in England until it was time to fly out to Cologne with, I seem to remember, his batteries fully recharged. The press had been hungry for interviews and photographs, all of which Mike relished.

The German GP of '57 was a classic. There are numerous detailed reports of how this was the greatest demonstration of on-the-limit driving by the reigning champion, Fangio. From what I heard, it wasn't too shabby an effort by Mike or Pete, either. For half the race, the two friends tried in vain to close the gap on Fangio who had established a decent lead. Fortunately, the Vanwalls were not set up well for this undulating circuit and, even in the hands of Stirling, Tony and Stuart, they weren't ever in contention.

Fangio was obliged to take a pit stop of nearly a minute while the mechanics changed the rear wheels and refuelled his car. Fangio actually got out of his car and had a drink. Mike told me afterwards that because Fangio had lost so much time the whole team believed it was impossible for him to regain his lead. He'd have needed to be lapping eight seconds or so per lap, every lap, to stand a chance. Having received information from the pit boards that Fangio was forty-eight seconds behind, Pete signalled to Mike that he would be happy with second, indicating Mike should take the victory. Although not wittingly taking their feet off the gas, the next information they received was that Fangio was only thirty-six seconds behind. They were incredulous. How had he managed to gain twelve seconds in one lap when they were driving so well?

Mike and Pete pulled out all the stops, and yet Fangio kept eating into their lead. He broke the lap record ten times. For those who were lucky enough to be there, they saw the Old Man driving like a man possessed. Even Mike said he'd never seen anything like it. The car was often sideways, on two wheels, off the track...even airborne. Fangio reeled them in like an expert fisherman, beating Mike to the line by 3.6 seconds, with Pete a further thirty-two seconds behind.

When Mike congratulated him, Fangio said, 'I did things out there I have never done before, and I don't ever want to drive like that again.' An impressive drive by any standards, but from a driver in his late forties – amazing!

It turned out that Fangio never did drive like that again for, after the German, he had established a practically unassailable points lead and went on to take his fifth and final World Championship. During the 1950s, in addition to five outright victories, Fangio came a close second in 1950 and 1953, and was forced out of practically the whole of 1952 due to an accident in which he suffered a broken neck. His record of Formula 1 races entered and won – twenty-four outright wins from fifty-two races entered – remains unbeaten.

After the race, Mike said, 'I tell you what, Tom, no matter how long I live, no matter what I do, or don't do, I'll never be in the same class as Fange. He's simply incredible.'

That German GP was Juan Fangio's showcase race, and Mike and Pete would talk enthusiastically about it for months afterwards.

Chapter Twenty-Two

Ferrari Favouritism

Mike offered to fly Pete and Louise up to Malmo in Sweden for the next GP. The first leg to Hamburg, where they stayed overnight, was uneventful. When they took off the next morning, the plane reached about 2,000 feet before the engine died. Mike decided to turn straight back and glide back to land. As he did so, the engine began firing but only on half the cylinders. There was no radio to warn the control tower of his actions, and so he picked out the longest runway and brought the plane down, much too fast. Local mechanics diagnosed that dirt had got into the fuel lines and blocked a main jet. When it was all ready to be tested, Mike rang the control tower and asked for permission to do a test flight.

The controller agreed, adding, 'That was a pretty hair-raising thing you did just then!'

Mike apologised and explained the reasons for his actions. The controller admitted he'd been quite anxious, but probably not half as anxious as the captain of the Convair coming in to land on the same runway but in the opposite direction.

Mike said he never even saw the Convair. Of course, when Mike was hamming up this story, he'd omit specifying which model of Convair it was, for the most notorious Convair was the 'B-36' Peacemaker, an absolute monster with six 28-cylinder engines and a wingspan of 230 feet, designed to carry nuclear bombs! I asked him directly what type of Convair it was, and he said it was most likely a 440 Metropolitan – a relatively small fifty-seater passenger plane.

The three friends spent two days in Malmo before hiring a car and driving down to Kristianstad for the GP. Mike was, by all accounts, in a cheerful frame of mind before the race, which was probably just as well. Upon arrival, he found he was to be partnered with

Luigi again despite the management being cognisant of the growing tension between them. Then Mike managed to repeat his accident of the previous Swedish GP by driving into a cornfield, albeit this time in a Ferrari rather than a Jaguar. Bernard Cahier (the photographer and friend) had told Mike in advance that he'd be waiting for him by the cornfield in order to capture the repeat performance. Mike's reply was unprintable. When Mike looked around, he was relieved not to see any photographers. Bernard, however, was as good as his word: he took his photographs from a helicopter. To be fair, this time the accident was entirely due to the Ferrari's failing brakes.

To compound matters, the pit stops had become a shambles, mostly because the mechanics were feeling the pressure of failure. The team had so far failed to win a single GP, a situation very unfamiliar to Ferrari. After Luigi had also driven into a cornfield and the car's rear brakes had gone completely, Mike and Luigi still managed a respectable fourth place. The race was won by Stirling and Jean Behra in a big Maserati, with Pete and Phil Hill second in their Ferrari.

If Mike was already feeling ill-disposed towards Ferrari in general, and Musso in particular, it was about to get a lot worse. The whole Formula One shebang traipsed down to Italy for the Pescara GP. However, when Mike and Pete pitched up at Modena, they learnt that Ferrari was still sulking about his treatment over the Mille Miglia affair. As a consequence, he was sticking to his guns that no Ferrari would ever again race on Italian soil. The Englishmen were accordingly dismissed and, as their next race was not for nearly a month, they returned home. Once home, they heard that Ferrari, who'd been the recipient of several emotional phone calls from one particular driver, had partly relented and had decided to send one car to Pescara. Its driver was to be Luigi Musso.

On the morning of Saturday 17 August, the day before the race, a peripheral Member, Nick Syrett, and I found Mike stomping around the TT Garage. We duly kidnapped him and went off to The Bush for a couple of 'sharpeners'.

A few beers, brunch, always a film, and then more beers had become a bit of ritual on the Saturdays when Mike wasn't racing. That morning, he wasn't in the mood – he was pensive and still mightily pissed off with Enzo Ferrari.

'He's a conniving bastard, that man. Why Musso over me or Pete?'

'Because he's an Italian...?' replied Nick, with a smile.

'It's bloody favouritism, that's what it is. If we'd had exactly the same cars, and the same mechanics as Musso, we'd both have more points than him.'

That was the heart of it. Musso had amassed sixteen points to Mike's thirteen and Pete's eight and a half, and here was an unopposed opportunity for Musso to jump further ahead – as much as nine points, if he was to win the race, and bag the fastest lap.

I was certain Mike was right. Ferrari was forever playing drivers off against each other and showing favouritism. I was tempted to point out that Pete had been Enzo's favourite up until he got married, but decided to be more diplomatic.

'Look,' I said, 'if present form's anything to go by, Stirling or Fange will win anyway. The other Vanwalls'll be right up there, and then there's Behra and the Yanks who are also in with a shout.'

'Yeah, yeah, I know all that, but even if Musso gets fourth, that's still three more points.'

'He can't win though, can he?' I asked.

'No, he can't, not now. The Old Man's out of sight. But second is, or rather was, up for grabs.'

He was right to be angered, but there was little he could do about it in Farnham. I decided a change of venue might lighten proceedings, 'Ready for breakfast, chaps?'

With that, we downed our pints and strolled down to Deeley's, a greasy spoon on West Street, for a late brunch of sausages, egg, chips and baked beans. That seemed to do the trick. Within no time, we were back to happier topics: planes, girls and music. From Deeley's we piled into the Regal to watch *Woman in a Dressing Gown*, a new release starring Anthony Quayle and Sylvia Syms. We had been teasing each other beforehand that it was probably going to be racy. Naturally, it wasn't. But it was a good film, albeit a sad one. It was all about unhappy families and affairs, which made me think it hadn't been the best thing to take Mike to.

I needn't have worried for, when we came out, Mike said, 'Well, she was a bit of all right!'

'Who was? Sylvia Syms?' asked Nick.

'Absolutely. In fact, the other one wasn't so bad…for her age.' The 'other one', a married lady whose husband goes off with Sylvia's character, was Yvonne Mitchell who would have been all of forty-two. But I had to agree – she was still pretty attractive, despite being too well covered up by a dressing gown.

We marched back to the Duke of Cambridge for a few more pints and to play darts while we decided what mischief we'd get up to that evening. Mike invented some new rules for the darts which, as no one could quite follow them, assured him of victory. As was usual, by seven o'clock, we'd already had six pints (including two in The Bush) and felt we were just getting started.

I remember trying to find out what happened in the Pescara GP the following day. It wasn't easy, partly due to an all-day hangover and partly because the BBC only gave the briefest of headlines: 'Stirling wins a second Grand Prix for Vanwall – and for Britain. Fangio comes second, to clinch his record fifth World Championship.' Of Musso, there was no mention.

I had to wait until Monday to discover that Musso had retired halfway round, after his car burst its oil tank. He had been on the front row of the grid, alongside Stirling and Fangio, so Mike had, of course, been right to be concerned. There was no point in letting Mike know this as he would have telephoned Tavoni or someone else in the team immediately after the race to find out.

The papers made the race sound terrifically exciting. The sixteen-mile circuit, not dissimilar in length to Nurburgring, was comprised of closed coastal public roads which contained numerous tight bends and undulating sections. Although Pescara is about 100 miles east of Rome on the Adriatic coast, it attracted a massive crowd of over 200,000 spectators. By comparison, 125,000 spectators watched the 2012 British GP.

Whilst at work the following week, I was greatly looking forward to the weekend. The Members were going en masse to Goodwood where Mike would be presenting the Brooklands Memorial Trophy which he'd won back in '51. It was a cracking day for us as spectators, although there was also some participation – racing down there and on the way back, and at one point to see who could down a pint fastest.

Mike stayed really quite sober until after he'd presented the winner, a chap called Innes Ireland, with the trophy and a cheque for £75. He made up for it later. Although we took the mickey out of Mike, when it came to public speaking, and looking the part, he was bloody good. He was always engaging and generous with his praise.

As I looked at him, all spruced, immaculately groomed and smiley, I asked myself: is this a man who's in conflict with his employer; who's lost his dad and umpteen close friends in the last couple of years; been turned down by his truest love and who's suffering from a fatal kidney disease? A man who knows he'll soon be dead? There wasn't even a hint of his inner turmoil or frailty. I looked around at the audience. They loved him.

Chapter Twenty-Three

Moving Goalposts

Enzo Ferrari was still intent on boycotting all Italian motor sport and announced that his cars would not be attending the Italian GP at Monza. Mike encouraged Pete to see if he could change the Old Man's mind. Pete duly went to see him and, in a forthright manner, asserted that Enzo's real problem was that he was still upset about the loss of Dino, and that he should start living in the present.

Mike asked how he'd reacted.

'He just sat there and said nothing. It was awful. I don't think he'll ever speak to me again. I'm probably out of a job,' Pete replied.

Far from being out of job, Enzo summoned Pete and Louise to his office the next day, thanked Pete profusely for his advice, and insisted that Pete and Louise move into a villa he owned on the outskirts of Maranello. He also announced that the team would race at Monza. What's more, a few days later, the Ferraris caught up with the Collinses in Milan and presented Louise with a large three-diamond ring, apparently without explanation. Pete was obviously right back in favour.

His unexpected break over, Mike flew back to Italy once more, headed for Monza. He had hoped that, during the intervening period, the Ferrari engineers might have found a way for their cars to be more competitive, if by nothing more than switching to disc brakes. However, the moment practice started, it was apparent that they were no match for the Maseratis, let alone the Vanwalls. Mike was kicking himself for not staying with Tony Vandervell. The sensation of the practice sessions was Stuart Lewis-Evans who finished up on pole, ahead of teammates Stirling and Tony Brooks, all of them driving Vanwalls.

What happened next was farcical. The standard Grand Prix grid formation internationally was 3-2-3, which would have meant the three British green Vanwalls lining up on the front row, ahead of all the Italian red cars – at Monza, the home of Italian motor sport! The race officials therefore decided that the 'new' formation for this GP was going to be 4-3-4, thus allowing Fangio's red Maserati to appear on the front row. When Mike told me this, I was speechless. I asked him what they'd have done if a couple of BRMs and Connaughts had all hit form at the same time. Would they have made it 8-7-8 and widened the track accordingly?

Pete, in his distinctive white shirt, was the quickest of the Ferraris at seventh, giving him a second-row start, whereas Mike, Musso and Taffy were all lined up behind. Mike refused to acknowledge Luigi as they sat in the heat waiting for the off.

The Vanwalls were pressed hard by the old hands of Fangio and Behra, but Stirling was able to control the race from the twenty-first lap to the chequered flag on the eighty-seventh.

Mike had said his only hope of some championship points coming his way was through the retirements of other drivers, and so he'd 'just keep pedalling for all he was worth'. When both Stuart's and Tony's Vanwalls stopped for long periods and Pete and Jean Behra and Harry Schell all dropped out with engine problems, Mike found by the sixtieth lap he was in third place, by default. All he needed was for his car to remain intact.

Petrol started spraying everywhere. Mike knew it couldn't be a repeat of the Naples incident, because Ferrari had done away with fuel pressure gauges. When he brought the car into the pits, it was found to be a fractured main fuel pipe. As Mike waited for his car to be repaired, he could see his potential four points slipping away – four vital points to put him above Musso in the championship points table.

Taffy's Ferrari was still going well enough and had inherited third place. Mike urged Girolamo Amorotti (whom everyone addressed as 'Mino' – but Mike wrote as *Meano*), a Ferrari henchman and sometime technical director, to allow him to take over Taffy's car. It wasn't that Mike thought he was going to finish better than Taffy; it was simply that Taffy had no points whatsoever, and therefore the four points would be neither here nor there to him, but could be vital to Mike. Mino refused. Mike was hopping mad, and showed it which, with hindsight, was probably not sensible. He told me they'd had a 'right set-to' – which, knowing Mike, would have included a fair smattering of Anglo-Saxon vocabulary, if not lapel grabbing. All of which would, of course, have got back to Maranello.

Mino happened to be a dear old friend of Enzo, and was a wealthy retired landowner. By '57, he'd been involved with Scuderia Ferrari for several years, holding various job titles, but effectively was now a loyal lieutenant to Enzo. It is said he never took a salary from Ferrari. At Monza, at that race, he was second in command to Tavoni. That Mino had never raced and looked like a stuffed shirt – always a white shirt, bow tie and 'stupid' round cap – really irked Mike.

The race reports made me feel sorry for wee Stuart Lewis-Evans. He was a funny-looking chap: slight of build, with a large head, and a crooked boxer's nose, which oversailed an occasional pencil moustache or goatee beard, but he was proving to be very competitive indeed.

My friend Nick took a picture once of him and me and captioned it: 'Little and Large'. He was five foot four to my six foot five. I'm not sure whether I look like a giant, or he a dwarf. In terms of being able to fit into racing cars, and weighing less than nine stone, Mike was jealous of his physique. 'The little blighter's got a twelve-gallon advantage over me,' he once remarked. But, of course, there's more to being a quick driver than having a weight advantage – as Fangio, who was no lightweight, proved time and again.

Stuart had served his apprenticeship in the little Coopers of Formula Three – six straight successful years – before he joined Connaught in May of '57 for his inaugural Formula One race. Four months later, having fleetingly represented Ferrari at Le Mans, he was on pole with Vanwall. He was more than just a quick driver: he was a likeable, self-effacing man who deserved a long and illustrious career.

Chapter Twenty-Four

Whacky Races

Mike flew back to England for the Daily Express International Trophy at Silverstone, a fixture which had been postponed from May due to the Suez Crisis. This was quite a departure from Mike's day job and another eagerly awaited Members' day out. Here, he'd be competing with other top-flight drivers, albeit in 'touring cars' – meaning lightly-modified ordinary saloon cars such as Jaguars, Fords, etc.

The day dawned beautifully bright but there was a cold wind. We knew it was going to be an unfair contest as the 'new' Jaguar 3.4-litre was superior to everything else in the field. And although this model of Jaguar was now Mike's own regular transport, he was not going to have it all his own way for also driving Jags were Archie Scott-Brown, Ivor Bueb and Duncan Hamilton. I wouldn't have missed it for the world.

Archie (he of the missing hand) was driving brilliantly. He and Mike were both vying for supremacy, and they shared the fastest lap of the race. It was fantastic to watch Mike being put under this sort of pressure. From a spectator's point of view, it was terrific to watch these softly-sprung, heavy saloons being pushed so hard through the corners it looked as if they would roll right over. Disc brakes were not permitted, and their drum brakes were barely up to the task. Archie experienced complete brake failure as he went into Woodcote Corner at ninety miles an hour. He whacked it into second gear, the engine screamed as the revs shot up, and somehow he managed to get safely round, albeit in a cloud of brake fluid smoke before coming to a halt. The other Jaguar drivers had more luck, but no one was able to catch Mike. Duncan finished eleven seconds behind him and Ivor nearly a minute later.

To see the joy on Mike's face was fantastic. I think I enjoyed that victory every bit as much as he did. It seemed like real racing, only slower and safer and somehow a lot more fun. The Members were unanimous: it was the best racing we'd seen all year. And, from Mike's perspective, there was none of the big team politics, scheming and backbiting which seemed to be happening increasingly with Ferrari.

While Mike was back home, Pete and Louise remained in Italy in anticipation of the Modena Grand Prix, for which Enzo had only selected Pete and Luigi. No clue was given as to whether these were Ferrari's two favourite drivers or whether Mike had blotted his copybook.

For the race, Pete was in a small-engined Formula Two car and so did exceptionally well to finish fourth. Fortunately, championship points were not at stake, so Musso's coming second to Jean Behra was no more than an irritant to the English contingent.

With the Spanish GP cancelled, Mike had to wait three weeks before his next race, the Moroccan GP at Casablanca. Pete and Louise meanwhile remained in Maranello doing up their grace and favour villa.

However, they did get together with Mike in London for a special event: Stirling's marriage to Katie Molson. Whatever their alleged differences, Stirling had invited both Mike and Pete as ushers. The late afternoon wedding took place at St George's Church in Eaton Square, and the reception at The Savoy Hotel. The wedding attracted huge media attention. Pictures appeared all over the press, not only of Stirling and Katie but of all the famous racing drivers present as well. Apparently, the crush of photographers outside the church was something the like of which even Mike had never seen. Mike and Pete were photographed looking particularly mischievous, despite the formality of their morning suits, top hats and pipes. More salacious pictures could have been snapped well after midnight as at least two of the high-profile guests left The Savoy in pairs having arrived alone, Mike being one of them. Today's paparazzi would have had a field day.

I would have loved to have been invited but, although it felt like I knew Stirling – like we all feel we know our favourite radio presenter – he probably wouldn't have remembered my name if we'd have passed one another on the street.

When I was pumping Mike for information about the wedding, such as who was there, what was the crumpet like, etc, he stunned me by saying that Pete was thinking about giving up racing. Mike told me that Pete was thinking about building an American-style house on an elevated site near Kidderminster and possibly about going into business with Donald Healey. The two of them would build fast cars and speedboats in the Bahamas ('of all places') and export them to Florida. I asked how Pete could be in two places at the same time. Mike said that he thought it was all hot air. He said that behind all these grandiose plans was really Pete's deep-seated concern about his own mortality, something they both shared. Pete, he said, was truly happily married and didn't relish the prospect of either dying soon or becoming paralysed.

In an interesting twist to the team selection saga, Enzo decided to leave Musso out of the team for the Casablanca GP. Mike wasn't sure of Ferrari's motives, but it was well-judged. Mike had been talking about telling Ferrari where to go. After all he'd only managed fourth place in the Championship, and now both the latest Vanwalls and the Maseratis were demonstrably quicker than Ferraris, he was sorely tempted to jump ship. Plus he and Luigi were barely tolerating each other. However, Pete felt he couldn't possibly leave Enzo, having received such generous treatment. In the end, the draw of staying with Pete as his teammate trumped all other considerations, and Mike signed up for the 1958 season.

As it turned out, Luigi must have been mightily relieved not to go to Casablanca, for most of the drivers immediately contracted Asian flu. It affected some more than others. Poor Stirling was very unwell and had to be flown back to London on the day of the race.

The Moroccans treated the visiting drivers extremely well, and Mike raved about their hospitality, especially that of the King of Morocco, even though Mike too fell victim to the flu. He said that he left the royal reception and went straight to bed, swallowed pills, and hoped to sweat it out.

In an effort to be more competitive, Ferrari gave Mike and Pete Formula Two cars with new V6 engines, much smaller and lighter cars than they had been driving.

However, neither of them should have started as both were still feeling decidedly unwell. The 'Ain Diab' circuit was brand new, built in just six weeks, and comprised a combination of public roads and purpose-built track. Pole position and third grid position were again occupied by the Vanwalls of Tony Brooks and Stuart Lewis-Evans. Between them was Jean Behra in his Maserati. Pete and Mike were fourth and sixth on the grid. Pete got off to a terrific start and briefly led the race. Unfortunately, his violent coughing caused him to spin out of control three times. Twice, he was fortunate to stay on the track. On the third time, he hit the straw bales and his race was over. Mike fared even less well. His braking was all over the place. Realising his judgement was seriously impaired, when Harry Schell alerted him to oil pouring from his car, Mike was only too pleased to retire and take himself off to bed again. Jean Behra won the race by thirty seconds from Stuart Lewis-Evans. Behra's victory in the legendary Maserati 250F marked the last ever win for a Maserati in Formula One – not that any of us knew that at the time.

I remember reading reports to the effect that Fangio had had a 'lacklustre' race, finishing an absurdly lowly fourth. My take was the exact opposite. He'd already sewn up the Championship, he was feeling terrible from the effects of the flu, and yet he recorded the fastest lap of the race. I particularly liked that – he didn't put pressure on himself for the full two and half hours – in one lap, he just quietly demonstrated how much better he was than everyone else.

There was the inevitable accident, of course. Jean Lucas, who'd started at the back of the grid, was blinded by the setting sun and consequently drove his Maserati off the track. It hit a spectator's car, bounced into a group of spectators, and left him badly injured. I like to think of him as one of the Fortunates. He recuperated, never raced again, and lived to the ripe old age of eighty-six.

The last race of the season was something of an afterthought, and it was to be staged in Caracas, Venezuela, a week after the Moroccan. Notwithstanding that the cars had to be shipped over there some weeks before, it remained a logistical challenge for the teams, but it was considered important as it would settle the Sports Car Championship. This was finely poised between Ferrari and Maserati, and in which there was only three points' difference – in Ferrari's favour.

Mike, still feeling unwell, flew straight to Lisbon taking Pete and Louise as passengers. They had an overnight stop in Lisbon before catching a plane to Caracas, the capital of Venezuela, and surprisingly close to Caribbean islands such as Grenada. Mike was blown away by Caracas. It was a newly oil-rich city where money flowed like the oil out of the ground. There was stunning ultra-modern architecture, newly constructed motorways, and conspicuous consumption by the nouveau riche. The latest, flashiest 'Yankie mobiles' were everywhere. Mike told me that I'd be shocked at the attitude of the people he met. If anything broke or malfunctioned, they would just throw it away as it was cheaper and easier to buy a new one rather than get it mended. Mike was equally conscious of, and affected by, the poorer citizens – those with no access to this wealth.

Once again, Mike and the Collinses experienced extraordinary hospitality, this time by the British air attaché and his wife, who picked them up from the airport and put them up in luxurious hotel accommodation. Shortly after arriving, the lads went to inspect the circuit. They were astonished to find that it incorporated all sorts of roads, from broad motorway intersections and flyovers to narrow single carriageways, level crossings and high concrete barriers. The other drivers agreed it looked dangerous and asked their representative body, the UPPI, to protest. Some changes were effected, and it was only good fortune that none of the inevitable accidents had fatal consequences.

I heard numerous anecdotes about double-booked hotel accommodation, impounded cars, entry taxes, no car transporters – necessitating the cars to be driven from the port to the circuit, and needing licence plates, etc! My favourite was Stirling and Tony having their passports confiscated. They refused to drive unless they were returned, which happily they were.

During practice, Phil Hill in his Ferrari took a wrong turning and only realised that he'd left the circuit proper when he encountered a petrol tanker and several cars coming straight towards him.

The grid looked promising: Behra and Stirling on pole and second, both in big V8 Maseratis, and Mike and Pete third and fourth in their Ferraris. Both teams had sent four cars and a full complement of drivers. For Maserati, which was in dire financial straits, this was effectively the last roll of the dice. It was rumoured that Maserati owed $155,000 for tyres alone. When the Ferrari boys heard that their principal rivals, the Maserati drivers, had been told on the eve of the race to 'please take it easy on the cars because they've all been sold', they literally fell about laughing. How, they asked, were they meant to win the Championship for Maserati, in order to save the company, by taking it easy?

Race day dawned hot and bright, ideal for racing, but even before the start, one of the four Maseratis, Tony Brooks's, went out with a defective gearbox. The pressure on the three remaining Maseratis became all the greater.

The next casualty was Masten Gregory, who got off to a great start in his Maserati, and was being pursued by Ferraris. He went into a corner on the second lap too fast, slid into some sandbags, rolled over twice, and landed upside down. Mike saw this happen. He said it was as if it happened in slow motion. He was terrified for his American friend. Masten had struggled to get out while the car was airborne but had failed. Fortunately, he was able to crawl out from under the car, his face covered in blood, before the car caught alight. The only reason he didn't die was the rollover bar he'd insisted be fitted the previous day.

Stirling then had a lucky escape, as did the driver of an AC Ace sports car. Stirling, who'd been making incredible progress after a stalled start, had been hammering along at about 170mph when the little AC, estimated to be travelling at just over 100mph, suddenly pulled over in front of him. Stirling's Maserati rammed the Ace up into the air and into a lamp post which crudely cut the car in two. Mike saw a cloud of dust and thought he saw two cars fly through the air, not one that had been bisected. How the American driver, Hap Dressel, wasn't killed, Mike said he'd never know.

Stirling, having been given the once-over by the medics, insisted he was still fit to drive and so went back to the pits. Stirling's teammate Harry Schell brought in his and Behra's Maserati. He saw Behra hop in and heard Ugolini, Maserati's team manager, shout, 'Go!'

Behra pressed the starter, and immediately the rear of the car was on fire. Flames shot out of the nozzle of the recently used petrol hose. Behra's clothes were ablaze. Behra threw himself out of the cockpit and landed heavily on the concrete floor, hurting himself as he did so. He suffered nasty burns to his neck and arms. Bertocchi, Maserati's chief mechanic, also sustained painful burns as he tried to combat the flames with an extinguisher. Mike had a ringside seat for all this drama as he was in the neighbouring pits taking a welcome drink. The fire had only lasted a few seconds, and the car still seemed driveable so, rather than ask Harry to go back out, Ugolini instructed Stirling to hop in. The latter was soon back complaining that the car was still on fire! As he got out, it was obvious that the seat was still smouldering and had singed the backside of his overalls. After more use of the extinguishers, poor Harry was despatched again. The car was still in a respectable third place, trailing the Ferrari of Mike and Pete.

The big Maserati was going well, and Harry managed to resume the lead. As he was about to lap Jo Bonnier's smaller Maserati on a bend, one of Jo's rear tyres burst. His car went sideways, struck Harry's, and smashed into a concrete lamp post. Anticipating an uncomfortable coming together with a lamp post, Jo decided to get out fast. Even while the car was travelling quickly, he wriggled out and fell heavily onto the circuit, in time to watch the upper part of the lamp post topple down onto the cockpit of the now driverless car.

The normally happy-go-lucky Harry was less lucky. His car slammed into a wall and burst into flames. He was able to get out, but not before his clothing was well alight. The innovation of fire-retardant drivers' suits was still a few years away. One quick-thinking spectator rushed over to Harry and threw a coat over him, smothering the flames. Although Harry suffered burns to his face and arms, this probably saved his life – or at least granted him the two more years before his fatal crash during practice at Silverstone.

With all four Maseratis out, the Ferrari could 'take it easy' for the remainder of the race to claim a comprehensive first to fourth victory. Pete and Phil took the chequered flag and Mike and Luigi claimed second place. It was a resounding success for Ferrari, a disaster for Maserati. Two weeks later, Maserati announced that it was retiring from Formula One due to crippling debts. It seemed a particularly sad announcement as Fangio had just won the driver's Championship with the firm's best car in years.

Mike's eagerly anticipated homecoming party had to be delayed by two days as he was forced to stop over in the Azores on his transatlantic flight. Apparently, the Constellation in which he and several of the drivers were flying developed control problems, and so they were forced to wait there for a substitute aeroplane. Mike said that the facilities on the island were basic, to say the least, with only one hut-like hotel with camp beds for them to sleep on. It must have been some contrast from their luxurious hotel in Caracas. However, their initial despondency was eventually completely reversed, initially by being shown an old black and white film, and later when a beautiful Spanish belly dancer was conjured up, and some alcohol consumed.

After a roller-coaster season, Mike was delighted with the prospect of six reasonably uninterrupted weeks before his next official engagement: Ferrari's annual lunch in Modena just before Christmas.

There were over 500 diners at the lunch, including drivers, trade representatives, journalists and numerous friends of the firm, but notably no Pete Collins who'd gone to America to spend Christmas with his in-laws, or women. Enzo was ebullient because Ferrari had won the Sports Car World Championship, and made a long and impassioned speech about the excellent prospects for the year ahead. Mike said it was dull there without Pete, and, without Pete, Ferrari definitely wouldn't have won the Sports Car Championship.

Mike also noted that nothing was said openly about '57 being the first year in which no Ferrari had won a Grand Prix race. He returned in a wistful mood, wondering whether he'd done the right thing, signing for the next season.

Chapter Twenty-Five

Jesus Launches Sputnik

No sooner were the Christmas decorations down than Mike was off to Argentina once again for the start of the new season. All through the autumn, the South American series had been in doubt: one minute on, the next cancelled. It was only confirmed by the sport's organizing body, the Commission Sportive Internationale (CSI), before Christmas. This caused a right furore as the two strongest British manufacturers, Vanwall and BRM, had no chance of getting their cars over there in time. The RAC registered a formal protest, demanding that the races be removed from the list of those which would contribute towards the Championships. The answer came back that they would consider the matter, once the races had taken place. As you can imagine, many on this side of the Channel took a very dim view of that. The Members were, naturally, measured in their response. It was, I think, Neil who said that was 'just typical of the effing French'.

Another talking point in racing circles – and therefore in the pub with Mike – were the changes being introduced by the CSI. The most significant of these changes, for the drivers, was that Grands Prix would now be shorter races: two hours or 300 kilometres, as opposed to three hours or 500 kilometres.

Almost as important was that from, hereon in, for a driver to score championship points, he needed to stay with the car in which he started. Although there was a lot of bitching about how Fangio had forever jumped in and out of others' cars, the Ferrari boys were almost as guilty. The general feeling was at least this would be a level playing field. Alcohol fuels were finally banned, and all teams would have to use high-octane aviation gasoline.

Mike thought that a shorter race, one without pit stops for fuel, might reduce the drama of a race and thus turn off spectators. Most of us felt that, in general, a two-hour race was plenty long enough, and that all the time the cars were of roughly similar performance there would still be plenty of drama. Of course, if someone had speculated that pit stop times might one day come down to below two and a half seconds, we'd have thought they were either joking or insane.

I'd spent a couple of extremely late post-pub whisky drinking sessions with Mike discussing his thoughts about the coming year, or more particularly about his prospects driving for Enzo again, given his love/hate relationship with the man. He was surprisingly optimistic. In his view, three things were changing for the better. Firstly, there was the new car – the Dino 246 – lighter and faster than big Ferraris of previous seasons. Secondly, there was standardisation of fuel which he felt would favour Ferrari. And thirdly, Fangio had announced his retirement.

'With the Old Man out of the way, it'll be between me, Pete and Moses,' he said.

'And Luigi...?'

'Not if Pete and I can help it,' was his ominous reply.

I welcomed his positivity, even if I couldn't quite share it. In a theoretical situation, where all the drivers had identical cars – and identical luck – I would have placed Stirling first, Pete second, with nothing to choose between Mike and Luigi, and even Tony Brooks and Stuart Lewis-Evans. Moreover, Harry Schell and Jean Behra were seldom ever also-rans. Even without *El Maestro*, the competition would be fierce, and Mike's health was only going in one direction.

Pete and Louise went directly to Buenos Aires from New York by boat, whereas Mike flew out with most of the Ferrari team from Italy. Mike had become adept at travelling all over the western world, packing lightly and moving off at a moment's notice but it's worth remembering that, in those days, many things were planned well in advance. There simply wasn't the opportunity to book things online or by fax. And whilst Mike was very resourceful, a lot of his travel arrangements were made for him by the team's management. In this instance, Mike had been given all his travel arrangements – times, places, flights, etc – when he attended the Christmas luncheon party.

For the first Grand Prix of '58, Stirling pitched up with a curious little car belonging to the 'privateer' Rob Walker (whose wealth was derived from Johnny Walker Scotch whisky). It was a 1.9-litre Cooper-Climax, nicknamed Sputnik III by the press – or Spunknik by us. Stirling himself appeared with a bandage over one eye after Katie had 'accidentally bashed him'. Accident, my foot, I thought.

The practice sessions were, as usual, dominated by Fangio who had entered a non-works' Maserati. I asked Mike why Fangio was still competing when he'd so publicly announced his retirement. Mike said that the race organisers had pleaded with Fangio to appear in front of his partisan home crowd as otherwise half the spectators would not have attended and the organisers would have lost a fortune. Fangio for the entrance gate was what Harry Potter is now to the box office. So marginal was the viability of the Argentine race, it was only staged twice over the ensuing twelve years.

Thankfully, this year's race was free of major accidents, although perhaps this was not so surprising given that there were only ten entrants, all top-flight drivers. Pete's race was over before it began, due to failure of a half shaft on the starting line. Fangio, after setting the fastest lap of the race, wasn't able to stay on the pace when his engine began to misfire. Mike fleetingly led, before experiencing oil pressure problems, plus he had a minor coming together with a driver called Menditeguy.

The big surprise to everyone was Stirling's victory. Credit must also go to the Coopers, the constructors, and Rob Walker as this was the first time a private entry had ever won a Grand Prix, and the first time a rear-engined car had won a Grand Prix since an Auto-Union before the war. Their Sputnik was quick, reliable, and, what's more, by Stirling conserving his tyres, didn't require a pit stop. The Ferraris were faster, but less reliable and hampered by needing to pit. Behind Stirling came Musso, then Mike, then Fangio.

After the race, there was quite a row. Tavoni believed Luigi could have won, if only he'd tried harder. Tavoni understood that Stirling's tyres had worn down to the canvas. He maintained that if Stirling had been harried a bit more, his tyres would have disintegrated. Luigi alleged that he didn't get any pit signals, protesting they were all for Mike. Pete rejected that, stating that he'd personally given Luigi updates on the time advantage Stirling had over him. This was undoubtedly the moment when the simmering resentments between the three drivers boiled over into something more overt, and quiet battle lines were drawn according to nationality. It may have been that night that Mike and Pete decided that, come what may, they would share their winnings fifty-fifty, thereby tacitly putting Luigi at a disadvantage.

It was ironic that the RAC had lobbied for these races not to count towards the Drivers' Championship, believing this would seriously damage Stirling's prospects as his Vanwall was not present. Now that Stirling had potentially got off to a flying start with eight points, the RAC was seriously wrong-footed. Fortunately, BRM, who'd also protested, sportingly withdrew its objection, and the decision was made to allow the Argentine to retain its World Championship status. That was one piece of good fortune to Stirling.

The system of awarding World Championship points according to where a driver finished was not so different from today. For first place, it was eight points; for second, it was six; for third, it was four; for fourth, it was three; and for fifth, it was two. I've never understood why one point wasn't awarded for coming sixth, but I'm sure they had their reasons.

With a week off before the 1,000km, Mike sought out Pete and Louise who had checked out of the team's hotel and were staying at a friend's 'jolly nice house' in the Buenos Aires suburbs. Much to Mike's delight, the friend, Tito Reynal, also had a Piper Apache aeroplane, complete with pilot. It was decided they would fly over to Uruguay for the day, to swim, sunbathe and sail. Knowing his fair skin was susceptible to sunburn, Mike read the papers under the shade of a large beach parasol for the four or so hours they were on the beach at Punta del Esta. He maintained he could only have been in the sun for a few minutes. Back then, there was no appreciation of how the sun's UV rays might penetrate cotton.

The pilot allowed Mike to fly part of the way back, a joy tempered by a sensation like pins and needles in his legs. By the time Mike reached his hotel, his legs were swollen and really hurting, so much so that, in the night, he called out a doctor. Mike said the doctor gave him 'some sort of jollop' to put on them. The sunburn was so bad he spent the next two days in bed, missing the first day of practice.

Tavoni wouldn't hear of Mike totally missing qualifying and insisted that he participate. Because of the length of the race, the

Ferrari drivers were again paired off: Pete and Phil Hill (the two fastest in qualifying), Luigi Musso and Gendebien, and Taffy and Mike. Mike said no one was very sympathetic towards him as it was deemed self-inflicted. Tavoni at least accepted that Mike could act as a relief driver to Taffy, perhaps driving only half-hour stints.

Feeling and looking dreadful, Mike watched as the cars tore away from the start. At the first corner, there was a big cloud of dust, signalling an accident of some sort. Luigi had shunted Trintignant and then smashed into a concrete wall in front of the grandstand. Luigi took a whack on his crash helmet but otherwise he was in one piece. The car, however, was a write-off. Mike immediately went to find Tavoni and suggested that Gendebien, Luigi's co-driver, should take his place, supporting Taffy. Tavoni agreed, and Mike was off the hook.

Apart from the novelty of seeing Fangio spin off and terminally damage his Maserati, the rest of the race was uneventful. Pete and Phil led from start to chequered flag. Taffy and Gendebien took second, and third went to Stirling who competed in a tiny 1600cc Porsche (roughly half the engine size of the V12 Ferraris).

Notwithstanding that Mike said his legs continued to be uncomfortable, he still managed to pick up a 'very nice' Argentinian girl called Martha. She acted as chauffeuse and physiotherapist – and she had a penthouse apartment with its own tiny swimming pool! I was so green when he told me that, and then, to make matters worse, he showed me a picture of her. Mike said he was soon feeling better. I bet he was.

The third and final race of what was known as the Temporada Series was the Buenos Aires Grand Prix which was to be run in two heats. Stirling entered the Sputnik again, and this time everyone took him seriously. It was a twisting circuit, and it was raining, both things which suited the little Cooper.

For once, Mike got off to great start and led Fangio into the first corner. He expected to see Stirling before long, but there was no sign of him. Apparently, just as Stirling was negotiating the first bend, 'Jesus walloped him up the arse in a Chevrolet Special'! Fortunately, Stirling was unhurt but his car was undrivable. This Jesus turned out to be Jesus Iglesias, an Argentinian driver of limited experience. Mike led the first heat from start to finish. His teammates were less successful. Pete broke a half shaft again at the start, and Taffy caught a big puddle and smashed into a concrete post – thankfully sustaining only minor injuries.

The second heat from Scuderia Ferrari's point of view was a disaster. In theory, Mike should have had victory in the bag, only this time it was his turn to have a half shaft break on the starting line. 'One's so pumped up for a race,' Mike said, 'that when something like that happens it's as if your body doesn't know how to react. The flag drops, the adrenalin is flowing, and then you just sit there, going nowhere. It's quite the strangest sensation.' Tavoni, he said, was very understanding, adding that he probably wouldn't have been had it not happened twice before to 'Precious Pete'.

Mike wandered out onto the track to see what was happening. Musso had managed to overtake Fangio but needed to extend his lead if he was to win on aggregate. Mike tried to signal Luigi not to go overly fast and risk spinning off. Mike said the silly bugger ignored his gestures and, if anything, seemed to speed up. 'I'm sure he thought that I didn't want him to win.'

A few laps later, when Fangio was beginning to catch him, Luigi duly went too fast into a corner and spun off. He did manage to get back onto the track but finished in third place behind Fangio and Menditeguy.

That evening, Mike and the Collinses went to a nightclub called the Riviera, and met up with the likes of Jean Behra, Jo Bonnier and Horace Gould. There, they had a rare old booze-up and ended up being thrown out – quite politely, apparently. After a full day of recuperation, the friends, together with the rest of the Ferrari contingent, flew back to Milan. To pass the time, Mike played gin rummy against Luigi for most of the flight, and was fortunate enough not to lose more than a dollar.

From Milan, Mike flew back to London while Pete and Louise went down to Ferrari HQ by train. A few days later, Pete and Louise drove across the mountains to the little Mediterranean city of Viareggio with the express intention of buying a boat. They commissioned a forty-three-foot motor launch on which they planned to live in Monte Carlo harbour, before returning to Ferrari's fold at Modena.

Normally, when I caught up with Mike, the first thing we'd

speak about was the race in which he'd taken part – either that or crumpet. But not this time. That very afternoon, there had been an horrific air accident which later was simply referred to as the Munich Air Disaster. It was a huge story. The whole of the Manchester United football team had been on board a flight bound for Manchester from Belgrade. The plane with its complement of thirty-eight passengers and six crew had stopped over at Munich Airport for fuel. It was snowing at Munich, and there was slush on the runway. Twice, take-off had to be aborted. On the third attempt, the plane failed to reach sufficient speed to get airborne and careered on, ploughed through a perimeter fence, across a road, and ended up crashing into a house, tearing off a wing in the process. Of course, we didn't know any of those details when we were having a beer in The Bull. All we knew was what we'd heard on the radio: twenty passengers and crew had died, including seven Manchester United players.

As a pilot himself, Mike speculated why such an accident might have happened. He assumed, wrongly, that it must have been engine failure. As far as I was concerned, flying simply provided me with yet another reason to worry about Mike. His response was predictable: 'Flying's a sight safer than what I do for a living. You know, McBride, you worry too much.'

Chapter Twenty-Six

Headline Priorities

The Cuban GP held at the end of February carried no championship points and, perhaps for that reason, Scuderia Ferrari chose not attend. It turned out to be a fortuitous decision for the likes of Pete and Mike. Some non-works' Ferraris were entered, whose drivers included Stirling Moss, Masten Gregory and a chap called Cifuentes. The man to beat, still, was the previous year's winner, Fangio, in his Maserati.

Cuba was a troubled country. Fidel Castro's revolution was just burgeoning, and the rebels were strongly opposed to Batista turning Cuba into a playground for rich Americans – an alternative to Las Vegas with handsome hotels and glittering casinos. They took exception to the vast expense of staging a Grand Prix when the country's unemployment levels stood at 500,000.

On the eve of the race, Fangio was walking through the lobby of the Hotel Lincoln on his way to the dining room when he was accosted by a man brandishing a pistol. The man declared himself to be a member of the 26th of July Movement and then ushered Fangio outside to a waiting car. The rebels asked Fangio for the whereabouts of Stirling Moss. 'You mustn't take Stirling. He's on his honeymoon,' was Fangio's quick-witted and untruthful reply. Surprisingly, they decided to stick with just Fangio.

It is said that they treated Fangio deferentially and, although he was temporarily kept under lock and key, he was given a fine steak dinner and a television to watch. Stirling and the other drivers had national guards posted outside their bedrooms who were ordered to check on the occupants at three-hourly intervals through the night. Not the ideal preparation for a Grand Prix.

Immediately prior to the start of the race, Fangio was delivered to the Argentinian embassy in Havana, safe and well after his twenty-seven-hour abduction, but too late to take part.

The race itself, so typical of South American events, was well attended and poorly organised. The course was run over the seafront roads starting in central Havana. Stirling and Masten quickly established a commanding lead, and were well out in front on the fifth lap when Cifuentes, in another Ferrari, hit a patch of oil, skidded off the circuit, and slewed straight into a group of spectators at 100mph. The 150,000 spectators were spread out all along the circuit, sometimes with no protection between them and the speeding cars. Cifuentes's Ferrari killed seven spectators and badly injured at least forty others, including himself.

One can't help but reflect on the inexcusability of these instantly extinguished lives: husbands, wives, sons and daughters, fathers and mothers. It was as if nothing whatsoever had been learnt from the Mille Miglia, or from Caracas as recently as the previous November... not to mention all the other spectator deaths, including Le Mans of '55. It also shows how times have changed: the brief, non-violent kidnapping of Fangio was an international headline story whereas the seven spectators who were killed and the forty or so badly injured warranted no more than a couple of inside columns.

By the waving of red flags, the drivers were signalled to cease racing and bring their cars safely round to the start/finish line. Masten was slightly ahead of Stirling when the red flags came out but, as their slowing cars were about to pass the finish line, Stirling speeded up to cross the line first, and thereby claim the prize money for winning. Masten challenged Stirling about this unsporting behaviour, which led to Stirling volunteering to split the prize money. Mike, as you might imagine, was very disparaging about Stirling's conduct.

Incredibly, Cifuentes was charged with manslaughter. I thought it should have been the circuit administrators who were charged – not with manslaughter, but murder.

I also find it extremely curious that, over the intervening fifty-plus years, the Hotel Lincoln has never relet, nor altered in any way, Fangio's bedroom, keeping it as a shrine to a great driver – and a night of high drama.

Chapter Twenty-Seven

Threesome…

Whilst the Cuban debacle was going on, Mike returned to the TT Garage and busied himself in its affairs. Or, at least, that's what he said he did. My impression was that he irritated his mother in matters of administration, annoyed Bill Field in the workshop, and terrified most of the junior staff. It was at times like this that one saw his two sides most starkly: the more common bonhomie for friends, media and the public, and the occasional frustrated egotist, desperate for adulation. One facet was charming; the other embarrassing.

He was also searching for love. During this interval of nearly a month, I saw him walking out with three different girls. Two I'd not seen before, and one was an old flame – a perennial, a cast-off from the pre-Cherry era. I don't think it would be unfair to describe these as liaisons of convenience, judging how they didn't seem to impinge too much on Mike's many other social commitments, such as driving around the county drinking copious amounts of ale. I knew that he felt little for them because he confided to me one night, when we were both half-cut, that if he could find a girl like Louise he'd marry her straight away.

'You practically have,' I said.

'What's that meant to mean?' he shot back,

'Your little *ménage à trois*? The press always takes photos of the three of you together…and it's rumoured that you've even shared a bed.'

'Rumoured by who?' His tone suddenly much sharper.

'I don't know…just gossip.'

'Well, there's no truth in it. None *whatsoever*.' His enunciation of 'whatsoever' was an instruction that the topic was now closed.

'Are you saying you wouldn't want to…?' I was enjoying my dangerous fishing expedition.

'You can't ask me that. Pete's my best friend.'

I changed the subject. I'd been enjoying his discomfort, and I was going to push him further. I was certain that I could have got him to admit that he really had got the hots for Louise, but that last sentence stopped me dead. He hadn't said 'one of my best friends'; he'd said 'best friend'. I fleetingly thought about challenging it – saying something like, 'Don't you remember that time when we went to Brooklands, when we were about eight or nine, and we swore we'd always be best friends?' but that sounded pathetic, so clingy, that I said nothing. What Mike had said was undoubtedly true, although I suspect, if I'd protested, he'd have replied mollifyingly that, of course, I was *also* his best friend. I wasn't a driver, and that was the thing.

I shouldn't sound bitter, however, because this was to become a very significant moment in my life. One of the two 'new' girls with whom Mike walked out during that brief spell was a striking auburn-haired girl called Sally – Long Tall Sally we called her. The day Mike flew off to Italy, en route for Sebring, I called her up. To cut a long story short, fifteen months later, Sally became Mrs McBride. For that, above all else, I remain eternally grateful to Mike.

I would have preferred that my wife had not been one of Mike's exes; however, the pragmatist in me accepted that he was a necessary catalyst. Without Mike, I would probably never have had the chance to get to meet such a lovely girl. Naturally, I wanted to know what Mike was like as a boyfriend. She said that she only went out with him half a dozen times and had barely got to know him. He was, she said, 'mostly a charming gentleman'. After further persistent questioning, she said he was 'very persuasive'. She didn't elaborate, and I found I couldn't enquire further in that direction. Apparently, on a couple of occasions, he'd cried, seemingly without obvious reason. Sally thought this was most strange. Through loyalty to Mike, I didn't express any opinion on this until after we were engaged when I told her everything about Mike – or at least nearly everything (I might not have told her about Paris…until now, of course!).

I asked her why they broke up. I remember the way she looked at me, as if I was mad. 'He was great fun, but he wasn't exactly the faithful sort.' Sally said she thought at the time he was two-timing her. I didn't like to suggest it was probably a bigger multiple than that.

She told me she'd ended it one night, after they'd been to the pub. Apparently, I was there – and was implicated! A mutual acquaintance of ours, a right smoothie, David Dodd, was also there with a classically beautiful girl. She caused quite a stir, and it was rumoured that she was a Hardy Amies' model from London. According to Sally, Mike couldn't take his eyes off her. She said, at one point, Mike whispered something to me, whilst looking lasciviously at the girl. Sally was furious at this discourtesy and immediately realised that life with Mike would always be that way.

Having Sally in my life was fantastic. It meant I had more to worry about than simply my job and Mike's welfare. Not that I ever stopped worrying about him.

Chapter Twenty-Eight

Sherbets in Sebring

There was a collective sigh of relief from the TT Garage when Mike left for Sebring. To get there, he was first required to fly to Milan where he met up with Taffy and another driver, Taffy's chum Wolfgang Seidel. Siedel was another pleasant German, by all accounts, but couldn't drive for toffee. The three of them flew to New York from where they were to fly straight on to Miami. Somehow, they missed the connection, forcing them to 'endure' a night out in New York. I suspect they were not up bright and early the next morning, but they did manage to catch a plane to Miami, and from there hired a big ol' Chevy in which to drive the three hours or so to Sebring.

All the Ferrari drivers had been booked into Harder Hall, a grand Spanish colonial hotel on Little Lake Jackson, famed for its golf and tennis facilities, and somewhere that Mike described as 'fabulously expensive'. Mike baulked at the expense and proposed to check himself into a nearby self-catering motel. His German compatriots tagged along as, of course, did Pete and Louise. Musso, for whom money was of little consequence, stayed put.

Mike and Pete enjoyed the novelty of going shopping at a self-service grocery store and inevitably bought far too much food. Louise, so Mike maintained, was happy cooking for the three of them. The evenings were passed with another novelty: the threesome watching television together. Mike admitted he'd become a 'goggle box addict'.

Neither Mike nor Pete took traffic regulations seriously, both picking up speeding and parking fines almost daily. Mike said of the parking fines: 'It's an easy system. All you do is put the tickets and the money in the envelope and post it off.'

The Sebring race was exclusively for sports cars, nearly all of which were built as two-seaters, and so when Mike was given a left-hand drive car, he complained to Tavoni. He felt it was unfair that Pete had been given a right-hand drive car. Tavoni told him to get on with it and, to his surprise, Mike realised that he actually enjoyed it. The new Testa Rossa ('red head') Ferraris were great-looking cars, and were fast, but there was the perennial problem: they still had drum brakes whereas all the opposition had moved on to disc brakes. The new Aston Martin DBR1s, to be driven by Stirling and Tony, were equally fast and were fitted with disc brakes. Mike was still grumbling about this when he got home. At least, he was pleased that the driver pairings remained: Pete and Phil, Musso and Gendebien, and he and Taffy. He would rather partner a German than he would Luigi Musso. Tavoni eventually cottoned on that putting Musso with Mike or Pete was not a good idea.

One-hand Archie had a lucky escape in his Lister-Jaguar. On only the fourth lap, his engine 'threw a rod', and the car stopped dead. Gendebien, who was right behind him, ran straight over the top of him, missing his head by a few inches. Incredibly, after a pit stop, Gendebien was able to carry on. Not so, wee Archie.

Few cars were able to withstand this gruellingly long race. Both Stirling's Aston and Mike's Ferrari developed transmission problems way before the end of the twelve hours, and none of the Jags were able to finish. Once confident that Pete and Phil were assured of victory, Mike went in search of consoling company. He found it in Briggs Cunningham's caravan where, amongst the mostly Scottish contingent of drivers, Scotch was being consumed like tea. An hour or so later, Ivor the Driver told Mike that he knew of a little pub on the way home. So, while Pete, his 'best mate', was notching up his second Sports Car Championship win, Mike and Ivor set about literally drinking beer and playing skittles.

They drove, somehow, back to the motel to find a small impromptu celebration party in full swing in the Collins's suite. Louise had run a bath for her tired but victorious husband, who was still chatting to friends and having a drink. Mike arrived wearing an inane grin, marched straight through the partygoers, didn't utter a word to anyone, and climbed into the bath still fully dressed – his dusty clothes ballooning above the water and his bow tie well askew. A young married woman called Robin witnessed this, thought it was hilarious, and ventured into the bathroom. Mike reached up and grabbed her, pulled her down, kissed her, and simultaneously soaked her using the shower attachment. With that, Mike stepped out of the bath and squelched his way out of the apartment, all without saying a single word.

Ivor remembered what happened thereafter rather better than Mike. Mike went to his own rooms, changed, and, with Ivor, went out in search of even more beer. Their night out culminated in playing poker in a hotel bedroom with three armed motorcycle cops at six o'clock in the morning.

Undeterred, but not feeling great, Mike and Taffy drove their Chevy back to Miami the next day, and then, with Ivor, went on to West Palm Beach in search of yet more mischief – successfully, apparently.

From there, Mike caught a plane to New York to join the Collinses for a party at Louise's parents' home in Great Neck, Long Island (the location for F Scott Fitzgerald's novel *Great Gatsby*), at which many United Nations' dignitaries were present.

Chapter Twenty-Nine

Goodwood Giggles

Mike was back for the Easter meeting at Goodwood only days after returning to England, and naturally I was keen to take Sally along to see him in action.

Mike flew down from Chobham to Goodwood on Good Friday as he'd been asked to try the modified car and provide some feedback to Carlo Chiti, Ferrari's chief engineer. When he arrived, Tavoni told him the cars weren't permitted to go out because it was Good Friday. He flew back home, and we met up that evening. Far from being upset by having a wasted journey, Mike was in great spirits. I think he enjoyed having an excuse to fly somewhere. He did so love that aeroplane.

Mike was up early the next morning and again flew down to Goodwood, this time for official practice. It was now snowing and bitterly cold. He said his 2.4-litre Dino seemed to handle well and was pleased that they'd remembered to fit his trademark four-spoked steering wheel. Chiti (you can imagine how we puerile Members pronounced his name) also reassured Mike that the half shafts had been beefed up and should no longer break. Mike was happier with the car, but was dismayed to find that he'd been allocated the number '1' by the organizers. Mike tried to persuade the secretary of the BARC to change it. The programmes had, of course, all been printed by then, and so his pleas were in vain.

Practice must have gone well for Mike told us that he'd 'just' made the front row of the grid. Alongside him, on pole, was Stirling in his 'Spunknik' and, next to him, Jean Behra in a BRM. Use of the circuit wasn't permitted on Easter Sunday, either, but this didn't stop Mike flying down to Goodwood yet again, mostly 'just for the hell of it'.

Mike told us the Duke of Richmond and Gordon had recently constructed a tunnel under the circuit near to the start/finish line for cars and a pedestrian subway linking the airfield interior with the Lavant Straight, features which greatly aid latter-day events such as the recent Revival Meetings.

Sally and I had an easy run down from Farnham that chilly Easter Monday morning and had a very welcome cup of coffee when we arrived. The first race of interest to us was the twenty-one-lap Sussex Trophy for sports cars of more than 1100cc in which Pete Collins was to drive a 2-litre Ferrari Dino 206S. There was great disparity between the cars, and Pete was up against much more powerful opposition. Stirling was to drive a 3.8-litre works' Aston Martin DBR2 and little Archie a 3.5-litre Lister Jaguar. Mike hadn't entered, and so spent some of the race standing with us giving us a running commentary.

Archie comfortably led the race for eight laps, and it looked for all the world as if he would win until he abruptly stopped at the pits. We learnt that the steering had tightened up so much that he was forced to retire. I'd been cheering loudly for him, because not only was Archie a good lad but he'd been prevented from driving in so many races due to his disabilities. With Archie out, Stirling had it all his own way, with Pete coming home a respectable second, ahead of Duncan Hamilton's D-Type and two larger-engined Ferraris.

The main event, however, and the one to which we were all looking forward, was the Glover Trophy. This was a forty-two-lap race run along Formula One lines, featuring one John Michael Hawthorn.

As the starting flag fell, Jean Behra shot in front, closely followed by Mike. Stirling just sat there. He'd stalled on the line. We watched as the two leading cars flowed round together. Behra looked smoother through the corners where he gained ground on Mike, and then Mike would claw back some distance on the straights.

We had an excellent view from the grandstand situated between the chicane and the start/finish. Behra came flying round Woodcote and appeared not to brake for the chicane. Instead of slipping past it, he slammed into it, side on. The noise was terrific. He half bounced out of his seat and then slumped back down. It was truly frightening. And in the next instant, Mike came barreling through, avoiding

Behra's stricken BRM and the chicane, and, miraculously, stayed on the circuit. It was a moment of very impressive car control.

I honestly thought Behra had bought it. He remained quite still. I turned to look at the gang with whom we were seated. There was about twenty of us all together. The girls looked horrified. Sally had her hand over her mouth, and her eyes were wide open in disbelief. I think in those few seconds she realised what life as a racing driver really entailed, and perhaps was grateful to no longer be going out with one. I then saw Behra move around in his seat.

Without thinking, I said, 'Look, Behra's okay!' Fortunately, I was right. His car was moved away, and we saw Behra being helped out of the cockpit. He looked groggy but was still in one piece.

The race continued apace, with Mike comfortably out in front. Stirling was working his way through the backmarkers like a man possessed, including his own teammate Jack Brabham in another little Cooper. I assumed we were in for an epic tussle between Stirling and Mike.

Sadly, it was not to be as Stirling's engine gave out, allowing Mike to cruise home to win. There was a euphoric reaction from our little party. We were on our feet, cheering and waving programmes, as Mike came past on his victory lap. Everyone looked happy and relaxed. I noticed David Dodd's stunning young girlfriend – the model – waving particularly enthusiastically.

Some of us ran through to the pits to congratulate Mike. This was his first major win for a couple of years, and it showed: he was beaming. He must have been exhausted for, despite the cold weather, when he pulled off his helmet, his blond hair was flattened by perspiration. Sally observed that drivers who favoured goggles over visors had funny blackened faces, and consequently got the giggles.

Mike agreed with me that his win deserved serious celebration, but protested he couldn't leave his plane down at Goodwood. We discussed various options before he bet me that he could fly back to Fairoaks Airfield near Chobham, jump in his Jag, and drive back down to Midhurst before we could drive there.

Midhurst from Goodwood is barely ten miles by road so, obviously, we accepted his ridiculous challenge. Pints were at stake. However, it took us an age to walk from the pits and out of the circuit, and then we had to endure a long queue to get out of the car park. By contrast, it was a minute's walk from the pits to where Mike had left his plane at the end of the newly reopened landing strip. We were then further thwarted by the crowds leaving a polo match at Cowdray.

We did win but, considering how much further Mike and his young passenger Neil Maynard had travelled, it was still surprising to arrive at The Spread Eagle only fifteen minutes before them. And we heard them arrive before we saw them. Mike's dark green 3.4-litre Jaguar saloon had been subtly race-prepared: the engine had been 'breathed on', the suspension stiffened, a limited slip differential fitted, and the rear track slightly widened. Which, coupled with Mike flushed with a Goodwood victory at the wheel, meant there was little if anything on the public roads to touch it.

Mike appeared to have got a second wind whereas Neil looked shattered. He practically fell into the bar and downed his first pint in a matter of seconds. There were a few of us there – drivers and old friends – and the atmosphere was fantastic. None of the drivers had been badly injured, Mike had driven brilliantly – and beaten Stirling. A couple of the girls, including Dodd's girlfriend, were obviously flirting with the champion – and being rewarded with much attention.

What was it about my newly wealthy, and now famous, old friend that beautiful girls found so attractive? I then realised what a mean sentiment this was, and how I genuinely did want the best for him. I'm happy, I thought, so, for God's sake, let him be happy.

I'd expected Pete and Louise to come along too, but apparently they'd had the good sense to retreat to their hotel on the coast.

There was earnest discussion about the race, particularly as to whether or not Stirling would have overhauled Mike had his Spunknik kept going. Mike, of course, pooh-poohed the idea. I wasn't so sure, and I suspect others likewise kept such thoughts to themselves. The BRMs came in for some serious ribbing. We all respected that they were quick; there was no doubting that. It was their unreliability that was still at issue.

We'd learnt that while Jean Behra had experienced complete brake failure with his BRM, his teammate, the ever jovial Harry Schell, had come into the pits because the brake pads weren't being released, causing clouds of blue smoke. I'd seen a BRM mechanic frantically try to douse the brakes using a fire extinguisher. At first, the extinguisher wouldn't work and then, with a bit of fiddling, it erupted and foam was indiscriminately shot over everyone within about fifteen feet of the car. Harry resembled an animated snowman.

Our party moved en masse from The Spread Eagle to the Duke of Cumberland at Henley-on-the-Hill. This was a tiny, quaint old pub, where a dozen of us ate the 7/6d steak with onions and chips, drank yet more beer, played darts and generally misbehaved.

We didn't so much leave as get thrown out − in a friendly way. After saying unnecessarily loud goodbyes to one and all, oblivious of the pub's poor neighbours, we got into our respective cars. I began to follow Mike and Neil too briskly down the lane going north which joins the A286. I glanced across at Sally and was surprised to see that she was already asleep in the passenger seat. I was suddenly mindful that my circumstances and those of the late Les Hawthorn's were frighteningly similar: it was late, I was seven-tenths drunk, and tired, and was returning to Farnham from Goodwood after a day's racing. I immediately gave up any thoughts of trying to keep up with Mike and watched his tail lights disappear into the cold night.

Chapter Thirty

Two New Loves

If I hadn't been going out with Sally, I would have travelled up to Oulton Park in Cheshire the following weekend to watch Mike race. I'd also have tried to hitch a lift in his plane – assuming he had passenger space. As it was, he did take a passenger: an old flame by the name of Carol Seyd.

'Well, everyone else was busy, and I didn't want to go by myself,' is how he explained it to me. In the afternoon, they watched Stirling Moss win the British Empire Trophy in a sports car race, and stayed over that night with the Palmers, some friends living just outside Warrington. The Palmers kept a boxer dog which had just had puppies. As Mike was obviously smitten, Ian Palmer offered him a boy puppy by the name of Boris – a name Mike wasn't too keen on, mostly because of its Russian connotations. Mike accepted the gift with alacrity.

Upon their return to Fairoaks, Mike took Carol and Boris straight into the Aero Club for a much needed drink – in his case, a pint of light and bitter. At one point when he was chatting intently to Carol, he looked round to find that Boris was lapping up his beer...his grog. It was at that point that Mike decided to rechristen the dog Grogger.

The moment Mike got home, he was on the phone telling me I had to drop whatever I was doing and come and meet Grogger. He was in love again.

As these things go, it wasn't the worst time for Mike to acquire a dog, for he had almost a month to kill before he had to fly off to the Continent again. Typically, rather than ask his mother, he assumed she would look after Grogger in his absence.

*

As luck would have it – our luck, that is – Mike's weekend prior to his May Silverstone meet was free. So what did we do? We persuaded him down to Goodwood again for the fiftieth BARC sports car meeting – a busman's holiday.

It wasn't really so difficult as Mike's pal Pat Massey-Dawson was racing a Lotus XI. Again, there were a lot of the old Farnham crowd there, and it was good to have Mike with us in the stands instead of worrying about him on the track. We saw a few good races, and it was exciting to see Pat finish fourth in the 1500cc class. I was touched to see Mike cheering like an ordinary spectator.

Afterwards, a whole bunch of us piled into The Richmond Arms, practically next door to the circuit. Those present included: Neil, Tim Ely, Nick Syrett, David Dodd *and* his delectable girlfriend we now knew as Jean, and Mike and Carol. As we left, Mike checked out Tim's blue pre-war Riley Ulster Imp, a close cousin of the cars in which Mike began his career, and commented that if it had been green he'd have liked to have bought it.

Our next watering hole was The Spread Eagle, right in the centre of Midhurst. Mike asked Tim if he might drive the Riley, 'for old times' sake'. Tim agreed and, leaving the rest of the party, they drove a few miles back towards Goodwood. As he shot past The Greyhound Inn, Mike spun the little car round and proposed a 'sausage and fluids change pit stop'.

As they approached the pub, Mike dropped down into third gear at about 70mph, which sent the rev counter shooting up into hitherto unexplored territory.

Suitably refreshed and walking back to the car, Tim enquired, 'That was a bit strange. It all went a bit quiet when we walked in.'

'Maybe that's because the last time I came here, I had a bit of bother with one of the regulars,' replied Mike, striding on and not looking at Tim.

What that 'bother' amounted to, Tim never did find out because seconds later Mike was screaming off again. He was going so fast as they approached the The Spread Eagle that he overshot the entrance. Poor Tim looked petrified as he entered the bar. He told me that Mike had driven there and back using the full width of both carriageways of the road, as if it were a race track.

From there, we went on to The Bricklayers Arms, with Tim

now safely back behind the wheel of his Riley, and from there to Wanborough Manor off the Hog's Back, or at least those of us who were still capable of walking and driving. By then, it'd been a ten-pint day for most of the chaps, with one unlucky soul modifying the bodywork of his Morgan on the way home. Two things which may have been related.

Looking back on that most enjoyable excursion, or at least what I can remember of it, I must hand it to Mike, the old smoothie, for somehow he managed to obtain, and keep safe, the telephone number of Jean Howarth, David Dodd's stunning Hardy Amies' model girlfriend. Weeks later, I asked Mike directly how he and Jean had started going out with one another.

'It wasn't exactly difficult. I phoned her up and asked her if she would like to go out with me.'

I wondered whether it wasn't what was said but who was asking that made all the difference. 'Weren't you at all concerned about Doddy?' I ventured.

'Funnily enough, that's what she said!'

'So what did you say?'

'I told her that David was nice, but he was boring, and I was a lot more fun.'

'You actually said that?'

'More or less.'

'And so did she say yes?'

'She said that she'd think about it, but she also said she'd never two-time David.'

'And then what?'

'I told her that she should have a really good think. I then called her again two days later and, of course, she said yes.'

'So, she finished with David?'

'I guess she must have done.'

May that year, containing four major races, was always going to be a bit manic, but Mike seemed up for it. The first of the four, the Daily Express Trophy at Silverstone, was relatively local, straddling the counties of Northamptonshire and Buckinghamshire, right in the heart of England. Like Goodwood, Silverstone is a former Second World War airfield.

For this race, Enzo had decided to swap roles for Pete and Mike. Pete would drive the Grand Prix car and Mike the sports car. I didn't even suggest to Sally that she might like to go up for the practice sessions. I was just pleased that she agreed to go up for race day. We were able to have a brief word before Mike went out, and he was not optimistic about his chances.

'The car,' he said, 'is great in a straight line but it doesn't like going round corners – the understeer is lethal.'

We discussed how the big Jaguar-engined cars were nearly 1000cc bigger, which was going to be asking a lot of the Ferrari.

Sally wanted to know what understeer and 1000cc were. This proved harder to explain to someone who knew nothing whatsoever about cars than I thought it would be. I just hoped Mike wouldn't start talking about axle ratios or carburation mixes. Thankfully, he didn't.

We left Mike so that we could watch the start. It was of the Le Mans style where the drivers run across the track and jump into their cars. This generally provides a more staggered start than the grid formation starts. 'Disabled Archie' got his Lister Jag off to a flying start and led the two Astons of Tony Brooks and Roy Salvadori, with Masten Gregory fourth in another Lister. Stirling and Mike were fifth and sixth respectively. Compared to Grand Prix standards, twenty-five laps wasn't a long race. Mike was clearly finding his 3-litre Ferrari a real handful. It was more than capable of making up ground on the straight bits but wobbling like a drunk through the twisty bits. Several times I thought he was going to lose it – fortunately, he never did.

Everyone was a bit disappointed when Stirling's Aston coasted into the pits after twelve laps due to engine failure. When Tony Brooks's Aston also gave up the fight, Mike inherited fourth place. At the front, Masten had a great drive and overhauled Archie to take the chequered flag. After what seemed to be a Herculean effort, Mike managed to overtake Roy Salvadori to take a creditable third.

Mike was always happy to race for Lofty England, and had jumped at the opportunity to drive his own Jaguar saloon, suitably fettled by Lofty, in the touring car race. However, it meant back-to-back racing: jumping straight out of the hard-sprung Ferrari and into the relatively softly-sprung Jaguar.

Sally looked incredulous at the array of different-sized cars:

thirty-three of them, all standard production models, with various degrees of modification. There were big saloons such as Mike's 3.4-litre Jaguar and 2.5-litre Ford Zephyrs lined up with tiny cars such as Morris Minors and Austin A35s.

'Surely,' she said, 'the big cars will win easily.'

I told her that she was probably right, but she'd be amazed by how quickly some of the little ones could be persuaded to go.

As the flag fell, we saw Mike, in his distinctive green windcheater and white trousers, dash across to his Jaguar and jump in. As the cars' engines roared into life, one by one they shot off – except Mike. He was the last to leave.

Sally turned to me and mouthed, 'Poor Mike'.

I smiled back. Well, I thought, he might have a fight on his hands but he won't stay last for long. Within three laps, he was at the front with Tommy Sopwith who was driving a similar Jaguar. Mike and Tommy established a huge lead over the rest of the field and were dicing for all they were worth. It was a great spectacle, seeing those big green Jags leaning right over, practically side by side, as their drivers applied opposite lock, tyres screaming. The two of them were racing with great finesse – so close and yet never touching.

At one point, Mike took the inside line of a corner with such brio that Tommy had to steer outside a corner-defining black and white fence only to rejoin the circuit at the end of the corner. The crowd went wild. Right to the very end, Mike managed to keep his nose, or rather the car's radiator, just in front, and won by less than one second. Involuntarily, I jumped up and down, and, to my delight, Sally did too. What a driver!

Behind them, there were other duels going on. Two of the big Fords were repeatedly bouncing off each other, and two cars – an MG and a Riley – both tipped over. The driver of the Riley was caught on a TV camera being flung from his car as it went over. Fortunately, no one was badly hurt. Two round little Riley 1.5s that had been neck and neck for the whole race, admittedly more than two minutes behind the leaders, came haring across the line to finish sixth and seventh, ahead of several big Jaguars and Fords. Sally was thrilled by the David and Goliath aspect of their performance. The saloons were again the highlight of the day's racing.

We wandered over to Copse, the first corner and a sharp right-hander after the pits, where we'd arranged to try and meet Mike. He made it in time to see Pete taking part in the Trophy race. Pete had managed to grab a place on the front row of the grid – a lone Ferrari alongside three Coopers, one of which was Stirling's. It was another packed field, with thirty-four starters. As the first cars came screaming towards us, I was thrilled to see that the leading car was red – it had to be Pete, and it was. In second and third were the BRMs of Behra and Flockhart. There were no Coopers to be seen.

Behra was clearly going all out to overtake Pete and did so after five laps. Stirling, who we were told had stalled on the line, was slicing his way up through the field but had left himself a lot of catching up to do. By the time he was up to sixth place, his car's gearbox failed.

Inexplicably, Behra slowed right up and then disappeared into the pits for seemingly quite a long stop. We later heard that a stone had smashed his goggles, resulting in a cut eye. Replacement goggles were found, but he'd lost so much time he was unable to contest the lead. We were beginning to think that Pete was going to have it all his own way when he came towards us at Copse and suddenly spun off sideways due to oil dropped from his own car. Fortunately, he kept the engine going and, such was his lead, he was able to rejoin the circuit, retaining the lead. Coming in behind Pete by twenty-odd seconds was the works' Cooper driven by Salvadori, who had been on pole position, and in an unlikely third place was Masten Gregory driving a Maserati 250F.

I said to Mike that it had been a very good day for him and Masten, both having a win and a third place, but not so good for Stirling. Mike wasn't going to crow. He said he felt sorry for Stirling, and that all drivers get unlucky days.

It had been a great day's racing and a terrific event to which to take Sally. I was surprised not to see Mike's new girl Jean there, but Mike explained that her modelling assignments took her off all over the place. He seemed strangely unconcerned. Sally and I were still buzzing when we eventually got home – happy yet exhausted, our ears ringing and our faces grubby.

Mike had booked himself into a little local pub called The Jersey Arms where several of the other notorious hellraisers, such as Duncan Hamilton and Peter Walker, were also staying. I hated to think what time and in what state they finally got to bed.

Chapter Thirty-One

Halcyon Days

Forty-eight hours later and Mike was flying off again to Italy, this time in readiness for the Targa Florio – a sweet-sounding name for a seriously tough 1,000km event, staged over the wild ruggedness of Sicily. The Florio, at that time the oldest race in the world dating from 1906, was named after Vincenzo Florio, a wealthy Sicilian car enthusiast who put up a gold plate as a prize (the word targa meaning plate or plaque). The circuit was fourteen laps of a seventy-two-kilometre circuit of rock-strewn, sinuous public roads which twist and turn up from sea level to 2,000 feet, full of hairpin bends and sheer drops. It had the well-deserved reputation for being hard on both cars and drivers.

The travel arrangements which had been passed to Mike at Silverstone by Tavoni broke down after the flight. There was no one to pick him up from Catania and take him on to Palermo. Instead, he tagged along with his old pal Bernard Cahier in a car driven by a friend of Bernard's. On arrival in Palermo, they were introduced to Count Florio himself, who Mike described as a 'wonderful old man'. As charmed as he was by the race's originator, he wasn't so keen on the course.

Mike hadn't driven the Florio before, and let it be known he wasn't impressed. Pete told me later that Mike wouldn't allow himself to be driven by anyone but Phil Hill, and the two of them drove sedately around the circuit a few times in a little Fiat hired by Pete. Phil was about as different in temperament from Mike as it was possible to be. Rather than indulge in boozy sessions in nightclubs, Phil was just as happy to retire to his room after dinner and listen to soothing classical music on his Concertone reel-to-reel tape recorder – a machine he also used to record long letters to his family back in the States.

Mike announced that he had no wish to die in a car driven by Pete in practice.

'He point-blank refused to come out with me, no matter what I promised,' Pete told me later.

Also available was a superseded Ferrari, the 'mule car', in which the boys were meant to practice. Given the donkey track nature of some of the roads, this term was particularly apt. One corner Mike described sounded truly frightening. They'd christened it 'Coffin-for-England' Corner. Descending through some short sharp bends, suddenly there was a tight right-angle bend with no barrier on the outside, merely a 200-foot drop onto jagged rocks. Mike said even the luckiest driver wouldn't be able to walk away from that one.

After the race, Phil Hill quoted Mike as having said, 'That's another race I'll never have to do again.' Phil took that to mean Mike had made up his mind to quit motor racing. It could, of course, have been that he would refuse to ever compete again in the Targa Florio. As Mike had never mentioned retirement to me, I was inclined to think it was the latter. Certainly, his appetite for competition seemed only to increase as the season went on.

The three days before the race were a strange combination of carefree holidaying with the occasional foray into the mountains, hoping not to hit something or someone as the roads were only closed for the race itself. When they were not out playing 'Do or Die Dodgems', the Collinses, Mike, Phil Hill, Taffy, and Siedel and his wife spent their days languidly on the beach, swimming, sunbathing and having picnics. It was a golden, magical time – all friends, all young, all fit and, seemingly, healthy.

Naturally, in such dangerous circumstances, not everyone was lucky. A private entrant swerved to avoid a lorry during practice and was killed. Fortunately, word of this didn't reach the Ferrari drivers until practice was nearly finished.

The Ferrari camp was optimistic about their overall chances of a success – if not their individual survival – for they'd entered four cars to Aston Martin's one, to be piloted by Stirling and Tony Brooks. The other fancied cars were the little Porsches which were probably better suited to the course.

Mike, who was to take over from Taffy, had to wait patiently for the cars to return from their forty-five mile-laps. Those waiting with Mike fully expected to see Stirling come through first, but it was Luigi Musso, who'd started in last position. Luigi was followed by Pete and then Taffy who'd already restyled the front end of his and Mike's Ferrari by crashing into a wall.

Stirling's delay was caused by needing to change a wheel whilst out on the circuit. After he'd received attention from the pits, which included the removal of a crankshaft damper, he positively flew – setting three consecutive lap records – and caught up well. He was, as we used to say, driving as if his pants were on fire – which was, of course, once true. It must have been enormously disappointing for both him and Tony, who'd completed sixteen practice laps, when their car's transmission failed on the fifth lap.

Another driver motoring as if his life depended on it was Luigi. He'd been telling everyone that he was the world's best driver on mountain roads. And, to be fair, he and Gendebien did lead the race from start to finish. Luigi did, however, have a very hairy moment when, towards the end of the race, he went to pull in at the pits only to overshoot considerably. He ran back, screaming, 'Niente freni.' No brakes! The brake fluid tank was found to be completely empty. They refilled it, and off he went. If I'd been Luigi, I wouldn't have trusted the brakes not to fail again, perhaps on Coffin Corner. However, Luigi was on a mission…he'd set out his stall. By such small margins of fortune are races won, and lives lost.

Jean Behra took second place in a silver RSK Porsche, a lithe little sports car not dissimilar to today's Boxster. Taffy and Mike finished in a respectable third place – a remarkable result given the extent to which Mike loathed and feared the circuit. When he arrived home the following day, he admitted he was completely shattered.

Chapter Thirty-Two

Rat Droppings

Monaco was but a week away and yet Mike still returned to England, and to Jean. I was surprised to see him as he was home for barely forty-eight hours. When he phoned, he seemed keen that we meet up as a foursome. I wasn't sure it was a good idea. I'd only recently let on about Sally and me. However, I was pleasantly taken aback by his kind wishes and words of encouragement. He said, 'Sally's a lovely girl…far too good for the likes of me.'

I was more concerned about Sally and Jean – an ex and a current – but Mike insisted the girls would 'get along famously'. When I asked Sally about this, she said she was more bothered about spending an evening with Mike than she was about meeting Jean properly for the first time.

Neither of us need have worried because the evening could not have gone better. There was no denying it: Mike and Jean made a stunning couple. Jean was tall and slender, with dark hair and big brown eyes, high cheekbones, flawless skin and fine features. It had been a long time since both he and I had girlfriends simultaneously, and it was a state of affairs I wanted to last.

Sally and Jean got on well from the start, despite Jean being a fair bit younger. Jean's father had done well in business in India before returning to live in a ten-bedroomed house near Huddersfield. His wealth had made it possible for Jean to attend a Swiss finishing school, then a private domestic science college in Edinburgh, and finally to Lucie Clayton's in London to learn deportment and from where the modelling contacts were made. Jean said she just 'fell into modelling'. It wasn't exactly hard to see how or why.

Unusually, Mike and I were both restrained on the beer front that evening and for once parted at a reasonable hour, almost in accordance with the licensing laws.

It was around this time when I noticed a small but discernible change in Mike – he wasn't in constant search for the next boozy session. In fact, Louise talked about the three of them sometimes eschewing a party in favour of quietly reading detective novels. However, when he did go out drinking with the likes of me, he was invariably still centre stage.

I thought a lot about his upcoming race, Monaco, probably for no reason other than it was one of the few circuits with which I was familiar – and its reputation for multiple pile-ups. It was also an important race in terms of the Championship, Stirling having already amassed twice as many points as Mike.

Louise, who'd taken a break from pandering to Pete, collected Mike from Nice Airport in her little Vespa motor car. Mike said he'd prefer to drive than be driven. Louise let him, thinking it was only a tiny car with a 400cc motorcycle engine, so surely it couldn't be too frightening. Wrong! She said he tried to drive it flat out from the start, and he got frustrated when the locals overtook them going uphill. However, when it came to the run down into town, Mike floored it, determined to overtake every car that had passed them. Louise said that she kept her eyes tightly closed for the last five minutes of their journey. Sally asked her if she felt he was showing off. She said that she believed he'd have driven like that even if he'd have been by himself – maybe more so. I'd have to agree, although on a different day he'd have been content to dawdle.

There was only capacity for sixteen cars on the grid and, as twenty-nine cars had been entered, practice sessions were crucial, for nearly half the entrants were going to be eliminated before the flag dropped. Two of those who failed to qualify are worthy of mention. One was Bernie Ecclestone; the other was Maria Teresa de Filippis – the first woman ever to compete in an F1 race – driving Fangio's '57 Championship-winning Maserati. There have only been four women competitors in F1 since – and not one in the last twenty-plus years.

Competition amongst the Ferrari drivers was fierce and, according to Pete, no one was happy with their engine's oomph, except Mike – which was a first. Pete was probably right, because Mike was able to bag the best grid position of the four Ferraris. However, as that was sixth, it was a pretty miserable showing all round. Tony Brooks was on pole; next to him was Jean Behra; and then there were three Coopers, all ahead of Mike. Stuart Lewis-Evans and Stirling were Mike's neighbours on the third row, ahead of Pete and Luigi on the fourth row.

It proved an auspicious day for one small racing team – Lotus – who managed to get two cars onto the grid. It marked their first foray into Grand Prix. The drivers were Graham Hill and Cliff Allison.

Race day, a Sunday, was a perfect summer's day. Prince Rainier and Princess Grace were first sedately driven round the circuit in a vast open American 'automobile' before taking their seats in the Royal Box. A mass of coloured balloons were released and then the sixteen cars were assembled on the grid.

The race was full of incident and accident, mostly affecting the smaller, quicker cars. Behra and Brooks commanded the first part of the race but, only a quarter of the way through the 100 laps, both drivers had retired – Brooks with a missing sparking plug and Behra without brakes. At this point, Mike inherited the lead, with Stirling hard on his tail. A tussle ensued for half a dozen laps, with the lead swapping repeatedly. And then it was Stirling's turn for trouble. His engine belched black smoke, and he limped round to the pits.

For six laps, comfortably in the lead, Mike thought victory was in the bag. All he needed to do was keep the car in one piece. If only it had been that easy. His engine began to misfire and then cut out altogether. He felt that he might be able to push-start it back into action. Mike spotted two photographers: Michael Tee from *Motor Sport*, and a Frenchman. He shouted across to them asking for a push. Michael Tee rushed over straightaway whereas the other man carried on taking pictures.

Tee was unable to get sufficient momentum by himself, and so Mike was left stranded. By his own admission, Mike 'lost it' and leapt out of the car with the intention of thumping the Frenchman. Fortunately for both parties, two other bystanders had noticed Mike's predicament and rushed forward to help. Despite their best efforts, the Ferrari still wouldn't fire. Mike lifted the bonnet, but it was Michael Tee who noticed that the petrol pump was hanging loose, effectively spelling the end of Mike's race. Mike wasn't exactly best pleased when he realised the mechanics had omitted to fasten the nuts with split-pins – a simple omission and similar to that which could have cost him his life in a BRM at Aintree two years previously.

It was a hot, tired and grumpy Mike who began to trudge back towards the pits. However, as could only happen to Mike, as he passed the station hotel, he spotted 'a lovely young blonde' leaning out a ground-floor window spectating the race.

'*Avez-vous une tasse d'eau?*' he shouted in his schoolboy French. I'm guessing he probably turned on the smile too. 'And would you credit it...? She only invited me to come in! So I did the decent thing and climbed in through the window.'

This may sound like an unlikely story – well, it did to me – but it was actually captured on film. Mike was adamant that all he did in the girl's bedroom was drink water. Given the circumstances – Mike, lovely young blonde, hotel room – I'd venture that if he was telling the truth that would be another first.

From there, Mike walked on round to the gas works to see little Maurice Trintignant drive smoothly to take the chequered flag once again for Rob Walker's diminutive 1.9-litre Cooper. Luigi and Pete followed him in, picking up second and third places respectively. And what of the Lotus debut? Sadly, Graham Hill's chances were totally scotched when a wheel fell off whereas Cliff Allison managed to survive to the end, albeit finishing in sixth and last place.

Although Mike took comfort from Stirling's failure also to finish, he wasn't so happy about Luigi picking up another six points for his second place. At least, the single point available in every race for the fastest recorded lap went to Mike who, when dicing with Stirling, managed to beat the other Briton's time by a mere 0.1 of a second. The Championship scoreboard at this point read: Musso 12, Moss 8, Hawthorn 5.

I was shocked when Louise told me that the race had been won by the oldest entrant, Maurice Trintignant, at the age of forty.

'What is it about these ancient men?' I asked, thinking also of Fangio.

'He's a lovely man. He has a dear little moustache and he's always smiling,' she said, adding, 'He comes up to Mike's armpit.'

'Which is why he won...he's tiny!' I said with feeling, before I remembered who'd recorded the fastest lap.

'The boys call him *Le Petoulet*,' remarked Louise.

'Is that like a little pet or a mascot?'

She giggled. 'No, it means *rat droppings*!'

'You're kidding?'

'No, seriously. Apparently, he stored a racing Bugatti in a barn during the war, and on his first outing afterwards its engine stopped. It turned out the fuel filter was clogged…totally blocked by…You guessed it!'

I laughed. '*Le Petoulet…Le Petoulet…*' I practised the name, wanting to remember it for some appropriate time with Mike, probably in a bar somewhere.

Incidentally, Maurice Trintignant may have been a diminutive, ageing driver, with an Inspector Clouseau moustache, but he was one of the few to enjoy a racing career in 1950s Formula One and make old bones. He competed at the highest level for fourteen years and raced in eighty-two Grands Prix. After retirement, he grew grapes, made wine and lived to the respectable age of eighty-seven.

The other thing Louise was keen to tell Sally and me about was the after-race party. Mike had watched the prize-giving and seen his 'mon ami mate' get covered in champagne and spray those around him with the stuff. They all then headed straight for Pete's boat, the curiously named Mipooka, which was moored in the harbour. An impromptu party began, and they were joined by lots of friends. Very much later, some of them, Mike included, ended up in Monte Carlo's Tip Top Club and some, Louise reported, in the harbour itself! I asked Mike about that night but he couldn't remember a thing.

Chapter Thirty-Three

Going Dutch

I learned of Archie Scott Brown's death even before Mike. While Mike was racing in Monte Carlo, Archie was competing in the Belgian Sports Car Grand Prix, in a Lister-Jaguar. I caught the announcement by chance on the radio that evening. It was ironic that this was the first continental race that he'd been permitted to enter. All previous entries abroad had been denied on the grounds of his disabilities – citing safety issues: the same disabilities that had so disadvantaged him the year before when he won eleven out of the fourteen races in which he drove the Lister-Jaguar! Archie had car control down to a tee. He had considerable experience – this was his eighth year of competitive driving, and he had courage to match his skill. And, to cap it all, he was modest, popular and amusing.

Only the day before the race, Paul Frère, the retired Belgian Formula One racer now journalist, drove the Spa circuit to see if there was anything dangerous about it. He was sufficiently concerned about a concrete signpost to tell the organizers that, due to its position, it should be removed. It was not removed. Needless to say, it was that post Archie's car struck when he was engaged in a tight battle with another Lister-Jaguar driven by Masten Gregory. His car flipped over, trapping Archie by his legs, and then burst into flames. He was severely burned but just alive. He was taken to hospital where he died six days later. Archie had overcome so many challenges to get where he had. This accident was one of the cruellest I ever knew.

It was another pit stop at home for Mike. He had just three days to 'turn his bike round' before he was off again to Holland, for the Dutch Grand Prix at Zandvoort. I suspect he only bothered to return to see Jean and Grogger.

I telephoned the garage on the off chance of catching him

there, and I was in luck. I commiserated with him about Monaco and wished him well for the Dutch. He asked me whether I'd be going. I told him I couldn't afford it – that I'd be going to the Whitsun meeting at Goodwood instead. He harrumphed at that. Then he called me a tight-arse. He said that he had a good feeling about the Dutch race and, if it was at all possible, I should come. Zandvoort was apparently a circuit which would suit the Ferraris.

'It'll sort out the men from the boys,' he said.

I took that to mean it would suit the bigger-engined cars, rather than the little Coopers and Lotus. He explained that, unlike Monaco, it was a fast, open course set amongst the sand dunes, with a mile-long straight and only two tight corners.

'Have fun,' I said, ignoring his entreaties. 'Just make sure you beat Moses.'

Given Mike's optimism, I was surprised when, far from dominating practice, the three Ferraris (Taffy had been excluded) were down in sixth, tenth and twelfth place on the grid. Clearly, there was something fundamentally wrong with the cars, though I was pleased to see that it was Mike in sixth, with Pete in the row behind, and Luigi in the row behind that. As it was, the three green Vanwalls were together, side by side on the front row – Lewis-Evans just pipping Stirling to pole. It didn't stay that way. The press reports that followed were all about Stirling's brilliance, how he dominated the race from start to finish, and how British cars had taken the top four places. Mike's fifth place was referred to like an afterthought.

I didn't have to wait long to hear all about the race in person, for Mike managed to meet up with a group of us who'd been at Goodwood that day. It seemed incredible then, and mildly surprising even now, that Mike had caught a plane back to England within a couple of hours of the race ending, driven down to Farnham, collected Grogger from his mother, and driven on down to the Duke of Cumberland at Henley in West Sussex, where he imagined, correctly, we'd be. I was so astonished to see him that I didn't believe he'd been to Holland. How was it possible to have raced in a Grand Prix on the Continent that afternoon and get practically all the way down to Midhurst to join us for a few beers?

'I drive quickly for a living, remember,' was his smiling, well-received answer. Of course, everyone desperately wanted to know how he'd fared.

'Fifth!' he said. 'We were bloody awful.'

'How come?' asked someone.

'The engines were rough, the brakes were as useless as ever, and, to cap it all, the steering was downright lethal. Around the hairpins, there was so much understeer you'd think you weren't going to get round. And then, if the car did manage to start cornering, it would suddenly develop a massive oversteer, so you risked going right over. I've never known such a lousy handling Ferrari. And it wasn't just me – the other two were in all sorts of bother too.'

He also told us about the start which had been delayed by half an hour. The attending firemen had gone on a lightning strike because they'd not received their gratis sandwiches between the morning's races and the start of the Grand Prix. Needless to say, that brought forth jokes about going Dutch. One lad, who didn't know Mike well, asked whether he regretted not staying with Vanwall (in whose car Stirling had won) or BRM (whose cars had come second and third). The lad got such a withering look in return.

Fortunately, before anything else was said on this subject, someone else raised a toast to Archie Scott Brown, the news of whose death had just percolated through the pub. Many warm things were said about Archie, and I remember thinking how much his parents would have loved to have heard those tributes: genuine, heartfelt feelings for a super, gutsy wee character.

The rest of the evening was subdued after that, not helped by Mike being uncharacteristically quiet. Apart from the Ferraris' performance, another taboo subject was championship points. I was only too aware that as Stirling had won, he'd now accumulated seventeen points. Musso, despite finishing seventh and therefore out of the points, still had twelve points, whereas Mike only had seven.

Mike told us that he left Tavoni in no doubt whatsoever how he felt about the state of the Ferrari. He quoted himself as having described the cars as 'fucking useless'. I don't know whether he would have actually used those words. I only hoped that Tavoni's vocabulary didn't include too much English vernacular. It was because of outbursts like this that I feared for my pal's career.

When we next met, he told me that he'd written to Enzo the

following morning, criticizing the cars' steering, the engines and the brakes. I didn't like to ponder what kind of letter a tired, emotional and hungover Mike might have penned. I was tempted to point out that the Ferraris' abysmal results were probably sufficient incentive alone for Enzo to seek dramatic improvement, but I thought that was another conversation best avoided.

Chapter Thirty-Four

Fencing at Nurburgring

It may have been a woeful time for Scuderia Ferrari as far as Grands Prix were concerned but, having established a comfortable lead over Porsche and Lotus, the team was enjoying considerable early season success in the Sports Car Championship. Accordingly, Mike was upbeat about his next assignment, the Nurburgring 1,000km. It helped that it was also his all-time favourite circuit, not only for the course but also the facilities.

Over yet another farewell late beer, on the Wednesday evening before his departure for Germany, he casually mentioned that he'd decided against flying there in his Vega Gull. Instead, he would drive the Jaguar.

'So, catching a ferry to Calais?' I asked.

'The ferry? Good God, no you pillock – far too slow. No, I'm driving to Southend where I'll pop the car on a plane, fly to Rotterdam, and drive to the circuit from there.'

'Sorry...put your car *in* an aeroplane?'

'Absolutely!' He was smirking.

I was momentarily speechless. I had no idea such a service existed. 'Have you done this before?'

'No. I only heard about it recently from Jo (Bonnier). It sounds a laugh.'

I wanted to ask him about the cost. It must have been fantastic.

I found out subsequently that this short-lived service was operated by Freddie Laker's air charter company. To say it was exclusive would be an understatement. The lower part of a Bristol Superfreighter's nose, below the cockpit, opened up to expose a hold capable of stowing three cars in a line. That was one of those moments when I realised that Mike's world and mine had diverged beyond measure.

This was film-star travel, and he took to it like a duck to water.

On arrival at the Nurburgring, Mike checked into the Sporthotel having specifically requested a room next to the Collinses. As his neighbours hadn't yet arrived, Mike took the opportunity to take out a Ferrari before official practice began. One might have thought he'd had enough of driving, having left Farnham that same morning.

The thing about 'the Ring' is that, at fourteen miles long and with 176 corners, it's impossible for most drivers to memorize the circuit. Consequently, it requires drivers' total concentration.

Enzo had issued instructions that the driver pairings were to be changed again, or at least Phil Hill was directed to share with Luigi, leaving Pete and Mike to share. Mike, of course, was delighted. When I asked him why Ferrari had done this, he said, 'It's obvious isn't it? Musso's probably gone snivelling to the Old Man, complaining about our little arrangement, and this is Ferrari's answer.'

Mike's 'little arrangement' was the unofficial agreement between him and Pete to split any prize money fifty-fifty. Of course, such an arrangement was completely contrary to Ferrari's modus operandi which was to play off his drivers against each other, and also was clearly against Musso's interests. For instance, apart from championship points at stake, if Pete or Mike was ahead of the other towards the close of a race, there was no incentive for either to overtake. And when that scenario featured Musso as Mike's co-driver, the former would miss out financially. By putting the two Brits together, any shared winnings were automatic. There couldn't really be any other explanation, because up until then the Collins/Hill partnership had been the most successful.

The principal external competition came from Aston Martin and Porsche. The former had a formidable line-up of driver talent: Stirling and Jack Brabham, Tony Brooks and Lewis-Evans, and Salvadori and Shelby. The Porsche representation was reduced by two cars on the first day of practice: one crashed into a tree; another left the track and burst into flames. Fortunately, neither driver was seriously hurt. The 3-litre V12 Testa Rossa Ferraris were every bit as capable as their opposition as far as speed and handling were concerned, but not so when it came to stopping. They still had drum brakes – something that was now widely considered passé.

The weather for Saturday's practice was dry and bright, and lap times started to fall. The best time of the day went to Mike, with Stirling two seconds slower. Two seconds over a lap time of nearly ten minutes may not sound like a lot – indeed, it isn't – but bettering Stirling is what would have been all-important.

The race deployed the familiar Le Mans type start, with all the drivers lined up, waiting for the countdown, before sprinting across to their cars. Maybe conscious of his slender two-second advantage over Stirling, Mike shot off before the countdown finished. As he crossed the tarmac, he heard Stirling behind him shout, 'You bastard, Hawthorn!'

Mike thought that was so hilarious he got a fit of giggles and consequently couldn't get his car started. He had to watch while Stirling and many of those around him took off before he did. Within a lap, however, Mike had got up into second place and was trying desperately to keep up with Stirling's Aston.

Stirling was really flying and successively breaking lap records. Stirling's teammate Jack Brabham, who took over, was unable to keep up the pace, and Mike was soon able to inherit the lead. Putting Stirling with Brabham appears to be an inexplicable decision for not only was it the Australian's first visit to 'the Ring' but it was also his first drive in a sports car of this ilk. At the time, we all thought that if Tony Brooks had been paired with Moss, they would have been unbeatable.

Unfortunately, on unlucky lap 13, Mike had a tyre burst on him immediately prior to handing over to Pete, which cost the pair a lot of time.

In theory, Mike was going to be relieved of driving duty for over two hours, but it was, I thought, still grossly irresponsible of Mike to wander off back to his hotel, mid-race, have a bath, and even have his overalls washed, dried and pressed! What if Pete had been taken unwell?

It was therefore a freshly laundered Mike who sauntered back to the pits in time to inherit the car from Pete on lap 28. By coincidence, this changeover coincided with a pit stop in the adjoining pit where Jack Brabham hopped out of the Aston and Stirling got back in. The Aston Martin crew also changed the tyres and refuelled the car. The Ferrari pit stop was far slower so that

Mike had to watch Stirling shoot off while his car's tank was still being filled.

Reg Parnell, one-time renowned driver and now manager of the Aston team, shouted across to Mike, 'Go fetch, boy!'

Mike responded with a two-fingered salute as he took off. This was not only noticed by an *Autosport* journalist but reported. Fortunately, in those days, it was printed in code. The sentence read: 'Mike gave what might be described as a jocular wave to Reg Parnell.'

Mike admitted to me that Reg's taunt spurred him on to such an extent that he pushed too hard and consequently spun the car and crashed into a ditch. He climbed out and tried to push the car out of the ditch. It was beached, straddled across one bank, and wouldn't budge. Ever resourceful, Mike spied a wooden fence, wrenched off a long plank and, with it, successfully levered the car back onto terra firma. He received such loud applause from the watching crowd that he gave them a quick bow before climbing back in and screaming off.

When I heard about this, I thought, What a show-off! Though I'd love to have seen that myself.

The lost time meant Stirling was never going to be catchable. He'd secured a lead of over four minutes, but at least Mike was able to hold on to his and Pete's second place to the end. And then, as a result of some rotten luck for Tony Brooks and Masten Gregory in a Jaguar D-Type, all the other Ferraris finished in the points: Taffy and Gendebien third, Luigi and Phil Hill fourth, and Seidel and Munaron fifth.

It was very much a case of Ferraris' overall capability and durability versus the brilliance of one driver, Stirling Moss – more than making up for his inexperienced partner. Stirling had driven thirty-six of the forty-four laps – over six hours on what was considered to be one of the most testing and tiring motor circuits in the world. Even loyal Members had to concede that in the Hawthorn v Moss supremacy debate, there was little debate.

Although there had been plenty of accidents and incidents elsewhere, none was so tragic as what happened to poor Erwin Bauer. The forty-five-year-old German, driving a privately entered 250 TR Ferrari hadn't noticed the finishing flag. On what should have been his slowing down lap, Bauer, still racing, crashed and died of his injuries. My pals back in Farnham, united in our bigoted youth, were of the opinion that he shouldn't have been racing at such an advanced age. In fairness to Mike, he did not share that view, and would always cite Fangio as an example of brilliance in his forties. No, Mike's beef, once again, was about the gulf of performance in the cars permitted to compete in these races.

'It's bloody madness…those Peugeots and Volvos are barely capable of 100 when we're travelling at 175. When you come up to them, it seems like they've stopped.'

'Can't you overtake them…pretend they're not there?' I ventured.

'It's not only the cars that are the problem; it's the drivers. They're simply not good enough. Poor old Tony was second on the last lap when he was taken out by a 403 (a Peugeot). The prat driving it moved right across in front of him on a corner…forced him into a ditch. If he'd have done that to me, I'd have thumped him.'

And, guess what? He would have done too.

After the race, some of the Ferrari driver entourage found their way back to the Collins's hotel room for a drink. Louise was wonderfully long-suffering. In anticipation that this 'early drink' might develop into a major party, Pete had thought to get in gallons of beer and a few bottles of whisky. Lots of people drifted in and out, including a very happy Stirling and Katie, Taffy, Phil Hill, Jean Behra and his wife, but unusually it remained something of a quiet affair. Mike put that down to two things. One: they were all totally knackered – 'even Moses'; and two: news reached them that the charming American driver, Pat O'Connor, had died that day in a fifteen-car pile-up in the Indianapolis 500-Mile Race. Apparently, his car had flown up into the air and landed upside down before bursting into flames. The following year, it became mandatory to have steel hoop protection above the line of the driver's head. Pat was twenty-nine years old.

After too little sleep, Mike returned home in the same manner in which he had left: by road and air charter. We met up the following lunchtime at the Duke of Cambridge in Farnham. His body language wasn't encouraging. I asked if he'd had a good journey.

'S'all right.' That was as much as I got.

'But the Jag must be great on those continental roads,' I prompted.

'Yeah, the Dutch roads are the best,' he said. 'Until the German border, I was doing a steady 120, 125. Once, the speedo hit 135. However, Germany was dire.'

'You reached 135?' I was incredulous.

'That was on the speedo, so it was probably closer to 120. I'd have much rather flown myself. The roads are so crowded, especially over here. You've always got to slow down for some bugger.'

'Aw come on. It's not that bad, surely?'

'You know that England has forty cars for every mile of road – and that's the average. Think what it must be around London and down here.'

If Mike was alive today, I wonder what he'd make of that statistic now being 150 cars per mile of road.

Mike had a letter with him. To my surprise, and I think his, it was a personal letter from Enzo Ferrari, addressing some of Mike's concerns with the Grand Prix cars. It was brief and clearly had been translated to English. In essence, it said that Enzo agreed that they had experienced problems and had been working really hard to address these, particularly the understeer about which Mike had complained so bitterly. He predicted that Mike would be much happier in the next race: the Belgian Grand Prix at Spa. There was, however, no mention of disc brakes.

Girlfriend Jean was periodically back on the scene and, on the now rarer occasions we all met up, Mike seemed in pretty good spirits. I wasn't convinced they would last as a couple. They were clearly mutually smitten, but Jean was more 'her own woman' than many of her predecessors (and peers!), and it didn't help matters that Winifred Hawthorn didn't seem to take to her.

Jean told Sally that the first time she stayed at the Hawthorns' they'd had supper on their laps in front of the telly. Mike had sat between Jean and his mother. Apparently, Winifred would pointedly say things such as, 'Pass that woman the salt' or 'Does that woman want more vegetables?' Jean, who at the time was barely twenty-one, found Mrs Hawthorn's hostility quite inexplicable – as did I – because she had positively worshipped Cherry, and the two girls weren't so different, at least not superficially.

Chapter Thirty-Five

Luigi's Luck

Having discovered there was an aerodrome just outside Spa, Mike had intended to fly to the Grand Prix in his trusty Vega Gull. His plan was scuppered at the last moment when he also discovered that the Gull's Certificate of Airworthiness (akin to an MOT for a motor vehicle) had expired.

Instead, he was obliged to take a commercial flight to Brussels from where he'd catch a train to Spa, a beautiful little town in the heart of the Ardennes Forest, close to the German border. Mike showed me a few photographs he'd taken of some grand buildings, including the impressive Spa baths, the world's oldest casino, and the Hotel Britannique where he and the Ferrari Scuderia all stayed.

The Spa-Francorchamps circuit had not hosted a Grand Prix for two years, and in the intervening time it had been improved considerably. The pits and paddock had been rebuilt, some corners eased, bumps erased, and the whole thing resurfaced. It was now one of the fastest circuits in the world. To give some indication of just how fast and furious most of its eight and three-quarter miles was, Mike was able to complete a lap at over 132 miles an hour, which included a thirty-mile an hour maximum hairpin bend.

Mike was immediately heartened to find that their Ferraris had improved commensurately with the circuit and were finally competitive.

Over the three familiarisation sessions, there was considerable shadow-boxing, with the drivers of the two fastest marques, Vanwall and Ferrari, not wishing to show their full potential, and yet anxious to be sufficiently competitive to gain good grid positions.

First, Tony Brooks set the best time; then it was Mike; then Stirling; and then Mike again finally, giving the latter pole position.

Meanwhile, the other Vanwalls and Ferraris were jockeying for position, and so the front row featured Luigi alongside Mike, Stirling next to him, ahead of Pete, Tony and Gendebien on the row behind: two Ferraris and a Vanwall on each row.

It was a nice touch that Ferrari had Gendebien's car painted yellow, the Belgian national racing colour, in the same way that he'd once had Mike's car painted British Racing Green.

Qualifying in last place on the grid was Maria Teresa de Filippis in what would be her first F1 drive. Poor Maria – she had to put up with so many chauvinistic taunts, it's a wonder she continued at all.

Besides the cagey tactics of practice, the principal talk was of a miraculous escape by Jean Behra. Halfway along the very fast Masta straight there was a little S-bend. As Behra's BRM entered the bend at 150mph, he touched the brakes. An oil breather pipe had broken and was spraying a mist of oil over the rear tyres, giving them almost no sideways resistance. The car weaved around as Behra fought to control the car with opposite lock, one way and then the other. He piloted the car through the bends at all angles, somehow missing everything in its path, until the bonnet struck a hedge, sending the car into a spin until it finally stopped. Jean Behra was shaken *and* stirred, but completely unhurt.

Someone remarked that Behra must be a cat in disguise as he really did seem to have nine lives. In fact, Jean survived twelve crashes in his career, and suffered all manner of broken bones, burns and concussion. He even lost an ear in one incident in 1955. His luck finally ran out in 1959 when the stocky little Frenchman lost control of his Porsche in the rain, was thrown out of the car, and flew directly into a flagpole. He died of a fractured skull and crushed ribcage. He was a feisty character, too. A month before his death, following a forced retirement from the French GP, he had an argument in a restaurant with Romolo Tavoni and another chap. He got so agitated he punched them both and, as a result, was summarily dismissed by Enzo Ferrari.

The Spa circuit itself may have been improved, but it didn't sound as if the administration had caught up. The new regulations specified a Grand Prix had to be of at least two hours' duration or 300 kilometres in distance. As the circuit had become so fast, the proposed twenty-four laps, totalling some 338 kilometres, could now be covered in about one hour forty minutes. Accordingly, the organizing club printed the programme showing the race would be run over thirty laps. Confusion reigned until someone made a last-minute decision to stick with twenty-four laps.

Then, when the grid formation was disclosed, it appeared that the organizers had put Mike on the wrong side of the track for pole position. Moss, on the other side, would have the advantage going into the first corner. Mike made a big fuss about this and was successful in getting his and Stirling's cars swapped over. Of course, when it came to start, Stirling's invariably faster getaway meant that it was he who swept through the first corner, much to Mike's embarrassment.

Mike's composure wasn't helped by the start. Under a hot sun, the drivers were careful about choosing when to start their engines – sometime after the two-minute signal and before the one-minute signal. The final signal board, indicating thirty seconds to go, would then go up – as would the adrenalin. On this occasion, shortly after displaying the thirty-second board, the two-minute board was inexplicably shown – for the second time. This was eventually followed by the one-minute board, which itself was repeated a minute later.

No one had a clue what the delays were for. It was a total shambles. All the engines were getting too hot, none more so than Pete's. He had to sit there, enveloped in steam with his Ferrari boiling over.

Mike was concentrating so much on his temperature gauge – which had ventured well into the red – that he missed the starter's eventual flag dropping. It was consequently an incensed Mike who tore after and quickly caught up with the leaders.

After Stirling's tremendous start, he missed a gear selection halfway through the first lap which sent the revs sky-high, effectively killing the Vanwall's engine and ending his race. Tony Brooks, in the second Vanwall, inherited the lead. Behind him were the three Ferraris of Pete, Gendebien and Mike. Tony was hounded first by Pete and then Mike for the rest of the race, but he managed to keep everyone at bay to win the Grand Prix. On paper, it was his second win but, given that his first – the British in '57 – resulted from Stirling taking over his car, I feel this was really his first. And it was a damned fine effort.

There was a moment of panic for Mike early in the race. As he swept through Stavelot, a sharp right-hander where Stirling missed a gear, he saw bits of red Ferrari strewn all over the place. Aware of how overheated Pete's engine had got at the start, Mike assumed that Pete's car had blown up and spun him into some concrete posts. The bulk of the car, however, was out of sight, down in a field on the outside of the corner. Mike admitted that for the ensuing half-dozen or so laps he was simply 'going through the motions'. All he could think was that Pete had probably been killed. And then, as he passed the pits, he saw Pete standing next to his car. Mike said afterwards that he felt an immediate flood of relief sweep through him until he realised that, if the crashed car wasn't Pete's, it had to be Luigi's, for he had seen Gendebien on the track.

This was, of course, relief tinged with guilt. He should have cared equally for his teammates, but he didn't. Mike made a point of looking out for the car on the next lap, and did spot it, complete with Luigi standing on the other side of the circuit. It was a miraculous escape. Luigi had a tyre burst when he was decelerating from about 160mph which sent the car spinning into the posts and off the circuit. His injuries, however, amounted to little more than a strained back.

Once Mike knew for certain that all his teammates and friends were okay, he got the bit between his teeth and set off after Tony. It was a good effort, but he had too much to do. He did manage to halve Tony's forty-second lead and bag the fastest lap for a bonus point. Should he have won? Who knows?

The finish itself was almost as chaotic as the start. Tony Brooks's gearbox failed, right at the last knockings; Mike's engine blew up as he crossed the line; and Stuart Lewis-Evans, in another Vanwall, came over with a drunken front wheel, lurching left and right. Had the race been one lap longer, it would have been won by the fourth-placed Lotus of Cliff Allison.

The retirement of both Stirling and Luigi from the race meant that Mike's second place, plus bonus point, brought him straight into contention as far as championship points were concerned. The leader board now read: Moss 17; Hawthorn 14; Musso 12. With the next points race being the French GP, a circuit he liked and at which he had excelled in '53, Mike was starting to feel more bullish.

Chapter Thirty-Six

Two Speeds to Le Mans – And One Back

I didn't know whether I might catch Mike between Spa and his next commitment, Le Mans, with there being only a week apart. Customarily, he would return home as soon as possible after a race, preferably in his own plane or car. At Spa, he had neither.

He was therefore a little lost when Pete and Louise pushed off with Harry Schell and his wife Monique early the following morning in order to attend a party in Paris to which Mike had not been invited. He kicked around for a while and then decided to wander into town in search of company. He headed straight for Pierre Le Grand – 'a great little restaurant where everyone goes'. There he bumped into Rodney Walkerley, the then Sports Editor of *The Motor*, and asked him if he was heading anywhere near Paris. Rodney was already committed to giving a motor racing artist a lift to Paris and welcomed Mike to join them.

Rodney was never in a rush and always sought out back roads, country lanes or 'nibbles', rather than main roads. He also prided himself on never going above 40mph if he could help it. After bumbling around like this for nearly five hours, Rodney chanced upon Dinant, a small Belgian town only ninety miles from Spa. They'd averaged 18mph.

Rodney and his other passenger decreed that was quite enough motoring for one day, and voted to stay put and head on to Paris the following day. Mike reckoned that, in the time it had taken them to reach Dinant, he could have driven to Paris, a distance of 260 miles. The stop did, however, allow the three chaps to thoroughly 'unwind' and toast their many absent friends.

They were slow to get going the following day, but still Rodney didn't alter his 'blistering pace', meandering through the rural lanes of Belgium and the Ardennes. Mike told of their need for innumerable refuelling stops en route. I enquired what sort of car it was that needed such frequent fuelling.

'Oh, no it wasn't the car…it was Rodney. He's rather partial to a gin and French. And to not join him, well…it wouldn't have been polite, would it?'

Seven hours later and the little party had only got as far as Reims, a distance of little over 100 miles. Mike said that, as much as he was enjoying the pace of the journey, if he wanted to get to Paris before midnight, he had to switch his mode of transport. He asked Rodney to drop him at the railway station where adieus were said and Mike hopped on a train to Paris. He arrived in time to catch Pete, Harry and co for 'one or two bevvies before bed' – something he confessed was not terribly wise given what he elected to do the following morning.

Bernard Cahier had offered to drive Mike to Le Mans in his much modified Renault Dauphine. The contrast in pace between Bernard's 'quick peddling' and Rodney's 'pottering' was about as extreme as it gets. Mike arrived at Le Mans 'a nervous wreck' – not helped, I'm sure, by the excesses of the previous day.

The extraordinary thing was how, as I've commented before, Mike's own driving was either flat out or dawdling, nothing in between – and it didn't seem to matter whether he had a passenger on board or not. But, as a passenger of a fast driver, he was dreadful. It was a good analogy of his life: he was either in a tearing hurry or he was ambling about, looking for amusement, or trouble. And he was never passive.

After checking in at the Hotel de Paris, Mike went off to see whether their cars might at last be fitted with disc brakes. They weren't. With the Astons' current form and drivers including Stirling and Tony, he and Pete didn't have a good feeling about their chances – unless it rained.

The Ferrari drivers' team was already weakened by the omission of Luigi, who was still recovering from his battering at Spa, and Munaron, a second-string driver, was also out with injury. Knowing Tavoni to be a worrier, Pete decided to pitch up on the first day of practice with his arm in a sling. Tavoni wasn't best pleased when Pete finally revealed he was only larking about. Neither was he amused when he heard reports of Pete and Mike saying that they weren't going to 'mess around with this twenty-four-hour nonsense' and they 'would be back home in time for Sunday lunch'.

Practice was telling. All three works' Astons, driven by Moss, Brooks and Salvadori, posted quicker times than the Ferraris. Not that it mattered for the race itself, as there were no grid positions up for grabs. The 4pm Le Mans start was a dramatic affair. With half an hour to go, the cars were pushed into position, and a host of gendarmes were deployed to clear the pits. At five to four, the drivers took up their positions within little painted circles opposite their cars. As the minutes ticked down so too did the hubbub from the tens of thousands of spectators. So quiet was it that, in the grandstand, they said you could hear the swish of the starter's flag followed by the pounding footsteps of the drivers as they sprinted to reach their cars. Within seconds, the pervading silence was displaced by an explosion of unsilenced exhausts, and they were off.

Once again, Stirling shot off first, with Mike trailing the other Astons. By the end of the first lap, Mike had hauled himself up into second place yet couldn't make any ground on Stirling. In fact, the Aston was gaining four seconds a lap. On the hour-mark, Mike was still in second place, and Stirling's lead had grown to half a minute. Mike lost and regained second place a couple of times, but Stirling was controlling the race.

When the skies darkened and a few spots of rain appeared, Mike made a concerted charge and recorded the fastest lap of the whole race —his fourth successive fastest lap of Le Mans: 1955 to 1958, a fantastic achievement of which he was justifiably proud. This going-for-broke spell, coupled with his admitted slipping of the clutch at the start, probably marked the beginning of the end for his Ferrari's clutch.

Shortly after this, Stirling's Aston blew up on the Mulsanne Straight, putting Mike briefly in the lead before handing over to Pete. As the two drivers swapped over so the heavens opened. A thunderstorm was directly overhead, and diluvial rains began to fall. Mike dived for cover and shouted over his shoulder, 'Looking good for lunch!' Within minutes, the track was deluged and visibility negligible.

Mike said, 'I was as lucky with that timing as Pete was unlucky… I really felt for him.' And then he laughed like a drain.

Sections of the track were beneath standing water, and in other places, there were rivers of wet mud. It was treacherous. Poor Pete had a torrid time. He hated driving when he couldn't see properly. In contrast, the American Phil Hill seemed to thrive on it and took his Ferrari into a dominant lead, which he and Gendebien maintained right to the finish.

To give some perspective to the inequality of performance between the participating cars, the winning Ferrari completed 305 laps in the twenty-four hours, compared to the slowest finisher's 202 laps.

The conditions decimated the field. Only twenty cars completed the course. Thirty-five didn't make it. And one of those was Mike and Pete's. The pair continued for a while but, despite the endeavours of the mechanics, the slipping clutch got worse. They knew they were going slower and slower, but this was mostly due to the awful visibility. The design of the car, so Mike said, was such that everything – rain, dirt, oil, debris – was directed straight onto one's visor. He desperately wished they'd been in a D-Type.

All around the circuit were crashed or burning cars. One Frenchman, with the unfortunate nickname of 'Mary', was killed.

Approaching the halfway point of the race, at 2am, during another Pete stint, the Ferrari's clutch finally gave out. Wet through and tired, Pete trudged back to the pits to tell Mike the 'good news' – it was all over.

Hugely relieved, they jumped into Pete's car, drove to the hotel, and had a couple of drinks before grabbing a couple of hours' kip. In the morning, Pete drove Louise and Mike up to Paris where they all caught the boat train to England.

I got a phone call that evening. On answering it, I heard a click as the caller pressed Button A to be heard. 'Tom, what are you up to?'

'Mike…? Are you okay? I heard you had trouble—'

'Yeah, bloody clutch went. Enough of that. You up for a beer later?'

'Later?'

'Well, not now, obviously, we're in London. Pete's staying at the Pond tonight. Fancy joining us?'

I was staggered. In my mind's eye, Mike was still either driving Le Mans or hanging around the Ferrari pits, and now we were about to meet up in Farnham. 'Righto. What time?'

'We're aiming to get there by ten. Call some others. With luck, we'll get a lock-in.'

'I take it you're okay?'

'No, I'm bloody not. I'm thirsty! I'll tell you all when I see you.' And, with that, he hung up.

I rounded up a couple of Members and got to the Pond barely half an hour before Mike screeched to a halt in his Jag. Our little reception committee went outside to welcome him back. I was portering a spare pint of light and mild which disappeared in three gulps and twenty seconds. He was in an uproarious mood and, absolutely right, the Pond was only too happy to allow Mike and Pete to host a 'private party'.

At some point, an older chap I didn't recognize asked Mike whether Stirling was as good as he was cracked up to be. I was conscious the press had started using more and more elaborate words to describe Stirling's 'phenomenal' abilities, and I was keen to hear what Mike thought.

He replied, 'I guess we'll never know. We always drive different cars. I like to think that, when it comes to taking the fastest lap, I can match him any day, anywhere – but it's just that the little blighter can keep it up, hour after bloody hour.'

I looked at my ebullient, healthy-looking young pal and asked myself whether he really was, as the quacks prophesied, on the way out. It seemed unfeasible. Had he somehow recovered?

The boozing, the chatting and the laughter went on until well after two o'clock, by which time Louise had sensibly been asleep in bed for at least two hours. Thankfully, the roads were deserted by the time Mike and I drove to our respective homes.

Chapter Thirty-Seven

Musso's Monza

Tucked up in the Frensham Pond Hotel, Pete was blissfully unaware of Enzo's fury at his behaviour. Tavoni's loyalty to his boss was absolute, and thus he had no choice but to report that whilst one Ferrari had won, the other two had been abandoned by their drivers.

Wolfgang Siedel, Taffy's partner, had gone into a ditch around midnight and had tried in vain to dig it out. Enzo wouldn't hear about half-hearted attempts. As far as Enzo was concerned, Siedel should have stopped at nothing to get his car out of the ditch, monsoon rains or not.

Pete's plight was worse, for Tavoni had passed on the rumour about the English pair being determined to get back home for a Sunday roast. When the mechanics went to recover Mike and Pete's car at the end of the race, the clutch, which had had twelve hours to cool down, appeared to be fine, and they were able to drive the car back to the pits. This only strengthened Enzo's conviction that Pete had deliberately abandoned the car in order to go home early. As far as Enzo was concerned, that was a slight and a disloyalty that he'd not forget.

Mid-morning the following day, Mike showed up at the TT Garage. The staff were quite bemused, especially when they found out he'd spent the night in his own bed. The first thing he asked was whether anyone knew the result of the race in which he'd participated!

We met up fleetingly once more that week. The rest of his time was spent closeted with the Collinses, even inviting them round for meals with his mother.

The boys were to go in different directions for the weekend, and Mike had the short straw. While Pete went to Oulton Park to drive pre-war racing cars for fun (one of which was a 1939 monster Mercedes with a straight-eight 5.6-litre engine producing a whopping 646bhp – more even than a 2011 McLaren 12C), Mike went from one event he knew he disliked straight off to another that he thought he would: the Monza 500.

Ferrari had been obliged to enter the race. He prepared two cars and lined up three drivers: Mike, Luigi and Phil Hill. Also in the race were Stirling and Fangio. The European cars, particularly the Italian ones, were not built for the rough pounding of the high-speed banked sections of the track. Mike said it was terrifying, hurtling round at such an angle, the whole car viciously vibrating, trying to shake itself apart – lurching uncontrollably from side to side. His helmet was threatening to come off, his vision was blurred, and even his teeth were chattering involuntarily.

He told me, 'It's like riding the Wall of Death only it's not all over in five minutes. All you can do is keep your right foot pressed down, your eyes wide open, and hold onto the steering wheel like your life depends upon it…because it does! You could get bounced right out of the cockpit, it's that rough.' He complained so bitterly to the mechanics that they installed a fighter plane-type harness to keep him strapped in.

Despite these protestations, Mike posted the fastest lap of the first practice session in a V12 Ferrari with a three-speed gearbox – at an average speed of 164.49mph. But that was before his Italian teammate had a go. The following day, Luigi, having only just recovered from his horrific crash a fortnight before, went out in the same car and smashed Mike's lap record – recording a lap speed of 175.73mph.

The continental press lauded the Italian and were critical of the Englishman's commitment. In praise of Luigi, even *Motor Sport* wrote:

Musso's most amazing display of courage and determination… Watching this effort from the north banking was almost as frightening as it must have been for Musso driving it, for by no stretch of the imagination could the Ferrari be said to have suitable suspension, and it was in full-lock slides right around the top of the banking, with inches of daylight showing under its wheels. Whilst Musso wrestled with the steering in a win-or-bust battle, Hawthorn just would not put his heart into driving the Ferrari and could not approach Musso's times or speeds…

This endurance race was again held over three heats, each now bearing sponsors' names: Esso, Mobil and Shell. Each heat was sixty-three laps, and the smaller-engined V6 Ferrari failed to even complete the first. As a consequence, all three drivers took turns to drive the V12 and, between them, they managed to pick up third place, finishing behind two Yank Tanks. But it was no thanks to Mike. By his own admission, he had been out-driven by the other two: Luigi for speed, and Phil for perseverance.

I can't help feeling that Luigi had wanted to prove something to someone – Enzo perhaps? Also worthy of note is that Musso was forced to stop early in the first heat, having been affected by methanol fumes. As he handed the car over to Mike, he was almost unconscious. He was helped to the pit counter where he practically fell over. He was duly bundled off to hospital 'to be revived'. To his credit, he was 'revived' sufficiently to drive the first twenty laps of the second heat. Mike likewise succumbed to the methanol fumes and, through sheer exhaustion, came in after twenty-four laps of the final heat to hand over to Phil to finish the race.

Fangio had two cars break down on him and never completed a heat, and Stirling had both offside tyres burst against the top retaining wall when travelling at 160mph, which caused him to slither all the way down to the inside of the track. He was certain he was going to die. Amazingly, he was completely unhurt.

It had been a glitzy, razzamatazz of a motor race, thrilling for the spectators, but one which would never be repeated. It began in controversy in 1957 and ended in 1958 due to lack of finance. It also never saw a fatality and was, at the time, the fastest race in the world. Mike hated every second of it.

He returned home the following day, looking dreadful. He was shattered and clearly in a lot of pain. He complained bitterly that his insides hurt, and that was despite having worn two body belts (something his younger self would never have done). His only compensation was that the rest of the season would be exclusively Grand Prix racing – six races over four months. The endurance stuff was over, thank goodness.

Chapter Thirty-Eight

A Woman's Helmet and Morto Musso

Mike hardly had time to draw breath let alone recuperate. After only one night at home, he was flying off to Paris, en route to Reims, again – this time for the French.

In Paris, he checked into the Miami Hotel where, by chance, Stirling and Katie Moss were also staying. Mike persuaded the Mosses to come with him to the Crazy Horse Saloon, a popular nightclub which offered striptease acts. It was bursting at the seams, and the smoky, alcoholic atmosphere was warm and intoxicating.

During the evening, Stirling asked Mike how he was getting to Reims. Mike had planned to fly, but at that stage hadn't any fixed arrangements. Stirling offered him a lift in his elegant Mercedes 220S. Rather than reply directly, Mike turned to Katie and asked, 'What's he like on the road now?'

'Oh, he's very good and drives quite slowly.'

Turning back to Stirling, Mike said, 'Thank you, Stirling, I'd love to come.'

The three of them set off for Reims the next morning, stopping for lunch at the ancient town of Soissons where they met up with Stirling's manager, Ken Gregory, and Harry Schell and their respective wives. Mike told Ken that Stirling seemed to have got the hang of this driving lark. By mid-afternoon, the party had arrived at Reims and were checking into their hotels.

The hot topic in the Ferrari camp was that Pete, winner of this race two years previously – in a Ferrari, had been dropped by Enzo. The four drivers chosen for the GP were Mike, Luigi, Taffy and Olivier Gendebien.

Ferrari's instructions to Tavoni were that Pete was to compete in a Formula 2 race over thirty laps, instead of the Grand Prix race.

Pete was livid, and demanded an explanation from Tavoni.

I believe this was the gist of Tavoni's extraordinary answer: 'Luigi complain to Mr Ferrari that you and Mike are such close friends that you drive against him. So, Ferrari he say, "Musso, in Reims, you will have no problem." Then he ask Peter to do Formula Two race only, but for same money as Formula One. He say to Peter, "You are not just a driver, you are part of my family. This is protection for Musso."'

As it happened, this was a most unfortunate sentiment.

Pete argued that if he was to finish the Formula 2 race in a good position and was still feeling capable, he would like to be given the opportunity to race in the Grand Prix.

Tavoni thought this was not a good idea as it was forecast to be a hot day and Pete would be too tired.

Pete pleaded that he at least ask Enzo. Curiously, Enzo must have relented because he threw it back to Tavoni, saying that he could make a snap decision at the time.

Tavoni's explanation wasn't accepted by everyone. After all, Pete was comfortably one of the top three drivers for Ferrari, so why would Ferrari drop him at the request of another driver when Ferrari relished competition within his team? The more plausible explanation postulated was punishment. Ferrari had been furious with the English contingent for ruining the clutch at Le Mans, and Pete in particular for abandoning the car. There was also speculation that this decision was a way of expressing Enzo's disappointment that Pete and Louise had moved out of Maranello, that they had deserted him.

Pete was not the only one to be snubbed that weekend. The Italian driver Maria Teresa de Filippis had entered to race only to be told by the race director: 'The only helmet a woman should wear is the one at the hairdresser's.' He refused to allow her to compete.

The lure of champagne to be won during practice clearly again pressed all the right buttons in Mike, for he was the first driver to lap at over 200kph and consequently won 100 bottles of bubbly. He was also the first to lap at over 210kph, thus bagging himself another 100 bottles, and as his lap speeds were not beaten during the whole of practice, he won another 100! He could literally have bathed in the stuff.

Mike was very impressed with the performance from the engine

– at 8,600 revs, he was hitting 180mph down the straight. Fangio had entered too, putting in a guest-starring role in a Maserati but, unlike its driver, the car could not compete with the latest models from Ferrari, BRM and Vanwall.

In practice for Formula 2, Pete was second only to Stirling Moss in Rob Walker's Cooper. Pete enlisted Ken Gregory's help to appeal Ferrari's decision to bar him from the Grand Prix. Ken spoke to Tavoni and insisted that it was Mike, by his own admission, who had 'buggered up' the clutch, and that neither driver would have walked away from a car that had any prospects of finishing. Moreover, argued Ken, Stirling was competing in both races. Why not allow Pete to do likewise?

Tavoni relented, and Pete inherited Taffy's car for the end of the GP practice, and managed to bag himself a second row slot on the grid, ahead of Stirling's Vanwall. The musical chairs effect of this development was not kind to his teammates. Poor old Olivier was deprived of a drive, and Taffy, who would inherit his car, had to start right at the back of the grid as he hadn't practised in that particular car.

Aside from these travails, the practice days for the Ferrari boys were jolly affairs, with some bloody good lunches and the 'odd sherbet' later on. Mike recounted a story from one such lunch. Harry Schell, whose BRM was going fantastically well, had announced that once he'd finished his good steak and the fine bottle of Beaujolais, he was going to take Monique, his wife, upstairs for 'one of the best experiences of her life'!

Mike was sitting next to Tony Rudd, BRM's chief engineer, and with whom Mike had made his peace. Mike made as if to go to the toilet and whispered to Tony, 'Keep him talking.' He was gone a while.

Apparently, he and Pete systematically removed everything from Harry's room – the carpet, the curtains, the bed, the table and chairs, the wardrobe, the couple's clothes and toiletries – everything except a vase of flowers they placed in the middle of the floor. They waited out of sight, and once the Schells had entered, they locked the room door from the outside.

'It was priceless,' he said. 'Harry went ballistic. Naturally, we did unlock the door…once he'd finished shouting that he wanted all his possessions brought to his room at once!'

The following morning, Mike rounded up Pete, Taffy and Luigi, and between them they managed to carry Harry's Vespa 400cc – a two-seater microcar – from outside on the street, where it was parked, up the stairs and dump it on the landing near the Schells' bedroom, with a 'For Sale' sign on top. Apparently, it was too wide to get into the bedroom, but they explained to Harry they'd done their best to 'bring him all his possessions'.

Practice was not such fun for Maurice Trintignant who, like Pete and Stirling, had entered both the F1 and F2 races. For the F2, he was to drive a Cooper-Climax for Rob Walker. On the last day of practice, his Cooper caught fire, and Maurice managed to jump out whilst the car was still moving. He was swiftly attended by a brand new safety innovation: the helicopter ambulance. Despite suffering minor burns to his neck and back, he was insistent that he could still race for BRM the next day. As it transpired, for all his stoicism, both his cars let him down to the extent he was unable to complete either race.

There were three full races that weekend. First up was a twelve-hour endurance race for GT cars which started at midnight on the Saturday. Fortunately, the recently 'bumped' Olivier, partnered with Paul Frère, won this comfortably for Ferrari. Mike spent the whole of this race in bed, only getting up for the Formula Two race which started at 2pm. This was predicted to be a three-horse affair: Stirling in a Cooper, Jean Behra in a Porsche, and Pete in a Ferrari Dino. Behra dominated from the start. He was briefly challenged by Stirling until the Cooper packed up. Pete was never quite able to catch the Porsche, and brought the Ferrari home in a respectable second place, ahead of six other Coopers.

By the end of the race, Mike was concerned about the amount of spilled oil on the track, after nearly thirteen and half hours of racing, and expressed his concern to the organizers. He was grudgingly permitted to do an exploratory lap to spot the hazards. Rather unnecessarily, Pete offered to lead Mike round in his GP car and point out any spills.

With the Ferraris placed first, second and fourth on the grid, there was at last a sense of optimism in the team. Sure, the Vanwalls of Brooks and Moss were in fifth and sixth position but neither they nor Harry's BRM had any element of superiority over the latest offerings from Maranello. The real competition was going to be between the Ferrari drivers themselves. Bang next to Mike on pole was Luigi Musso.

Seldom one to get away quickly, Mike was outgunned by Harry, Tony Brooks and Luigi – in that order. Nevertheless, Mike was in tremendous form, and even before completion of the first lap he'd taken the lead. Looking in his mirrors, he could see a phalanx of pursuers. These included the three he'd overtaken, plus Fangio, Stirling and Pete. But none of them could catch him. By the second lap, the Ferraris were looking in control. Luigi had bagged second place, and Pete third.

By the fifth lap, and clearly with something to prove to the Old Man, Pete was really getting into his stride and began catching his teammates. Then, as he approached the tight Muizon corner, he found the brake pedal was locked solid. A metal air scoop had fallen into the footwell and become lodged underneath the pedal. Pete rapidly changed down to first gear and was lucky to run off into the escape road. He needed to reverse out, but found the gear lever now wouldn't budge. Using the scoop, he banged it against the lever until it was freed. This little 'moment' lost Pete fifteen places. So incensed was he that, as he passed the pits, he lobbed the air scoop at the Ferrari pit mechanics.

The order of the race leaders remained unchanged after nine laps, but Musso was now snapping at Mike's heels. As they embarked upon lap 10, Mike led Luigi past the pits and under the Dunlop Bridge, both cars approaching 160mph. Immediately after the footbridge, the circuit curved gently into a long right-hander, a corner that taken with care could be driven almost flat out. Once he'd rounded the bend, Mike glanced in his mirror to see Musso's car going sideways and then disappear in a cloud of dust. He knew it was bad, but there was nothing he could do about it, and so pressed on regardless. On the next lap, he saw the small helicopter in action for the second time that weekend.

Meanwhile, Fangio, in what would be his last ever Grand Prix race, had inherited second place – an extraordinary feat considering the inferiority of his outdated Maserati. Pete too was doing well. He managed to work his way through the traffic to join Messrs Fangio, Moss, Behra, von Trips and Schell in a battle royal for a place.

A while later, when Mike thought he had a comfortable lead,

he came up behind Fangio who'd had to stop at the pits. Out of deference to the great driver, he decided not to lap him but instead follow him round for a bit. Mike told me that he was happy just to study the racing lines he took, and note the smoothness with which he controlled the car. 'His placing of the car for a corner was calm and precise – always an immaculate line'.

Mike continued to lead the field and, in the closing stages, decided to go for the fastest lap bonus point. This he achieved, albeit he'd been even quicker in practice.

Amongst the chasing group it was, unsurprisingly, Stirling who, once Behra's BRM had retired, prevailed to take second. Behind him was Taffy, then Pete. However, as Taffy crossed the finish line, Pete ran out of fuel. If he hadn't led Mike round that recce lap prior to the race itself, he'd have been fine.

Mike said, 'I even warned the daft bugger that might happen. His car had smaller fuel tanks than the rest of ours, but he wouldn't listen.'

Stranded, Pete jumped out and pushed his car to the finish line. It says something for his stamina that he was able to do that after not one race but two. While Pete was pushing for all he was worth, Fangio came whooshing past to claim fourth place. Pete's consideration of Mike had cost him one championship point and, more importantly, £500 in prize money.

In answer to his teammates' enquiries, no one in the pits was able to say how Luigi was after his accident. All they knew was it was serious, and he'd gone straight off to hospital. Mike suggested that, after the prize-giving, he drive Pete and Louise and Phil Hill there to see how he was. They'd seen Luigi emerge from similar crashes with barely a scratch, so they were determined to remain optimistic. The roads leading away from the circuit were, as always, jammed, and Mike became frustrated at their lack of progress.

Phil told me Mike's behaviour had really shocked him. 'He was shouting at everyone to get out of the effing way. There was this little old lady on a bike, wobbling in front of us, going very slowly. Mike was so impatient he nudged her, admittedly gently, with the car's bumper, causing her to fall off onto the grass verge. He didn't stop to find out how she was. He just drove on. I doubt she was badly hurt, but it was one of the most callous things I've ever witnessed.'

When they eventually reached the hospital, they met a friend of Luigi's who told them that Luigi had recently passed away. He died of a fractured skull. He was thirty-three years of age.

Tavoni had reached the hospital first, and when he heard the news, he collapsed. He'd been awake for the whole of the twelve-hour race, the Formula 2 race and the Grand Prix. He was completely exhausted, and this news was too much. The doctors decided to sedate him and put him in a hospital bed.

It's possible that Tavoni had seen this coming. What he'd omitted to tell Pete, when recounting Luigi's plea to break up the Hawthorn/Collins allegiance, was that Musso was in deep financial trouble. Earlier in the year, Musso had committed to import 1,000 Pontiacs a year into Italy. There was scant demand in Europe for large American cars, and consequently he was heavily in debt. His business partner had sent him a telegram the day before the Grand Prix, telling him that he absolutely had to win in order to stave off their creditors. The French GP prize money was the largest purse of the season.

To be truthful, I don't think that anyone was much surprised. Pete said he'd seen Luigi leave the track at the very spot where he had crashed three times before his accident. He'd been really pushing his luck. Remembering Luigi's bravura performance in the Monza 500 and the Targa Florio, Mike said it was only a matter of time.

Accepting there was nothing they could do at the hospital, the foursome piled into the car and headed back to the hotel. According to Mike, they just sat down, and no one spoke for what seemed like ages. In this maudlin silence, I am sure they were thinking about their teammate, their rivalry, of the good and bad times past, and of their own mortality. Mike apparently announced he would have to pack up racing soon or he would end up morto like Musso.

Then they began to discuss how the accident might have happened, and concluded that, by and large, it was Luigi's own stupid fault; how it almost served him right, the way he'd tried to get Pete demoted to Formula Two. Pete recalled how Musso had refused to let Fangio take over his car back in '56 – despite team orders. Mike remembered the occasion when Luigi had wheedled his way into a drive at Pescara when they were both told that Ferrari would not be entering.

And then all it took for the mood to change completely was for Mike to say, 'Look, he's gone and that's it – there's nothing we can do about it. Let's go out and have a drink.' Although, of course, in their case, there wasn't much chance of it being one drink…

Later that night, Tony Rudd wandered down to Bridget's Bar where he found Mike and Pete and a few others rather well lubricated. He said no sooner had he walked in than Mike grabbed him and began winding a fire hosepipe round his waist and stuck the nozzle down the front of his trousers. He only just managed to extricate himself before Mike was able to turn on the water.

After closing time, the jolly party sashayed their way back to their hotel, and Mike and Pete started kicking an empty beer can about in a mock game of football, larking about and laughing loudly.

It was the worst possible timing because passing them in a car, also on her way back to the hotel, was Musso's girlfriend, Fiamma Breschi, who was returning from the hospital having said a final goodbye to her dead fiancé. The scene confronting her confirmed her belief that Luigi's death meant absolutely nothing to his former teammates. From that moment on, she developed an absolute and obsessive hatred for the pair of them. She spoke of wanting to see them die too.

It may have seemed unbelievably inappropriate behaviour to Fiamma, but those young guys had already witnessed a lot of fatalities, and they knew full well that, but for the grace of God, it could be them next time. Yet all the time they were spared, there were celebrations to be had. It was not insignificant that Mike had picked up 5 million francs – or nearly £5,000 (the price then of two semi-detached Farnham houses). He'd won Ferrari's first Grand Prix since the German of '56, and he'd drawn level on championship points with Stirling – at twenty-three points apiece. There was an awful lot to celebrate.

Chapter Thirty-Nine

Meeting Sir William

There was to be a two-week interval between the French GP and the British GP on 20 July. Almost immediately when Mike arrived home, he announced he was going to take a holiday. I wasn't alone when I teased him that his whole life was one long holiday. He had the good grace to agree, but said that he fancied going to Ireland, to forget all about motor racing for a while.

Whilst Mike was delighted with another victory at Reims, he and Enzo were pilloried by the magazine *Civiltà Catolica*. It said the win meant nothing, because it was built on dead men. These harsh words got to Enzo Ferrari who went to see a priest about his intention to retire. He was told: 'God gives each of us a way. Sometimes it is difficult, sometimes it is easy. You have chosen the difficult way. You must have the courage to follow it.'

Taking time away from racing may have been Mike's aspiration but it didn't work out like that.

Firstly, Lofty telephoned him the next day with an offer he couldn't refuse: Would he travel up to Silverstone to test a brand new car?

Once Jaguar had withdrawn from racing, Lofty was promoted from race team manager to a director of Jaguar Cars. Mike's justification to us for helping Lofty was that there was a rumour Jaguar might return to racing the following year, and he wanted to make sure he'd be their number one driver. There may have been some truth in that, though what was undeniable is that of all the 'authority' figures in Mike's life it was Lofty for whom Mike would do almost anything. Lofty was like Mike's favourite uncle. Plus Mike genuinely liked driving Jaguars, probably more than any other marque of car.

Mike reckoned that he could go straight from Silverstone to

Birmingham Airport from where he could catch a commercial flight to Dublin. I asked him how he intended to get to Silverstone.

'That's easy,' he replied. 'You're going to give me a lift.'

As this conversation was taking place on a Monday evening and he was intent on going up in the morning, there was no way I could oblige: I would be at work. He read my expression. 'Aw, come on... just ring up and tell 'em you're not feeling too clever. Say, you've got a stomach bug.'

I'd never feigned sickness before, but the thought of spending the day with Mike *and* seeing a new Jag put through its paces was too tempting. I agreed and said I'd call for him at eight thirty. I hoped I wouldn't be seen by anyone.

When I drove up to his house a few minutes early, I was surprised to see Mike standing outside his front door. He was dressed, suitcase in hand, and clearly raring to go. He told me to park up and hop in the Jag. He'd be driving. He was on great form that morning due, I'm sure, to the prospect of spending time with Lofty, doing what he did best, and knowing there was no racing for nearly a fortnight.

It was great to have some time alone together. We devoured a packet of assorted Spangles as he regaled me with some of the high points of the French GP, not least his description of the 'sexy little crumpet' who kissed him when he was presented with the trophy. She was, apparently, '*ooh la la*'.

He was honest, too, about Luigi. He said that he hadn't much cared for the chap, and spoke of how Luigi had always jostled for supremacy within the Scuderia. But I didn't get the impression he was triumphant at his teammate's death. He was more relieved that the infighting was over.

I asked him whether there was any truth in the story about Graham Hill almost wriggling out of his cockpit whilst going round a 160mph corner. It was true, apparently. Mike said that the oil in Graham's Lotus gearbox had got so hot it had melted the solder holding on the filler cap and, as a result, boiling oil was slopping onto his legs.

To say Mike didn't hang about on that drive would be an understatement. We covered the ninety-odd miles to Silverstone in a little under an hour and a half. When we arrived at the circuit, I walked behind the car and glanced down at the exhaust. The inside of the gleaming chromium pipes were milky white – not a hint of black or sooty brown deposit. No car driven by Mike would ever need a decoke – a new engine periodically, perhaps, but not a decoke.

The circuit was relatively deserted; so different to the Silverstone I was used to seeing on race days. We drove around until we spotted a small group of men standing around half a dozen cars. I'd expected to see Lofty, of course, and one or two of the design engineers, but I never imagined that Sir William Lyons, 'Mister Jaguar', himself would be in attendance. I recognised him immediately from the many photographs I'd seen. This must be important, I thought.

Mike screeched to a halt and jumped out. I got out more slowly.

'Good morning, Sir William,' said Mike, in his politest voice. I thought it interesting that Mike was formal and deferential towards the company's founder and chief executive, especially by contrast to the greeting of his old friend Frank England: 'Morning, Lofty!'

Not forgetting his manners, Mike introduced me to the assembled Jaguar personnel. In addition to Sir William and Lofty, there was the legendary Bill Heynes, the company's designer and chief engineer, and three or four others whose names now escape me. All but one were dressed in dark suits – the exception was clearly the 'spanner man', and he wore smart white overalls. I guessed his job was tuning: to micro-adjust the timing or carburettor jets, perhaps at the instruction of Bill Heynes.

Sir William, despite being dwarfed by Lofty, was unquestionably the boss. I'd never before seen big Lofty in a subservient role. And although Lyons had quite a reputation as an autocrat, his intelligence was easily apparent and his authority quietly exercised. He'd clearly earned his respect. He was to Jaguar what Enzo was to Ferrari.

It was only as I stepped forward to shake his hand that I remembered something so awful I felt myself falter. It related to that dreadful crash at Le Mans in '55. Naturally, everyone at Jaguar had been upset by that tragedy, but it was far worse for Sir William than anyone else I'd met. His only son, christened John Michael, exactly like Mike and within a year, the same age as Mike, had crashed his car and died whilst driving to watch his father's Jaguars compete at Le Mans.

As far as the press were concerned, it was a minor story, overshadowed by the scale of all the spectator deaths, but I remember asking myself how Mr Lyons (he was knighted the following year) could possibly carry on in the car industry after something like that. And maybe Jaguar's decision to withdraw from motor sport a year later wasn't completely unconnected with Lyons' own loss.

What Mike had come to drive was in front of us. It was a fabulous looking car – not dissimilar to a D-Type, but softer and even more graceful. The dorsal fin at the rear had gone, and the cockpit now resembled a conventional luxury sports car. As a prototype, there were places where it was obviously unfinished, but there was no denying its seductive shape. The thought that one day even someone like me might be able to buy such a car from a showroom and drive it home was…well, it was unthinkable. It was too gorgeous. Little did I know then that I was seeing a nascent E-type, a car that was to bring more fame to Jaguar than any other model. And, in the eyes of many commentators, the most beautiful car in the world. It was to be another eighteen months before it would be ready for production.

This meeting was, however, very evidently Lofty's, and soon the conversation became earnestly technical. A lot of jargon went straight over my head. I soon began to feel like a spare part, and so volunteered to wander off in search of coffee for everyone.

As I walked past the circuit's many buildings, I thought back to the '55 crash. Halfway through the race, hours after the main disaster had occurred, Mercedes' team manager Alfred Neubauer had sought out Lofty to request Jaguar's retirement from the race, saying the Mercedes' board had met and that was their wish. It was reported that Lofty argued that there was still a race to be won and that he had gone there to race, and unless the race was to be officially stopped, that's what his team would continue to do.

When I first heard that, I was surprised Lofty did not feel compelled to refer the question to his immediate superior, William Lyons. But what if Lofty had learned that his boss's son had just been killed? Might he have thought that he couldn't possibly burden his grieving employer any further? I meant to ask Mike about this once we were alone, for I was sure that if Lofty would talk to anyone about such things, it would be Mike, but I confess I forgot about it until it was too late.

Poor Sir William, I thought. Not only had he had that double tragedy to endure but a large part of Jaguar's Browns Lane works had burnt down eighteen months later, taking with it many nearly finished cars. Incredibly, the man's face gave away none of this. He did not appear broken or angry or in pain. His countenance was simply business-like. If one ever wants an example of English stiff upper lip, I give you Sir William Lyons, the son of an Irishman.

The rest of the morning I spent mostly on my own, watching Mike hammering round Silverstone in the prototype. Momentarily, I would fancy that I could swap places with him and do just as well, and then I'd get realistic. He was probably one of only twenty drivers in the country who could take that car's handling right to the limit, stay relatively safe, *and* give technical feedback.

I drifted back and forth to the pit area to glean how things were going. The 3-litre prototype was being developed for comfort as well as speed and therefore had power-assisted brakes, softer suspension, and no limited-slip differential. Notwithstanding its concessions, everyone, Mike included, seemed to be delighted with the results. Mike's best lap, 1 minute 49 seconds or just shy of 97mph, was a mere three seconds off Silverstone's sports car lap record – something which was fittingly held jointly by Stirling and Mike.

I was loitering in the pits when Mike came in for the final time. Sir William fired a lot of questions at him, some about the novel features of the prototype, and others about the potential customer demand for such a car. It was clear that Sir William had a healthy respect for Mike, even though they'd not had many face-to-face encounters. It may have been more than that. There could have been another coincidental parallel between Lyons and Enzo Ferrari: both men might have unwittingly been searching for surrogate sons.

Then, to my great surprise, Sir William suddenly asked who Mike would like as teammates should Jaguar ever decide to return to sports car racing. Mike didn't hesitate: 'Peter Collins and Phil Hill.' I wondered what Ferrari would make of such a suggestion – all of his top Grand Prix drivers driving for Jaguar.

I was fairly certain that Mike, if forced to choose between Ferrari and Jaguar now, would choose Jaguar, even if it meant no more Grands Prix. I wasn't so sure about Pete, and certainly not Phil who'd only recently begun to drive sports cars for Ferrari and was likely to be next in line for a Grand Prix car. Sir William emphasized that it was very much an 'if' rather than a 'when' question.

Lofty kindly invited me to adjourn with them to the White Horse, a nearby pub, for 'a spot of beer, bread and cheese'. I was already beginning to feel like an interloper, and so I said I ought to be getting back. Fortunately, no one asked me what for. Lofty said he'd be happy to take Mike on to Birmingham Airport where he would catch his Dublin flight.

Mike walked with me to retrieve his suitcase from the car, threw me the keys, and with a smile said, 'Try not to bend it.'

I got in, adjusted the seat a fraction, and then got out again. I slowly took off my jacket and lay it on the back seat next to a folded British Racing Drivers' Club (BRDC) green blanket. All the time, I was waiting for the others to get into their respective cars and go. It was an odd feeling. I knew I was a totally competent driver, and yet I didn't want to risk crunching the gears, or stalling, or over-revving the engine, or any one of a number of things I hadn't done since I was learning. I was also acutely aware that 'Mike's car' actually belonged to Jaguar – it was merely his to use. Fortunately, they didn't hang about, and first away in their little convoy were Lofty and Mike in Lofty's befittingly whale-like two-tone grey Jaguar Mk VIII.

Driving back alone, I was so caught up in my thoughts I even forgot to turn on the radio. For the first few minutes, I *was* the Farnham Flyer. I sat up straighter, leant my elbow out of the window, drove a bit quicker, and smiled broadly. But it wasn't long before slight euphoria gave way to slight embarrassment, and I reverted to being Tom.

I did, however, nearly run out of petrol. Mike had left me about a gallon to get home. Bloody typical. For a moment, I debated whether I should fill it up and seek reimbursement when I next saw him, or put in just enough fuel to get me back to Farnham. I chose the latter as getting money out of Mike wasn't easy.

When I arrived at the TT, I went to retrieve my jacket, only to find it had slid off the dark green leather bench and was lying on the floor. As I reached down to pick it up, I noticed a tan coloured ball just visible under the passenger seat. Not recognizing what it was, I picked it up. The moment it was in my fingers, I realised, to my horror, it was a balled nylon stocking. I quickly looked around to see if I was being watched and, confident I wasn't, shoved it straight back under the seat – where I spotted a suspender belt clip. I locked the car and hurried off to buy some cigarettes, in order to avoid being asked why I was looking so flushed. I felt so naïve for having made Mike laugh earlier when I'd asked him if he kept the BRDC blanket for picnics.

After Mike had lunched with Jaguar's top brass, Lofty drove him to Coventry where they watched the Coventry Air Pageant together. Mike then caught an early evening flight to Dublin.

Chapter Forty

Motor Racing – Irish Style

So much for 'forgetting all about motor racing'. Mike's arrival in Ireland coincided with the Leinster Trophy Race – an event he'd won six years earlier in a skeleton-dismantling pre-war Riley. I don't know who he thought he was kidding. The moment he arrived, he was latched onto by that good old friend of ours, Pat Massey-Dawson, who was there campaigning in his little Lotus 1100.

According to Mike, the new Dunboyne circuit was only better than the old one at Wicklow in one respect: the pits backed onto a Guinness-serving pub. Mike spent many happy hours, and Irish punts, shuttling to and fro both places.

He said that, for the race itself, he was positioned at a right-angle turn immediately past the pits. The scene he described would be unthinkable today. It was pouring with rain, and many of the enthusiastic amateur drivers in their Irish 'specials' came hurtling past the pits, left their braking too late, and failed to make the corner. Almost none utilized the escape road, preferring instead to mount the pavement and clobber the various shopfronts or, more worryingly, to come to a slithering halt on the petrol station forecourt. Incredibly, not one car hit any of the pumps.

After steadily drinking Guinness all day, Mike attended a major party in one of the hotels where most of the out-of-town drivers were staying – a party from which he doesn't remember leaving. It is a testament to his constitution that the next day he went flying with another old friend in a little Chipmunk. Not only that but there was an instructor present who encouraged him to do all manner of aerobatic stunts including stall turns, barrel rolls, loop the loops and even 'beating up the airfield at naught feet'.

Chapter Forty-One

Toast to the Crowd

Mike flew home on the Monday to give himself 'a couple of days to dry out'. Most things are relative, and it must be admitted that on one of those nights we each put away the best part of a gallon of ale. As we parted, I wished him well for Silverstone. Although I intended to be there, I thought it unlikely that I'd see him before the race.

He was fairly bullish about Ferrari's chances, citing the fact they had won every Silverstone GP for the past seven years. It was a thing with him: he would almost never speak about his own chances, only those of his team.

He again booked into The Jersey Arms and then went off to find Pete and Louise. Once out on the circuit, he and Pete revised their optimism because, although their cars were quick, they were still experiencing problems with handling through corners.

There was one amusing novelty for Mike, who up until now had always had difficulty squeezing his large frame into small Italian cockpits. This time, his car was actually too big – a career first. A makeshift rubber cushion was provided to bring him closer to the steering wheel.

Practice times were all very close, with no team demonstrably better than another. This gave rise to an unusually diversified grid. In pole position was Stirling's Vanwall. Next to him was Harry Schell in a BRM. Then came Roy Salvadori's Cooper, and beyond him was Mike's Ferrari. On the second row were Cliff Allison's Lotus, Pete's Ferrari, and Stuart Lewis-Evans's Vanwall. The third row contained the same four marques as the front row.

In the aftermath of the Reims race, Mike and Pete had discussed tactics. It was typically generous of Pete to acknowledge that his chances in the Championship were not as good as those of Mike, and so he would do everything he could to help his teammate. His plan, such as it was to go flat out from the start in order to put pressure on the vulnerable Vanwalls, reckoning that if he blew up his own car in the process that would be too bad. At least, that was Mike's understanding of the plan.

There was some speculation that Pete's offer wasn't entirely altruistic. It was barely a fortnight since Pete had been demoted by Enzo, and thus he might have had another agenda: to show the old man just how capable he was. Pete was an absolute charmer, more so than Mike, but no one gets to the top level of motor racing unless they've got a steely quality. Pete could have handled demotion, if deserved, but he wouldn't stand being demeaned.

As spectators, Sally and I had a great view of the grid although, frustratingly, we couldn't make out the drivers' facial expressions. Without binoculars, they were just too far away. We were, however, able to see the unmistakable figure of Tavoni come from the pits and have a quick word with each of his charges. He was followed by Earl Howe, president of the British Racing Drivers' Club. As the earl started towards the cars, we saw an official bound up to him and whisper something. It may have been something to do with smoking not being the safest activity when surrounded by high-octane fuel. Earl Howe immediately took his long cigarette holder out of his mouth and threw the cigarette onto the ground, extinguishing it with his shoe. Mike said he was a nice old chap who had successfully raced Bugattis back in the thirties.

After the race, I asked Mike what both men had said.

'Tavoni always says the same thing to everyone: "*In bocca al lupo*".'

'What's that when it's at home?'

'Essentially, good luck. Literally, it means "in the mouth of the wolf".'

'Is it rude?' I was genuinely perplexed.

'Nah, it's the equivalent of "break a leg" to an actor.'

'Only that's more likely in racing car, isn't it?'

'One's expected to respond by saying, "*Crepi*".'

'Creppy?'

'It means "to die" – apparently you wish the wolf dead.'

'Bloody strange. Johnny Foreigner, if you ask me.'

'Tavoni's all right. Actually, I've rather got to like him. You've got to watch him though. He feeds every single word back to the old man.'

'And what about old Curzon (Lord Howe)? What does he say? "Best of British"?'

'No, he's got the message. He kept wishing me luck, and I never had any after speaking with him, so I suggested he just shake my hand in future...so he did. I was impressed he remembered.'

After all the dignitaries and mechanics left the grid, the race started bang on two o'clock. As usual, Stirling started well, and Mike didn't. It was an exciting first lap – a shakedown of the race order to come. Pete quickly stole the lead from Stirling, and Mike whipped past Harry's BRM to lie in third, a situation that prevailed for three quarters of an hour.

An early casualty of the race was Jean Behra whose unlucky season continued when his car hit a hare and caused him to have a slow puncture. On lap 26, Stirling, who had been looking secure in second place, was forced to retire with a broken con rod. If trying to stay with Pete had forced Stirling to push the Vanwall too hard, part one of the boys' plan had worked.

Although now up to second place, Mike was facing a dilemma: should he stop for oil or press on to the end? He had been aware of a periodic puff of blue smoke emitting from the bonnet for some time and a corresponding drop in engine oil pressure. However, in similar circumstances at the beginning of the season, he had chosen caution, perhaps unnecessarily, and had as a result probably lost vital championship points.

He held on for another half an hour before feeling sufficiently confident that if the pit stop was quick enough he'd be able to retain second place. At a mere thirty seconds, it was and he did, but only just, for third-placed man Roy Salvadori was now right behind him. With his oil pressure partially restored and with the spur of Roy on his tail, Mike decided to let rip and put some distance between him and Salvadori. On lap 50, Mike recorded the fastest lap of the race and thereby secured the bonus championship point.

For us mere spectators, the spectacle of the three leading cars processing around separately was unexciting. The drama was amongst the drivers behind: Stuart Lewis-Evans and Harry Schell, and Taffy and Jack Brabham. Unfortunately, Taffy wasn't as circumspect as Mike, and his Ferrari did run out of oil. He went out on lap 60. Stuart began to catch Roy and was pressing him hard for third place.

Notwithstanding that Mike was gaining a couple of seconds on Pete with each closing lap, Pete never did relinquish his lead. He finished twenty-four seconds ahead. Thirty seconds behind Mike came Roy and Stuart seemingly side by side. Despite Stuart's best efforts, Roy was judged third by one fifth of a second. Britons taking the top four places at the British Grand Prix – the crowd loved that. Of the twenty cars that started, only nine lasted the course.

Sally and I were still watching the lower placed cars cross the finish line when Pete who was completing his lap of honour came past, waving to the crowd and receiving enormous applause. Less than a minute later, it was Mike's turn to parade past, only he wasn't waving to the crowd, he was toasting them with a pint of ale!

'Where in goodness did he get that?' she asked.

'I haven't the foggiest.' I replied.

'Is he sponsored by a brewery?'

'Not yet, but he should be, shouldn't he?'

Everyone wanted to know the story, and it wasn't long before we heard that Mike had been watching a couple of his old cronies, including the renowned bon viveur and former Le Mans winner Major Tony Rolt, conspicuously drinking beer whilst carrying out their marshalling duties at Beckett's. Feeling thirsty, and no doubt a little euphoric, Mike stopped at Beckett's, removed his crash hat, and demanded a pint 'to take away'.

As you can imagine, this stunt did Mike's PR no harm whatsoever. Not an eyebrow was raised, however, at the thought of the marshals quietly enjoying the odd libation whilst supervising the British Grand Prix.

I urged Sally to hang around until after the prize-giving. I knew that Mike and Pete would be in good spirits, and I was not disappointed. We found them, together with Jean and Louise, predictably enough in a beer tent. The presence of Jean was a pleasant surprise as we didn't know whether she and Mike were still 'officially' together. She'd only seen him race a few times before, and then hadn't usually hung around afterwards.

There was much good-hearted banter, which included Mike

demanding to know why Pete hadn't ceded his lead as per the plan. I realised this was all said in jest for although Mike picked up only seven points, rather than nine for a first place plus fastest lap, more importantly, Stirling had garnered none. Mike now had thirty points to Stirling's twenty-three.

After several beers, Pete and Louise said their goodbyes and drove off to Pete's family house in Kidderminster, accidentally taking with them Mike's sports jacket containing his wallet, his pipe and his car keys. When we all went to leave, Mike was convinced someone had stolen it from his car. All was not totally lost for Mike kept a spare key in the boot, which he seldom locked, and was at least able to drive home – after he'd persuaded us to join him for 'a couple of sherbets' in the White Horse.

Chapter Forty-Two

Pete's Off

Mike was grateful for the fortnight's break before his next big race: the German GP at the Nurburgring. Of course, the nett time available to spend at home was a little over a week, much of which he spent at the TT Garage, getting under the feet of the full-timers, and some of which he spent getting to know Jean Howarth much better. He even managed a couple of sessions with his old muckers.

It was a lovely optimistic time for Mike and all those who held him dear. Not only was he leading the Championship but he was optimistic about the next race, telling us that 'the Ring is a Ferrari circuit', one not at all suited to the Vanwalls of Stirling and Tony. He even began saying things like, 'Chaps, when I'm world champ, I'll...'

It was around this time that Mike had a very clandestine assignation; one about which he confided in no one, or at least no one to my knowledge. He met up with Jacqueline and their four year-old son Arnaud in London. He mentioned it a few weeks later, saying how he'd driven Arnaud quickly in his Jaguar and how it had made the young Hawthorn smile. But as for Jacqueline and Arnaud's future, he wouldn't discuss it. As far as he was concerned, Arnaud was Jacqueline's problem, not his. Certainly, there didn't seem to be much paternal interest in the boy. I wondered whether Mike was actually being considerate. Should Arnaud get to know his father, indeed maybe to love him, then it would be really hard on the boy when Mike died.

After Silverstone, Pete and Louise spent the weekend with Pete's family. They'd invited Tony Brooks and his Italian fiancée Pina to come back to his parents' place for a victory party and to generally unwind. Pete offered to book the couple into a nearby hotel. He was flabbergasted when Tony, the twenty-six-year-old Grand Prix racer, requested separate rooms. Tony couldn't have been more different to Mike or a Pete in that regard, but he was likeable and well respected as a talented driver. In fact, Pete spent the weekend trying to persuade Tony to join Ferrari, saying how well he'd fit in with Mike and himself.

The Collinses also excitedly bought a house that weekend, or at least agreed to buy a house. It was a handsome but run-down Georgian pile set in four and a half acres some five minutes' drive from his parents' house. The sum agreed, £4,500, was not a lot more than the prize money he'd just won. Their plan was to continue living onboard Mipooka in Monaco and do up Honeybrooke House over the course of a year, mutedly speaking of its suitability for bringing up children and keeping pets.

Electing not to drive, Mike had a tortuous journey to Nurburgring on the Wednesday prior to the race weekend. First, he flew from London to Amsterdam and then on to Cologne. From there, he caught the slow train to Koblenz before taking a taxi to the Sporthotel. By his own error, he arrived a day early as practice didn't begin until the Friday. Fortunately, the day wasn't wasted as the Ferrari cars had already arrived, and he was able to have a few quiet familiarization laps.

The Collinses had spent a quiet week relaxing back in the Mediterranean before they too flew to Cologne, on the right day. There, they hooked up with Harry and Monique Schell, rented a Mercedes, drove straight to the Ring, and also checked into the Sporthotel.

The thing about this hotel which was unique, so Mike said, was that it was practically incorporated into the main grandstand and opposite the pits, so there was no messing about driving in and out of circuits as the competitors had to do elsewhere. One could practically fall out of bed and into one's car – which is exactly what he did. He described the whole weekend as spent either lounging around in his pyjamas or driving in his overalls, oscillating between high-adrenalin driving and doing 'bugger all'.

Louise was remarkably sanguine about Mike's familiarity. She spoke of how Mike would enter their room before they were awake, stare down at them, and demand to know where his early morning cuppa was. After copious cups of tea, the threesome would order a brunch of boiled eggs, toast, bread and jam from room service and hang around until it was time for practice.

The results of the practice laps were an unwelcome surprise. It wasn't going to be a Ferrari walkover. In a nutshell, the Ferraris had got quicker in a straight line; the Vanwalls, in addition to having superior braking courtesy of disc brakes, had improved their suspension and now cornered brilliantly; and the small-engined Coopers continued to be highly competitive everywhere, despite the fast nature of the circuit.

The organizers had decided to incorporate the Formula Two race with the Formula One in order to make the circuit fuller for the spectators' benefit. This led to some peculiar, not to say unfair, decisions in terms of starting grid positions for the mid-placed cars. The front two rows were unaffected. At 9 minutes 15 seconds, Mike had gone very well and had secured pole position. Alongside him were the Vanwalls of Tony Brooks and Stirling. Pete's Ferrari, on the outside, completed the front row. Taffy and the Coopers of Salvadori and Trintignant were on the next row. Phil Hill, in the best placed of all the Formula Two cars, was on the third row.

Phil wasn't actually the quickest in a Formula Two car. It was the Australian Jack Brabham. However, because Jack had only driven five laps, not the regulation six, he was placed an arbitrary nineteenth on the grid rather than tenth. A similar fate befell Jo Bonnier whose qualifying time in his Formula One Maserati should have placed him ninth but he ended up twenty-first on the grid. To all but the organizers it all seemed quite illogical.

According to Mike, Pete again volunteered to help him in his quest for the Championship.

An enormous crowd had assembled to watch the race. The numbers were undoubtedly swelled by the closeness of the contest between Stirling and Mike. And although the two men didn't come right out and say it, they both knew it was a two-horse race for the Championship.

By now, it'll come as little surprise to hear that once the starter's flag had been dropped, Stirling shot away and Mike messed up. He slipped the clutch so badly, he feared that his car would probably not last the distance. Tony Brooks made the best start but by the end of the first lap a firm race order had been established: Stirling, Mike,

Pete. And really, from that point on, Stirling ought to have won.

As a staunch Hawthorn ally, I refused to recognize it at the time, but Stirling's drive here exemplifies why many thought he was the best driver in the post-Fangio years. In a car thought to be 15mph slower than the Ferrari, Stirling broke the lap record on his second lap and took a further 7.4 seconds off it on his third.

Try as they might, the boys' trailing Ferraris were getting further behind. It must have been an enormous disappointment to Stirling when, on only his fifth lap, his engine suddenly died on him. The solder holding the magneto in place had broken and caused it to short. This was excellent news for Mike and Pete, now side by side, for not only did they have about thirty seconds in hand over third-placed Tony Brooks but it meant Mike could be gentler on his clutch in the hope it would last the distance.

It seemed as if it was going to be a repeat of Silverstone: Pete leading, Mike following. However, Tony Brooks was slowly getting the hang of the 'Ring', and with Stirling out, the Vanwall challenge fell to him. By lap 9, Tony had caught the Ferraris, and dived inside Mike on the North Turn to take second place. Using his superior speed, Mike managed to regain second only to lose it again the next time they reached North Turn. Tony's lap times had got down almost to Stirling's best, and on lap 11, again at North Turn, he slipped past Pete to take the lead. The crowd roared with approval and waved their programmes.

Determined not to let the green Vanwall get away, the boys had to drive close to their limits, and those of the cars. Pete, it seemed, was the more determined. Mike hung back a little as he watched Pete throw everything at trying to overtake the Vanwall. He told me afterwards that whereas he'd only tried to reel Tony in on the straights, courtesy of his superior speed, Pete was prepared to attack everywhere. At one corner, Mike thought the other two would touch – they were that close.

As the three leaders, barely a few car lengths apart, approached Pflanzgarten, a demanding fast right-hand corner, Pete, in a desperate effort to repass Tony, overaccelerated coming out of the dip. As a consequence, he wasn't able to turn into the corner sufficiently to get round safely.

Mike foresaw the danger immediately. He said Pete was maybe

only a yard too wide but, once there, no one would have been able to stop the car drifting onto the outside of the bend where there was a low bank. One of the Ferrari's back wheels made contact with the bank. Mike braced himself for the car to spin onto the circuit and take them both out. But, in the next second, he saw the Ferrari flip over and Pete thrown out. As Mike flashed past, he saw the car bounce over again. He braked hard and tried to look back but he could see nothing but a great cloud of dust.

Mike drove on, trying to convince himself that Pete would be fine. A few broken bones perhaps, concussion even? He stopped thinking about the race. The thought of Pete being seriously hurt was too much to contemplate. He passed the pits without stopping, aware that word of Pete's condition wouldn't have reached them. Instead, he decided to drive on round to the accident scene and stop if he thought he could help.

Unfortunately, the 'Ring' was over fourteen miles long. It was the longest GP circuit in the world. Less than three miles later and the clutch on Mike's Ferrari went completely – he could push the car by hand when still in gear. Stranded at Aremberg, he begged a marshal to telephone the pits to enquire about Pete. The answer came back that he was 'a bit bruised, but all right'. Mike could breathe again.

A conventional ambulance had taken Pete first to the pit area. From there, a helicopter took him on to a hospital in Bonn. Thankfully, Louise remained completely oblivious to her husband's accident. She was in the Ferrari pit area engrossed in completing her lap charts which she did right up to the moment a triumphant Tony Brooks crossed the finish line, well ahead of the Coopers of Roy Salvadori and Maurice Trintignant. She knew that both Pete and Mike were out of the race, but retirements weren't exactly uncommon.

In the days before live television feeds and mobile phones, communication – especially hurried and passing through many hands – was often chaotic and unreliable. As the race was finishing, Louise was told that Pete had had an accident, but no one knew how he was. This was followed up by another report giving the wonderful but totally inaccurate news that he was now walking back to the pits. It was Tavoni who eventually had to inform her that Pete had been seriously injured and was being airlifted to hospital.

Tavoni drove Louise to the hospital in tortured silence, largely because Louise couldn't converse in Italian. They were also extremely slow getting out of the circuit, along with the thousands of other departing spectators.

Meanwhile, Mike could do nothing but wait by his car until the race was over. He was given orange juice by the marshals and some cigarettes by English spectators, but no further news. A German marshal volunteered to drive him back to the pits. Mike asked to stop at the scene of the accident. Pete's Ferrari was upside down. Beside the car lay Pete's blue crash hat, one shoe and one glove. Mike saw that the helmet had been pierced, although he was relieved not to see any blood on it.

Mike asked his German driver to enquire of the Red Cross officials standing around what they knew of the accident. At first, the driver relayed dreadful stories of horrendous injuries, and then another interrupted to say that the others were talking rubbish and in fact Pete had been taken to hospital with a broken arm. All claimed to be eye witnesses, and each had a different story.

Mike made to leave with Pete's hat, shoe and glove but was stopped by the police. Once he explained he was a Ferrari team driver and would sign a receipt for the items, he was allowed to take them. When he finally arrived at the pits, he learnt that Louise and Tavoni had already left for the local hospital at Mayen. Mike felt impotent. There was nothing he could do other than wait upon more news.

He went to his room and started packing. There was a knock at the door. It was Artur Keser, Mercedes' amiable press director. Apparently, the latest word was that Pete was very seriously injured and had been flown to Bonn University Clinic, not Mayen Hospital.

As Mike had arrived at Nurburgring by public transport, he was unable to jump in a car and set off for Bonn. Thinking quite rationally, Mike sought out Harry Schell and asked him whether he would give him a lift to Bonn – in the car Harry and Pete had hired in Cologne. Harry immediately agreed. Mike then went into the Collins's room and packed up all Pete and Louise's belongings. Harry then drove round to his lodgings to pack his own things.

The race had finished before five o'clock, and yet Harry and Mike didn't reach the clinic until ten thirty. On arrival, they spotted Taffy's mate Siedel, 'the other Wolfgang', sitting with his wife in his car outside the entrance. Mike jumped out to speak with him. It was the shortest of exchanges.

'How is he?' asked Mike.

'He's dead,' replied Siedel.

They went into the clinic to find Tavoni and Louise, and already lots of reporters. Louise was trying to be brave, and Tavoni was showing her great tenderness.

Incredibly, Louise had been informed not by the clinic but by her father back home in New York. Once Louise had identified herself to Reception, a doctor handed over the handset he was holding and said gravely, 'Your father is on the phone.' I guess if anyone had to be the bearer of the worst possible news it couldn't have been anyone better, but it must surely have thrown her. How could he, thousands of miles away and in a different time zone, know more than she did when she was on the spot? The answer was that her father, Andrew Cordier, was a major player in the United Nations, and wherever in the world Peter was racing, he had contacts able to reach him in New York.

Tragically, as Tavoni and Louise had crawled towards the hospital, and the crowd watched Tony Brooks lift the trophy for his second solo Grand Prix victory, Pete had passed away in the little helicopter overhead.

Mike asked Tavoni whether it was possible to see Pete. Tavoni said that Louise had asked the same question but had been told by Reception that there was no point in seeing a dead man. Mike, however, was insistent, and, with Tavoni and Louise, was eventually admitted.

Mike said afterwards that there was no logic to his request. It was as if he believed the hospital had made a grotesque mistake. Louise saw one white foot protruding from beneath a white sheet and left the room. Tavoni and Mike stayed while the doctor pulled back the sheet. They said Pete looked as if he was peacefully asleep.

According to Tavoni, Mike turned around, walked out to the corridor, leant against the wall, and then slid down to the floor. It was minutes before he could speak.

Tavoni and Harry were, by all accounts, wonderfully considerate towards Louise and Mike. Gently, Tavoni proposed that they couldn't stay at the clinic all night and, despite the hour, successfully set about finding hotel accommodation for them all. Mike proposed that he take Louise back to Peter's parents, and so the following morning he set about booking flights to England and said his farewells to the other two.

Back in Farnham, I didn't hear the news about Pete until first thing the following morning, a Monday. I could only imagine how distraught Mike would be. I waited until just after seven thirty when I thought someone would be at the TT Garage, and telephoned to enquire if they'd had any information on Mike. I figured that Mike couldn't let everyone know his movements whereas anyone close to him would expect his mother, or at least the garage, to know his whereabouts. It was a calculated guess which proved correct. I was told that he was intending to fly into London Airport later that day. I asked how he was intending to get home as his car was still in Farnham.

'We believe he's going straight up to Kidderminster,' I was advised. I recognised the voice as belonging to Bill Morgan, the general manager, and told him who I was. I suggested that Mike might appreciate having use of his car. Bill agreed, but said they couldn't spare the personnel to get it there and return in another vehicle.

On the spur of the moment, I volunteered. 'I'll drive it up, if someone can drive me back. I've driven it before,' I said.

The speaker went quiet for a few seconds, and then Bill said, 'Okay, let me have your number, and I'll call you when we know which flight he's on.'

I came off the phone wondering what on earth I had done. It was a new working week, and I was expected in the office within the hour. I toyed with asking for a no-notice day off or calling in sick. Neither was a good option. I'd hated myself for the 'sickie' I'd only recently taken and decided I would try to beg for a day's leave. If that didn't work, I'd have to face the music and tell Bill that I couldn't get the time off work. I didn't much relish the prospect of messing Bill around.

As it transpired, I needn't have worried. My boss seemed in an unusually good mood and actually recognised that I had recently worked considerable overtime and was sympathetic to my reasoning. At the time, I thought he was merely being kind and appreciative of me. Looking back, I wonder whether, by coming to the assistance of Mike Hawthorn, the now famous racing driver, however distantly, he was seeking some vicarious glory. And that is how I ended up driving Mike's beloved Jaguar for the second time.

Bill had instructed one of the garage lads to follow me up to Heathrow in an old Austin. This obliged me to drive sedately, or word would have got back to Bill, or worse, I could have lost the kid for, by his own admission, he'd never been further than twenty miles from Farnham in his life.

Once we'd parked at the airport, I made my way up onto the observation platform in order to spot them coming into the terminal. I wasn't the only one with that idea – there were literally hundreds of others, mostly reporters and photographers. I suppose this was the moment when I first appreciated how big the names Hawthorn and Collins really were in the eyes of Britain's media.

We didn't have to wait long for the Bonn flight to discharge its passengers. As they filed across towards us, the blond couple – him tall and striding, her shorter, slim and elegant – were unmistakable. Louise was wearing dark sunglasses, I guessed so that no one could see if she was crying. As Mike got closer, I saw that his face was expressionless. I remember thinking it was the same blank expression he'd had at Julian's funeral, and Don's, and his dad's. It was a funereal expression.

I snapped out of my reverie when I realised that all the press were streaming downstairs to a special press reception area. I tried to follow but was stopped when I couldn't produce a press card. I made my way round to where I thought Mike might exit and waited there. Eventually, I could make out the couple trying to walk towards me. There were flashbulbs going off nineteen to the dozen and lots of reporters shouting questions over each other.

'Mr Hawthorn…what have you to say about Pete Collins?' bellowed one hack.

'As a friend, he was my best friend, and that is it.' Mike's voice was choked, almost unrecognisable.

If I'd have heard that 'best friend' eighteen months earlier, I'd have been devastated. Now, having got together with Sally, I was far more sanguine about such things.

They emerged from the throng, Mike blinking from the flashbulbs, tears streaming down his face. He didn't notice me. In fact, he could have walked straight past me.

I touched him on the shoulder. 'I'm so sorry, Mike…'

He took another step and then stopped and turned, looking puzzled. Half a smile tried to form on his lips. He quickly turned back to halt Louise and said, 'Wait up, it's Tom.' Turning to me once more, he said, 'We've got to get out of here. It's a bloody nightmare.' He looked dreadful, vulnerable. He hadn't shaved, and his wet eyes were bloodshot.

'Yer wee Jag's outside, bo,' I said as I held out a hand from which the keys dangled. I glanced at Louise. There was nothing discernible from behind those large black sunglasses. She was leaving everything to Mike.

'Oh, Tom!' he said wearily, 'That's marvellous…that's really kind. I can't thank you enough…' He paused and looked worried. 'Only I'm not going home. I said I'd take Louise up to Pete's folks.'

'Don't worry,' I said, 'I have my chauffeur waiting outside.'

Mike looked bemused.

I picked up the more girly of the two suitcases Mike had been carrying. 'Follow me, sir,' I said, and started walking.

We didn't have much of an opportunity to talk then. It wasn't the right time or place, and I had to get Junior back to the garage. There was just time enough for me to express my sorrow, and for Mike to express his shock and disbelief.

Louise was very sweet when we parted and kissed my cheek and thanked me for being such a good pal to Mike and Pete. I didn't like to tell her that I'd hardly got to know her husband. Even in grief, I thought ashamedly, she's one great-looking girl. I know I shouldn't have, but I did wonder whether Mike might chuck his new girlfriend Jean and get together with Louise. And then I thought why would any girl want to risk losing a second husband to motor racing? It wouldn't make any sense.

On the drive back to Farnham, I simply wanted to silently empathize with Mike and Louise. All bloody Junior wanted to do was talk about football. Worse than that, as a keen Reading supporter, he was actually crowing about the recent deaths of the Manchester United players in the Munich air disaster. I didn't know whether to shout at him or punch him. I did neither, of course. I turned on the radio and feigned interest in everything that was being broadcast.

Mike must have been in a real state because, when he got to Kidderminster, he couldn't remember how to find Shatterford

Grange, Pete's folks' place, somewhere he'd been many times. Mike's solution was to go to a pub. They arrived about sevenish, and Mike bought himself a pint and a double brandy for Louise. Louise was feeling so raw that she couldn't face anyone and so stayed outside in the garden. Mike bought another round and explained their predicament to the landlord. The landlord knew the house and volunteered to lead them over to Shatterford in his own car.

I didn't hear all the related stories at the time, but I was rocked when I heard how Louise was treated by Pete's father, Pat Collins. Both Pat and his wife Elaine were naturally warm and supportive in their words to Louise when she first arrived. However, the following day, Pat asked that Louise sign a document renouncing any rights to Peter's share of Kidderminster Motors Limited, adding, 'Well, you'll no doubt go back to acting, so you won't have to worry about this sort of thing.'

Peter's shareholding in the business would have been valuable, and indeed it was his stated intention to quit racing in the very near future, initiate a Ferrari dealership, and ultimately take over the business completely from his father.

I was therefore pleased, patriotically, that Louise also experienced some British kindness. The ninety-year-old retired bishop and his wife who had agreed to sell Honeybrooke House to the Collinses wrote a most charming letter of sympathy to Louise and enclosed with it a cheque for five hundred pounds, which had been their non-refundable deposit.

Pete's funeral was a small private affair, held the following Thursday at St Mary's Church in the village of Stone, just outside Kidderminster. Mike was one of the few outside the immediate family to be invited. He confided it was one of the most painful experiences of his life. He couldn't get over the idea that Pete had been so close to packing up racing, after which he and Louise would undoubtedly have settled down and had kids. 'They'd only known each other for nineteen months...'

It was probably just as well he did attend the private funeral, for three days later a memorial service was held at the same tiny thirteenth-century church, and that was a much more public affair. I offered to accompany him from Farnham, an offer he willingly accepted. We spoke almost non-stop all the way up there.

Mike drove, automatically and distractedly. 'Nothing's the same anymore. I can't see the point of it,' he said.

'The point of what?'

'Carrying on. What's the point? How can I have plans? I could die next week, next month...'

'Come on...you've always known that. Only recently, you said you'd rather risk dying than seeing out the rest of your days in poor health.'

'But that was when I was enjoying it...having a laugh. He's gone...'

'What about Jean?'

'What about her? She doesn't like racing any more than my mother.'

'So, what will you do?' I asked.

'I should quit – right now. Tell Enzo.'

'You'd really do that...mid-season?' I glanced across at Mike.

'How do you think he'll react?' he asked, still staring dead ahead.

'You're asking me? I've no idea. You know him. I don't.' Obviously I didn't know Enzo, but everything I'd heard suggested he wouldn't take kindly to being dumped.

'I'm only a driver to him. Just a pawn in his game,' said Mike.

'More like a castle or a bishop,' I ventured. 'Don't forget you're about to win a world title for Ferrari. He won't be happy. You can be sure about that.'

'Yeah, but it's not like he's facing death week in, week out, is it?'

'Fair point. But you need to think about it. You've come this far. You're so close to winning. It's the thing you've always wanted. I think you'd come to regret it – and you are six points clear of Moses (Stirling had earned one point at the Nurburgring).' I couldn't believe I was saying this. How I'd changed my tune!

'So you think I should continue?' He paused and then said, 'Even you don't care if I die.' He was starting to play me.

'Of course I do, you daft ha'p'orth. That's not what I'm saying, and you know it.'

And so the conversation went on, and around, with Mike continuing to examine his mortality and me either challenging him, if I thought it would help, or trying to mollify him, if I didn't.

Even though we arrived in good time, we'd arrived too late to stand a chance of getting inside the church. Mike and I stood outside listening to the service which was relayed by way of a loudspeaker. The churchyard was overflowing with wreaths. Some were huge, elaborate affairs such as those from Enzo Ferrari and Tony Vandervell. I didn't count them, but it was thought there were over 200.

Canon Rees Jones's address was powerful and poignant, and reduced most of the congregation to tears. Naturally, he spoke at length about Peter's warmth, charm and courage, and of his ability to make friends wherever he went. He also spoke of the inherent and unacceptable dangers of motor racing circuits and 'the lightness of today's Grand Prix cars'. I wasn't sure whether he meant that if the cars were heavier they would be slower – which would be true – or if they were heavier they wouldn't roll over – which would be untrue, for Ferraris were the heaviest of all current Grand Prix cars.

Later, I learnt that he must have picked this up from something attributed to Fangio, although it was widely thought he had been misquoted. Either way, as Canon Jones was saying those words, I noticed Mike twitch as if reacting to a small electric shock. Canon Jones was far from the only clergyman to renounce motor racing: the Pope too had said it must stop.

It was lovely to see so many of Mike's fellow racers demonstrate their compassion, not so much with words but by putting their arms around his shoulders or simply shaking his hand, in a silent acknowledgement that 'there but for the grace of God...'

As we left the church, two small lads with autograph books in their hands came walking towards us. For a second, I feared for them, thinking that Mike, who was still tearful, might brush them aside, or worse. I needn't have worried. He asked them their names and then bent down and duly wrote in one: *Barry, All the best, Mike Hawthorn* and in the other boy's book: *Gordon, All the best, Mike Hawthorn.* I should never have doubted him.

The conversation on the way back to Farnham, such as it was, was more wide-ranging, but Mike did return to the canon's comment about the lightness of Grand Prix cars. He said that only recently he and Stirling had been discussing the matter of weight, the mass of the car, and had concluded that a lighter car was less likely, not more likely, to flip over. But, it was more complicated than weight alone, so many other factors came into the equation: sideways force, ride height, wheel size and wheel construction, obstacles, suspension, tyre width and composition...the list was endless.

The sole cause, according to Mike, for the fatal crashes of both Pete and Luigi was driver error. They'd both been driving on the limit, and had both made minor errors of judgement. I think it was Stirling, who'd been talking to Mike at the wake, who cemented this notion. It was probably the only way either man could look at it, if they were to carry on driving at that level.

To allow the thought that any Grand Prix car, at any time, was a lethal accident waiting to happen could invoke such nervousness that it could itself be dangerous. A driver could only really carry on if he had sufficient conviction that he was above making any driver errors. One had to have supreme confidence in one's abilities – that was Stirling's view. It wasn't logical, but it does explain why they carried on racing in the face of frightening odds.

Chapter Forty-Three

Stirling Behaviour

It was fortunate there was a three-week break before the Portuguese GP, which was to be staged in Porto, Portugal's second city. Without such an interval for Mike to come to terms with motor racing, he might not have continued, or continued whilst suffering mental turmoil. For a fortnight or so, no one knew whether he was quitting. At different times, he told nearly everyone he met he'd had enough. Jean, Bill Morgan, Charlie from the Duke, and most of the Members all heard him swear that he was stopping.

Mike didn't spend all this time in Farnham. Some was spent in London with Jean and his old friends, the Hume-Kendalls. But, on the odd occasion I did see him, he remained close to tears. Moreover, I never again heard him laugh his inimitable, uninhibited, full-throttle laugh. That had gone with Pete. It was as if some of the luminescence within had been snuffed out.

It was another driver, I can't be sure who it was, maybe it was Harry, who posed these searching rhetorical questions of Mike: 'What would Pete want you to do?' and 'Wasn't it because Pete so wanted you to win the Championship that he lost his life?'

Finally, Mike alighted upon the only reason to continue that made sense to him: to do it for Pete. Once he'd fixed on that simple notion, he was able to depart for Porto. At the same time, he widely broadcast that, come what may, win or lose, this would be his last season of racing. It was, he said, three more races, and then he was out for good.

Although Mike was clearly mourning Pete, I saw little evidence that he continued to think about Louise. Fortunately, her father, with whom Louise was very close, had flown over from the States for the funeral services and had stayed with Pete's parents at Shatterford

Grange for the duration. Given Pat Collins's behaviour, I shudder to think what the atmosphere was like between the fathers.

Aware that she needed to move on from Kidderminster, Louise faced the prospect of returning to Monte Carlo and Mipooka alone. Fortunately, the Cahiers, throwers of those wonderful Riviera parties, invited her to stay with them rather than by herself on the boat, surrounded by memories of Pete. She accepted, and not wishing to outstay her welcome, she also decided to move onto Modena, to see Enzo.

She wrote to her parents on the day of the Portuguese GP saying that she'd never seen Enzo so upset, how he viewed Peter as his own son, and had intended to give him the villa – even a stake in the business! What she found most confusing was he'd decided to pull out of motor racing altogether *after* the next one, the Italian at Monza – one race before the end of the season. He also insisted that Louise accompany him to Monza as his guest. Louise protested that everyone knew Enzo *never* attended Grands Prix. He'd not watched a race for fifteen years.

He would not take no for an answer, and became excessively sentimental about how it would the last ever race for Ferrari – for Italy. It would, he said, mark the end of his career. He declared that he'd be sending only one car, and that would be for Mike. She asked for time to think about it, but implied she would probably attend.

Sweetly, she added in her letter to her parents how concerned she was for Mike who was racing that same day, saying that she hadn't been able to sleep for fearing the worst.

Whilst in Milan, Louise went with Enzo to visit Phil Hill who was in hospital. He was suffering from a kidney ailment. The significance of his condition didn't occur to me at the time. Phil remembers Enzo weeping when he spoke about Pete and confirming that Monza would be the firm's final Grand Prix, and how he wanted Louise by his side.

It took Mike three flights to get to Porto: London to Paris, Paris to Lisbon, and Lisbon to Porto, all organised by Scuderia Ferrari. There he checked into the Grand Hotel where he met up with another of Pete's good mates, Taffy, and the two Lotus drivers, Cliff Allison and Graham Hill. They would all have been aware how much more the loss of Pete meant to Mike than the loss of Luigi a month earlier.

I was happier knowing that Mike had found a *raison d'être* for finishing the season, but I was still nervous thinking about whether he would be able to focus adequately. I knew that errors came from lack of concentration, and a two-hour race on a hot day wasn't easy for the fittest of drivers. I hadn't had any recent reports of how he was feeling – or more particularly whether his 'waterworks' were okay.

It seems that Pete's death had affected nearly all the drivers, for practice started off a very muted affair. The early lap times were proof of their tentative, exploratory driving of an unfamiliar circuit. The Boavista circuit was a true 'road' circuit, tree-lined in places and criss-crossed by tramlines, and it was hilly. There was even a slippery cobbled section. All the normal immovable hazards of a road circuit, such as kerbstones and lamp posts, were present too, of course. I was glad I didn't hear what it was like before the race.

Mike was again exasperated with the lack of attention to circuit safety. His concerns about such matters had never been so acute. He complained that where a fast, downhill twisting section passed between trees, the organizers had placed straw bales about a yard apart. He said to Tavoni, and anyone else who would listen, that if a car's rear wheel was to get caught by the edge of a bale it was likely to flip the car over. If the bales were continuous, the cars were more likely to bounce off. Tavoni knew he was right, but all he could do was sympathize.

Tavoni did change Mike's race number though. Mike had been allocated 22, and both Pete and Luigi had died driving cars bearing the number 2. Mike thought this was a bad omen, and successfully petitioned to swap numbers with Taffy who'd been allocated number 24. I don't think it's disloyal to say that Mike probably gave scant consideration about the uncaring implications of this request upon his remaining teammate. Mike was not one of life's natural empathizers, and it's highly likely that he didn't think it through.

As I've noted before, he and Pete also had their different perceptions of Taffy, despite the three men's apparently warm camaraderie. Pete had unreservedly embraced the gentle German aristocrat who spoke Americanised English and whose life had been anything but sugar-coated. By contrast, Mike never forgot that Taffy had once been in the Hitler Youth – even though Taffy had been fifteen years old at the time, and had simply been complying with his parents' wishes. Mike couldn't help himself. He had this conviction, encouraged by his father and Lofty, that the old enemy was still the enemy.

In practice, it was Stirling who established the fastest lap. Harry then knocked it down by a couple of seconds. Then the gloom-laden atmosphere was not helped when Cliff Allison almost wrote off his Lotus by catching a hay bale, and poor Maria de Filippis then spun her Maserati and crashed into a concrete lamp post. Fortunately, neither driver was badly hurt.

Mike went out again and posted a time three seconds quicker than Harry's. Clearly spurred on, Stirling went out and took it down again – this time by over five seconds. Ambition and innate competition must have begun to trump their fear and caution for Mike then shaved a little off Stirling's time, both men hunting that prized pole position. Before the first day of practice was over, Jean Behra had fleetingly taken the best time only for Stirling to reassert his dominance by close of play.

It was much the same on the second day of practice, albeit both Mike and Stirling kept their powder dry until the end. Stuart Lewis-Evans, Stirling's teammate, put in a blistering time, beating Stirling's best. Fearing a second-row position, Mike shaved a fraction of a second from Stuart's time. Leaving it right to the last moment, Stirling managed to better even that time by one twentieth of a second. All the top drivers, Mike included, were now fully engaged in the fray.

Sunday, race day, dawned, and the fine weather of the practice days had given way to rain. Fortunately, the start wasn't until four o'clock by which time the rain had eased, although the track was still wet. Porto may have been a small city by global standards but, despite the miserable weather, the race attracted a gate of over 100,000 spectators.

Stirling told Mike that he was going to take the first lap 'nice and easy', and, surprisingly, he did. In fact, all the cars went uncharacteristically gently for the first lap. Mike was the first to break ranks and nipped past Stirling on the second lap. However, as the surface dried so Stirling got quicker and resumed the lead on lap 7. Even at that point, Mike was anxious whether his brakes would last. The pedal travel was getting longer with each lap, and, in order to stay with Stirling, he was having to brake hard.

By the halfway mark, Stirling had a lead of nearly a minute over Mike and was repeatedly setting new lap records. Tony Brooks and Graham Hill, both points' contenders, spun off, which was good news for Mike. Increasingly anxious about his brakes and now with less immediate competition, Mike decided to risk a pit stop, and in so doing handed second place to Jean Behra.

Anxious not to concede more points than he could help, and with his braking restored, he set off in pursuit of Jean who was only eighteen seconds in front. Not only did he catch him but he established a new lap record.

The Vanwall pit needed to advise Stirling that not only was Hawthorn gaining but he had taken the lap record. Consequently, they put out a board which read: HAW-REC. Stirling saw this as HAW-REG – HAWthorn lapping REGularly – and therefore could relax. It was a big mistake.

Another piece of luck befell Mike when Jean Behra's BRM lost a sparking plug, and he had to continue slowly with only three cylinders.

Mike believed his inherited second place was now under serious threat from Stuart Lewis-Evans. The Ferrari pit had advised Mike that Stuart was only trailing by four seconds, whereas he was in fact a full lap behind. With less than two laps to go, Mike noticed a Vanwall coming up quickly in his mirror. He assumed it was Stuart's.

Mike's brakes were now on their last legs. Even pumping the pedal didn't help much. He had no choice but to brutally change down for corners and trust he could steer round without spinning off or hitting a backmarker.

Unable to slow sufficiently for one left-hander, Mike ran too wide and hit a straw bale. Unlike Cliff Allison, he simply bounced off it and was able to drive on. With seconds lost, the approaching Vanwall drew up level. As Mike glanced across to acknowledge Stuart, he found himself looking at Stirling: he was being lapped.

Stirling elected not to overtake and dropped back. With a lap in hand, he knew then all he had to do was nurse the car round and finish. Mike no longer posed a threat. Stuart meanwhile had caught up with the two leaders, and so it was a Ferrari-Vanwall-Vanwall procession until Mike's final lap.

Immediately after Mike crossed the finish line for the penultimate time, Stirling took the chequered flag. If only Mike had realised, as Stirling had done, he had a lap in hand over Stuart, he too could have coasted round. Instead, he pushed on. This was to prove disastrous because, at exactly the same corner as he'd hit the straw, his brakes gave out totally. He knew he wouldn't get round and so aborted up an escape road. Desperately trying to turn the car around, he stalled the engine. He leapt out, hoping to attempt a push-start. Unfortunately, it was slightly uphill. A well-intentioned spectator ran over to give Mike a push.

At this stage, after two hours racing and having given it everything, Mike was hot, exhausted and stressed. However, none of that really excuses Mike thumping the helpful spectator! The poor chap was probably oblivious to the fact that if Mike had received third-party assistance, he'd have been disqualified.

While all this was going on, Stirling, on his lap of honour, came past, slowed up and shouted, 'Push it downhill. You'll never start the bloody thing that way!'

Mike bump-started it in reverse — only for it to stall again. He'd now run out of escape road. However, with some amazing, super-human effort, he managed to turn the car around, again, and bump-start it forward — successfully. Suspecting he was now in last place, he nursed the brakeless car round to the finish. As he came up to the Ferrari pit, a smiling Tavoni greeted him with these words: 'You're second, and you made fastest lap!'

Mike couldn't believe it, or at least couldn't until he was invited to hop into a large convertible Yank Tank. Stirling was on the top of the back seat with Stuart on one side. 'Hop on, you jammy bugger,' shouted Stirling, patting the other side. 'We're going for a ride.'

As the car took them off for their final lap of honour, the crowd gave them a fantastic standing ovation. Stirling and Mike had done it again: eight points to the former and, by the skin of his teeth, seven points to the latter. With two races to go, there was just five points between them: Mike on thirty-seven; Stirling on thirty-two. But the difference in brakes between the two cars had assumed a huge significance.

As Mike filed up to receive his award, an official intervened and asked him to report to the Automobile Club's offices later that evening. He'd been spotted pushing his car against the direction of the race, the penalty for which would be disqualification.

After dinner, Mike duly went along to face the music. He said it was like being sent to the headmaster's study, only instead of one disapproving old man there were many. Fortunately, Tavoni was already there – Mike's only ally, perhaps. Mike was asked to give his own account of the incident after which Tavoni made an impassioned plea on behalf of his driver. Mike was hoping that, as he'd pushed the car up onto the pavement, it wasn't technically on the track. It seemed this was his only possible mitigation.

'Thank you,' they said, 'and would you be good enough to wait outside for half an hour?'

'Half an hour?' I exclaimed when he told me. 'What on earth for? Were they trying to torture you?'

'God knows,' he said, 'but it was one of the longest thirty minutes of my life.'

When he was finally summoned, he was told that Stirling had volunteered his observations. He'd said that, as Mike had restarted his car on an escape road, he could not be described as going against the traffic. It was apparently this argument, rather than Mike's pavement one, which persuaded the committee to exonerate him. It should be stressed that Stirling's opinion had not even been requested: he'd simply volunteered to speak up for Mike. It was an extraordinary, altruistic gesture which would cost him dearly.

Stirling said, 'I spoke up for Mike because it looked as if they might disqualify him and I didn't want to win the Championship by default. I liked Mike, so I volunteered the information. If it had been someone else, I might have waited to see if I was asked.'

Chapter Forty-Four

Quiet Nights In…

The penultimate GP of the season was the Italian at Monza, to be held a fortnight after Porto. These two weeks provided little rest for Mike. No sooner was he back in England than he flew off to Italy to see Enzo on two matters. One was to establish which road-going Ferraris the factory would be sending for the TT Garage's stand at Earl's Court in October, and the other was to argue passionately for disc brakes to be fitted to his Grand Prix car.

Mike wanted Ferrari to take the disc brakes off Pete's personal Ferrari 250 GT and fit them to his Grand Prix Dino car. He was hopeful that, as the post-construction modification had been commissioned by Enzo's 'surrogate son', and it would be a one-off, he might get his way. Ferrari was not convinced, primarily because the disc brake was a British innovation and, like the German-invented fuel injection, anything not invented by the Italians was to be resisted, even, seemingly, at the expense of success!

Ferrari did at least agree to meet with Dunlop representatives. So, two days later, when Mike got back to England, he telephoned Harold Hodkinson, a Dunlop technician he knew, to ask whether Dunlop would do the work. Needless to say, Harold got the green light and flew out to Maranello the very next day.

It proved impossible to transfer the brakes from a road car to a Grand Prix car, and so the whole of Saturday was spent persuading Enzo to agree to start from scratch. Initially, he would only consent to the front brakes being changed but, eventually, with endorsement from Carlo Chiti, Enzo's chief engineer, the Dunlop team was instructed to design, fabricate, fit and test a bespoke system – within four days. It was a remarkable collaboration of British and Italian design and manufacturing under immense time pressure. Finally, it seemed Mike would be competing on level terms.

While this was going on in Italy, Mike was involved in yet another race − not as a competitor but as a celebrity guest. Nick Syrett, a great chum of ours, and the then secretary of the British Racing and Sports Car Club, had asked Mike if he would present the prize for the Kentish 100 Trophy, a Formula Two race at Brands Hatch. The race had attracted a surprisingly strong field, including many of Mike's principal rivals: Harry, Maurice, Roy, Jack, and even Stirling.

It had been a bloody good session in Farnham the night before, taking in four pubs and rather more pints, notwithstanding that the majority of Members had every intention of attending Brands Hatch. Most of us made it there, eventually, but I suspect few of my peers were up to see the dawn of that beautiful summer's day. Mike was no exception. Driving his own Jag, he arrived at Brands so late that he missed the whole of the first heat. I was so looking forward to the day, I woke very early, but then had to wait for Sally to be ready. I drove her and two of her friends in my car, and we arrived about halfway through, with some twenty laps still remaining. It was terrifically exciting and, for us Hawthorn devotees, it was brilliant to watch Jack Brabham lead Stirling over the line.

The second heat was just as exciting, only this time the order was reversed, with the indomitable Stuart Lewis-Evans finishing between them in second place. The conclusion was that Stirling won the trophy with his first and second places, compared to Jack's first and third.

From our vantage point, which wasn't close, Mike looked a million dollars, even though I could be sure he wasn't feeling it. He'd probably partaken of a couple of 'stabilizing' beers before he made a short, polished and very witty address to the crowd. As Stirling stepped forward to receive the trophy, Mike bent forward as if he was going to whisper something. Instead, he very theatrically planted a wet kiss on each cheek and gave a little curtsey. Stirling's face was a picture, and there were great peals of laughter and clapping from the crowd.

A week later, and these two adversaries would be facing each other in the Italian GP at Monza. The circuit there had been built in 1922 within the grounds of a royal park, a short distance from Milan, where most of the drivers would be staying. Mike flew out midweek and checked into the Palace Hotel. Enzo Ferrari had arranged for Louise to stay there as well.

Afterwards, I asked Mike what it felt like to be around Louise again without Pete. It had been three weeks since they'd seen each other at Pete's memorial service. In truth, I was impatient to discover whether there was anything behind the many stories still circulating on the rumour mill about their *ménage à trois*. It was clear Mike didn't want to talk about Louise. He said he was too preoccupied with practice, that it wasn't the same without Pete, and that she reminded him too much of all the gay old times they'd enjoyed together.

I've since heard that Louise said Mike's attitude changed completely after Pete's death, and that he was cold and uncaring towards her. Was he simply trying to shut away his memories of Pete, or was he almost too attracted to Louise, but felt that wouldn't be doing right by his old mate and, of course, feared for his own mortality? I guess we'll never know.

What we do know is the press were still hyping the Moss v Hawthorn battle. It was widely reported that Mike's disc brakes and Stirling's new-fangled Perspex 'bubble top' over his cockpit were signs of serious intent on both sides. As it happened, the Perspex bubble was extremely short-lived. It was both deafening and heat-intensifying. Stirling would have passed out well before the end of the upcoming 250-mile race.

Enzo Ferrari attended the practice sessions looking incongruous in shirtsleeves, braces and baseball-type cap. Whereas he'd told Louise, unequivocally, only a few days earlier that he would be sending only one car to Monza – for Mike – he had in fact sent four. The others were for Taffy, Gendebien and, for the first time in a Grand Prix car, Phil Hill.

Enzo sought to explain this extraordinary U-turn by publicly quoting Mike as having said, 'I am responsible for myself and I know the risks. If I don't have a Ferrari, I will race another car, but I want to race a Ferrari for the rest of the season.'

'But I thought he was he was only going to enter the one car – for you alone?' I protested to Mike.

'He was. Quite how my outlook on this justifies his change of mind, from the whole team quitting to carrying on, I'll never know. Only now I've got another three Ferraris to contend with.'

Seasoned commentators expected Mike to go well in practice. He now had disc brakes, and he also had a tuned engine giving him even more horsepower. But, once again, the Vanwalls, in the right-hands, proved to be every bit as quick.

At the end of a second hot day of practice, the grid positions had been established: Stirling was in pole position, with his teammates Tony and Stuart on either side of Mike. The second row was all Ferraris – a mere point 0.1 of a second separating those three drivers.

Following events from England was nowhere as easy as it would be today. There was some live broadcasting prior to the race, but this was pitched for a lay audience rather than enthusiasts. One such programme, *Sportsview*, included an interview conducted by Ronnie Noble of Stirling and Mike together at the end of practice. The end of the interview went something like this:

'So, Mike, what will you be doing tonight?' asked Stirling.

'I haven't actually given it any thought. I suppose I'll go back to my hotel, wash and brush up, have dinner with some friends, and then probably wander around Milan hoping to bump into some decent crumpet.'

'What a jolly good idea,' said Stirling. 'I think I'll do the same!'

I nearly fell off my chair. The thought of Stirling being out on the town like Mike was not simply risible, it was impossible.

Ronnie Noble and his television crew decided to shadow Stirling, by invitation, and a little more footage was broadcast showing Stirling having a refined dinner with Katie and his parents and then going to bed and turning out the lights at ten o'clock. It was some hours later, as Ronnie was turning in, that he spied Mike in the Palace Hotel bar.

'Goodnight, Ronnie,' Mike boomed as Ronnie passed by, and raised what was probably not his first nor his last glass of the evening.

Ronnie put the word out that Mike had been surrounded by pretty girls. The truth was that it was probably only three or four, one of whom would have been Louise. The others were most likely the wives or girlfriends of Mike's driver friends. But, then again…

Louise recorded that she went to Mike's room early on the morning of the race to take tea with him, but declared 'it was a bitter mistake'. To this day, I wonder why was it a mistake? What ambiguity. What intrigue. I never did ask Mike about that final encounter of the two of them alone, although I doubt he'd have been very forthcoming.

Michael and Noreen Irving Swift, old friends from Farnham, also called on Mike that morning. They were holidaying in Italy, and hence Mike had invited them to come as his guests. Michael Irving Swift said that when they arrived at the hotel Mike was still in bed and wasn't looking forward to the race. By then, it had gone noon. Mike could only manage a very light brunch. Like the majority of drivers, he wasn't able to eat much prior to a big race. Indeed, it wasn't uncommon for drivers to feel or even be sick whilst waiting for the off.

Mike slowly roused himself, and then drove his four passengers in a Lancia Aurelia out to the Monza circuit. Cramped inside the car were Louise, the Irving Swifts and Jack Dunfee, 'a lovely old gentleman' and one of the legendary 'Bentley Boys' who'd raced Bentleys around Brooklands before Mike was born.

As Mike disappeared off to the pits, the Irving Swifts kindly escorted Louise to her grandstand seat. However, poor Louise was in for more disappointment: she'd been stood up. Having pleaded with Louise to accompany him as his special guest, Enzo Ferrari didn't show up. When I heard that, I was incensed. What selfishness. What a bastard!

Enzo wasn't alone in his absence for, although Ferrari was represented with four Grand Prix cars, the Italian fans stayed away in their droves: none of the Ferrari drivers was Italian. The crowd of a mere 20,000 would have been doubled, more likely trebled, had Luigi Musso or Castellotti still been alive. There were only two Italians driving in the race, and they were on the last row of the grid.

Tavoni assembled his team for a short briefing. Mike's teammates were to press the Vanwalls as hard as possible as this was likely to help Mike. As the drivers dispersed, Taffy turned to Mike and said, 'I don't think I can get round any faster than I did in practice. I'm sorry.'

'Don't worry,' said Mike. 'You did fine in practice. Do your best, but don't take any chances. And, for goodness' sake, don't have an accident.' He meant well.

Because Mike was so anxious about his record of poor starts, he probably tried too hard and messed up yet another one, slipping the clutch and then letting it in too abruptly. The three Vanwalls shot away from him as did Phil Hill who'd come up from the second row.

Mike's teammate Gendebien fared even worse. He stalled on the line and consequently had Jack Brabham plough into him, finishing his race.

On the very first corner, Taffy drove straight up the back of Harry's BRM and was launched up into the air. Mike was directly behind and saw the horrifying spectacle of a spinning, airborne Ferrari throw out its driver, when it was about ten feet off the ground. The car disappeared over a barrier, and Taffy was catapulted into some bushes. Mike didn't wait. He pressed on, intent on chasing Tony Brooks, the nearest of the Vanwalls.

By the end of the first lap, Phil Hill had established a slender lead over Stirling and Stuart. Mike, having overhauled Tony, was in fourth place.

By the end of lap 4, Mike was well into his stride and had overtaken all three cars in front. The Vanwalls were still very much in contention, however, and it looked set to become a classic battle. No sooner than Stirling had been overtaken than he came back at Mike to resecure the lead.

For the next dozen laps or so, it was Mike, the three Vanwalls and Behra's BRM all going as hard as they could, the lead swapping several times. Phil Hill appeared to have vanished – a tyre had disintegrated, obliging him to pit for a new wheel.

Of Mike's three supporting Ferraris, one hadn't left the start line, one had crashed badly, and one had 'thrown a tread'. He was now without protection. Mike knew he needed to establish a lead as he'd need a fresh set of Englebert tyres, whereas the Vanwalls' Dunlops were likely to last the distance.

On lap 18, everything changed. Stirling's gearbox failed, and suddenly he was out. If Mike now won the race, he'd win the Championship. If he didn't win, all he needed to do was to finish in the top five and his lead would be extended. The pressure was off, which was just as well for his clutch was giving out.

This really did seem to be his lucky race: Stuart was forced to retire, due to engine overheating; Tony slowed down, concerned about losing oil; and Behra dropped out with clutch trouble. Everyone thought Mike was going to cruise home unchallenged.

However, Phil Hill, having slipped down as low as tenth because of a shredded tyre, had been working his way up through the field, and by lap 25 had taken second place, and recorded the fastest lap on lap 26. It was now Ferrari first and second.

The big surprise was that another American, Masten Gregory, in a Maserati 250F, had also been going well and was starting to challenge for the lead. Ten laps later, and the leaders were joined by the only remaining Vanwall, that of Tony Brooks, who'd presumably had a refill of oil. The pressure was right back on.

It was an excruciating time for Mike. He was trying to save what was left of his clutch and consequently driving more slowly. By contrast, the Vanwall pit were urging Tony to drive faster.

Masten's challenge was short-lived as sheer exhaustion forced him to hand over his car to Carroll Shelby.

On lap 60, of the seventy-lap race, Tony Brooks managed to pass the Ferraris and began to pull away. By the penultimate lap, the three leaders were well distanced from each other but, whereas Mike had slowed right down, Phil Hill was still charging. With less than a lap to go, it looked as if Phil was going to nip past Mike and deny him second place. Phil understood that Tony Brooks was catching him whereas, because Tony was one lap ahead, it was actually the other way around.

As Mike saw Phil's red car rapidly approaching, he waved his arm up and down, signalling for Phil slow down. Afterwards, Phil said it was only because of Mike's unique bottle-green jacket sleeve that he realised who was driving and then worked out why he was trying to flag him down. That, Phil acceded, was very magnanimous. First to cross the finish line was Tony, then Mike, Phil, Carroll Shelby, and Roy Salvadori. There were only seven finishers.

Mike's second place provided him with another six points: an eleven-point lead over Stirling in the Championship and a seemingly unassailable lead. Except there was still a slim – very slim – chance for Stirling.

Louise and the Irving Swifts hung around after the race to see the trophies being awarded. They caught up with Mike briefly to congratulate him and to hear about the trouble he'd had with his clutch, and how it was all his 'own bloody silly fault'. Mike then made his excuses as he needed to wash and change, and doubtless have a 'well-earned beer' or two as he was attending a UPPI reception in honour of Fangio's retirement from the sport.

That was the last time Louise saw Mike. That very weekend, she'd received a cable from Peter Ustinov, famed actor, broadcaster, film and theatre director, etc, who also kept a boat in Monte Carlo. He offered her a starring role as Juliet in his Broadway production of Romanoff and Juliet. It was a lifeline. Louise flew back to New York the next day, and within a fortnight she was part of a cast that would tour Canada for ten weeks. She later said, 'It was the best thing that could have happened to me. I had to be on stage, looking good, feeling good, and knowing my lines at eight thirty every night. At that difficult time after Peter's death, that kind of discipline and purpose was just what I needed.'

Mike, together with every other top racing driver past and present, attended the reception in honour of Juan Fangio. Mike told us that Stirling had looked in but left early to catch a plane. Considering how close Stirling and Fangio had been as teammates, Mike thought that was rather poor form. He also told us that Fangio rattled on at great length in Spanish which few of the assembled understood – although Mike did comprehend Fangio thought the Italian Grand Prix had been a 'good race' as nobody had died.

In case you're wondering what happened to Taffy and Harry after they collided, they both survived. Despite receiving cuts and bruises, Harry, who'd remained in his car, was able to walk away. Taffy was considered extremely lucky to have been thrown out of his Ferrari, for the thing broke up completely. He ended up with a broken leg and multiple contusions.

He was fortunate on that occasion. Monza wasn't a kind circuit to him. He'd crashed and been injured there in the '56 Italian Grand Prix, and at this same event three years later, he would have a horrific accident which not only accounted for the loss of his life but also the deaths of fifteen spectators.

At the time of his death, he was still driving for Ferrari and was leading the Championship points table. He'd led a helluva of a life in his thirty-three years. It's odd to think that Taffy was considered a bit 'girly' when he was young.

After the Fangio reception, Mike went out to dinner with a few chums, including the Americans Phil Hill and Carroll Shelby. Celebrating their various successes, the chaps decided they would 'do' a few Milanese nightclubs. It's funny how this latter part of the evening was differently recorded. Mike told me afterwards he thought it would be fun to see if the Yanks could hold their booze, and it had ended up 'quite a night'.

In his memoirs, Mike wrote about going to the nightclubs and implied he was a little groggy in the morning. Carroll Shelby expressed it thus: 'We got real drunk and raised hell all night with a bunch of American models.'

I'm guessing the models referred to were there because of their fashion work, not the lure of the Grand Prix drivers, but whatever the circumstances it would have been a heady mixture.

It was only with a supreme effort, and almost certainly a few Alka-Seltzers, that Mike managed to catch the two o'clock afternoon bus to the airport for his flight back to London, with his Championship hopes in a considerably better state than he was.

Chapter Forty-Five

Come in Number 6…

The final Grand Prix of the '58 season, the Moroccan, was now five weeks away, and it proved an agonizing wait for Mike and Stirling. On the face of it, with only one race left offering the victor a maximum of nine points, and with Mike eleven points clear, it might have appeared all over. And yet, due to the arcane nature of the competition's rules, if Stirling was able to get maximum points and Mike finished in third place or lower, the Championship would be Stirling's. This was because only the competitors' best six (out of ten) races would count towards their tally. There were many different computations, but in essence it meant Stirling absolutely had to win in Morocco to be in with a chance.

Emotionally, it was a roller-coaster time for Mike. On the downside, he was repeatedly asked about his prospects of winning the title – about which he could do nothing but fret. On the upside, he was, at last, able to spend time with Jean Howarth, reacquaint himself with what was happening at the garage, and attend various functions as a sporting celebrity.

Before settling back into English domesticity, Mike flew to Italy for a brief meeting called by Enzo. He wasn't exactly sure what to expect. When he returned, he recounted something of their extraordinary exchange.

'The Old Man was really friendly – it was pretty disarming. He said he wanted me to stay with Ferrari next year. He said I could even write my own contract – and he would sign it without reading it! Can you believe that?'

'Bloody hell! That doesn't sound like Enzo Ferrari,' I exclaimed.

'It's the truth, I'm telling you.'

'Well, hopefully you thought of a figure and then doubled it,' I said.

'No, what I actually said was, "Thank you very much for the offer, but first I have the battle for the Championship. Then, when I come back, we can have dinner and discuss such things".'

'What did he say?'

'He said okay, and then asked me what I was doing until Casablanca.'

'So, you lied, presumably?'

'Naturally! I told him that I would be very quiet before the race, and I wouldn't be going anywhere near a pub.'

'What's this,' I exclaimed and looked around, 'if it isn't a pub?'

He simply laughed.

Later that evening, I reflected on our conversation and asked, 'What if the Old Man changes his mind? Aren't you worried you might have let the moment pass?'

Mike pulled a bit of a face. 'Not really,' he said. 'I'm ninety-nine per cent sure that I want out.'

'But what about the money?' I couldn't help blurting out the question, even though the last thing I wanted was Mike to continue racing.

'You can't spend it from the grave, can you?' he replied.

Finally, I thought, he's picturing his own mortality. Pete's death had changed everything.

Of the many diversions to come Mike's way was a PR event in Coventry to launch ERNIE, the Government's new Premium Bond selection machine. Preceding that, Mike had the onerous duty of helping choose a 'Miss Triumph' – a title pertaining to the marque of car rather than a brassiere, although I'm sure Mike could happily have turned his hand to either. The girl who won Miss Triumph would become one of the nine young women each representing the Midland's nine car makers.

Mike was one of three judges to interview the contestants. Another judge was the television presenter Eamonn Andrews who was filmed seated in a TR3 open sports car. Mike said the three judges had fierce arguments between themselves about which girl to choose. The criteria were meant to encompass looks, poise, personality, interest in motoring, experience of motor sport, whether they drove, and so forth. Mike said the girl they eventually chose was 'so-so', but she certainly wasn't the one he'd have taken home.

Up in Coventry for the ERNIE launch, Mike was required to drive a vintage car across the first floor of one of the city's leading department stores, Owen & Owen, before pushing the button to start the October Premium Bond draw. The beauty parade girls were then required to walk on, each bearing a number or a letter, which together would comprise the jackpot winner's combination – for a prize of £1,000.

When Mike told me what he'd been up to, I was insanely jealous. 'Just you and *nine* beautiful models?' I protested.

'They weren't all that much,' he said nonchalantly, 'If pushed, I'd have plumped for Miss Standard, but frankly none of them was a patch on Jean.'

It was said Jean who persuaded Mike to go to Paris a week later. While there, they visited Le Salon to view an exhibition entitled *Toutes les Voitures Françaises 1958*, to admire the beautiful form of French automobiles. And so typical of Mike, he took her to the Crazy Horse Saloon – the cabaret show famed for its beautiful choreographed female nude dancers – alleging it was a similar aesthetic pursuit.

Whilst in Paris, he learnt he'd been awarded the coveted Driver of the Year by the Guild of Motoring Writers. Mike was well chuffed by this for not only had he had his ups and downs with the press as a whole but he was succeeding Fangio from the previous year, and Pete from the year before that. The citation which accompanied the award included these words: '...difficulties of such a nature that many less courageous drivers would not have gone on trying as he did.' This struck me as coded recognition of how much Mike was known to have grieved for Pete.

By mid-October, Mike was readying himself for Morocco. He was keen that Jean should watch his final race and probably see him crowned Britain's first World Champion. Mike was equally keen the press didn't latch on to them as a couple, and so insisted they travel separately.

Tony Vandervell hadn't enjoyed the cramped flight with Air France the previous year, 'with barely a fromage sandwich' for sustenance, and so decided to charter a plane from British European Airways for his Vanwall team, and invited other racing luminaries to tag along, including Mike.

It was perverse that Mike, Vanwall's chief opposition, was on board whereas Vanwall's top driver, Stirling, wasn't. Also on the flight was Lofty. He'd told Mike some cock and bull story about his needing to check out Jaguar's sales organization in Morocco, and how it was a happy coincidence that his trip would coincide with the Grand Prix. Mike told me he was delighted that Lofty would be on hand, even if it was completely unofficial.

Stirling and Katie Moss had elected instead to fly out on 'the Grand Prix Special', another privately chartered plane. Mike suggested Jean took this flight and asked the Mosses to take good care of her.

Once there, most of their crowd checked in at the Marhaba Hotel, at the time a swanky American-styled establishment. They were joined for dinner by Romolo Tavoni who'd brought with him the allocated race numbers.

Mike saw he'd been given the number 2. 'Oh, for crying out loud!' he exclaimed. 'Is this someone's idea of a joke?'

Phil said Mike was so angry he half expected Mike to lash out, or storm out.

Tavoni looked most embarrassed as he remembered the furore Mike had made over being allocated number 22 as recently as August. But '2' – oh boy, for Mike that was the worst possible number: the number of death.

Fortunately, Olivier Gendebien came to the rescue and said he wasn't in the least superstitious and volunteered to swap his number 6 for the fated number 2. As time would testify, Gendebien was indeed one of the lucky ones for he retired from the sport in 1962, still in one piece, and comfortably outlived his allotted three score and ten.

There was a secondary competition going on – lower-profile than the Hawthorn-Moss one – and that was between the constructors. Given how much was at stake for Ferrari, it seems bizarre that Enzo would send out three cars with three different braking systems: two fitted with discs, by different makers, and one with drums. Mike had the choice of the disc-braked cars, and plumped for Dunlop over Girling. The latter went to Olivier, while the drum-braked car with a Formula Two chassis for some reason went to the arguably quicker driver, Phil Hill.

Suitably mollified with his number 6, and enjoying decent

braking for once, Mike went well in practice and got himself on pole. Stirling was closest of the Vanwalls and bagged second, but not without first blowing up his car and needing to commandeer Tony's. Stuart, in the other Vanwall, took third place on the grid.

BRM were there in force with four cars and four top-flight drivers, the quickest of whom, Jean Behra, was fourth on the grid.

I wasn't going to miss this race for all the tea in China. I thought it would be Mike's last Formula One race and was almost certain to be his Championship-winning race. Fortunately, there was so much demand from British supporters because, come what may, the Champion would be British, for the first time in history, it didn't prove difficult to get flights. However, they weren't cheap. The word went round at work that I was a Flash 'Arry, but everyone knew how important it was to me to go. I couldn't afford to take Sally, but she was gracious about that, adding it didn't appeal greatly because it would be very hot and the food would be funny.

Unfortunately, I arrived too late for the practice sessions, but did track Mike down on the eve of the race and joined him for a couple of sundowners, or 'nerve-settlers' as I called them. He was looking terribly smart as he was taking Jean on to a party hosted by the British Ambassador, Sir Charles Duke, at the consul's residence. I asked him how he was feeling.

'Bloody nervous, of course.' he replied.

'Nah, you're not. It's in the bag.'

'Look, you know what a balls-up I keep making of these starts. What if I bugger up the clutch and don't even finish?'

'You'll be okay. You told me Ferrari has sourced extra-strong clutch linings. Anyway, how about you do "a Stirling" and go easy on this stuff, for once?' I said, raising my glass.

He smiled. 'You know, I'm feeling knackered already. I'll definitely have an early night.'

I wanted to stay up chatting, and yet I felt the decent thing to do was to feign tiredness so I bade him goodnight and set off back to my hotel, but not before wishing him the very best of British. I sensed he was more nervous than knackered.

And did he do 'a Stirling'? No, of course he didn't. Stories went flying round the next day claiming he'd been spotted around midnight returning to his hotel with Jean Howarth on one arm and

Mary Taylor Young – a young lady friend of his who'd flown out on the same flight as Mike – on the other.

Race day dawned a lot earlier than Mike, and although a little overcast, doubtless a lot brighter too. Mike's pal, Rodney Walkerley (he of the Spa to Reims meanderings), must have had a more sober night than either of us, and wrote this wonderfully evocative scene-setter for *The Motor*:

> The desolate landscape on the southern outskirts of the vast, white city of Casablanca, alongside the long breakers of an Atlantic shimmering blue and sparkling with diamonds in the misty sunlight, was that day transformed with colour. The grandstands and enclosures seethed with a record crowd of some 100,000. Figures which might have stepped straight out of some Biblical illustration jostled with women clad with all the elegance of Paris. In the royal box sat King Mohammed V and his entourage, gorgeous in their Arabian garments, and before the grandstands paraded units of the Moroccan army, smart and picturesque in white tunics, huge baggy pantaloons, white gaiters and boots, some turbaned, others haughty in their red tarboosh (a Fez-like hat) head-dresses.

Mike, however, was irked because all the top-brass transportation was German. The royal cars were all Mercedes and the King's bodyguard unit all rode BMW motorbikes.

He was even more irked by the actions of Raymond 'Toto' Roche. Despite his history of ineptitude, Toto, an official of the Automobile Club de France, had been chosen to start the race. He managed once again to delay proceedings, waiting for one of the Coopers to get started. Although Toto had some 'form' for this kind of thing, I doubt that many sane people volunteered. The race starter was required to stand in the middle of the front of the grid and bring down his flag as a signal to go. Toto wasn't a small man either: from the rear, he looked similar to Alfred Neubauer, the Mercedes' boss. It's a wonder he was never hit.

I'd found a good seat, about two thirds of the way up one of the grandstands, some hundred yards or so past the start/finish line from which to watch Toto's antics. Most of what I could see around me was common to all major circuits around the world: cars, people, white-overalled mechanics, and lots of advertising banners promoting companies such as BP, Total, Esso, Shell, Dunlop, Englebert, Martini and Campari. I still found all this advertising a bit of a novelty. I wasn't sure whether I liked it or not.

Looking down the circuit towards the first corner, I saw straw bales spaced about a yard apart. That'll annoy him for a start, I thought.

As the grid started to grow so too did the expectation of the crowd. There was usually a buzz of excitement before the off. however, this definitely felt special.

When the flag went down, Stirling, as usual, shot away with Phil hard on his tail. Mike, taking it easy on his clutch for once, went off more slowly.

By the end of the first lap, Mike had caught up to take third place. It was just the start I was hoping for. Phil was clearly going to push Stirling to make a mistake, but even if Stirling won, I was sure that Phil would crucially once again allow Mike to take second place, right at the last knockings.

On the third lap, Phil tried braking at the same place as Stirling but his drum brakes were not up to it. Unable to negotiate the corner, he ran off down an escape road. What was Ferrari thinking of – giving Phil the least competitive car? Management ineptitude doesn't begin to describe it.

This gave Mike second place, with Jo Bonnier third. Phil may have gone off, but he wasn't out. He managed to get back on the circuit and fight his way back into contention within three laps. When he overtook Bonnier, and Mike waved him past, I could breathe again. The Ferraris were back in charge.

The status quo lasted for a few more laps until Tony Brooks, often slow to get going, decided he'd got the hang of the circuit and began charging up the field. By lap 12, he was challenging Mike for third place. It was obvious that Mike had better outright speed but, when overtaken, Tony would slip in behind the Ferrari on the straights for a bit of a tow, and then, using his greater power out of the corners, he'd reovertake the Ferrari.

This ding-dong battle lasted for half a dozen laps during which I was on the edge of my seat. Unfortunately, by lap 20, Tony had not only passed Mike, but had a lead of three seconds. If the race order stayed like this, with Mike in fourth, the title would be Stirling's.

An impartial spectator might have described this situation as thrilling. Sitting there, living every second of the race with Mike, I can only describe it as excruciating. Looking around me, it was clear that the majority of spectators also knew just how close it was. Their attention was rapt, their eyes flicking back and forth between the track, the leader board and the pits. The tension was unbearable.

In the Ferrari pit, I could just make out Jean. Her head was bowed. I guessed she was busily recording her boyfriend's lap times. I wondered what she was thinking.

On lap 21, Stirling, having established a commanding lead, then piled on the agony by posting the fastest lap.

The only comfort I could take from the situation was that Tony's Vanwall was occasionally puffing blue smoke. I was willing his engine to blow up. However, to my enormous relief, Mike hadn't given up, and he and Tony were soon at it again, swapping places every lap.

And then, on lap 30, Mike got a lucky break: Tony's engine did blow up and oil poured from his car. The back wheels lost all traction, and the car spun violently at great speed, fortunately coming to a halt without hitting anything. Thankfully, Tony was able to walk away. Mike was now third, but there were still a lot of miles to cover.

At lap 39, and with fourteen still to go, Tavoni signalled for Phil to slow down in order that Mike could pass into second place.

Ah, the relief! We could relax a little. It looked as if no one stood a chance of catching Stirling, but at least Mike's second place was now guarded by Phil. The only potential fly in the ointment was Jo Bonnier, in fourth place, who was having a great drive in his BRM, and had caught up with the two Ferraris. Thankfully, Phil and Mike drove so defensively that Jo was never able to pass them.

On lap 43, out of sight from where I was standing, there must have been a big incident because a huge plume of ominous black smoke rose above the circuit. I wasn't able to work out whether one car or more were missing. A while later, the commentators announced over the tannoy that Stuart Lewis-Evans's Vanwall had come off the track.

Mike knew that it wasn't Stirling's car for, if it had been, his pit would have signalled he was in the lead. So, for the remainder of the race, right to the chequered flag, the status quo was unchanged: Stirling first, Mike second, and Phil third. The sweaty-palmed drama was replaced by breath-holding tension.

I was standing a little beyond the finish line as the dark green Vanwall flashed by, Stirling with his arm raised in a salute to the crowd. He'd driven the perfect race. Again. He really couldn't have done more. And yet, hopefully, he was going to be beaten into second place overall by a single point. It seemed ages – well, it was nearly a minute – before the two red Ferraris hove into view, almost side by side. I could make out the taller driver well before I could read the car numbers, and then, a few seconds later, a car length in front of the other, number 6 whooshed by, its driver wearing the biggest smile you ever saw and pumping his clenched fist up to the sky.

In a moment of unguarded emotion, I began to do the same. He'd done it! He'd really done it. It almost felt like I was the World Champion, not him. As he disappeared out of sight, on his lap of honour, I realised there were tears in my eyes. I needn't have worried about feeling self-conscious. The crowd around me were waving and cheering madly. It didn't matter whether you were a Moss supporter or a Hawthorn supporter, it had been an exciting race with three British successes – two drivers and one constructor, Vanwall. At long last, there was a British Champion.

I looked across to where the royals were sitting. On the front of their box-like enclosure was a large Star of David. Inside the box, they were all on their feet, applauding enthusiastically. In the end, it hadn't been the closest of races, but it was always going to be dramatic, and the atmosphere of the crowd was infectious.

I rushed towards the start/finish line hoping to get a good vantage point for the presentations. I couldn't get very close because of the crush of all the other Brits, but it didn't matter too much – on account of my height: I was about a head taller than most folk around me. Nothing seemed to happen for ages. I couldn't fathom what was taking so long.

As I stood there, I began to think about how Stirling must be feeling. He'd won four Grands Prix that year compared to Mike's one, and was only beaten in one race – that same one. Of the other five Grands Prix, three times his engine had blown up, once his gearbox had broken, and once his magneto had failed. He'd had the most miserable luck. By contrast, Mike had finished all but one of the ten Championship races, notwithstanding near misses through his clutch abuse. Then, when I factored in Stirling's generous support of Mike over the Portuguese disqualification debacle, all of a sudden the season's outcome couldn't have seemed more unfair.

And then I caught sight of Mike – wreathed in smiles, and admirers – and felt guiltily disloyal. He hadn't made up those silly rules – he was simply the benefactor of them. After all he was *nearly* the best driver of the season…if, of course, you didn't count Tony Brooks who'd won three Grands Prix outright and suffered five retirements. I see it much more clearly now. Our Golden Boy was lucky – very, very lucky.

Chapter Forty-Six

Celebrating the WC

Of course, not everyone was so lucky in Casablanca. There'd been a number of crashes. Olivier's Ferrari had spun on oil dropped from Tony's Vanwall, causing a Cooper to slam into him. Both cars went off the circuit, and Olivier's Ferrari hit a large rock, neatly slicing off the rear of the car just behind the driver's seat. Incredibly, all he suffered was shock and a couple of broken ribs.

Because we spectators were almost exclusively packed in grandstands around the start/finish line, only a handful of people witnessed the worst accident of the race: that which befell Stuart Lewis-Evans. Due to the new fuel regulations, his Vanwall engine seized, causing him to spin at Azemmour, a tightish right-hander which turned down towards the sea after a long straight. His car had finished up on the inside of the track where it hit a small stand of trees and burst into flames. Eyewitnesses said he managed to get out of the car, his clothing ablaze, and in panic ran directly away from the marshals who, with their extinguishers and blankets, could have helped him. After he collapsed, he was taken to hospital immediately with serious burns.

Outside the pit area, there was an excited throng gathered around Mike and Stirling as they climbed out of their cars. I'd never seen Tavoni so animated. He was patting Mike so hard on the shoulders I thought Mike might fall back into the cockpit. I saw Lofty making giant strides towards Mike and then shake his hand. And then, much to my surprise, David Yorke of the Vanwall team did likewise, old animosities clearly forgiven.

Mike told me afterwards that Tavoni had said, 'Next year, we will do it again!'

Mike had replied, 'It'll have to be without me. I've retired!'

Romolo simply laughed and said, 'Of course you'll be racing.'

The race winners' names were announced, and the King presented trophies to the top three placed drivers. A pretty girl then placed a laurel wreath over their grimy, grinning heads, giving each of them two kisses. It can't have been very pleasant for her. I noted there was an equal amount of clapping and hollering for both Mike and Stirling.

I then noticed Stirling whisper something to Mike. After much more clapping and general posing from the drivers, they left the little podium and were soon lost in the crowd. I thought it peculiar that there was no mention of the World Championship. I was expecting Mike to be called back for another presentation but the crowd started to disperse. A chap standing next to me must have read my thoughts because he said he'd heard the official prize-giving was going to be held in the evening, and that it was a ticket-only affair. I felt quite cheated. It was a massive anti-climax that the prize-giving was not held then and there.

I was determined to be amongst the first of Mike's friends to offer my congratulations. I was a sufficiently familiar face to talk my way into the Ferrari pit, only to be told I'd just missed him. I reckoned he'd either head straight for a bar or to his hotel to clean up. I decided my best bet was to walk briskly to his hotel. I hadn't got far before I heard Lofty England's stentorian tones from within a tented structure on the perimeter of the circuit. I pulled back a canvas flap and, sure enough, there were Mike, Jean and Lofty raising their glasses to one another.

'Congratulations, champ!' I hailed as I ducked under the flap.

Mike swung round, his smile immediate and generous. 'We did it!'

'Best I buy you a drink, then?'

'That's very kind old chap, but this is my second already, and I suspect it's going to be a long old night.' Rather than looking supercharged with success, Mike looked exhausted, which I suppose was to be expected after a 250-mile race, and even a little deflated. 'What I ought to do is head back for a soak and a shave and then get ready for dinner. I suspect we'll be going on somewhere. Shall we try and meet up later?'

I told him that unfortunately I was flying back that evening so I'd have to pass.

Lofty was clearly delighted for Mike. It was as if his own son had won. Not, of course, that he had a son – Lofty's issue was limited to one daughter. Equally, in the absence of Leslie, Lofty was the nearest thing Mike had to a father figure.

We chatted briefly about the race. Mike was generous in his praise of Phil, who had risked and sacrificed much to help him to victory. I asked whether there was any news about Stuart. They told me that he'd been taken to hospital and was thought to be badly burnt, but he'd come through.

I also asked Mike how it had felt driving round for his lap of honour. He said that all he could think about was that it would be the last time he'd ever drive a Grand Prix car, and that had felt strange. He loved racing, but hated the races – for all the risks and the pain they represented. He didn't look as happy as I thought he would. In fact, Jean looked happier – maybe because she could see a safer future for them together. Before I left, I broached a difficult subject: Stirling.

'What did Stirling say to you on the podium?'

'He said, "You did it, you old so and so!".'

'All things considered, Stirling was a bit unlucky, don't you think?'

'What d'yer mean?' Mike shot back.

'Well, he did win four Grands Prix…' I said, thinking but not saying, …to your one.

'Ah, it's all about consistency, Tom,' Lofty interjected, sticking up for his protégé. 'Don't forget, Mike got points in nearly every race.'

'Yeah, and without me around, Moses will have it all his own way next year,' added Mike.

I dropped the subject. There was little point in saying anything about Stirling's rotten luck with Vanwall's reliability. It wasn't as if Mike had cheated: he was simply fortunate.

As Mike made to leave, I went to shake his hand. Instead of extending a hand, he suddenly threw his arms out and hugged me. 'Thanks for everything, Tom.'

'I haven't done anything,' I protested, pulling back a little. He had this uncanny knack of making me feel guilty whenever I wasn't being 100 per cent loyal. It was if sometimes he could read my thoughts.

'You've always believed in me. That's enough.'

I watched them leave together: Mike, uncommonly diminished

by Lofty's big frame, and Jean, tall and elegant alongside them. I felt a surge of pride. And then it hit me – he'd actually survived motor racing! This race was his swansong. There would be no more fear that I could lose my best friend umpteen times a year. The relief was immense. Feeling almost tearful, I hurriedly finished my drink and went in search of a snack, knowing I only had an hour or two before my flight back to London.

Mike duly attended the award ceremony which he described as 'a lavish affair', and at which he was presented with a 'stupidly heavy' trophy comprising two chunky discs of marble separated by four tall columns on top of which sat – most inappropriately – four bronze models of a Connaught racing car surmounted by a large silver bowl.

Mike said he felt very mixed emotions at that dinner: massive elation and relief at having won, and sadness that neither Pete nor his dad were there to share it.

He let on he was feeling a bit flat when he, Jean and Lofty and the Martineaus all convened back at the hotel bar for what someone proposed would be the last drink of the night. In this lull in proceedings, Mike must have been in reflective mood for he thought to send Louise Collins a telegram which read: WE HAVE DONE IT MON AMI MATESS. WILL WRITE SOON. LOVE MON AMI MATE. MICHAEL.

Of course, today that would probably be a text message – vastly simpler to arrange and much cheaper to send. I've since speculated whether this message was prompted by his true feelings for Louise, or whether it was essentially a communication to his late friend. Perhaps it was both.

Needless to say, it wasn't one last drink back at the hotel, and when eventually a Shell representative bowled in and said that a whole bunch of drivers were having a whale of a time at a local nightclub, Mike's threatened early night turned straight into an extremely late one. Mike admitted that by the time he crawled into bed he was completely done in.

When boarding the Vanwall chartered plane the following day, Mike was shocked to see Stuart Lewis Evans being carried on by stretcher, accompanied by a French nurse. Not only was he apparently well enough to travel but he was surprisingly cheerful despite being in considerable pain. His repatriation was all thanks to a Shell employee whose excellent command of French had made it possible to fly Stuart back to England and the specialist burns hospital at East Grinstead.

It was a sombre flight for Tony Vandervell, winner of the Constructor's Championship, considered himself responsible for Stuart's accident. Stuart was a driver of whom he was particularly fond. Amazingly, until now, none of his drivers had been badly hurt, although several had crashed, and now Vandervell blamed himself, apparently because of his 'stupid hobby of building racing cars'.

Mike returned to Farnham that same evening and, although we couldn't meet up, we did have a few words on the telephone. I asked him how he was.

'You know – up and down. I'm not sure about all this fuss, though.'

'You mean the press?'

'Yeah, I've never seen anything like it,' he said, referring to his arrival at London Airport. 'There were reporters and cameramen everywhere. You'd have thought I was the President of the United States.'

'You'd better get used to it. Britain's never had a World Champion before.'

'It's the same here at the garage. We've had stacks of letters already, and the telephone doesn't stop ringing. God knows how our customers will get through.'

'Has the press cottoned on to you and Jean yet?'

'I don't think so. She's not back yet. The plane she was on with Stirling and that lot had engine trouble, so they had to stop over in Paris.'

'How is it with Jean?' I asked tentatively. He didn't reply. I think he feigned not to have heard the question. 'You know, Mike, you could do worse. She's a lovely lass. D'yer think she's the one?' With his retirement planned, I was certain he'd be thinking about settling down, maybe even starting a family.

'Mind your own business, McBride! Now I'm World Champion, all the girls will be after me.' His tone was mischievous. He clearly wasn't in the mood for confidences.

'They already were, you greedy bugger,' I said, hoping not to sound too jealous.

Chapter Forty-Seven

Stuart's Turn, Then Grogger's

The days and weeks that followed were a whirl for the new World Champion. He had never experienced attention like it and, to his credit, he tried his best to fulfil every invitation – whether that was appearing on television or radio, or being a guest of honour, an after-dinner speaker, or an opener of *fêtes* and shows. In one week alone, he had twenty-seven engagements, in addition to which he was expected to be on the TT Garage's stand at the Earls Court Motor Show where he had two fabulous Ferrari 250 GTs on display.

He complained that it was all right for the likes of Stirling, who had a manager and staff who would handle such matters, but the burden of all this administration fell to him and the girls at the garage. I said that, if he wasn't such a tight Yorkshireman, he too could have minions.

All these obligations meant I hardly saw him in person until Christmas, which was odd because it was as if I'd never seen more of him – he was everywhere. And, what's more, he was very good at it. Not only did he photograph well but his modulated, public school speaking voice was perfect for broadcasting. His ever-ready smile flashed for the cameras, and his ability to appeal to a diverse audience of class and age made him ever more popular. He was a natural. And he *never* looked anything less than totally fit and healthy.

Of course, the media back then were much less intrusive and prurient. Mike's private life still, by and large, stayed private. The press were even considerate as to what was, or was not, broadcast. He told me that one interviewer wanted to know about his driving style, to which Mike replied, 'I haven't bloody well got a driving style'. Fortunately, that and many similar such quotes never went public.

Mike was unwavering about his retirement and, in my opinion, he did the decent thing by advising Enzo formally before going public. In a letter, he thanked the Old Man for all that he done for him and said politely, but unequivocally, that he would not be signing up for 1959. Whilst writing, he asked whether he could purchase his winning Ferrari, in the certain knowledge that it would not be used in the forthcoming season.

Enzo never replied, nor did he try to contact Mike again. Some weeks later, Tavoni wrote saying that Enzo was devastated about Mike's decision, and thought he was wrong to retire. Mike's request for the 1958 Formula One car was never mentioned. I knew Mike intended to keep it as a memento, not to drive it. With hindsight, Mike should have said as much in his letter.

One of his first public engagements, and to which he took Jean, was the British Racing Drivers' Club dinner at the Park Lane Hotel. There he was presented with the BRDC Gold Star, its highest award, and the British Automobile Racing Club (BARC) Gold Medal in recognition of becoming Britain's first World Champion. Apparently, when Stirling was making a short but generous speech, about how pleased he was that the title had gone to his very good friend, etc, Mike was standing off, discreetly raising two fingers in Stirling's direction. All in jest, naturally.

A couple of days later, Mike and Stirling, amongst others, attended a two-day seminar at the RAC in Pall Mall to debate the future of motor racing and its governing rules and regulations. Representing the Formula One drivers, Mike, Stirling and Maurice Trintignant all spoke up against radical changes.

On the evening of the second day, there was the official prize-giving ceremony at which Tony Vandervell and Charles Cooper (John's father) received trophies for winning the Constructor's Championship in Formula One and Formula Two respectively, and Mike received his driver's trophy. The press were there in force, and the following day, pictures of Mike holding his simple, bucket-like silver cup appeared in every national newspaper. I thought it amusing that the official FIA World Championship trophy was so modest in comparison with his Moroccan one.

The seminar itself ended in uproar, however, when, directly against the wishes of the drivers and the British constructors, the governing body voted to limit engine sizes to 1.5 litres; impose a minimum weight for all cars; and introduce a number of other safety measures which included anti-roll bars and safer fuel tanks.

Although some of these safety measures had merit, the restriction of engine size was considered by many as little more than an anti-British ploy by various European countries – such was the dominance of the big-engined British and Italian cars.

It hadn't been a week since Mike's return from Morocco when I learnt of more tragic news. Stuart Lewis-Evans had passed away; his burns had proved too severe.

Having heard how chipper he'd been when flying back with Mike only a few days earlier, I really hadn't expected this outcome. To think I'd seen him, admittedly from a distance, only minutes before the Casablanca GP, so full of beans – the little chap with an over-sized head and boxer's nose. Managed by Bernie Ecclestone, he'd rapidly become one of the most competitive racers in the world and then, aged twenty-eight, it was all over. The poor wee lad. I don't recall whether Mike went to Stuart's funeral. I didn't. I had no holiday left, and, in any case, I couldn't say I knew Stuart well.

On one of those rare occasions that Mike and I did meet up, it was for a classic Sunday lunchtime at The Barley Mow at Tilford. It was a jolly gathering of Members and newer friends alike. I still have an old black and white picture of the scene. We're all smartly dressed in our Sunday best suits. If you saw a group of men dressed like that today, you'd think they were going to a wedding.

Mike arrived in a bright red Ferrari 250 demonstrator. Parked amongst our humble jalopies, it couldn't have looked more incongruous if it had been a spaceship. Jean was in the passenger seat and Grogger, Mike's boxer dog, was sitting between them, his smiling, slobbery face craned forward. Talk about cutting a dash – they could have come straight off a Hollywood film set. Amongst the Members, there was much interest in the Ferrari and, after a little badgering, Mike agreed to take a few of us out for a spin, just around the immediate lanes.

On the second such outing, and on hearing the raucous Ferrari returning, Grogger, who'd been sitting quietly between Jean and Sally, suddenly dashed out of the bar to greet his master. Sadly, neither Mike, who was driving quickly, nor Grogger, who was running, were able to stop in time. Grogger was killed outright.

Fortunately, most of our party was inside the pub when it happened, but the gruesome news spread in seconds. The majority didn't know what to say or do, and so left quickly. I wanted to stay with Mike, and I was glad I did. It was awful to see such a euphoric atmosphere collapse so quickly into deep tragedy. It was as sudden as the bursting of a balloon.

Mike was inconsolable – he couldn't stop crying. Jean, Sally and I did our best to console him but he just wanted to go home. I suggested that Sally took him and Jean back to his mum's while I would follow slowly in the Ferrari. Mike was so shaken up he just wanted to be told what to do. Sally was great – she ushered them out of the pub and into my car. I asked Mike for his keys which he handed over wordlessly. Luckily, I managed to follow the others without incident. It was the one and only time I ever drove a Ferrari, and I don't think I went above 25mph.

Sometime later, I heard on the grapevine that Mike had gone to his mother's room that night in floods of tears, clutching Grogger's lead, saying, 'What *have* I done, Mother? My lovely Grogger is gone.'

Mike didn't remain without a boxer dog for long. Within days, he and Jean drove up to Yorkshire to see her parents, and used this opportunity to call in at the kennels from where he had bought Grogger. He saw two puppies that he liked and chose a nine-week-old boy that bore a close similarity to Grogger, except for a white patch on its face. Showing all the imagination of an American movie-maker, he decided that the new dog should be called Grogger 2.

As they were driving home, Mike suddenly turned to Jean and said, 'Would you like one, too?' Jean said she would, so Mike stopped, turned the car around, drove the thirty miles back to the kennels, and bought the other puppy – this one ostensibly as Jean's early Christmas present. As it was named Ferrari, I suggest Jean received both the dog and its name with scant consultation.

Chapter Forty-Eight

Honour Pending...?

Of all the adulation and recognition that came his way, it was an invitation from Buckingham Palace to a private luncheon party for seven selected guests on 6 November 1958 with the Queen and the Duke of Edinburgh which meant most to Mike.

For a time, whenever I saw him after that he was insufferable. It was all: 'Oh, when I was at the Palace...', and 'I was only saying to the Queen the other day...' and 'Of course, Prince Philip shares my interest in young fillies...'

About the only formal function which I managed to attend was a civic dinner hosted by Farnham Borough Council in mid-November. The chairman of the council made a generous and stirring speech, finishing off with a sentiment that he hoped it would not be too long before Mike was back behind the wheel of a *British* racing car. I studied Mike's face looking for a reaction but there was none – just his fixed grin.

I was probably the only one there, besides Jean and Winifred, who knew of Mike's intention to retire. However, I began to wonder whether Mike really would retire if he was offered a place with a top British team. Was his resolve weakening?

And, of course, in the short time since Mike's decision, there was now an unexpected as well as a tragic vacancy at Vanwall. But that would mean Mike and Stirling being teammates, and I couldn't see that working out.

Mike's reply speech was first-class. He spoke about how much his home town meant to him and of his wonderful formative years spent at Barford School. He paid a heartfelt tribute to his late father, and to his mother for having taken such good care of the garage while he was away 'enjoying himself'. I glanced around the room at all the people I knew, and their expressions seemed to reflect my own feelings: pride and an illogical belief that all of us had won a tiny part of that World Championship. The master of ceremonies wrapped up the speeches with these words: 'All the best, Mike, and may God bless you and keep you safe.'

I mouthed a silent 'Hear! Hear!' to that.

It seemed an interminable wait until Mike went public about his retirement. He told me that he would announce it at the prestigious British Racing Drivers' Club annual dinner dance, early in December. Not being a BRDC member, I wasn't able to attend, but I was on high alert the following day waiting for the announcement to come on the news, convinced it would be important enough to make national headlines. I must have listened to six news bulletins, but there was nothing. So, when I next spoke to Mike, the first thing I asked him was whether he'd changed his mind.

'No, not at all, old chum. It's just the timing was awful. Before I was about to speak, the *Daily Express* handed over a cheque for ten thousand quid.'

'Ten thousand quid? But that's surely good news?' The *Express* was a big sponsor of motor racing.

'It certainly created a stir – except it was designed to soften the blow that they were pulling out of motor racing altogether. I thought it would spoil a very nice evening if I said I was quitting, too. Plus, maybe I'd have been expected to shell out likewise?' He smiled weakly.

It was a few days later that Mike contacted the Press Association to make his formal announcement. It was clearly orchestrated, almost certainly by Tavoni, because on the same day Enzo held a press conference in Italy. Enzo paid a handsome tribute to Mike, saying, 'Hawthorn's decision to quit is an intelligent one. I am entirely in agreement with him. As he explained in a letter to me, he wishes to get married to a beautiful girl and dedicate himself to his promising business interests. I am really sorry to lose Hawthorn, who is irreplaceable. But I respect his judgement.'

That was the public story. The private one was markedly different. From things that Tavoni let slip, Enzo was still furious that Mike was leaving, and wouldn't entertain Mike's request to keep his Championship-winning Ferrari Dino. Mike said he thought Enzo would rather scrap it than sell it to him.

One oft-repeated quote of Mike's was his reply to why he had decided to retire when he appeared to be at his prime and still a young man. He said, '"Why have you retired?" is so much nicer a question than "Why don't you retire?".'

Hawthorn announcements seemed to be all the rage. A week or so later, Mike proposed to Jean, and, unlike Cherry before her, Jean accepted straightaway. What I didn't know at the time, and only learnt much later, was that Mike did the decent thing and told Jean about the existence of Arnaud, his son – something I wasn't sure he'd do, especially after Cherry's reaction.

Much later, Jean told Sally that they'd been motoring down the A3 from London towards Farnham, passing Wisley Gardens, when Mike suddenly asked her whether she had 'any skeletons in the cupboard'.

Jean said, 'I didn't know where on earth he was going with this. I was barely twenty-one. I'd been in full-time education nearly all that time. It certainly rung alarm bells. I replied, saying, "No. Why, have you?" And that's when he told me about Arnaud…or at least some of the story!'

Two days afterwards, they were on the road again, headed for Yorkshire, in order that Mike could ask Jean's father for her hand in marriage – something which at the time was quite normal.

It seemed everything was happening at once for Mike. Duncan Hamilton, who just six years earlier had considered Mike a 'bumptious little upstart', proposed that, as he too was retiring as a driver, they should go into partnership, trading as Hawthorn and Hamilton Limited. With Mike now holding an official Ferrari concession, as well as other marques, they had grand plans. It was a prospective partnership that appealed greatly to Mike as he'd always got on well with Duncan.

My opinion, which I kept to myself, was that, as they were very similar characters, the chances of it being successful were probably slim. In fact, I thought they'd probably be half-cut most of the time. But I did think it was telling that Duncan, who was not always known for his humility, was shrewd enough to realise that Mike's surname would have the greater commercial impact and hence it should precede his own.

As a double celebration of engagement – a marriage and a business partnership – the Hamiltons treated Mike and Jean to dinner at the Ivy in London. Their partnership was to start sometime early the following year, and the wedding was planned for a year hence, although they sensibly decided to bring this forward to June of '59, primarily for the better weather. Sally was none too pleased about this as we too planned to get married in July, and she knew that a Mike and Jean wedding would completely eclipse our own humble affair.

Inevitably, Mike wasn't able to carry on that relentless amount of travel, PR engagements and partying without his body saying 'enough is enough', and so, by Christmas, he was exhausted and really quite poorly. Jean had been invited to stay with Mike and his mother at Green Fields, Winifred's home, but had not expected to have to nurse her fiancé. Mike's kidneys were the cause of so much pain and discomfort that he spent the whole of Christmas Day in bed.

Unaware he was sick, I telephoned the house that afternoon, ostensibly to wish them all a happy Christmas, but mostly to confirm arrangements with Mike for the following day's motor racing at Brands Hatch. The Boxing Day races were legendary back then. Many of the spectators were tipsy and, more worryingly, so were some of the drivers.

Mike had committed to going, not to participate, but to watch me and Neil compete in a little Mk IX Lotus 1100cc that Neil had found and somehow convinced me to co-fund.

Winifred answered the phone in her usual dour way. If she was pleased to have her only son and her future daughter-in-law staying with her, she certainly didn't show it. Reluctantly, she handed over the telephone to Jean. I asked Jean whether she expected Mike to be better by the morning.

'I never know. One minute he's at death's door, the next he's like a jumping jack. This morning, the poor thing was writhing around on the floor in agony. He's feeling a bit better now.'

'Look,' I said, 'we'll call round at eight, and if he's feeling okay, we'll drive you both there. If not, we'll just leave you in peace. Does that sound reasonable?'

*

It was barely light when Neil and I pitched up at Green Fields. Privately, neither of us thought Mike would want to come. It was a reasonable distance to travel even if you were feeling well. But no sooner had we pulled up than Mike appeared at the door, dressed, smiling and raring to go.

'So, y'er feeling better, bo?' I asked, as I walked up the path.

'Didn't think I had a choice. Who else is going to look after a couple of novices like you?'

Mike decided that he'd rather not be driven, and so off we went in convoy. Neil and I had to go slowly, due to the Lotus on a trailer. Mike and Jean trailed behind in his Jag.

It turned into a fantastic day. There was a sizeable Farnham contingent, and the craic was excellent. Needless to say, despite intensive coaching from Mike before our races, we were hopeless. I put it all down to our unfortunate power-to-weight ratio. I thought it was unreasonable to expect a wee 1100cc engine to haul around an eighteen-stone chap. Mike said that was a small but probably insignificant factor, and that we were just a pair of useless drivers – 'way too cowardly on the corners'. I couldn't imagine having gone any faster round the corners, or at least not without encountering certain peril. The banter carried on all day, as did the beer consumption. After which, of course, we all drove home.

It was always going to be slow leaving Brands as we had to pack up our stuff and load the trailer. Mike and Jean therefore set off back to Farnham independently. Whether it was the beer or the frustration of watching motor racing rather than participating in it, I don't know, but Mike positively flew home. My pal, Tim Ely, he with the old Riley, was driving along the A3 near the Hog's Back when Mike's Jag appeared from nowhere in the fog and shot past him, making Tim think he'd stopped. 'One second, he was behind me. Five seconds later, I couldn't make out his tail lights. If the car had had wings, it would've taken off,' said Tim.

Mike and I met up a few times afterwards, usually in larger groups, and always with our other halves. Whenever Mike was pain-free, which fortunately was more often than not, he was clearly having one of the best times of his life. He was on sparkling form when we all went over to Wanborough Manor near the Hog's Back – a hotel where Jean often stayed to avoid Mike's mother – for a New

Year's Eve party. I remember that being a very late one and was very appreciative of Sally driving home.

And so it was, through the fog of a hangover-from-hell the next morning, I learned that Stirling Moss had received an OBE in the New Year's Honours' List. I wondered whether the BBC had forgotten to mention an honour for Mike, or whether, in my dozy state, I had missed it. I waited until the next news bulletin, but no, only Stirling was mentioned. I was tempted to phone Mike, but decided I'd wait until we met up.

Around teatime, Mike telephoned me, primarily to propose 'a quiet hair of the dog with the girls'. He sounded a little jaded, as I suppose did I, but neither hurt nor angry. He asked if I'd heard the news.

'What news?' I asked warily.

'Bloody Moses – and his OBE.'

'You're kidding,' I replied, trying to sound surprised.

'Yeah, Nick phoned specially to tell me. "I see your mate's got the OBE then," he said.'

'That was kind of him. What did you say?'

'Oh, something like: "Has he really? The OBE? That must stand for Order of the Bald 'Ead?"'

I thought that was quite brilliant and laughed out loud. Had he made it up on the spot, or had he been planning that when thinking about the possibility of both of them being awarded something? 'But, Mike, I don't understand it. *You're* the bloody World Champion, not him.'

'No, I don't get it either. Maybe it was for *not* winning – like a consolation prize?'

'Maybe,' I said. Or maybe not, I thought. Hadn't Mike only recently been to see Her Royal Highness for lunch? The Honours' List would have been compiled well before then. Had Mike disgraced himself at lunch? No, that seemed most unlikely. As my old mother used to say, Mike knew how to behave when he needed to. He had exemplary manners, most of the time. The more I chewed it over, the more I thought it was probably due to his draft dodging. It may have only been a few years previously, but the public don't easily forget. Moreover, it would have been so easy for one aggrieved journalist, and there were a few, to pen a headline such as 'Draft

Dodger Gets OBE', and all the old resentments would flare up once more.

I don't honestly think Mike was overly bothered about this apparent snub. If he was, it was more about Stirling getting an honour and not him. He said, 'You know, Tom, sometimes I cannot believe how lucky I am. If it wasn't for my effing kidneys, I'd be the luckiest bloke I know.'

Chapter Forty-Nine

Planning the Future

It would be false to give the impression that everything in Mike's life now, apart from his health, was trouble-free. Believe it or not, the fallout from the Le Mans accident three and a half years earlier still rumbled on, despite Mike's official exoneration. Much of it was ignorable, but Mike wasn't able to ignore Lance Macklin. In their early racing years, Lance had considered Mike a friend although, by 1956, when Lance retired from racing, their paths crossed far less.

Their relationship changed dramatically when Mike's autobiography *Challenge Me the Race* was published in the spring of '58, absolving himself of all blame. Lance believed by implication that Mike was pointing the finger at him. He was so incensed that he brought a court action against Mike for libel. The case never came to fruition, yet it was an arrow which I know pierced Mike's armour, and upset him greatly.

Life after Christmas carried on apace: more engagements, more promotions, and more planning of his future as an ex-racing driver. Mike had even begun to think about a matrimonial home. He'd seen an old cottage, Well Cottage, at Dockenfield come up for sale and had put in an offer. I was most surprised when I found out. It was a modest property, in a sorry state, so I asked him why.

'It's within staggering distance of The Blue Bell. Just think of the mischief we could get up to, bo,' he replied.

I could – too easily.

'But it's tiny,' I protested. 'What does Jean reckon?' thinking what a comedown it would be for her, considering what I'd heard about her parents' palatial home.

'I'll extend it,' he said confidently. 'Jean says she likes it too. She likes the peace and quiet, and all the trees and fields around it.'

'I thought you'd buy something in Monaco, or Switzerland, or even the Bahamas.' Dockenfield wasn't the home of World Champions. It didn't sound right.

'And just how would I get to work from the Bahamas?' he asked.

I was so used to him being away all the time, often in exotic locations, that I hadn't thought of him actually settling down in Farnham. It had finally dawned on me that my pal was going to be back for good, albeit no longer as a single man. I pictured the many boozy sessions we'd have in The Blue Bell, with half a dozen Members piling back to Well Cottage to raid Jean's larder...and maybe trying not to fall over some infant's toys...Now there was a thought. What sort of a father would Mike be? Hopefully, not exactly like his father.

As often as not, our conversations at this time revolved around what he would do with himself now that he was 'retired' – after the celebrity hubbub died down – something he was realistic enough to recognize was inevitable. He certainly wasn't short of ideas. As far as the TT Garage was concerned, it would continue much as it was: selling Jaguars and other marques, offering servicing and repairs, and selling fuel. Privately, he acknowledged it didn't really require much of his attention. The proposed Hawthorn and Hamilton partnership with Duncan would initially concentrate on the Ferrari franchise, and in time would look to add other exotic marques.

To my amazement, Mike had also begun to write children's literature. I'd known about the autobiography, because he had been interviewed at length by the ghostwriter Gordon Wilkins, but I was quite thrown when he casually mentioned that he'd already completed two short books.

'What? Proper books?' I demanded.

'Of course.' He told me that he'd started scribbling away on odd occasions when he was on long flights or train journeys, and the rare times when he wasn't raising hell in some unsuspecting hotel somewhere.

'I hope they're not based on you,' I said with a smile.

'No, but they'll sound familiar. I've called the main character Carlotti. He's a young Italian boy.'

'Sounds like Castellotti to me,' I remarked.

'Good. I started with the name Carlo. It's a common name in Italy, and then I thought of Eugenio and decided that Carlotti would be my private tribute to him.'

'Are they racy?' I asked, enjoying the double entendre.

'Tom, they're children's books!' Mike said with mock exasperation. 'The first one's about a young lad who gets a lowly job in the pits and dreams one day of being a racing driver.'

'So, not *exactly* like Castellotti, then?' I didn't need to elaborate. All the Italian drivers I knew had been born into money – pots of it – which had accordingly afforded them their opportunities.

I did read one of Mike's two books – *Carlotti Joins The Team* (published posthumously by Cassell) – a long time ago. The language used and the innocent style seemed at odds with my knowledge of Mike. Later, I would discover the books had been written in collaboration with a professional children's writer, a Reginald Alec Martin. Clearly, Mr Martin didn't mind remaining 'ghostly' – by his death, he'd written under fourteen different pseudonyms.

I wasn't so surprised by my discovery. Mike's attention span was fairly short, and I suspect he'd have soon tired of this labour, especially with so much else going on in his life. It's another quirky parallel that, after Stirling retired, he too became involved in children's literature, narrating the popular *Roary The Racing Car* stories.

I saw Mike on Saturday 17 January 1959. It was back to the old Farnham routine: beer, flicks, grub, and more beer. I think it was only five of us that rolled on to the Regal Cinema: the World Champion, Neil, Nick, Tim and me. The newly-released film *Sea of Sand* proved to be a cracking World War II adventure, starring Dickie Attenborough and Michael Craig. It was right up Mike's street: British Tommies from the Long-Range Desert Group on a mission to blow up a German petrol dump in North Africa in 1943. We came out of there feeling uplifted, and thirsty. I recall everyone being on fine form, especially Mike who, after several further 'sherbets', entertained the last pub we visited with some particularly bawdy songs. Mike, smartly dressed in a tweed jacket with tankard in hand, in full song and with the occasional big grin on his face, is the abiding memory of my friend.

Before we parted, Mike told us how much he was looking

forward to a black tie dinner being held by the National Sporting Club in his honour at the Café Royal the following Monday. He sounded genuinely excited that most of Britain's top sportsmen would be present – including such famous names as Joe Davis, the snooker champion, and Henry Cooper, the heavyweight boxer. Also on the guest list was Donald Campbell who held the current record for being the world's fastest man on water – nearly 250mph!

Mike already knew Donald, and had begun negotiations with him about a joint attempt at the world land speed record – something Donald would achieve solo five years later. Hoping that Jean might not be free to accompany him, I cheekily asked if he was taking anyone. He said that the invitations were personal, and there was no mention of partners. I never did hear whether the occasion lived up to his expectations, but at least shortly afterwards I was able to watch a brief British Pathé News piece covering the dinner and naming many of the sporting legends present.

Chapter Fifty

Two-Finger Challenge

Five days later, Thursday 22 January 1959, began as a very ordinary day for me. A day without meetings, laboriously preparing accounts longhand. It was in stark contrast to the potentially exciting day in store for Mike. He had planned a hectic schedule in London which included meeting Louise Collins for the first time in months. Louise had returned from the States following her successful tour of *Romanoff and Juliet*, and had briefly visited Pete's parents before going up to town.

Mike's first appointment was to see a chap called Noble about some financial tie-up with his small car company, York Noble Limited. Noble had plans to build fast glass fibre three-wheelers. It was strange how many new 'friends' Mike had attracted since becoming World Champion.

From there, he was to go on to meet the holiday camp impresario Billy Butlin for lunch at the Cumberland Hotel, after which the two of them would judge a fun event for the Invalid Tricycle Association, involving more three-wheelers. His next appointment, at three o'clock, was at The Westbury, a recently opened, five-star American hotel, to see Louise before meeting up with Duncan Hamilton at teatime, with a view to concluding their partnership arrangements – a rendezvous that would, no doubt, necessitate a 'celebratory shandy' afterwards at the Steering Wheel Club.

As if that wasn't enough, he would be stopping off on his way home at the Hog's Back Hotel as the guest of honour at the Farnham and District Motor Agents' Association dinner.

The day did not, however, start well. Mike woke up feeling under the weather. Winifred had already left for the TT Garage by the time he got up. The only other person in the house was their 'daily', Mrs Taylor. Working downstairs, she said it was about ten thirty before Mike eventually appeared, smartly dressed in a grey suit, but looking decidedly peaky. She saw him come gingerly down the stairs and sit wearily on the chaise longue, holding his head in both hands. He stayed like that for a few minutes. Mrs T, as Mike always called her, asked him whether he'd like a nice cup of tea.

'No, thank you,' was all he said. Then the telephone rang, and he stood up to answer it. It was Jean. Mrs T said that he sounded pleased to hear from her.

Jean had gone up to stay with her parents for a few days, with the intention of trying to explain away the existence of Arnaud before they heard about him from any third party. She wanted to let them know that Mike would be seeing a Parisian lawyer the following weekend in order to offer a maintenance settlement to Jacqueline.

Mrs T overheard Mike say that he didn't really feel like going to London – in fact, he felt 'bloody awful'. But he had to go, he said, as he couldn't let down so many people. They only spoke for a couple of minutes. Mrs Taylor didn't see him leave, but as he left he called out, 'I'm off now, Mrs T. See you tomorrow.'

Mike drove his Jaguar, VDU 881, the short distance to the garage. It was a grim winter's day – sharp showers were being pushed along by a strong south-westerly wind.

Even though he was running late, on arrival at the garage he popped in next door, to the Duke of Cambridge Hotel, to let them know that he'd not be in for lunch. Whenever Mike was in Farnham, it was a given that he'd take lunch there each weekday unless he cancelled.

According to the workshop lads, Mike then spent around half an hour in the office going through correspondence. Also at this time he asked for his Jaguar to be refueled and the tyre pressures checked. While he was there, Louise telephoned him to confirm their three o'clock meeting at The Westbury. Her call appears to have perked him up considerably because Bill Morgan, the manager, remembers Mike being more cheerful as he was preparing to leave. Mike said that he needed to 'get a wiggle on', otherwise he'd be very late for Billy Butlin, and that would never do. He omitted to mention that he was already too late to see York Noble and, as Mike had no secretary or assistant, no one was any the wiser.

As Mike was readying to leave, he gazed out through the showroom windows just as an exotic sports car drew up and stopped opposite the garage. Who should it be but his old friend and sparring partner Rob Walker driving from his home in Somerset to his garage near Dorking in his new and decidedly swanky Mercedes 300 SL – finished in of all colours light silver. This was the perfect metaphoric 'red rag' to Mike – German, silver, svelte… piloted by an old racing hand.

Spotting Mike looking out, Rob without word or expression, opened the gullwing door, extended his arm upwards and flicked up the first two fingers of his right hand.

I must at this juncture, if it's not too late, point out that such a gesture was a common one back then between male friends. It was jocular – cheeky rather than offensive. But the gauntlet had been thrown down. Mike grabbed his mackintosh and bag, hurriedly shouted goodbyes and ran to his Jaguar, started it, and tore off after the Mercedes.

'What's that silly bugger up to now?' asked Joe Bickell, TT's irascible foreman, of no one in particular.

'That looked like Rob Walker in the Merc. I reckon Mike'll be trying to catch him,' ventured the forecourt lad, Brian Taylor.

Rob had established quite a head start, given his thirty-second advantage over Mike. By the time he'd stopped at the junction where the A31 joins the A3 at the end of the Hog's Back, he saw Mike closing in fast. Rob had been expecting to see the familiar dark green Jag in his rear-view mirror, but even he was surprised by how quickly Mike was travelling. There was no feeder lane at this junction, and so motorists were obliged to stop, or nearly stop, in order to give way to any traffic coming from the right.

Fortunately, there was nothing coming round the dual carriageway Guildford bypass to encounter the two friends' cars shooting onto the A3. From this point, there's little doubt both men 'floored it' – they accelerated to the maximum.

Mike, having needed to slow down less, had a slight momentum advantage. He also had marginally the faster car through the lower gears. It was now essentially a half-mile drag race.

Mike tucked in behind the Mercedes, using the other car's

slipstream. As they approached Coombs Garage, Mike pulled out to overtake, his car's engine screaming as the revs went to the red line. The weather was still foul. The rain had almost stopped, but the wind was still gusting across the carriageway.

A motoring enthusiast, John Farrow, was one of the few who was driving along the same stretch of road at the same time, and recalls travelling at approximately seventy-five miles per hour when two cars flashed past him.

The A3 here, beyond Coombs Garage, was a gently snaking, downhill dual carriageway, and the traffic was light. It is estimated that Mike had reached a genuine ninety-five miles per hour, possibly a hundred, by the time he swept past Rob's still accelerating Mercedes on the mildest of left-hand bends.

When Mike was passing, he had just enough time to reciprocate Rob's two-fingered salute. Rob recalled how the buffeting wind and wet road surfaces had been severely upsetting his Mercedes' normally sure-footed handling.

Mike was a few yards in front, as the road gently curved to the right and went further downhill. At this point, Rob began to lose his nerve and eased off the throttle, effectively conceding defeat. To continue the chase would have been madness, for everyone knew that Mike would never back down.

It is possible that Mike was still looking across at Rob when the rear wheels of his Jag began to lose their adhesion. However, the 'loss of the back end' was hardly a novelty to Mike: he'd practically made a career out of it.

Rob wasn't studying Mike's progress minutely. Instead, he was concentrating hard, trying to control his own car, and his vision had been temporarily worsened by spray from the Jag. He saw well enough however to see the rear of the Jag swing out once the car's rear tyres lost their grip. He assumed Mike would catch it in time. He'd seen Mike drive 'sideways' many times before. However, VDU 881 continued to swing out until it hit the nearside kerb.

Chapter Fifty-One

A Silly Thing to Do

Had he spent a second too long looking across at Rob? Or had he been taken by surprise when his novel Dunlop Duraband radial tyres suddenly lost their grip on that slippery concrete surface, augmented perhaps by a gust of wind? Or had he thought he had sufficient width of 'track' on which to recover the slide? Or was it simply that he was still feeling off colour, and his reflexes weren't quick enough? And does it really matter? It was probably a combination of all these things.

Mike's car continued to career downhill and towards the opposite carriageway, for there were no central barriers, touching a central bollard which divided the dual carriageways, causing the car to spin.

One of the few vehicles travelling in the opposite direction was a Bedford open-back lorry chugging slowly uphill, heading west. Its driver, Fred Rice, saw the Jaguar coming at him, sideways, with the driver madly flailing at the wheel. Fred accelerated as best he could, in the hope of missing it, and nearly succeeded. VDU 881 just clipped the rear of the lorry. Fred felt the slightest of collisions. Seconds later, he heard a most dreadful bang. It was the noise of Mike's Jaguar colliding sideways with, and practically felling, a slender tree some fifteen feet away from the edge of the carriageway. The front passenger door of the Jaguar struck the trunk with such force that the car wrapped itself around it.

The Jaguar came to rest practically on its side, and was stopped from falling down a steep bank into the ditch between the road and the field by the tree, which was now almost horizontal. The boomerang-shaped Jaguar lay alongside a *hawthorn* bush – a serendipitous gift for the headline writers.

One glance at the mangled wreck would have suggested that the driver's survival was nigh on impossible. And yet Rob Walker, the main witness and first man on the scene, stated to a television journalist nearly a quarter of a century later, 'I ran across the road, thinking to go up to him and say, "That was a bloody silly thing to do, Mike",' and 'I looked in the car, and he wasn't in the driving seat. Then I walked round the car and saw him lying full-length in the back seat, just as if he'd got in there to have a kip. His eyes were open, and I saw a trickle of blood coming from the back of his head. Then, as I looked down at him, his eyes suddenly glazed, and I realised he was gone.'

I don't like to doubt anyone's first-hand accounts, but I do have a problem with this statement. Firstly, from the pictures of the gruesomely contorted Jaguar, no one in their right mind would have been formulating the joshing greeting Rob recalls. The only sane reaction would be to contemplate whether the occupant needed an ambulance or a hearse.

Furthermore, the back seat of the Jaguar, as the car itself, was precipitously canted over – not exactly the place for a kip. Moreover, Mike was six feet two inches tall and the back seat little over four feet across. He couldn't have lain 'full-length' across the seat – in any circumstances.

In fact, I'd go as far as to say that Rob was extremely 'economical with the actualité' in respect of most of his accounts. He told the inquest, held four days after the accident, that he had 'no idea who the driver was'...which is strange when you think he had the intention, apparently, of addressing the unknown driver of the dark green Mk I Jaguar as 'Mike'!

He also told the inquest that the pair of them were most definitely not racing! This could be semantics. Did Rob consider their driving to be coincidentally and simultaneously testing their cars' maximum performance?

At the scene, Rob was soon joined by Fred, the driver of the lorry, who'd stopped his truck a hundred yards or so up the hill and run back to the stricken Jaguar. They were soon joined by a chum of ours, Ted Rumfitt, the assistant general manager of Coombs Garage, which the friends had passed some quarter of a mile or so before.

Ted had been sitting in his car just before midday, waiting to drive off the forecourt when he'd seen the two cars flash by. He saw the Jaguar overtake the Mercedes and then begin to pull over back to the nearside carriageway as the road started to curve right. He also witnessed the rear wheels begin to slide out towards the near kerb. It slid further, completing what Ted reckoned was about three quarters of a complete circle before it went out of sight.

Anxious to discover the outcome, Ted set off after them. Upon discovering Mike had crashed, he turned straight round back to the garage and telephoned 999 for the police and ambulance.

He was a good sort, Ted. I remember he told the inquest: 'The driver appeared to be travelling at what I would say was a normal speed for the type of car on this unrestricted road' – 'the type of car' being a souped-up Jaguar prepared for road racing by the reigning World Champion driver. I couldn't have put it better myself.

More people arrived within minutes. A local GP, Dr Bateson, had been buying petrol at Coombs when he heard that there'd been a terrible accident. Basil Putt, the manager of Coombs, offered the doctor a lift to the scene.

On arrival, Dr Bateson observed, 'Hawthorn was barely breathing. He had no pulse. He was deeply unconscious. He possibly breathed twice but it was too late to do anything.'

John Coombs, the proprietor of Coombs Garage, also arrived shortly thereafter and was advised by Dr Bateson not to look inside the car. 'He's gone,' said the doctor.

A police car arrived within five minutes of being called. PC Bartlett was one of two officers first on the scene. He recorded at 12.05 that two men were present, in addition to the casualty. One, who declared himself to be a doctor, pronounced Mike dead. The other, presumably, had to be Basil Putt, who'd chauffeured the doctor. As for John Coombs and Rob Walker, there was no mention. Fred Rice was described as being 'with his lorry' which had a damaged rear mudguard and cut offside rear tyre.

John Coombs knew the local police well and, once it was clear that Mike was beyond help, he suggested to another policeman, Douggie Brazier, that they, together with Rob Walker, return to his garage so that Walker's statement could be taken. It is not clear whether this little party had left before the first report of the scene was taken, or were somehow overlooked by the report. Either explanation seems peculiar.

Incidentally, it was PC Brazier who had the unfortunate duty of being the reporting officer on Leslie Hawthorn's fatal crash, four and a half years earlier.

Either by design or by fortuitous accident, Rob tucked his super-distinctive Mercedes round the back of the garage, out of sight to the public and, more pertinently, the press. While this was happening, John Coombs began telephoning various people. Coombs was himself a recently retired racing driver, albeit of a lesser standing than Mike, but nevertheless very well known in racing circles.

By a bizarre coincidence, Duncan Hamilton was not in London, but also in the near vicinity. He'd stopped en route at a friend's house near Guildford, from where he telephoned a contact at the BRDC about a completely unrelated matter.

The recipient of the call was learning of the breaking news from John Coombs via another line whilst speaking to Duncan. 'There's been a terrible crash on the Guildford bypass, just this side of Coombs Garage at Guildford. It's thought to be Mike,' he said.

Duncan shot back to his car, a stylish Jaguar XK150, and drove straight to the accident scene. He was there in barely five minutes, despite the 'awful conditions' limiting his speed to around 60mph.

On arrival, Mike was still slumped against the back bench seat. However, a couple of journalists and press photographers had already arrived and were busy taking pictures – pictures they knew would make international news. In those days, various individuals and agencies would listen around the clock to the emergency services' short-wave radio transmissions, hoping for a big scoop, exactly as this one.

Duncan was not to be trifled with, and promptly told the photographers to 'bugger off'. He was not of a squeamish disposition either – he'd seen many dead bodies during the war – and was willing to lend the police a hand lifting his old friend out of the wreck. I saw photos of him bearing Mike onto a waiting stretcher lain on the wide grass verge.

Another call Coombs made was to Bill Morgan. Bill had seen Mike less than half an hour previously.

'Bad news, I'm afraid. Mike's had a spill. Can you get down here straightaway?' asked Coombs.

Bill went off to find Winifred. 'I hope he hasn't done any damage,' he remarked to her.

A few moments later, Coombs phoned again and told them not to bother coming to the garage as Mike had been taken to Guildford Hospital. Consequently, Bill drove Mrs Hawthorn straight to the hospital. After announcing their arrival at reception, a doctor came to meet them.

Winifred knew instinctively, before he even had a chance to speak. 'My son's dead, isn't he?' She and Bill left at once and returned to the TT Garage. By this time, the forecourt was teeming with journalists and photographers. Winifred merely wanted everyone to go away.

Bill decided to close the garage early, and ordered all staff to pack up and go home immediately. Winifred told them under no circumstances should they speak to the press. This was not an instruction to be abused, not if you wanted to keep your job.

Another call made by John Coombs was to Jaguar Cars in Coventry. Because of who he was, he was able to speak directly to Sir William Lyons and Lofty England. 'There's been a bloody awful accident. It's Mike...'

Lofty thanked him and said he'd come down first thing in the morning. He was, of course, far too late to see Mike, but he did oversee the recovery of VDU 881 which, although Mike drove it, remained the property of Jaguar Cars. Lofty insisted it be pulled up sideways rather than lifted straight onto Coombs's tow truck. The possible sight – or more specifically press pictures – of a Jaguar practically broken in two would have sensationalized the story and would not have been a good advert for Jaguar.

Duncan was asked to go to the hospital to formally identify the body, which he did later that afternoon. Winifred was indebted to Duncan for doing that 'horrid task' and offered him a couple of Mike's personal effects. Sometime previously, probably when they'd been larking about, he and Mike had sworn an agreement that each would do that very task for the other's family, if so required – never, of course, thinking it was likely.

Shortly after visiting the hospital, Duncan was asked by the BBC whether he would pay a tribute to Mike, live on the six o'clock radio news. This he duly did, and then recorded another for the nine o'clock news.

Despite the phone lines buzzing all around West Surrey and London, no one called me. I was oblivious of the news until I heard it on my car radio. It was the headline story for the BBC, and I nearly missed it. If it hadn't been such a big story, I might have done.

I was returning home from work when the announcement came: 'Mike Hawthorn, Britain's reigning World Champion motor racing driver, crashed his car on the A3 near Guildford earlier today and died shortly afterwards. There were no other vehicles involved.' It took a moment to sink in. I pulled over to the side of the road, now listening intently, but the newscaster had moved on. I tuned out. That can't be right, I thought. Mike's not dead. He's retired.

For a second, I thought I'd dreamt it. I sat there dumbfounded for a minute or two, debating whether I'd heard it accurately. Could they have made a mistake? Had he just blacked out and was really only unconscious? Then came a summing up of the day's news, and the headline was repeated. This was news I had feared for the best part of a decade but which, in recent months, had become no more than an old shadow. I felt numb. And then I heard the tribute from Duncan. Duncan was magnificent, statesman-like and controlled, but warm and clearly deeply upset. And that's when it hit me – like a sledgehammer. In a state of almost suspended animation, I checked my mirror, indicated and motored on back to my parents' house, tears streaming down my face.

Chapter Fifty-Two

Whose Fault?

Even Louise, staying at the Westbury in Mayfair, heard before I did. I guess it was because Pete had been a friend of the hotel's manager. In anticipation of Mike's visit, she'd returned from shopping shortly before three in the afternoon and gone up to her room. A moment later, the manager called her on the phone to ask whether she'd heard the news. She hadn't.

There was, she said, so much left to resolve with Mike, and now there would never be that chance.

With the 'mon ami mates' both gone, none of us will ever know how things really stood between Mike and Peter, vis a vis the lovely Louise.

During the following forty-eight hours, the story only seemed to get bigger. The press was in frenzy. A typical headline read: 'Mike killed on A3!'. That they didn't even use his surname was a testament to his fame. Mike had cheated death for years, raced at speeds almost twice that fast. Of course, it all made great copy: 'Prime of his life'; 'About to marry the glamorous model...'; 'Crowned Champion only three months previously'; and, naturally, 'Was he racing Walker?'

The answer to *that* question, for anyone who knew Mike well, could never be in doubt. If Mike encountered any peer or contemporary known to him when he was driving, he considered them fair game. If they didn't respond to his taunts, they'd never hear the last of it in the pub.

It was easier for Members such as me as we didn't have powerful cars, nor did Mike rate many of us proper competition. But it was very different for the likes of poor Roy Salvadori. A couple of years earlier, Roy, when driving his Aston Martin, would occasionally encounter Mike in his Lancia on the Kingston bypass. When their routes coincided, which could be for as much as five miles, it was always 'game on'. Mike would flick two fingers at Roy, looking to initiate a race. Roy recalls those five miles and several roundabouts as being amongst the hairiest driving he ever did, anywhere in the world. He was always greatly relieved when he could peel off to his garage, still in one piece, leaving Mike to it. Were Mike and Rob racing on 22 January 1959? What a daft question.

That said, none of our friends could believe Mike had actually bought it – not in a saloon car. He'd seemed charmed on the race track, and invincible off it. Except, of course, to those of us who knew he wouldn't be cheating death for very much longer. But even that, we wanted to believe, was years away.

Amongst the press outpourings in the days which followed was the Pathé News coverage from the National Sporting Club's annual dinner, which had been held on 19 January, only three days before Mike died. I found this particularly harrowing to watch, not least because the footage was taken so soon before his death, emphasizing the 'one day you're here, full of life, the next you're gone' aspect of an accidental death.

The dinner had been an all-male affair, as Mike had anticipated, and most of the British sporting heroes were in attendance. It is shocking now to realise that not only were 'partners' not invited but there were no sportswomen present either. Charles Forté, the club's chairman, unveiled a huge cocktail cabinet, fully stocked with spirits, liqueurs and glasses, before presenting it to Mike. It must have stood six feet tall.

In Mike's brief and attractively self-deprecating acceptance speech, he issued the following invitation: 'I hope one day some of you will come along and join me, and we'll empty that lot.'

I smiled at the thought of how upset Mike would be that he'd never had so much as a single drink from that fantastic cabinet.

The inquest was held by the county coroner only four days later in Guildford and lasted just two hours. I'd taken half a day off work. Of course, I thought it would be difficult to get in, given the massive public interest, so I arrived ridiculously early and queued outside until the doors were opened at 4pm; an hour before the inquest started. The press area and public gallery were, naturally, packed. A couple of Mike's racing contemporaries had also come along. Although I wanted to learn the true story, what I most wanted to know was whether he'd blacked out.

Whilst the car was very badly damaged, experts reported that they could not identify any mechanical malfunction. Therefore, no fault whatsoever could be attributed to the car, or any other road users – notwithstanding the gossip doing the rounds. It was only later that Mike's questionable choice of tyres gained some credibility. The surface of the road was reported to be free of mud and chalk though the particular section of road was acknowledged to be dangerous. An Inspector Smith produced a list of accidents going back two years, many of them also in foul weather conditions. From the fifteen accidents on this stretch of road, three had resulted in serious injury, and in two there were fatalities.

As the various experts were discussing the Jaguar, my mind went back to the time I drove it up to London Airport to meet Mike after Pete's fatal crash. VDU 881 then had seemed exotic and special – reassuring almost – and now I was forced to picture it as a carriage of death.

Giving evidence, Rob Walker emphatically denied he was racing and had absolutely no recollection of the speed at which they'd been driving. It is only fair to say here that the only road speed limits in the country at that time, were the 30mph ones in built-up areas. Outside such areas, there was no speed limit. Even at 100mph, they would not have been breaking the law. There was, however, the offence of dangerous driving, and racing on a public highway would certainly have constituted dangerous driving. Nor did Rob let on that he'd passed the TT Garage earlier and 'waved' to Mike – something only two men other than Mike witnessed and had kept secret for fifty years. It was only in 2008 that the then eighteen year old Brian, disclosed what he and Joe had seen that morning.

Having called and heard from all witnesses to the accident, the coroner summed up thus: 'There is no question whatever that Mr Hawthorn was going quite fast.'

At this, I allowed myself a wry smile, thinking how Mike would have laughed, and probably blurted out: 'Quite fast? Damn it, old man, I was flat out!'

The coroner continued: 'There is no question that he hit

a bollard, and that set the car on the way it did till it came into a collision with this tree, with the result that the front of the car was very nearly severed from the rear.'

'Can't argue with that, old man,' Mike whispered in my ear.

PC Brazier then listed the contents of the car. Along with many predictable items, such as a tobacco tin, the BRDC blanket and a motor racing magazine, he'd found 'a pair of girl's blue slippers with gilt bubbles (sic) on the toes'. At that, I had to stifle a chuckle. I wondered whether the policeman had also found items of women's underwear, but had chosen to be discreet.

The worst part for me was listening to the pathologist's report. Some of it I didn't understand, so medically obscure was the language. But I did understand the lay terms: 'severe head injuries' and 'a fractured skull with fragments of bone having been driven into the brain'. Also apparent upon examination was evidence of kidney disease and a small coronary atheroma. The former was expected. The latter I didn't understand, but have since looked up. It is the furring of an artery, or arteries, by cholesterol plaque. Maybe he wouldn't have made old bones, regardless. The bottom line, though, was that the cause of death, unequivocally, was brain injury caused by a fractured skull.

There was only one thing revealed at the inquest that surprised me, and that was that Mike was wearing a support corset beneath his shirt. In a saloon car! He'd have kept pretty quiet about that, I can tell you.

'Speed was the cause of the accident...' the coroner said.

'I beg to differ, sir,' piped up Mike. 'It was not speed, per se. It was my own bloody silly fault for racing in treacherous conditions on the wrong tyres!'

The coroner went on, 'And there was no question of any other person being criminally responsible, or that the action was caused by the action of any other person – certainly not by Mr Walker or Mr Rice.'

The jury concurred that Mike's death was an 'accidental death'. Amen to that.

I walked away from the court with my mind in turmoil. It all seemed so straightforward, so matter of fact. I guess there'll always be a part of the bereaved that won't accept the finality of death. And yet, I began to conclude, with Mike's gruesome decline of health on the horizon, his might actually be a *good* death. On the downside: he'd not got married, despite having known women well; he'd not had children, or at least none he chose to recognize as his and he was well short of his three score and ten. On the upside: he'd led one hell of a life; he was well travelled; and he'd had a lot of fun – an awful lot of fun. He'd become famous, and he'd brought a lot of people a lot of joy. If he could have chosen that thrilling chase of an accident, or a slow painful death in a hospice, say a couple of years later, I know which he'd have chosen.

As the ensuing days and weeks passed so the media continued to search for a sensational reason for Mike's accident. It was as if a simple misjudgement couldn't possibly have been made by a world champion. Speculation ranged from defects with the car – though none was ever found – through to Mike having a hand throttle fitted (a crude version of today's cruise control), to Mike having been shot by a sniper! There was no convincing evidence for any of these theories.

My original concern that he had blacked out was more or less nullified by the autopsy, and the only other one I briefly entertained was a sticky throttle cable, but again I considered that unlikely.

Many an older Farnham resident didn't need any third-party justification. I heard more than one old boy carp along the lines of: 'It was only a matter of time before that young tearaway would kill hisself...'

For me, it became simple. It was Mike's fault and no one else's. He was feeling decidedly off colour, and he'd enhanced the performance of a standard saloon car to the point where it required the very best control of the driver. He'd arguably also made a massive mistake changing the predictable cross-ply tyres to the more all-or-nothing radial tyres. More horsepower, lower ratio gears, and Duraband tyres were fine in the dry, but lethal in the wet – especially for someone under par, and racing.

Chapter Fifty-Three

In the Aftermath

The death of Mike had a profound effect on the staff at the TT Garage. I popped in twice the following week, once for petrol, and once to see if I could be of any assistance to Mrs Hawthorn. The staff were busy enough, but the atmosphere was like a morgue.

I don't think I fully appreciated, for example, that Bill Morgan had known Mike for twenty-five years – longer even than I'd known him. Bill was another man who felt in part like a surrogate father to Mike, and who felt the loss most keenly – notwithstanding what a pain in the arse Mike had so often been at the garage.

It was the reaction of Winifred that I found most disturbing. She wanted to expunge all physical reminders of her only son as quickly as possible. I've since pondered whether this was a pragmatic 'get it over and done with' Yorkshire approach, or whether she was angry and felt utterly let down by the two men closest to her – her husband, for his fecklessness, and both of them for their needless and arguably selfish fatal accidents. There may have been one or two people close enough to Winifred to know how she really felt. Today, there would be few still alive.

What Winifred didn't quickly give away of Mike's, and that wasn't much, she systematically burnt. One evening, all alone, she took all his clothes from his bedroom, carried them to the garden, and made a bonfire of them. She gave instructions that everything at the garage which belonged to Mike should be brought up to her cottage. Young Brian Taylor was given the job. He took up about three or four carloads, only to be directed to throw them onto the fire. Not only were there private papers but mementos and small trophies – even his personal cine films. It greatly upset the lad.

I was completely taken aback when I learnt Winifred had

telephoned my mother to enquire if I wished to be a pall-bearer. Thankfully, my mother said she was sure that I would, and, if Winifred didn't hear directly to the contrary, she could rely upon me. I was grateful to Mum. I wouldn't have known what to say to Mrs H. She was never a particularly warm or 'mumsy' type of woman, even when both Les and Mike were alive. But, then, I didn't know what she'd had to put up with.

The funeral was held just two days after the inquest. I think the speed was in part because Winifred let it be known that she wanted it to be a private affair – ideally, or so I heard, with only her and Mike's few relatives attending. Some chance!

In many ways, it was very similar to Pete Collins's funeral. The little parish church of St Andrew's in Farnham was packed to capacity, something over two hundred. I reckon there was the same number again standing respectfully outside. If Winifred had not been at all successful in broadcasting her wishes, I shudder to think how many more folk would have turned up. As it was, the streets of Farnham were lined with spectators as the cortege passed by. The day had dawned fine but cold. Everyone was wearing their thickest coats and warm hats. As we trooped into the church, the weather had begun to brighten. I remember thinking how typical it was that the sun should come out for the Golden Boy's send-off.

I'd anticipated seeing several famous faces, but even I was surprised by how many big names from motor racing turned up to pay their respects, and a few minor celebrities too. I'd bristled slightly when I learnt that Rob Walker was to be another pall-bearer. However, he was actually charming towards me, and although a part of me wanted to blame him for Mike's accident, the more rational part firmly ascribed all the blame to Mike. I also reflected that it had been Rob Walker who had looked after Mike during the 1955 Le Mans disaster, and how grateful Mike had been for his support.

I was very pleased to spot Stirling Moss. They'd had their moments, and Mike hadn't always been fair towards his old rival, but that was probably due to a grudging respect for Stirling's dedication and his greater professionalism.

Another pall-bearer was David Dodd – Jean's ex. His inclusion gave me pause for thought. Surely, there was one man with a valid reason for not feeling well disposed towards Mike – unless, that is, he thought that the competition had now gone, and maybe he'd win back Jean. I don't know whether they did get together later. I suspect not, for Jean met and married a bobsleigh racer, Mike Davison, in 1960. Very much later still, she married former racing driver, Innes Ireland, another contemporary and old friend of Mike's.

I was delighted to see Lofty, who was kindly towards me, and, of course, Jean, Duncan, Louise and the Massey-Dawsons. In fact, everyone who should have been there – who wasn't already dead – was there. But what surprised me was the presence of so many young women, at least half of whom I didn't recognize. Now, that would have tickled Mike. He'd have been both amazed and flattered.

Notwithstanding that the service was somewhat impersonal, for the vicar hadn't known Mike, I found it greatly moving. Sentiments such as: '…a larger than life character', '…cut down in the prime of his life', '…having only just announced his engagement', 'so soon after his retirement from the dangerous sport of motor racing', and 'his wish to settle down and have a family' seemed to affect me cumulatively. I was soon in tears again. For this audience, there was no counterbalancing of sentiment: nothing relating to Mike's dire medical condition; nothing to suggest it might have been a blessing. It was all bleak, and black, and terribly tragic.

I looked ahead to where Winifred was sitting, and tried to imagine how she was feeling. She seemed so small and alone, despite having a few family members around her and Jean by her side. Her life for over thirty years had been dominated by the careers of her husband and son - and their Garage. She had no passion for the business; she was merely its stoic caretaker. Whatever was left, for her?

Many of the congregation went from the church directly to the cemetery for the interment, a distance of about half a mile. Having helped carry the coffin to the waiting hearse, I began walking towards one of the funeral limousines, in which I was to travel, when I caught sight of Winifred getting into a small Jaguar saloon – the very same model in which her only son had just perished. I couldn't believe my eyes. Were the funeral directors not aware of how Mike had died? If it wasn't their crass error of judgement, it could only be that Winifred had specifically requested that particular marque and model of car and, if that was the case, that was surely perverse.

Unlike many women of her age, she really *did* know one

car from another – it had been her livelihood for years. And then I remembered how Mike had chosen to drive a Lancia Aurelia, straight after his father had killed himself in one. Maybe Winifred had deliberately asked for a Mk I Jaguar. Maybe it was her way of being closer to Mike. They were a funny lot, those Hawthorns.

After the brief interment ceremony, I wandered alone amongst the hundreds of wreaths which festooned the cemetery. They were neatly laid out in parallel lines, each containing fifty or so wreaths. I concentrated at first on the most elaborate. Many, including a terrific one from the BRDC, were in the shape of a steering wheel. Other ostentatious ones were from Daimler Benz, which surprised me, and from Tony Vandervell and Enzo Ferrari, which did not. I'd clubbed together with the rest of the Members – whose number had already diminished considerably – but even our collective effort looked a meagre thing compared to the likes of Vandervell's.

At one point, I found myself standing close to Louise. I noticed her stoop down and pick up a card from a modest spray of white roses. After reading it for a moment, she slipped it surreptitiously into her handbag, before looking up and glancing left and right. It was only then she spotted that I was watching her. We held each other's gaze for a second or two.

She walked over to me, wordlessly withdrew the card from her bag, and passed it discreetly to me. It read simply: *A mon papa, Michael.* I realised at once it was from Arnaud, or at least Arnaud's mother, Jacqueline. Louise lifted her head to study my response. I whistled softly.

'I think it's best if neither Jean nor Mrs H see that, don't you?' she ventured in a low voice.

'Absolutely,' I whispered. I'm sure that, with the passing of time, both women would have heard about that wreath, but I remained impressed by Louise's compassion in doing what she did that cold January day to spare any unnecessary heartache.

The Hawthorn family and all close friends were expected back at Green Fields for tea and sandwiches. Winifred had specifically mentioned that this should include all of the Members. Accompanied by Sally, I drove slowly up to the cottage. It was the first time I'd been there since Mike died. The place was full of memories, most of them happy.

Over a tepid cup of strong tea, Sally had a quiet conversation with Jean, which she couldn't wait to relate to me. 'Did you know Jean's staying here?' she asked.

'No, but I'm not greatly surprised. Poor old Mrs H doesn't really have anyone else.'

'Okay, but what's a bit batty is that Winifred has insisted Jean shares her bedroom.'

'Urgh, that *is* creepy!'

With the benefit of hindsight, I believe Mrs Hawthorn was clinically depressed, and possibly mentally unstable, for it was not long afterwards that whenever Jean telephoned her out of concern, Winifred would be extremely curt and, later still, deny knowing her. It was alleged that no sooner had Jean placed roses on Mike's grave than Winifred would throw them away.

After about half an hour of uncomfortable small talk, Neil McNab came and found me. 'You thirsty, old chap?' he asked, sotto voce.

'Always!' I replied with a grin.

'The Pond? For old times' sake?'

'Why not?' I felt ashamed and juvenile as we sneaked out of the house without saying anything to Mrs H, not even goodbye. However, by going off for a couple of pints, it felt exactly like what Mike would have done. So, in our self-justifying manner, it was our way of paying him a tribute.

After Mike's death, Winifred became very distant. To my shame, I lost touch with her soon after the funeral. I could excuse this by being a generation apart, her son's generation, but by then I was thirty years old – it was more a case of not knowing how to engage with her. I did hear that it was only after the funeral that she discovered Mike had made her a grandmother. Apparently, she was none too pleased about it.

However, she soon travelled out to Reims, and appears to have softened, initially at least, because she made arrangements to help support Arnaud. A few years later, she and Jacqueline met up in Paris, although this time it ended in an almighty row. Winifred considered that Arnaud was not being brought up properly. The boy was, she thought, far too rowdy and undisciplined. That meeting was the last time Winifred had any contact with her only grandson or his mother.

Although conveniently adhering to the tragic theme of this narrative, it is scarcely believable that, within ten years of Mike's death, Jacqueline was herself killed when she was struck by a speeding motorcycle. That Arnaud would continue his passion for motorcycles, rather than reject them, should confirm his parentage just as surely as any DNA test.

When that terrible tragedy befell Arnaud, it was none other than the generous and wonderfully avuncular Lofty England who stepped in to administer financial matters between Winifred and Arnaud. Lofty, it should be remembered, had been a tower of strength to Mike in the aftermath of the world's worst motor racing accident, and now, fourteen years later, he was still picking up the pieces of his young protégé's life. Lofty was a big man, in more than just stature.

I stayed in touch, sporadically, with the lads at the TT Garage, although even this diminished over time. Some weeks after the funeral, I stopped by there for petrol and bumped into Bill Morgan. He seemed to have aged ten years in as many weeks. He was keen to share the contents of a letter he'd recently seen, written by the surgeon who'd removed one of Mike's kidneys back in '54. The surgeon had said that, whilst it was most regrettable that Mike should have killed himself, it really was for the best. He understood that Mike had died quickly whereas the death he would have experienced, had he lived, would have been excruciating and protracted. In his opinion, Mike would soon have been confined to a wheelchair. It was an opinion shared by the pathologist who carried out the autopsy.

I asked Bill whether it was commonly known by the Garage staff that Mike had been seriously poorly. Bill said they all knew that he was, because sometimes you'd go to his office with some query or other and find Mike writhing on the floor in agony or, twice to his knowledge, passed out. 'We're weren't ever to say nothing to nobody, or he'd have had our guts for garters. He was a very proud and private man.'

That his kidney condition, at that time, was considered incurable was never doubted. It was only a question of life expectancy where the medical profession didn't agree. Some said he had twelve to eighteen months to live – others said he had three to five years left.

There is, of course, a huge difference between one year and five years, but, whenever it was to happen, my feeling of loss would have been the same - just as acute.

Of course, my life carried on. In many ways, exactly as before: I continued to work for the next thirty-four years in accountancy and related fields; Sally and I grew even closer and had two lovely children – both now grown up, one of whom we christened Michael, and I carried on following motor racing. But, I lost something very special on 22 January '59. A little part of me died too that day – it was the joy that was John Michael Hawthorn.

I often think back to those exciting and occasionally wild times, a time before health and safety, and when things now thought mundane, such as air travel, were considered exotic, and contemplate the many losses and gains. I have a lot to thank Mike for: the places we went, the people I met, and for many of the best times of my life. I also experienced too much loss of life.

Occasionally, I go for long walks with my son Michael – he prefers not to be called Mike – and I talk to him about the things we did when we were young – younger than he is today. Well, not all of it, obviously. And I can see him thinking how naive we all were back then, but also what incredible thrills were had.

I'm not sure he believes me still when I tell him that Norman Dewis was clocked doing 192mph down the Mulsanne Straight in a Jaguar D-Type sixty years ago, especially since he's seen one of these 'basic-looking' open sports cars in a museum. He reckoned the tyres on it weren't as wide as those on his Ford Fiesta.

I've also taken him to visit Mike's grave in Farnham, where the headstone reads: A Gay and Gallant Sportsman. Last time we were there together, Michael asked me whether that was a fair epitaph. I thought about that for a while and replied, 'I think F-words would be more appropriate.'

He looked at me a bit old-fashioned and asked, 'Like what?'

I thought for a minute, and then suggested, 'Funny, fiery, flawed, and far, far too fast!'

Epilogue

It's now over half a century since my best friend died. Naturally, I was devastated by his passing, and yet took comfort from the knowledge that his kidney disease would have taken his life within a couple of years and, by having a fatal car accident, he'd avoided the agonizing death the consultants had so graphically forecast.

That should be all there is left to say on the matter – another bright, gay (in the old sense), reckless hell-raiser whose life was snuffed out – another good man who played hard, broke hearts, and died too young.

However, as a result of a recent chance discovery, I believe there is a possibility that his life could have ended very differently. So differently, in fact, that he could still be alive today – possibly even announcing his retirement, just as his old adversary Stirling Moss, now Sir Stirling, did at the remarkable age of eighty-one.

As a lifelong devotee of motor racing, I've continued to read about drivers, young and old, including Sir Stirling. In the book *All But My Life* written by Ken Purdy, I was amazed to discover that Stirling had also avoided national service because he failed his medical examination due to…a kidney condition! Exactly as Mike would later. That struck me as a bizarre coincidence, so I investigated further.

I read that Stirling missed a lot of schooling when he was around eleven years old, due to kidney problems. However, his condition clearly wasn't so severe that once he was a young man he couldn't drive brilliantly – like a fighter pilot, week in, week out, all around the world, for many years afterwards, and live healthily into old age.

In order to silence the allegations of his son's national service avoidance, Stirling's father made public a copy of his son's medical examination. Mike, with no such defence, had to endure years of haranguing by the press and politicians for draft dodging. This used to really wind Mike up. After all, the two of them were contemporaries, doing the same thing, leading virtually parallel lives, and yet Stirling was free to carry on, barely attracting comment, whereas Mike was branded a traitor and a coward.

The exact reason cited for Stirling's rejection from the armed forces was that they discovered he had Nephritis. Even if I had known that at the time, it would have meant nothing to me. Nephritis, I now know, is essentially inflammation of the kidneys. I suspect the screening medics found blood in Stirling's urine, and that was his armed forces career over before it started.

Nephritis is one of the leading contributors to chronic kidney disease (CKD) – essentially the condition from which Mike was told he would eventually die. The other two contributors are diabetes and high blood pressure. Whilst it is possible that Stirling, when he was young and fit, may have had diabetes or high blood pressure, there is little supporting evidence.

The coincidence that both Stirling and Mike were diagnosed with kidney conditions as youngsters made me wonder if there were any environmental factors common to both men. I didn't have to look too hard. Two well established causes of kidney damage are the inhalation of certain toxic gases, particularly engine exhaust fumes, petroleum and petroleum additives, solvents and lead, *and* excessive physical vibration – literally being shaken.

You may recall my accounts of Mike being shaken so hard in his early racing days that he was advised to wear a corset – which, of course, being Mike, he initially eschewed. Indeed, he was shaken *so* hard at Dundrod that he even passed out. That type and severity of harsh vibration, which he and his fellow racers endured, is no longer experienced in motor racing. But, I suspect kidney damage caused by shaking was more prevalent at the time than was appreciated.

Leslie Johnson, another British Grand Prix racer, who was born seventeen years before Mike but died in the same year aged forty-seven of a heart condition, had also been diagnosed with nephritis as a youngster. Even Dino Ferrari, Enzo's son, who died of muscular dystrophy, was found to have nephritis. It's a fair bet that for most of Dino's young life he'd been shaken about in cars, and inhaled considerable quantities of petro-chemical fumes.

Airlines today also appear conscious of the risk of vibration on aircrew. A US Army website states: 'Exposure to vibration over a period of time may cause injury to aviators...(including) kidney damage. Signs of overexposure to vibration include hematuria (blood in urine) and albuminuria (albumen in the urine).'

Mike, I venture, had even greater exposure to toxic gases than most of his driver contemporaries. Not only did he hang around workshops and pits for much of his working life, but the family garage where he spent long hours included a petrol filling station. Moreover, his father was renowned for his cocktails of super-high-octane racing fuels, including additives which are now recognized carcinogens and have been banned for years. Stirling, too, would have been exposed to high levels of dangerous chemicals.

Up until 1957, racing teams had no restrictions on the fuels they used. Stirling's employer, Mercedes, used forty-five per cent Benzene (a chemical now directly linked to a rare form of kidney cancer), twenty-five per cent methyl alcohol, twenty-three per cent aviation fuel, three per cent acetone, two per cent nitrobenzene – with the remaining two per cent kept secret to this day!

I accept that Stirling was said to be suffering from his condition before he started racing, but as someone who already had such impairment, his lifestyle could hardly be described as benign to his kidneys. My discoveries bought other revelations. They included:

- Nephritis can cause pain in the side or back, or both.
- Long-term effects of nephritis include irritability.
- Nephritis is common – sixteen per cent of the adult population have some marker of kidney disease – albeit it is more severe and more frequently found amongst the elderly.
- The great majority of patients with early CKD do not progress to renal failure.
- Most people who suffer from nephritis get better.
- I discovered a third potential contributor to nephritis: the ingestion of large quantities of alcohol! You will have gathered that Mike was no stranger to alcohol. Far from it. Stirling, too, enjoyed the occasional beer but, compared to Mike, he was a model of sobriety.

So, what can I establish as fact, and what is unscientific speculation? It is apparent that both these contemporaneous drivers had significant exposure to at least two recognised causes of kidney malfunction:

inhalation of toxic substances and being violently shaken, before and around the time of their national service medicals.

It's also well known that Mike complained of back pain and became increasingly irritable from his mid-twenties onwards – conditions commensurate with, among other ailments, nephritis.

My question is simply this: Without today's sophisticated methods of analysing kidneys, could Mike's consultant have misdiagnosed severe nephritis as congenital kidney failure? It strikes me that both men might have had congenital kidney weakness which developed into nephritis as a result of at least two of the known causes.

If that is the case, it could surely be argued that as Mike had greater exposure to toxic gases, had driven more in pre-war racing cars, consumed considerably more alcohol, and had been diagnosed later, so his condition had become more severe. Mike may well have had a congenital kidney defect but he almost couldn't have done more to exacerbate his condition.

Mike's physicians cannot have known about the causal effects of violent shaking or the inhalation of toxic gases on the kidneys, nor presumably, the extra risks posed by his marathon drinking bouts and heavy smoking – if they had, surely they would have advised him very differently? And if they had, might his condition, like Stirling's, have either receded or stabilised to allow normal living?

Today, I believe he would have been instructed to stop racing (ie avoid vibration and stress); to avoid petrol vapours and similar fumes; to give up or greatly reduce consumption of alcohol and tobacco; to reduce his salt intake; to exercise gently, but frequently; and to drink more water. He may also have been prescribed antihypertensive drugs to reduce his blood pressure – something which many sufferers of CKD experience. And, yes, if he'd had a kidney stone then that would be surgically removed.

It seems perfectly logical to me. If Sir Stirling recovered, perhaps by lessening his exposure to now banned fuel additives, and by driving cars with better suspension, and drinking in moderation… then surely with a little more of all of these then Mike too might have joined him in reaching a ripe old age.

And what if his diagnosis had been along these lines: 'I'm afraid you have nephritis. It's serious, your kidneys *are* in a poor state, but if you change your lifestyle enough you *may* recover significantly'?

Would he then have courted mortal danger less? Would he have thought more about his fiancée Jean, and their future lives together, and possibly that of their children? Would he have driven quite so recklessly? Would he still have chosen to race Rob Walker for all he was worth along the Guilford bypass to the point where he might have suspected the next moment would be his last? Would he? We'll never know.

The Lost and the Lucky

Predeceased: Those Close and Lost to Mike

When	*Who*	*Category*	*Age*	*Why/How*
June '47	Simon Hayter	Close friend	18	Member, Fell from motorcycle – allegedly looking at crumpet.
June '53	Tom Cole	Teammate	28	Driving at Le Mans.
July '53	Bobby Baird	Friend	41	Racing for Ferrari at Snetterton.
Aug '53	Mike Currie	Close friend	c24	Member, Fatal road accident.
Dec '54	Leslie Hawthorn	Father	52	Driving home from Goodwood.
May '55	Alberto Ascari	Mentor	37	Test driving for Ferrari.
June '55	Pierre Levegh	Sport elder	49	Racing in Le Mans 24 Heures.
July '55	Don Beauman	Close friend	26	Racing in Leinster Trophy.
Aug '55	Mike Keen	Close friend	26	Racing at Goodwood.
Aug '55	Julian Crossley	Close friend	28	Member, Riding Ulster GP.
Sept '55	Richard Mainwaring	Friend	26	Racing in the Dundrod TT race.
Sept '55	Bill Smith	Friend	20	Racing in the Dundrod TT race.
Sept '55	Jim Mayers	Friend	24	Racing in the Dundrod TT race; hit stone gatepost.
Jan '57	Ken Wharton	Sport elder	40	Racing in New Zealand.

Mar '57	Eugenio Casttelotti	Teammate	26	Test driving for Ferrari.
May '57	Alfonso de Portago	Teammate	28	Racing in the Mille Miglia.
July '57	Bill Whitehouse	Sport elder	48	Racing at Reims (F2).
July '57	H Mackay-Fraser	Friend	30	Racing at Reims (F2).
May '58	Archie Scott Brown	Friend	31	Belgian Sports Car Race.
May '58	Pat O'Connor	Friend	29	Racing at Indianapolis.
July '58	Luigi Musso	Teammate	33	Racing at Reims, French GP.
Aug '58	Peter Collins	Best friend	26	Racing at Nurburgring.
Sept '58	Peter Whitehead	Sport elder	43	Racing in Tour de France (cars).
Oct '58	Stuart Lewis-Evans	Friend	28	From burns Morocco GP.

Those Lost Thereafter:

When	*Who*	*Category*	*Age*	*Why/How*
Aug '59	Ivor Bueb	Teammate	36	Racing at Charade, France (F2).
Aug '59	Jean Behra	Rival	38	Racing at AVUS, Berlin.
May '60	Harry Schell	Teammate	38	Racing at Silverstone – in practice.
Sept '61	Taffy von Tripps	Teammate	33	Racing at Monza, Italian GP.
April '62	Ron Flockhart	Friend	38	Record distance flight attempt.
Nov '65	Peter Poppe	Close friend	c36	Member. Flew into sea, Malaysia.
June '72	Joakim Bonnier	Rival	42	Racing in the Le Mans 24 Heures.

Those Close Who 'Got Away':

Survived racing	Age (year died)	Retired from F1 racing in:
Sir Jack Brabham	88 (2014)	1970 – aged 44. Three times World Champion.
Tony Brooks	83	1961 – aged 29. Teammate and friend.
Norman Dewis OBE	94	N/A Sports car and Jaguar test driver. Good friend.
Juan Fangio	84 (1995)	1958 – aged 47. Five times World Champion.
Paul Frere	91 (2008)	1956 – aged 39. Teammate.
Olivier Gendebien	74 (1998)	1961 – aged 37. Teammate.
Jose Gonzalez	90 (2013)	1960 – aged 38. Sport elder.
Duncan Hamilton	74 (1994)	1958 – aged 38. Close friend.
Phil Hill	81 (2008)	1966 – aged 39. Teammate and friend.
Lance Macklin	82 (2002)	1955 – aged 36. Former friend.
Maglioli	70 (1999)	1957 – aged 29. Friend and rival.
Sir Stirling Moss	85	1961 – aged 33. Friend and rival.
Reg Parnell	52 (1964)	1954 – aged 46. Sport elder.
Major Tony Rolt	89 (2008)	1955 – aged 37. Sport elder.
Roy Salvadori	90 (2012)	1962 – aged 40. Friend and rival.
Piero Taruffi	81 (1988)	1956 – aged 50! Rival.
Des Titterington	73 (2002)	1956 – aged 28. Teammate.
Maurice Trintignant	87 (2005)	1964 – aged 47. Teammate.
Rob Walker	71 (2002)	N/A (F1 team owner not driver.) Friend.

Acknowledgements

In the process of trying understand another's life, especially someone of an earlier generation, one has to glean as much as possible from others, whether this be by conversation with those who knew the person, reading widely, watching films, documentaries and British Pathé clips or, of course, surfing the Web. And yet, instinctively, you realise that you'll never know every facet of another person — not purely from what has been said or written about them. After all, it's probable that you don't even know your best friend as well as you think you do! But it's fun guessing.

The factual information and anecdotes — that is to say, almost everything herein pertaining to Mike Hawthorn — has been derived from personal conversations, correspondence and a great many different publications — almost too many to list. But, in particular, I would like to pay tribute to Hawthorn's friends and contemporaries:

Sir Stirling Moss and Tim Ely — for their generosity, warmth and information and various members of the Hawthorn Appreciation Luncheon Club.

Principal publications:

Challenge Me The Race by Mike Hawthorn. Published 1958 by William Kimber and Co.

Champion Year by Mike Hawthorn. Published 1959 by William Kimber and Co.

Behind the Scenes of Motor Racing by Ken Gregory. Published 1960 by MacGibbon & Kee Ltd.

Mon Ami Mate by Chris Nixon — a superb dual biography of Mike Hawthorn and Peter Collins. Published 1991 by Transport Bookman Publications.

Mike Hawthorn – Golden Boy by Tony Bailey and Paul Skilleter — a wonderful compendium of facts and figures relating to Mike Hawthorn, containing many photographs. Highly recommended. Published 2008 by PJ Publishing Ltd.

Archie and The Listers by Robert Edwards. Published 1995 by Haynes Publishing.

The Chequered Flag by Douglas Rutherford. Published 1956 by Collins.

Bernie Ecclestone – King of Sport by Terry Lovell. Published 2009 by John Blake.

Enzo Ferrari by Richard Williams. Published 2001 by Yellow Jersey Press.

Stirling Moss by Robert Edwards. Published 2001 by Cassell and Co.

The Limit by Michael Cannell. Published 2011 by Atlantic Books.

www.mike-hawthorn.org – a vast resource of facts and photographs about Mike.

I am greatly indebted to Helen, Jo and Carol of SilverWood Books for their help and professionalism, and to Clare Christian, the Book Guru, for pointing me in their direction.

Sincere thanks must also go to Alison Chisholm and Chris Andrews, for their encouragement; Tim Fenner for his contacts; Sarah Higbee for her expertise; Jan Henley for her inspiration; and my amazing wife Janet Shepherd for her patience.

Lightning Source UK Ltd.
Milton Keynes UK
UKOW02f2327220616

276894UK00004B/245/P